Kit Media Co.

1801 7th Street, Suite 150

Sacramento, CA 95811

Tel: (916) 256-6266

Fax: (916) 447-0720

franckherman@hotmail.com

Ultimate Revenge
Involuntary Transsexual

By: Herman Franck, Esq.

TRAFFORD
PUBLISHING

Order this book online at www.trafford.com
or email orders@trafford.com

Most Trafford titles are also available at major online book retailers.

Printed in the United States of America.

ISBN: 978-1-4269-4696-7 (sc)
ISBN: 978-1-4269-4697-4 (e)

Trafford rev. 01/11/2011

 www.trafford.com

North America & international
toll-free: 1 888 232 4444 (USA & Canada)
phone: 250 383 6864 ♦ fax: 812 355 4082

Dedication

To my lovely, lovelier, loveliest wife, Sabrina Chen.

Acknowledgements

I acknowledge and thank the following individuals whom assisted me in the process of creating this book:

Paul Garton, the Transcripts Co-op, did a wonderful job typing the manuscript from my series of micro-cassette tapes. See transcriptcoop.com for more information.

Jamie Blair, did a wonderful job proofreading the manuscript.

Kip Ayers, did a wonderful job designing the front and back cover, and drawing and coloring the artwork on the front cover. See kipayersillustrations.com for more information.

About the Author

Herman Franck, Esq. is a mild mannered attorney at law practicing in the field of civil trials and appeals. He owns his own law office, Franck & Associates, in Sacramento, California.

He grew up on a ranch in Scottsdale, Arizona, where he learned to dig holes, put in fence posts, and how to install barbed wire and chicken fencing. He also learned a rule of life there, "the animals eat first." During his tenure as a ranch hand he managed to let loose into the wild a group of 9 peacocks, whose offspring can be found atop telephone poles in the Scottsdale area even to this day.

Mr. Franck attended high school in Scottsdale, Arizona before returning to Woodside, California, and graduated from the often overlooked Woodside High School in 1976, at the bottom third of the class.

After a second, third and fourth chance at several California community colleges, he managed to gain entrance into U.C. Berkeley, and received his B.A. (*honors*) from U.C. Berkeley in Political Economy in 1981.

Equally miraculous was his admission into the Georgetown University Law Center, Washington, D.C., where he received in Juris Doctor in 1985. He also received a Master of Arts in Economics from Georgetown University, and did a masters thesis in Anti Trust economics.

He recently self published his first economics book, *U.S. Grown, To Survive a Nation Must Feed Itself* (Booksurge 2009).

He is a member of the State of California Bar, and is admitted to practice before the Federal Courts of California (where he sometimes goes and argues cases), the State Courts of California (where he spends roughly each day arguing cases; the Court has considered charging him rent), the United States Court of Appeals for the Ninth Circuit (where he is occasionally found arguing to be a published case typically in the field of prison civil rights), and the United States Supreme Court (which has yet to invite him to argue a case).

He was formerly admitted to practice in Ukraine (1992-1995) under its foreign attorney program. Mr. Franck resided in Ukraine during 1992 in connection with an agri-business project, and from that, gained some insights from traveling throughout Eastern and Central Europe, Central Asia, and other far off locations.

Mr. Franck was admitted to practice before the U.N. Tribunal for War Crimes for Former Yugoslavia (but alas, never got a case).

Mr. Franck is the founder of The Entrepreneur Center of Sacramento (www.entrepreneur-center.net), and is the author of a book entitled *Entrepreneur by Necessity* (XLibris 2008).

Mr. Franck is a weekend writer of books and screenplays. "Ultimate Revenge Involuntary Transsexual is his 23rd book." His 19th book, *Supernatural CSI, Dead People Make Excellent Witnesses* (Booksurge 2008) received a positive review from the Sacramento Book Review (June 2009). ("This was an enjoyable read written by an author with an invigorating imagination.")

Mr. Franck lives in West Sacramento with his real life loveliest wife-poo, Sabrina Q. Chen, their children, Adam and Alex Franck, and Sabrina's daughter Ms. Lo Qin Romano, and four Dalmatians, Spots, Diamond, and two sons.

Other Works by Herman Franck, Esq.

Herman Franck is the author of the following other books, comic books, and screenplays:

Supernatural CSI. Dead People Make Excellent Witnesses. (Booksurge 2009) Trips to the otherworld reveal evidence of crimes here on earth.

Ice Dragon. [XLibris 2007] *Book I. Battle of the Longheads.* [google longhead and see what you find] Kit Media produced a completed 32 page English/Spanish language color comic book based on Episode I of the book. Comic artwork, layout, lettering by Atlantis Studios, Atlanta, GA. Online comic: www.icedragon.biz

Ice Dragon [XLibris 2008] Books II and III: The Case of the Stolen Cartoons; The Case of the Missing Toys. Vincent and Ice Dragon solve the most important crimes in the history of the world.

Star Boy. [XLibris 2007] Novella. Kit Media produced a 32 page Spanish/English color comic of the first third of this novella. An ET visited earth and left a little hybrid boy for somebody to take care of. Artwork, layout, lettering of the color comic by Atlantis Studios, Atlanta, GA. [Starboy's song: *I know it's true, I'm part ET, but please, don't hate me.*]

Katie Cranberry [XLibris 2008]. Novel. Traveling fruit characters attend Katie's world university of diplomacy. Bow and Arrow recommended. Book I: *Katie's Silk Road Adventure;* Book II, *Katie's Preview in South America;* Book III, *American Stonehenge* Completed Telescript for one hour series pilot, How to Earn a Kingdom. See www.katiecranberry.com for more information.

Katie Cranberry IV: *Katie's North American Peace Adventure.* [BookSurge 2009] Katie Cranberry and her entourage of worldly friends set out on a mission to eliminate the white man's annihiliation of the Native Americans.

Juan Bonderello Quatro Cinco Seis. Novella Book I: The Case of the Stupid Food. [XLibris 2007] Juan Bonderello is the perfect peoples' spy to save the United States from its first bout with agro terrorism.

Second Life [XLibris 2006]. Novella. Success and failure are but two sides of the same page. A failed alcoholic doctor's soul is transferred into the body of a totally successful doctor.

Cheetah Kids [XLibris 2007]. Novel. Two infants are raised by a family of Cheetahs, and become the fastest humans on earth. A Dubai sheik with a heart of gold, as in Olympic Gold, shows them the path to glory. In the process, they find the tragedy that left them with without parents. How fast can you spell revenge. See www.cheetahkids.com for more information.

The Post Debutante [iuniverse 2001] Novel. An innocent deb gets on the wrong side of a murder case. In the process she becomes an expert on injustice and disloyalty, even among family.

The Politician [Kiwe Publishing] Novel. A new country is formed on a series of super barges. And that's not treason.

The Family Business. [Emerson-Adams Press 2002]. Novel and screenplay. Between organized crime and corporate America, will the real criminals please stand up. Introducing Tina, Mafia spy girl, the story of Tony, who thinks he is leaving the criminal world for so called legitimate business.

The Nobel Prizener [iuniverse 2004] Novel and feature length screenplay. Rape is a hard charge to beat, especially when you're innocent.

Franck Tails. [Kiwe Publishing 2003] Collection of animal stories. *Winnie and Thunderose, The Lonely Leopard, Ca Ca Boy, Wolf's Law.* Also wrote a script for *Winnie and Thunderose.*

Relationship Agreement [Iuniverse 2005] A code of conduct for lovers. Example: you can say no, but you can't say no all the time.

Just Add Water [Kiwe Publishing 2001]. Novel. There had to be revenge for this killing.

Entrepreneur by Necessity [XLibris 2007] Booklet on how to start a business when you have to. No Ice Dragons, Starboys, or fruit characters in this one.

U.S. Grown. To Survive a Nation Must Feed Itself. The Impact of Food Imports on American Food Producers. Okay, so I wrote an economics book.

How to Marry and Keep a Supermodel, Lessons From a Mid Wife Crisis.(Create Space 2010) See www.midwife-crisis.com for more information.

Reptile Man [*Homo-Reptilius Criminalis*] Eliminate this specie and you eliminate crime. Completed 125 page feature length screenplay.

OOPS. Out of Prison Inc has a run in with the Christian right. Completed 95 page screenplay. Where is Martha when you need her?

The Conversation. They all died and lived happily ever after. 52 page script for a poltergeist/legal drama.

The Tehachapi Militia. Ex- military turned Prison guards plus mowed over by state bureaucrats equals militia that takes over a prison. Completed 120 page feature length script.

The Debt. Its like waking up and learning that you were Hitler in a past life. Completed 135 page feature length script. Received honorable mention in Film Makers screenplay competition, 2001.

The Shanghai Twins. Its nighttime in Shanghai, do you know where your children are?

Two part mini series [95 pages each] based on author's grand-parents' tragic experience of losing male twins in Shanghai during the 30s. We never did find them. Written in China [in English].

Mayflower. These are not the pilgrims we learned about in grade school. Completed 120 page scandalous feature length script.

Red Card, script. If you take the time to help a stranger. Geek American engineer attempts arranged marriage in Gobi Desert China. Oops, in the process he gets arrested for lying to Chinese immigrations authorities. His defense never worked before, but this is a new Red China.

The Family Business. Feature length script based on the author's novel.

The Nobel Prizener. Feature length script based on the author's novel.

Katie Cranberry. Script for a one hour pilot for a tele-series based on the author's novel.

Winnie & Thunderose. Script for a tele-movie based on the author's short story.

Illustrated Stories

Winnie and Thuderose is being produced into an illustrated book [forthcoming][Artwork by Maria Byerley].

The Dance of Isis [artwork by Maria Byerley].

New Books in Progress

Issues and the Beast. [in progress]. For example, the whale that was afraid of water.

The Fake Family [in progress]. Everything about this family is 100% fake, until something terrible happens that teaches them how to be real.

More coming . . .

List of Characters

(In Order of Appearance)

Ben Nightingale

Assistant U.S. Attorney Jaffey

U.S. District Court Judge Alan Wickenberg

Erica Lazarus

François (Tasterilla maitre d')

Henry Emerson II

Adolph Emerson

Alice Emerson

Henry Emerson III

Detective Malene (female detective)

Officer Ballati (male officer)

Eddie Fernandez (cook)

Dr. Weiss (attending physician)

Parsons (forensic nurse)

Profiler Donna Kuchins, Ph.D

Dr. Boyce (veterinarian)

Dr. Carl Rasmussen (veterinarian)

Detective Olson (male detective)

Dr. Salisbury

Dana Fuerenstein (public defender)

Judge Harold Ransom

Sam Nightingale (Ben's father)

Assistant District Attorney Ed Sinclair

Sgt. Neeley

Paula Router, DVM

Abigail Miller, PhD

French Hayes (inmate)

Stephen Lipsig (inmate)

Brian Tsaupolis (inmate)

Kevin Chambers (inmate)

Mayor Jack Cowens

Bill Sazevich (city attorney)

Malcolm Speagel

Michael Angelforth, Esq. (Attorney General's office)

Sonja Kingsberry (Appellate Public Defender)

Poncho (drug dealer)

Eddie (ex-con)

Enrique (Eddie's boyfriend)

Carlita (transgendered female)

Warden Warren

Lilith (Warden's daughter)

Hazel (the former Henry Emerson III)

Doctor McNalley

Alfonso Ramirez

Officer Bentley

Contents

CHAPTER 1   Ben Nightingale...1

CHAPTER 2   How Was Your Day?...5

CHAPTER 3   The Tasterilla...8

CHAPTER 4   The Incident..10

CHAPTER 5   The Aftermath..15

CHAPTER 6   San Diego Crime Scene Investigation.........................17

CHAPTER 7   Eddie The Sex Offender 22

CHAPTER 8   Mercy Hospital, San Diego...25

CHAPTER 9   The Investigation Begins...30

CHAPTER 10   San Diego's Veterinarian Clinics 33

CHAPTER 11   Cheerleader Turned Pharmaceutical Sales Rep 37

CHAPTER 12   Google: Military Class Ring 41

CHAPTER 13   The Journalist...43

CHAPTER 14   The Emerson Ranchette...46

CHAPTER 15   Henry Wilbur Emerson III...50

CHAPTER 16   How To Catch A Serial Rapist 51

CHAPTER 17   The Arrest Of Henry Emerson III 59

CHAPTER 18   Meanwhile, Back At The Mental Institution 61

CHAPTER 19   People Versus Henry Emerson III.................................63

CHAPTER 20   Ben's Father Lends A Hand...66

CHAPTER 21   Hearing On Motion To Exclude Illegally Obtained Evidence 68

CHAPTER 22   The Ad 87

CHAPTER 23   The First Call 93

CHAPTER 24   The Second Call 94

CHAPTER 25   Erica Gets A Visitor 97

CHAPTER 26   Consolidated Hearing On Motion To
Change Venue And Preliminary Hearing.....................99

CHAPTER 27   The Non-Plea Bargain 103

CHAPTER 28   The Seed Is Planted 108

CHAPTER 29   The Sentencing...110

CHAPTER 30   The Angel Returns... 116

CHAPTER 31   Sexual Offender Therapy: Day One..117

CHAPTER 32   Meanwhile, Back At The Newspaper 124

CHAPTER 33   The Penile Plethysmograph...127

CHAPTER 34   Relapse Prevention Plan 133

CHAPTER 35   Hearing On Motion To Dismiss The Rico Case 140

CHAPTER 36   Henry's Relapse Prevention Plan 143

CHAPTER 37   The Appeal 151

CHAPTER 38   The Polygraph..152

CHAPTER 39   Summit At The Mayor's Office..159

CHAPTER 40   Parallel Lives...164

CHAPTER 41   The Aftermath...169

CHAPTER 42   Appellant's Opening Brief..173

CHAPTER 43   Is There Anything I Can Do For You? 174

CHAPTER 44   Videocam Funeral 178

CHAPTER 45   A Letter To Henry's Father 181

CHAPTER 46   Sam's Prize 186

CHAPTER 47   Erica 187

CHAPTER 48   I Am You 188

CHAPTER 49   Oral Arguments In The Court Of Appeals.............................190

CHAPTER 50   Henry's Last Day In Prison...199

CHAPTER 51   Rapist Freed...202

CHAPTER 52   Dismissal..203

CHAPTER 53   Ben's Reaction...205

CHAPTER 54   Henry Is Home..208

CHAPTER 55   Ben Has A Plan 211

CHAPTER 56   Home De-Provement 214

CHAPTER 57   Stealing A Prisoner Right Out From Under The Sheriff's Nose.............217

CHAPTER 58   Meanwhile, Back At The Ranch 219

CHAPTER 59   Boat Trip 222

CHAPTER 60   What Now? 227

CHAPTER 61   Prison Is Not Enough 230

CHAPTER 62   The Rape Of Henry..234

CHAPTER 63   The Sensitive Non-Rapist..243

CHAPTER 64   Now What Do I Do? 249

CHAPTER 65   His Name Was Carlita 250

CHAPTER 66   The Emptiness Of Revenge..253

CHAPTER 67	Henry's Hormone Hell	255
CHAPTER 68	The Rape Of Hazel	257
CHAPTER 69	Jealousy	259
CHAPTER 70	What Can I Do For You?	261
CHAPTER 71	Knock And Talk	266
CHAPTER 72	The Warden's Daughter	268
CHAPTER 73	The Guitar Center, San Diego	269
CHAPTER 74	Fish Out Of Water	274
CHAPTER 75	Catatonic And Telepathic	277
CHAPTER 76	Can I See Your You-Know-What?	280
CHAPTER 77	Serendipity	282
CHAPTER 78	Twelve Hours Later	285
CHAPTER 79	What It's Like To Be Dead	291
CHAPTER 80	The Literary Agent Makes It Happen	295
CHAPTER 81	Ben Gets The Book	297
CHAPTER 82	Hi Honey, I'm Home	301
CHAPTER 83	Honesty Is Not The Best Policy	304
CHAPTER 84	Honey, I'm Home	307
CHAPTER 85	Let's Bake A Pie	310
CHAPTER 86	Shopping For Pie Material	312
CHAPTER 87	The Intruder	316
CHAPTER 88	Hazel's Reversion Back To Henry	325
CHAPTER 89	The Hospital	329
CHAPTER 90	A Day Later	333
CHAPTER 91	It Was A Dark And Stormy Night…	335
CHAPTER 92	Discovery, Revenge And Redemption	339
CHAPTER 93	The Revenge Part	344
CHAPTER 94	Redemption	347
CHAPTER 95	Epilogue	349

SONGS

Bridge of Sighs, by Robin Trower [Used with permission]

Bring Me to Life, by Evanescense [Used with permission]

I am You, by Henry Emerson III

Release the Demon, by Hazel

CHAPTER 1

BEN NIGHTINGALE

"I decline to answer that question on the grounds of the newsperson's privilege under the First Amendment to the United States Constitution." Ben knew his assertion would upset the judge and the assistant U.S. attorney questioning him.

"Your Honor --"

The U.S. Attorney did not need to repeat his request. United States District Court Judge Alan Wickenberg bolted.

"Young man, what did you say your name was again?"

"Ben. Ben Nightingale."

"Okay, Mr. Nightingale. Here's how we're going to do this. Do you see the clock over there on the wall?"

Ben nervously glanced at the clock embedded in the dark walnut walls of the courtroom. He studied it much longer than the judge expected.

"Okay. Note the second hand. It is right now at the number 5; do you see that?"

"Yes."

"When it gets back around to that 5, do you know how long that will take?"

"I do."

"How long?"

"Sixty seconds."

"Okay. By the time it gets around back to that 5, you are going to answer the question. If you don't answer the question, you see that gentleman over there with the badge on his shirt in the blue uniform? He's what we call a U.S. Marshal. I am going to direct that U.S. Marshal to arrest you, put handcuffs on you, and bring you down to the federal penitentiary, where you will be sentenced to 90 days of time. There will be no prosecution, there will be no indictment; you will be summarily sentenced by me. I am able to do that because you committed a crime right in my presence, the crime of contempt of court. I hereby order you to answer the question. By the way, you've only got 25 seconds left."

The second hand was one of those smooth moving second hands that did not make a sound as it proceeded through the remaining trip around the clock. Ben looked at the U.S. attorney.

"I have a privilege --"

The judge interrupted:

"You do not have a privilege to withhold information of a federal crime. I don't know how many newspaper folks I need to lock up before you guys get that through your thick heads."

"I was writing an exposé --"

The judge interjected, "I don't care about your exposé. You can write exposé until your heart bleeds out every last drop of its liberal blood. In the meantime, you need to answer that question."

It was true that several staff members of the *San Diego Chronicle* had been jailed. Ben visited his colleagues in jail and saw the impact of jail on them. They were frightened, cold, and worse than that - forgotten. Here they were making a huge sacrifice in the name of the First Amendment, and nobody cared. Did he want to make this self-sacrifice? The seconds were passed over by the clock. There were about four left. The judge was calm as he watched the final seconds of the clock.

The Marshal stood up, ready for cuffing. Ben decided against martyrdom.

"Okay, okay. I'll answer the question. It was U.S. Attorney Yonoko Suzuki."

This was a bombshell to all in the courtroom. The assistant U.S. Attorney had managed to force a newspaper person to divulge that his own office was guilty of a serious crime.

"No further questions."

The only possible way to get out of hot water, when you hear terrible answers to your questions, is to end the questioning. But sometimes it's not so easy.

"Wait a minute there," the judge of course intervened. "You may not have any further questions, but I certainly do."

"Your Honor, it's not how it seems --"

The judge put his hand up and stopped the U.S. Attorney in his tracks.

"It's not what it seems? You mean you know what it is? Are you telling me that you're part of this whole escapade, that you're eliciting testimony of the newspaper person, willing to get him held in contempt, and the whole time you yourself are holding back information? Please tell me it isn't so."

"It isn't so."

U.S. Attorney Jaffey sat down. The judge proceeded.

"Mr. Nightinhorse, are you telling me --"

"Excuse me, Your Honor, it's Nightingale."

"Oh, Nightingale. Fine. Are you telling me that --"

U.S. Attorney Jaffey interrupted the judge again, a precarious path.

"Former U.S. Attorney."

"The former U.S. Attorney divulged to you testimony given during a grand jury investigation?"

"No, I am not saying that at all. They asked me a question: where did I get the information leading me to the name of a witness. I answered that question. I got it from Yonoko Suzuki, the former U.S. Attorney."

"Did she divulge to you any testimony that this witness you've identified gave during the course of his grand jury testimony?"

"She did not. She gave me his name only, and as I understand it --"

"Mr. Nightingale, excuse me. I am not interested in your understanding of the law, I'm just interested in the facts. Next question."

"Yes, sir."

"In giving you this information, was she retaliating against the U.S. Attorney's Office for having been fired?"

"Do you think?"

"Excuse me?"

"Well, what do you think? After more than 22 years of service as a U.S. prosecutor, where she devoted her life and soul to the service to the United States of America, and some pipsqueak, unqualified Attorney General is appointed by a similarly situated President, who then fires her because she's not quite right wing enough, and you want to know if maybe she's retaliating? Duh!"

Mr. Jaffey made a pathetic attempt to stop the inquiry.

"Your Honor, I object, as the question calls for speculation."

"You're objecting to my question?"

"I am."

"Objection overruled. Here's what we're going to do from here," the judge proceeded to lay down the law. "You're saying you were only given the name of a witness."

"That's correct."

"And no information about what this person actually said during his testimony."

"Correct."

"And then you found that person?"

"I did."

"And then you interviewed that person?"

"I did."

"And they provided you with all the information you published in your article -- let's see, I have it right here -- 'Scandal from Above: Politics and Horseplay in the U.S. Attorney General's Office.'"

"That's correct. Your Honor, it may be that the information a witness gives during a grand jury investigation is off-limits. If that witness outside the grand jury is asked what does he know, such an inquiry is proper, legal, and fully consistent under the First Amendment of the United States Constitution."

Mr. Jaffey was openly angry that Ben spoke the truth. The judge knew it as well. He looked over at Mr. Jaffey.

"Any further questions, Mr. Jaffey?"

"None."

Mr. Jaffey was one of the extreme far wingers that was left unfired under the campaign to purge the U.S. Attorney's Office of middle of the road right wingers, as if there was something wrong about that.

"All right then, these proceedings are complete, the order to show cause for contempt is hereby discharged; Mr. Nightingale, you are free to go."

The judge slammed down his gavel. Nightingale was relieved to have his freedom. There would be another day when he was perhaps not so lucky. As he proceeded out of the courtroom, the judge studied Ben's attire and couldn't help but make a comment.

"Mr. Nightingale?"

"Yes, Your Honor."

"The next time you're in my courtroom, which I have a feeling will be soon enough --" The judge pointed down to Ben's Birkenstocks. The assistant U.S. Attorney Jaffey wore wingtips, as though they were still in style. The judge corrected what he was going to say. "Wear socks."

Ben nodded. He didn't say yes, he didn't say no, he just nodded and left the courthouse.

CHAPTER 2

HOW WAS YOUR DAY?

Ben drove perhaps one of the last convertible Corvairs on the planet. It had a three on the tree shift device right on the steering wheel column, but it was in excellent condition. He proceeded to his modest apartment in a fairly seedy part of downtown San Diego. He climbed up the fake white marble steps. Several Hispanic children were playing in the parking lot. Two men with tattoos and tank top t-shirts, wearing small hats, cooked hot dogs on a barbecue. They nodded at Ben as he proceeded to his apartment. Ben nodded back to his neighbors and went into his unit.

He could see right away there was trouble. On the living room floor were more than fifty crumpled up pieces of paper. His fiancé could not be seen, but he knew where she was. He hurried past the kitchen table, where the origin of the anxiety could be seen: a laptop hooked up to a laser printer. The book she was writing had the ominous title, *My Angst*, and had grown to over three and a half inches tall. The stack of finished papers was nearly as high as the two Red Bull energy cans. The blockage, in the form of crumpled paper strewn across the floor, was just another day in the life of an angst-filled writer.

Ben shook his head. He walked down the hallway to the bathroom. The door was closed. He could hear her whimpering.

"Honey, are you there?"

Of course she was.

"Go away!" she yelled out.

"Oh, come on, honey. I'm here."

"I'm sick of this!"

"Sick of what?"

"Not being able to go forward."

"But we are going forward. We're getting married in just two weeks."

"I'm not talking about us, you stupid, I'm talking about my book!"

"Honey?"

"Yes?"

"I love you."

It was amazing how those words could turn this hysterical, high-angst, coffee-filled, energy drink junky into a piece of melted cheese. The bathroom door unlocked. She opened it, and peered out with her beautiful blue eyes. Her eyes were not looking so pretty filled with tears and red. Ben went from memory and knew how beautiful they could be. He had seen them when she awoke in the morning. He had seen them when she was in the bookstore, touching the copy of her first book, *Her Angst: The Story of a Mother Who Would Not Let Go*, by Erica Lazarus.

He saw them again now, drooling with tears, coming from the woman that he was hopelessly, madly in love with. He was her rock. She was quicksand. As she peered out, she saw a man that she knew she could depend on. This was a man who was filled with direction, knew what he wanted out of life, was chasing down his own dreams, was achieving them, and was doing it all while being madly in love with her. She opened the door to show her entire self.

One of the good things about anxiety-prone women is they hardly ever eat. She had a gorgeous figure, the kind that most girls lose after high school. She had beautiful skin and a dark complexion, contrasted by her dirty blonde hair.

This is what happens when your grandmother is a Lithuanian Jewish refugee who meets a Portuguese Jewish refugee at Ellis Island. You get an outstandingly gorgeous girl filled with high levels of anxiety and angst, an extremely high IQ to boot, and an unstoppable desire to write all about it. The perfect woman, at least for Ben.

Ben, on the other hand, was none of these things. He was an American WASP, who had the privilege of growing up rich. He could afford not to be rich. It was not a question of "I hate my parents and all they stand for." Instead, rather than writing the law as his father had, he decided to write about the law, as no one had.

As it often happens, writers fall in love with writers, no matter how difficult they are. Erica hugged him, held him, kissed him.

"I'm so sorry."

He held her tight, as though her life depended on it, which it did.

"Honey, you don't need to be sorry for who you are."

She looked at him as though she had discovered some great secret of life.

"How do you know these things? How do they come to you like this?"

She put her finger to his mouth.

"Don't say another word."

She tore down the hallway back to her laptop and began typing. It was furious typing. Indeed, several of the keys on the laptop had fallen off. She used a butter knife to push them back on. She opened up another energy drink, took a big sip and gasped.

"God, this tastes terrible."

She typed furiously for the next hour and a half. Ben knew the drill. He picked up the paper, sat on the couch, and opened to a page he had nothing at all to do with writing: the sports page. About an hour and a half later, he heard the humming of Erica's printer. It took awhile, but sixteen perfectly written new pages came out. She took them from her printer and held them vertically. She smacked them lightly against the table to bring their edges all flush. She placed them at the bottom of the three and a half inch pile of completed papers, making it just slightly higher than the Red Bull cans.

There's something about a feeling of accomplishment which makes a girl feel sexy. Before writing those pages, sex would have been the furthest thing from her mind. Now that she had written them, she felt accomplished. Her day meant something, and she knew that Ben deserved all the credit for it. Ben was oblivious to her change in mood. He was on the couch sound asleep. She took this opportunity to put on something more comfortable.

The idea of an angst-filled Jewish girl having something in the realm of sexy clothing may seem like a contradiction. She really didn't have anything to wear in this way, other than her shout it out sexy body. She decided to skip the uniform, and walked out in her birthday suit.

She tapped his shoulder. He just moved a bit in his dream. She tapped again, almost getting angry. His eye opened. Then the other eye opened. Then his mouth opened.

"Oh!"

This was the most intelligent word he could come up with. She smiled. He knew the mood. He had been there many times before. If she can't write a page, she'll be forever angry, dry as a buried bone. If she can write a page, and especially sixteen of them, she will become a sex goddess.

She looked down at him as he looked up to her.

Mmm.

He got out of his horizontal position and sat up. He was trying to move the sports page away, as though to tidy up. She quickened the pace of this process by swiping it, slapping it with her hand and tossing it. It floated up, over, and down, turning it into a short-lived kite. Before it landed, she gave him, in her most sexy voice, the question:

"I forgot to ask, dear, how was your day?"

She did not wait for his answer.

CHAPTER 3

THE TASTERILLA

It was make-up sex, without ever having a fight. Ben was fairly well-behaved in these Olympic-style sessions; Erica was not. It was a window to a part of her soul that rarely saw the light of day. Once shorn of her "whatever it is" inside her, she was an absolute animal. It was something that Ben would never get used to. Every time was a first time. The afterwards was his favorite part. He loved to spoon and curled up into her backside. She thought it was rather feminine of him.

"You like to spoon?" she mentioned.

He laughed.

"What's wrong with cuddling with the woman I love?"

She smiled.

"I like to plate."

She rolled over onto the top of him, spreading his legs and arms out. She laid atop him, matching him arm for arm, leg for leg. He couldn't help but giggle. Giggles are contagious.

"What's so funny?"

"I don't know. Why are you laughing?"

"Oh, you."

"What, me?"

"I don't know."

"No, tell me."

She propped her head up so she could see him and gave him one of those, "you have to answer my question" looks.

"I've just never had anyone like me as much as you do."

She became less giggly, more serious. She placed his hand on her heart.

"You and me."

He pushed his hand over to her breast and touched her nipple. She quickly removed his hand and put it back on her heart.

"Oh no, dear, the store is closed."

He smiled, like someone who had been caught trying to steal something.

"No after-hours shopping?"

"Oh, no, no, no."

She did a gymnastic twirl off of his body onto the floor. He loved watching her practice gymnastics, especially stark naked. She sprung up to her feet without the use of her hands. She stood up and performed a cartwheel, somehow grabbing her panties with one hand in the process. By the time she finished her cartwheel, the panties were on. He inelegantly put his boxer shorts and pants on at the same time. She pretended to walk on an imaginary balance beam on the carpet, one foot after another, toe to heel, toe to heel. She proceeded to the kitchen, past the table where her laptop was. She opened the cabinets and stared at the food.

Sex made her hungry. There was peanut butter and bread.

"Mmm."

She pulled down the bread, pulled down the peanut butter, and made one of her favorite items: a slice of bread with peanut butter. He put on one of those Hawaiian flower shirts that you don't have to tuck in. Just as she was about to eat her slice of peanut butter bread, he grabbed her wrist.

"Honey, don't."

"What?"

"Let's go out. We'll have a nice dinner tonight. Let's go to the Tasterilla."

Her eyes lit up.

"Oh, can we? Can we really?"

"Yes, dear. Let's go."

She raced past the kitchen area, quickly passing over her imaginary balance beam, toe-heel, toe-heel, two skips and then a leap off the balance beam onto the floor with a near-perfect, 9.6 landing. He gave her an imaginary applause for her imaginary performance. Within minutes, she came out in her typically "show nothing" attire: Oshkosh overalls, a non-matching but feminine white blouse, and her single adaptation to his contribution of post-preppydom WASP non-culture -- a pair of penny loafers without the penny, and without socks. To Ben, even dressed in this way, she was the sexiest woman on the planet.

The Tasterilla was in a nice part of town, so they would have to drive. They hopped into his Corvair. Tattooed residents of the apartment complex were in the parking area, enjoying the barbecue process as much as the barbecue itself. They nodded at this fish out of water couple.

He carefully backed away, making sure the children had safely moved away from his path. He used the stick shift on the steering column to go from reverse to first gear.

They proceeded to the Tasterilla, a scenic drive along San Diego's shoreline. Seagulls rested on the masts of sailboats, as others fluttered jealously above.

CHAPTER 4

THE INCIDENT

Erica's moderate level of success with her first book, *Her Angst*, did not make her wealthy. But it did provide her with a local celebrity status that came in handy at popular restaurants such as the Tasterilla. This restaurant served what had become known as fusion food, with elements of Mexican, Southwest, Tex-Mex, and a little sushi thrown in for fun. There were more than twenty people standing in front of the restaurant, enjoying the cool breeze of the San Diego night, but not enjoying the lengthy wait for their table.

They walked past the well-dressed diners in waiting and made their way to the maitre d's podium. The maitre d' was a combed back, big-haired Mexican with a name badge showing the dubious name of "François." A Mexican French wannabe working in a fusion restaurant serving enchiladas and sushi. Not much fazed Ben and Erica, including this curious individual named François.

François was a busy man this evening, hustling patrons in and out, and did not take the time to make eye contact with Ben and Erica. He announced his greeting to his new customers:

"Welcome to the Tasterilla. I'm sorry that the wait is estimated --"

It was then that he made eye contact with Erica, which completely changed his attitude.

"Oh, my goodness, we have a celebrity among us. Look, it's Erica Lazarus!"

Erica was the last one to seek any kind of notoriety. Ben smiled. It was fun having a famous fiancée. François had a dream that someday he would work at a famous Hollywood restaurant, where he would seat movie stars, rock stars, and political stars. Tonight he would have to settle for the Tasterilla and a local writing star, Erica. But it worked for him. His radar eyes scanned the restaurant and saw table 24, a cozy two-seater near a bird of paradise plant, with one real flower opened. It looked quite nice against the faux adobe wall, painted to look as though it were built during the reign of Father Junipero Serra. It was a darkish Navajo white.

François saw that the diners at table 24 were getting up and leaving. Before any of the outside patrons could say, "Boohoo," he ushered Ben and Erica over to the table. While walking over, he telegraphed across the room to a fast-working busboy with that "get over here right now" look. As sweet as he was to the customers, he could be a real prick to the staff. The busboy quickly arrived, knowing that his life depended on it.

François spoke to him in Spanish with a French accent. "*Stop everything and clean this table at once!*"

Erica smiled at the busboy. He smiled back. François was not happy to share his stars with anyone, and snapped his finger at the busboy. The busboy worked at near super-burro speed to clear the dessert plates, the coffee cups, and the basket of tortilla chips. François stood by to watch every millimeter of this job. The busboy was about to take his leave, when François pointed with his eyes. There was the small corner of one tortilla chip that he had missed.

"Oh, I am so sorry."

He picked it up with his hand, put it in his busboy apron pocket, and walked away. François then sat Ben and Erica down and gave them the colorful, high-gloss menus.

"Thank you, François."

Erica enjoyed saying his name. She loved to speak fru fru.

They could see into the kitchen area. The busy chefs wore white chef coats and those black and white checkered chef pants. They were busy as fireflies, whizzing around the kitchen area. On the other side of the room, toward the front of the restaurant, was a bar area. Ben and Erica had not noticed that a man sitting at the bar had taken notice of her. Francois's excitement had caused several heads to turn, including the head of Mr. Henry Emerson III. He was an Anglo-Saxon with a perfectly shaved head, neatly dressed in a blue blazer, beige shirt and slightly darker beige pants. He wore a pair of brown leather tennis shoes that almost looked like dress shoes. He was in his early 20s.

Unfortunately for Erica, the man had a look of obsession. In his hyperactive mind, a movie played in slow motion. A man in a military outfit, his father, Henry Emerson II, was dancing with a dead woman, Henry's mother Alice. Her body was limp like a Raggedy Ann doll. She had been a beautiful woman, blonde, tall, thin, a little bit in the same realm as Erica. He danced with her to a classical symphony. When the drama of the symphony was over, he announced to the young boy, a boy by the name of Henry Emerson III: "*A thing of beauty must be destroyed.*"

Back at the Tasterilla, Henry was ready to seize the moment. It would not be his first. He was practiced, cunning like a wolf, patient as a tortoise, and watchful like a hawk. The human beast was careful not to be obvious in his glances over to Erica.

Erica remained oblivious to it all. Ben had his back to him.

They talked like true lovers do, about absolutely nothing.

She giggled, she fluttered her hair, and blew a kiss. Ben faked as though it nearly knocked him over.

Erica was drinking an iced tea, and not the Long Island type. Henry watched as she downed one, and then two. It was only a matter of minutes before the caffeine and water of that tea would wash through her stomach, go into her intestines, filter through her kidneys, and get into her bladder.

Henry prepared himself.

"Bartender."

"Yes, sir?"

"Check, please."

"Very well."

The bartender added up the night's meal: raw tuna, another order of raw tuna, and two margaritas. Henry paid cash. There would be no credit card receipt, no paper evidence of his ever being there. He put his jacket on and pretended to be watching the television. While looking at the TV, he could see over to Erica's area.

Erica got up to use the restroom. Ben did not spend even a half of a second thinking about it. The restroom was around the other side of the kitchen area. She had to walk in front of the kitchen, where the hard-working chefs took notice of her. One of them yelled out,

"Hola, Chiquita!"

She smiled at them. Meanwhile, Henry took another route around the perimeter, walking in a fast way but making it look slow. His tennis shoes were below radar quiet. He arrived just behind her. He pulled a syringe out of the chest pocket. Luckily for Henry and unluckily for Erica, the hallway was empty. The restrooms were unisex; supposed to be for one occupant at a time. She opened the door and entered the bathroom. She wasn't looking behind her, and had no idea that Henry followed her in. His rubber-soled tennis shoes allowed him to walk invisibly, quietly, like an Apache.

Before she could yell "stop," he forced his hand over her mouth, muffling her scream. He shoved the syringe into her neck, and injected her with a liquid drug cocktail. She went limp within seconds. He turned back and locked the door. She was now his prey to do whatever he wanted.

He pranced about like a fox in a cage, back and forth. Where would he start? The mouth? The breasts? The shoulders? Which part of her would he touch first? Would he smell her? Would he taste her? Or would he just look at her?

For the time being, just looking was perfect. He sat her on a toilet stall and propped her back up to the wall. He unsnapped her Oshkosh overall tops. The front part of the overalls fell down, revealing the white blouse. He unbuttoned the white blouse, which revealed a lacy white bra. Ooh, he thought. Very pretty. The bra had one of those front snaps. He undid the bra. Her breasts floated out. Oh goodness, she is a pretty one. He held her breasts, caressed her nipples. One at a time he squeezed them, he kissed them, he sucked on them. She was delicious.

He stood her up, and removed the rest of her overalls. She remained with her shoes on, underwear on, no bra, no blouse. Very sexy looking.

He danced with her limp body. One, two, three, one, two, three. He remembered the waltz as though it were played yesterday. Like father, like son. How could he forget? She groaned a bit.

"What's going on?"

She started to come to. He had purposely given her a cocktail that would put her out, but not for long. What he was about to do with her would not be nearly as interesting if she wasn't fully aware of what was happening. He took some cold water and doused it on her face. She shook her head.

"Good morning, dear."

"Who are you?"

"I am your new owner."

"Let me go..."

She was too tired to scream, but he wouldn't trust the power of the drug. He had in his coat pocket a spool of clear packing tape, the type that is two inches thick. Probably the noisiest part of this incident was the process of unwrapping that tape from its spool.

"Don't worry, you'll be able to breathe."

The taping of her mouth woke Erica up even more. Her eyes showed the terror of what was about to happen. She tried to fight, but she was too weak. She looked around for something to grab, but there was nothing. Her eyes lit up more as he removed his pants. He took out of his pocket a condom, and removed his underwear.

Oddly, he had shaved all of his pubic hair, perhaps to match the shaved look of his scalp.

He taped her hands together at the wrist, using more of that packing tape. He placed her over the bathroom sink, with her breasts and chest in the sink, her head over the other side, and her ass propped up. He had a small vial of hand cream. He dropped some onto her butt. He used his finger to massage it into her anus. He then placed the condom on. He placed cream on the condom and proceeded to jack off, while massaging her anus with his finger. She was groaning, not out of enjoyment, out of fright. He then entered her anus. The cream helped it slide right in. This was her first experience with anal intercourse. It was extremely painful. Her muffled scream could be heard only by him. Her back was arching up, down, sideways. She was trying to get free. He rode her as she wiggled.

She was too weak to fight him off. Her wrists were tied, so she was unable to flail around with her hands. One thing she could do, she did: she whacked him with her elbow, right in the gut. UMPH. It actually hurt him. He withdrew from her for a moment. This really pissed him off. He punched her in the jaw.

"Do it again, I'll snap your neck," he warned her.

She realized at that point there was only one way to get out alive, and that was just to submit. She cried, knowing that this was her fate. He put some more cream on her anus. He put some more on his cock. He had gone a little soft, so he jacked off a few strokes. He massaged her anus with his finger some more. He placed himself back into her, and continued with his fantasy.

Time is truly relative. For Erica it seemed like three days; for Henry it seemed like three seconds. It was in fact three minutes. At last he was done.

He withdrew from her and smiled at his cock, removed the condom, threw it in the toilet and flushed it away. He took her off the sink and neatly placed her onto the toilet seat. She sat there, delirious. He washed his cock off at the sink, and carefully dried it with hand towels. He flushed the hand towels down the toilet. He put his pants back on and zipped them up. The zipping sound bothered her. She looked up at him. It bothered him to have her look at him.

He gave her a second dose of whatever that drug cocktail was. She watched as he came out with the half-filled syringe. She shook her head. No, no, not another one. He stuck it into her neck and emptied the syringe into her. He took another paper towel and wrapped the syringe in it. He put the syringe into his pocket.

He opened the bathroom door and peered out in the hallway. A man was walking down the hallway. He closed the doorway and waited until he could hear the man go into the bathroom next to them. He heard that door lock. He knew it was safe. He peered into the hallway again.

There was no one there. On the back of the hallway was an exit door leading to the back part of the restaurant, where they kept the garbage cans. He very quickly and quietly walked out the back part into the garbage can area, where an open gate into the back parking lot awaited him. He got into his car, ironically a very police-looking Crown Victoria, and drove away without a screech, as though he was in no hurry at all.

CHAPTER 5

THE AFTERMATH

Ben was quite used to Erica having long visits to the bathroom, and hadn't become the least bit suspicious about this lengthy stay. An unsuspecting woman was next to use the restroom. Boy, did she get an eyeful when she opened the door.

The shriek shot across the restaurant and hit Ben like a ton of bricks. He knew it had to be about Erica. God knows what it was. It could have just been a psych relapse. The furthest thing from his mind was a rape. He ran to the restroom, almost running over François in the process. François was right behind him. He got to the bathroom door and saw with his own eyes two women, one crouched over Erica trying to remove the tape around her mouth, and the other, of course, being Erica. She was woozy, drugged, in a semi-conscious state. The woman looked at Ben, and could see that there was some connection between the two.

"Is this your wife?"

"She's my fiancée."

"I'm so sorry. I don't know how she got this way."

There was a crowd at the door of the bathroom. Erica was stark naked. Ben turned around and saw the crowd.

"Do you mind?"

François took two immediate steps. First he ushered everyone away from the door. Then, he called 911. Ben heard the 911 call and realized it was of course the right thing to do. Ben then focused on Erica.

"Honey? Honey? Are you okay? Are you there?"

She was obviously not dead; she was moving her head around, she was breathing loudly, she was groaning. That was the good news. The bad news was she was so semi-unconscious that she couldn't say a word, at least not one that made any sense. The woman helping out was kind enough to bring over Erica's clothing. Ben studied the wound on Erica's jaw. It had been struck hard, was bleeding, and had a mark on it. It had the mark of being hit by something metallic, something like a ring. Ben realized they should of course put Erica's clothes on. Ben snapped off a few pictures out of his cell phone.

The woman thought it was unusual until Ben explained, "I want to preserve the crime scene."

The woman nodded. Ben took a picture of Erica as she was, on the floor, naked, with tape around her wrists and an injured face. The only part that was not found "as is" was that the tape around her mouth; it had been removed. He photographed the sole item left behind by the rapist: an open condom wrapper. The woman was about to pick it off the floor when Ben stopped her.

"Leave it alone. There could be fingerprints on that."

She agreed, and stayed away from it. The police arrived. Three units pulled up almost simultaneously. One unit had a male and female officer; the other two units had two males each. François brought them back into the bathroom area. The feminine-looking female detective, Detective Malene, approached Erica cautiously. Ben was holding her.

CHAPTER 6

SAN DIEGO CRIME SCENE INVESTIGATION

Detective Malene could see that Erica was trying to say something. The small bathroom quarters were rather confining. The tile walls made it so that all speech echoed. Erica found a trust in Detective Malene, and was trying to mouth some words. Detective Malene got down on her hands and knees.

"Tell me. Tell me."

Everyone became quiet. Ben listened with great fascination at what Erica was trying to say. She began to utter a word:

"Cooc…"

It trailed off.

"What? She's saying 'cooc.'"

Suddenly this almost speech was interrupted by an exorcist-style hurl of liquid from Erica's mouth. It splashed against Detective Malene's chest, but didn't faze her even for a second. She hurled one time, two times, three times, and then went into a series of dry heaves. There was nothing more to come up. After the iced tea, the couple tortilla chips, the series of energy drinks from the day, and one peanut butter laden piece of bread, plus a bit of angst bile, her stomach was completely empty.

The dry heaves were particularly exhausting. Right afterwards, she went into an unconscious state and flopped into the wet arms of Detective Malene. She gently put her down into the arms of Ben. Detective Malene stood up, went over to the paper towel dispenser, got some towels, and cleaned off her chest area. Malene explained to Officer Ballati:

"I think she said 'cook.'"

Officer Ballati went into alert dog mode. He turned over to François and snapped his fingers at him, as though anyone was allowed to finger snap in Francois's little fru fru restaurant.

"I want you to give me the personnel files of all cooks on duty."

He turned to the other three officers present.

"To the kitchen, now. We must cage the cooks."

The kitchen was less than a few nightsticks away. There were four cooks, all of Latino descent. One of them, Eddie Fernandez, knew the dog alert look in the officers' eyes. His heart started beating. His adrenaline started flowing. They seemed to be coming at him in slow motion. They weren't looking at him, and didn't suspect him, but in his own paranoia he thought they were all looking at him and completely suspected him.

He did something he should not have done. He ran. There is actually a jury instruction given in criminal trials that a jury is permitted to consider the fact that a person flees as evidence of consciousness of guilt. Unfortunately, as is sometimes the case, fleeing can have nothing to do with guilt.

He ran out the back door, to the same area where the garbage cans are kept, where Henry had earlier fled through. He did not get far, as two other police units drove up to the back. In classic police pursuit, they placed several cars at the front and two in the back.

As he was running out, one resourceful officer opened his driver's side door, which Eddie smashed right into. He tumbled up and over the door, and smashed into the back passenger door. If the door had been open, he might have fallen right in the back of the police car. Instead, he fell down on his back by the door.

Two other officers were on him in a matter of tenths of seconds. One perhaps overreacted and tasered him, connecting him with two darts fired out of a plastic gun, with the help of a pressurized CO_2 canister. The darts are connected to wires that are connected to a regular D9 battery, the sort that you put in a radio. Once the two wires connect, about twenty-five thousand watts of electrical current are transmitted into the victim. Most people will be immediately incapacitated. Some of the exceptions are those under the effects of PCP or other drugs. Eddie, for all his failings and problems, was not a drug addict. He was a sex addict, and as will be seen, would be the perfect scapegoat for Henry's crimes.

Detective Malene was on the scene.

"Did you get his wallet?"

One of the officers showed it.

"Right here."

"Look at his ID."

They pulled out two driver's licenses. One was from the Republic of Mexico, Tijuana. The other was a California license.

"Run 'em."

The police had laptops right in their patrol cars and punched in his driver's license. Within seconds, his rap sheet came up.

"Ohh."

Malene wanted to know what that meant.

"Look at this. We've got four counts of PC 288(a), child molestation; one count forced oral copulation; one count rape; recently paroled from California Department of Corrections; and, for what it's worth, in good standing with his parole officer. Until now, anyway."

Malene walked over to this culprit. She did not wish to make any judgments. She surprised everybody by getting down on her hands and knees, putting both her hands on his cook pants, and ripped them apart, exposing his pelvic region.

"Aha!"

And what did they find? A man whose penis had, of all things, a condom on it. She put her hand up, like a surgeon does when he needs a new set of forceps. One of the officers handed her a pair of surgical gloves. Another officer handed her a pair of tweezers. She pointed at Eddie's face with the tweezers.

"Don't move unless you want a very significant injury. I never made it to medical school, and I've got pretty shaky hands." She held up her twitching fingers.

Eddie complied. She very delicately used the tweezers to grab the reservoir tip of the condom. She noted it was not full of semen, a fact that proved absolutely nothing. Many rapes occur without the man climaxing.

She removed the condom and placed it into a Ziploc bag and sealed it.

"Bag it, tag it."

The question would remain whether DNA testing of the outer part of that condom would match any DNA from Erica. Until then, of course, Eddie the cook was presumed one hundred percent, absolutely guilty. They placed him on a parole hold, cuffed him, and put him in the back of the car.

All this was under the watchful eye of a fairly large audience of the public. Malene turned around and saw that she had attracted quite a crowd. She turned to her fellow officers.

"Get 'em out of here."

They had to remove the taser darts from Eddie's abdomen. They had pierced the cook's jacket, and went right into him. They removed them, picked him up and not so gently placed him into the back of the patrol car.

Meanwhile, back in the bathroom, some unfortunate medical events were transpiring. There was a huge impact, both physical, emotional, and pharmaceutical, on Erica. She had received too much of the drug cocktail. It did not help matters that she was already a woman on the verge of an angst breakdown. On top of that was her now empty stomach, the combination of too many energy drinks, and the emotional impact of the sexual assault. All this placed her into a comatose state.

Ben held her head softly and figured she would wake up soon enough. Paramedics arrived with a stretcher. One of them had a flashlight. He opened her eye and saw that her pupils were not responding to the flashlight. Another put a blood pressure monitor on her. Another put oxygen over her mouth.

"On my count: one, two, three!"

They lifted her up and placed her on the gurney. They turned to Ben.

"We're taking her to Mercy Memorial. You want to ride with her?"

He got up, nodded, and followed. As she was leaving, one of the officers stopped the path of the gurney.

"Just a second."

He had a CSI team member, who snapped several photos of her body and her face. Malene came back and saw the mark on her face where Henry had struck her. It had a weird mark to it, one that was captured by a series of flashes from the CSI team. It was also captured by Ben's cell phone camera.

The indentation appeared to have wings, and eerily showed stars and stripes just above the wings. Malene couldn't help but call it out.

"It looks like some kind of American bald eagle with stars and stripes."

She got a quick idea and radioed to the officers that were driving Eddie the cook to his holding cell.

"Malene to dispatch."

"This is dispatch."

"Put me through to patrol car 644."

"Patrol car 644 here."

"You've got the cook in the backseat?"

"Sure do."

"You take a look at his fingers for me?"

"Okay, they are currently cuffed behind his back."

"Pull over. Check them out."

The officers pulled over. They exited the driver's side and passenger side front, opened up the back door, and roughly took Eddie from a seated position to a prone position on his stomach. His hands were now up.

"Okay, what are we looking for?"

"By any chance, is he wearing a ring?"

"Yes, he is."

She thought maybe she had hit pay dirt.

"What kind of ring?"

"Gold wedding band."

"Oh."

That is not what she had expected from a lifelong sex offender, but even they manage to get married.

"Any marks or engravings on the ring?"

They inspected it.

"No. It's your basic flat gold wedding band. Nothing different or unique about it."

"Any other jewelry?"

"He's got a watch."

"All right, check out the watch."

"What do you want to know about it?"

"What's it made out of?"

"Leather band, silver metal face, Timex."

"Any kind of wing-shaped, beak-shaped, or stars and stripes shapes on it?"

"None."

"Any tan line on a finger showing where a ring used to be?"

The officers looked, and found none.

"Negative."

"Hmm."

Malene now fully expected that the DNA extracted from that bagged condom would not be a match to Erica.

CHAPTER 7

EDDIE THE SEX OFFENDER

In the kitchen area of the Tasterilla, there was a garbage can. Police found in that garbage can a group of open condom packages, and used condoms. These condoms had semen in them. The officers took them out one by one with tweezers, and bagged them. The other cooks were interviewed:

"Eddie is a sex offender?" one asked.

"Yes."

"I had no idea."

"Do you ever see him do anything to girls?"

"Not a thing. He's a very hard worker."

"Come to think of it, though, I did notice him while cooking," one said, providing some guidance. "You see, from our workstation, you can see out to the restaurant area."

The officer turned around. Sure enough, it was a full view.

"You see over there on the oven?"

They looked over and could see a group of hot pads.

"I noticed Eddie tilting in to those hot pads. I thought he had just lost his balance."

"Oh?"

The officer went over and examined the hot pad. It looked like a regular hot pad used to pick up hot frying pans.

"This is where Eddie worked?"

"Yes."

They noticed on the floor there was one more condom wrapper. The officer picked it up with tweezers and placed it into a bag. All told, there were seven condom wrappers and six condoms from the garbage can. Number seven was found on Eddie.

Eddie was still in his post-prison sex offender therapy regimen and had been thought of as one of the better students. He had fully admitted to his past crimes and was participating in the sex offender therapy. He lived at a sex offender halfway house, a place where they put individuals after they are paroled from prison. They don't just dump them back into the street. Most people would be shocked to know that possibly down the street from your house is a house filled with umpteen registered sexual offenders trying to beat their demons and become positive members of society. The data is a bit daunting, as few succeed.

Eddie was one of those few, at least up until today. Back in the police interrogation room, they placed Eddie under video. Detective Malene placed the unwrapped condom package that was found in the bathroom in front of Eddie. She then placed another bag filled with other condom wrappers. As it happened, they were all Trojan brand.

"What other brand is there?" Eddie noted.

Eddie pointed out that the package found in the bathroom was silver, whereas his packages were gold.

"That doesn't prove a thing. It shows that you buy different packages," Malene said.

"Well, officer, I believe it's legal for me to have condoms. I am not aware of anything in my parole conditions that says I can't have a condom."

Outside the interview room was Eddie's parole officer. He looked over to the sergeant and the captain looking in through the mirror.

"He's right. He's allowed to have a condom. He's just not allowed to use it against anyone who does not consent."

The sergeant thought that to be a rather odd rule. Eddie tried to explain why he had those condoms in the kitchen area.

"Officer, I'm sorry to tell you this, but there are so many hot babes that come into the restaurant, and I get so excited. Now, I'm not going to touch one of them, I don't even talk to them, but you know what, I notice them. So I've had a couple accidents, shall we say, and I've figured out a good way to avoid accidents was to simply come to work wearing a condom."

Malene studied this pathetic man. As ridiculous as it sounded, it was unfortunately one hundred percent true.

"Eddie, will you take a lie detector test?"

"Absolutely yes."

"Will you do that right now?"

"I will."

A lie detector technician was brought in. One of the greatest ways of getting to the bottom of a 'he said she said' situation, especially where there is no 'she said' to hear, is a lie detector. The technician strapped it on to Eddie and asked him a few baseline questions.

"Is your name Eddie Fernandez?"

"Yes."

"Do you work at the Tasterilla?"

"Yes."

"Are you a registered sex offender?"

"Yes."

"Do you live at the Eternal Hope Halfway House?"

"Yes."

"Did you rape a woman today in the bathroom at the Tasterilla?"

"No."

Malene studied the horizontal lines of all of those questions printed out from the lie detector system. They all showed very consistent honest answers. She looked up at the two-way mirror, knowing her sergeant, the captain, and the parole officer were watching from the other side. She shook her head no. Eddie was not the guy.

CHAPTER 8

MERCY HOSPITAL, SAN DIEGO

Meanwhile, in the emergency room at Mercy Hospital, San Diego, Erica was undergoing a battery of tests to figure out what was wrong with her. Dr. Weiss was the attending physician, and had seen, unfortunately, many rape victims in the past. This one was a little bit different. Amazing. Not one single pubic hair left behind. Usually there's at least something.

One of the forensic nurses, a large female by the name of Parsons, pointed out some chafing.

"Look, Doctor. Right here around the outer part of her anus."

The doctor looked down, and sure enough, there were marks of chafing.

"This," the doctor noted, "could have happened from a couple things. First, if a man was there orally, and was slightly unshaven, that would cause a kind of sandpaper-type friction to the extremely tender buttocks, which would result in chafing."

The nurse came up with her own theory.

"Or, the man could have shaved his pubic area."

The doctor looked at the nurse and was a bit impressed that she would come up with such a theory.

"Excellent analysis, Nurse Parsons. I'll bet you right now that's exactly what we have: a culprit who shaves his pubic area."

"Which means what?"

The "what" of that would become the subject of a study done by a forensic profiler. She had just arrived into the ER room: Dr. Donna Kuchins, a diminutive Filipino woman with a super brain.

"A man who shaves is likely borderline or past borderline gay. He is trying to be effeminate. He is also one of these super-clean people. I would expect him to be short-haired, clean-shaven, with a perfectly manicured set of nails, fingers, and toes. I would expect his dress to be impeccable."

The doctor was inquisitive.

"You expect him to wear a dress?"

"No, I don't. I expect whatever he is wearing, though, to be impeccable: perfectly ironed, pressed, not a wrinkle or stitch out of place."

Erica was completely unconscious through all of this. They swabbed her body up and down with cotton swabs, hoping to find some mark or something that would show DNA residue from her assailant.

"There is usually something left behind," the doctor noted.

Profiler Donna Kuchins, Ph.D, noted:

"The chafing is all you may have. He used a condom," Profiler Donna Kuchins, Ph.D said.

"A wrapper was found in the garbage in the place where the incident occurred," the doctor said.

"But no condom?"

Dr. Weiss answered, "No."

"It was probably flushed."

"I also note two puncture wounds, both in the neck. This is where he drugged her."

The profiler questioned this,

"What was the drug?"

"According to our toxicology reports, it was a mixed cocktail of a pre-anesthetic known as Acepromazine, an anesthetic known as Sevo, and prescription grade Valium."

The profiler looked up in the air for answers.

"Here's the thing. First of all, Acepromazine and Sevo? Do you know what those are used for?"

The doctor looked to the profiler.

"They're used to put animals out."

Dr Kuchins said, "Yeah. That's a veterinarian's anesthesia."

Dr. Weiss knew, "Well, Valium isn't."

"I wonder if what we've got here is a shaved effeminate man, bisexual, employed or somehow connected to a veterinary clinic, and who is undergoing some kind of medical care where he receives prescription Valium."

The doctor nodded his head.

"We're getting a profile."

"The good news…just a second." the profiler said, left the room and came back within a matter of moments with the San Diego yellow pages. She opened to V for veterinary clinics.

"There are only seventeen clinics in the city."

The doctor studied the names of the seventeen clinics.

"A friend of mine is a surgeon at that one. His name is Carl Rasmussen. Give him a call."

Dr. Kuchins would delegate the interrogation task to Detective Malene. For now, her job was to call it in. She picked up her cell phone and went into the hallway as Dr. Weiss and Nurse Parsons continued their millimeter by millimeter examination of Erica.

She saw the fidgety, super-nervous Ben Nightingale in the hallway.

"You are the fiancé?"

"Yes. Who are you?"

"My name is Dr. Kuchins. I am a police profiler. I look at evidence and try to figure out what kind of perpetrator we're dealing with."

"Yes, I'm aware of what a profiler is."

Ben had done several articles about profilers. It is truly amazing what they can do with just a handful of evidence.

"Do you have any kind of profile here?"

"Yes. Why don't you listen in on this call."

Detective Malene had finished her interrogation of Eddie. She had crossed him off the list of suspects, but would wait until the DNA report came back from the one condom found on Eddie before making her final decision on the issue. Eddie would remain in custody until then. She took the call.

"Yes, Dr. Kuchins?"

"Is this Detective Malene?"

"Yes."

"You're the lead on this?"

"I am."

"Detective, I think you want to come down to the hospital. We have the beginning of a profile analysis."

Malene was pleased to hear of some progress.

"I'm on my way."

Within seconds, she was out the door in an unmarked police department issued Crown Victoria. It took her a matter of several minutes to make her way to the hospital ER room, where she met up with Dr. Kuchins, Dr. Weiss, Nurse Parsons, and Ben Nightingale. She saw through the window to the ER room, where Erica was sound asleep.

"How is she?"

"I'm sorry to tell you, she's in a coma," Dr. Weiss explained.

"A coma?" Malene shook her head.

"She has basically OD'd on the anesthesia given to her."

"The anesthesia, it turns out, is most commonly used by a veterinarian," Kuchins interjected.

"A vet?"

Malene was surprised to hear that one. Kuchins showed Malene the open yellow pages.

"Take a look: there's only seventeen in San Diego."

She looked down and saw vet clinics in the yellow pages. Indeed, seventeen vet clinics.

"Well, that narrows down the search."

· Ben pointed out something, though.

"You think it's an employee of a vet clinic? If that were true, yeah, it would narrow down the search. But I've got news for you."

Everyone looked at Ben. They didn't realize they were dealing with an investigative reporter that was quite resourceful in getting to the truth of matters.

"What's that?"

"It could be a client of a vet clinic. And how many dogs, cats, horses, sheep, goats, cows or whatever do you think these vet clinics deal with?"

Weiss had some input on that. His surgeon friend Dr. Rasmussen shared with him quite a few details of his daily regimen.

"Probably over a hundred a day."

"Okay. So maybe this guy had a dog or a cat or something, and somehow while there managed to swipe some Sevo and Acepromazine."

"Hmm. If that were the case, that would add another element to the profile."

"What's that?"

"A sneaky thief. I would expect him to probably have a conviction for shoplifting or something like that."

"Unless, of course, he's really good and never got caught."

"You know, the thing is, if you're at Wal-Mart, they're looking out for shoplifters. They've got a whole system of in-store detectives, security officers, cameras, the works. But at a vet, they completely aren't paying attention. They're so darned busy bringing animals in, animals out, you've got people at the front desk, answering the phone, doctors going from one surgery to x-rays to surgeries and this and that; it would actually be fairly simple for some guy to just casually walk to the back area, the pharmacy lab, and pull off several bottles of anesthesia."

"But he would have to know what it was."

"Not necessarily. He might just pile it in a bag, a knapsack --"

"It wouldn't be a knapsack," Kuchins interrupted. "Too messy. This is the kind of guy I would expect to have Ziploc bags in his coat pocket. I would also expect him to know exactly what he's looking for, not a random handful of drugs. It's not hard to figure this stuff out. All you've got to do is go online. He could figure out what a good anesthesia is."

"But why a vet clinic?"

"Maybe it's just because of how you said it: it's the easiest way to get this stuff."

"So what, he faked a sick dog?"

"No, maybe he had a sick dog or cat."

"Maybe he shows dogs," Ben interjected.

They looked at him.

"What?"

"Yeah. Maybe he shows dogs."

"What's that got to do with the anesthesia?"

"Show dogs need to undergo a process to have their hips x-rayed, make sure they don't have some kind of hip dysplasia or other malady. In the process, they give this kind of anesthesia."

Nurse Parson was impressed.

"Aha! So now the profile becomes a little bit more detailed. We've got a clean-shaven, bisexual, organized, meticulous man, who shows dogs."

Everyone looked at each other and wondered, how on earth would they find that guy?

CHAPTER 9

THE INVESTIGATION BEGINS

Ben took his cell phone out of his coat pocket and brought up the picture he had taken of the mark on Erica's face.

"What about this? What does this tell us?"

Weiss took a look at it.

"Yes, we have multiple pictures of that mark."

"Ben, I'm going to need that photo," Malene noted.

"Okay. I can upload it to my computer and email it to you. How about that?"

"How about you just give me your phone right now and I'll upload it."

"Well, do you have the connector?"

"No."

"How about you let me email it to you. Trust me, I want to help you."

"We've got plenty of photos of that mark," Weiss assured Malene.

"Yes, but Ben's may be the freshest."

"I took it immediately. It's within seconds of the discovery of her body," Ben noted.

Malene looked at him.

"I want that photo."

"I'll get it to you."

"You got any others on there?"

"Yeah."

He showed her seven other photos of Erica in the state that they had found her: tape on her mouth, propped up against a toilet seat, arms bound together, tears coming from her eyes, and limp like a Raggedy Ann doll. Her legs were apart, her Oshkosh pants were on the floor next to her. She was still in her shoes.

They all looked at this messy picture and wondered.

"So the guy punched her?" Malene thought out loud.

Ben knew Erica would have put up a struggle.

"Maybe she punched him."

Malene disagreed. "With her hands taped together?"

Nurse Parsons had an idea. "Maybe it was a head butt."

Dr. Weiss searched Erica's forehead, but found no evidence of trauma.

"I might add, if she's on this anesthesia, whatever she did to him would not have had much of an oomph."

"She's pretty strong. She's a gymnast. She can get a good jab in when she needs to," Ben pointed out.

"It was strong enough that the man reacted and hit her, and he left a mark," Dr. Kuchins noted.

They studied the photo of the mark.

"And here it is, it's got that weird eagle shape with stars and stripes. What is it?" Malene wondered.

"Any of you ever been in the service?" Dr. Weiss asked.

Surprisingly, no one had.

"Well, I have. That's how I got through med school. That could be a class graduation ring from one of the military colleges. Or some other college that has an eagle with stars and stripes."

Weiss looked over to Ben.

"You know of a college that has an eagle with stars and stripes as its mark?"

Nurse Parsons, amazingly enough, knew one.

"As a matter of fact, American University, Washington, D.C. Check them out."

Ben went right to business on that with the use of his touch screen phone. The iPhone can do many things. He went online, did a Google for American University, and pulled it up. At the site, he did a search for "class ring." Up came an ordering form for a class ring, which had on it a photo of a very lovely American University class ring. However, of note: no eagle, no stars and stripes. And, in rather brazen lettering, were the words "American University."

"I would expect to see a reverse image of at least one of those letters on her face," Dr. Weiss noted.

"So we can cross that off the list," Malene noted.

Profiler Kuchins took the momentum forward.

"I think we should follow Dr. Weiss's path here and look at the military academies. What do we have?"

Dr. Weiss knew them very well.

"There's the Air Force Academy, that's where I went."

He showed he had an Air Force Academy ring, and guess what: no eagle, stars or stripes on that one.

"Okay, cross that one off the list."

Ben went to the website of Annapolis. They looked at the class rings there. No stars or stripes, no eagle.

"Surprising. You'd think these military academies would have almost nothing else but that."

In fact, they looked at all the academies -- Annapolis, West Point, VMI -- these academies all had impressive class rings, but did not show any kind of eagle or stars and stripes.

"I just don't think we're dealing with a military person here," the profiler indicated.

CHAPTER 10

SAN DIEGO'S VETERINARIAN CLINICS

Ben and Detective Malene proceeded to the seventeen veterinarian clinics in the San Diego County area. The first one was called South County Vet Clinic and had a staff of four doctors of veterinary medicine (D.V.M.) who were hard at work, as usual. The receptionist greeted Ben and Detective Malene. Malene spoke first, and flashed her badge.

"We'd like to speak to who's in charge."

Ben looked over to the badge and smiled. The only thing he had to flash were his press credentials, which would hardly get him in anywhere. The receptionist smiled and asked a typical reactionary question.

"What's this about?"

Malene declined to give details.

"I'll ask the questions here. Let me speak with the doctor in charge."

The receptionist left and went to get Dr. Boyce. While she was gone, Detective Malene and Ben studied the lobby area and the area behind the reception area. The pharmacy area could be seen right behind the reception. There were shelves and shelves of unguarded veterinarian medicines. There was no cabinet, no lock and key, just regular white shelves, the type you might put canned soup on at home, with neat little bottles of medicine all lined up. And at that very moment, nobody was in the reception area; everyone was back in the surgery rooms.

"Look at this. We could just walk right back there right now and take any kind of medicine we would like," Malene noted.

Ben saw that there was a kind of half door, at the height of the reception desk. He noted the rather impressive construction job of this half door. It had a series of countersunk nails in it. This is where you take a pen nail with no head, lightly pound it into the wood, slowing down the process as it gets to the wood so that absolutely no indentation from the hammer is left on the wood. Then the nail is actually tapped into the wood approximately one-sixteenth of an inch. The small hole is filled with putty, and then sanded with fine sandpaper to make a perfectly flush face. There were a series of these, barely noticeable in the door. Ben put his hand over it and felt the smoothness. He looked over to Malene. She had no idea what he had found.

It was locked, but all a person had to do was reach over and unlock it. He did so just as a test. The door opened. Ben walked to the reception area, and back to the pharmacy area. Malene shook her head.

"Great security system."

Just then, Dr. Boyce and the receptionist walked out. Dr. Boyce was surprised to see Ben in the pharmacy area.

"May I help you?"

"Oh, sorry Doctor. I was just testing a theory."

Ben then walked out through the same half door, and joined Detective Malene. Malene introduced herself.

"I'm Detective Malene with the San Diego Police Department. We are here investigating an issue that may involve one or more veterinary clinics in San Diego. May we talk?"

The doctor was more than happy to cooperate.

"Certainly. I would invite you into my office, but I don't have one. Perhaps we could go outside; that's about as private as it gets around here."

"Very well."

The three walked outside, leaving the receptionist behind to wonder about the issue. Once outside, they stood in the parking lot. Several clients were showing up with their various dogs and cats, getting out of their cars and bringing their pets into the clinic. The doctor pointed over to an area where there was some shade, and a modest amount of privacy. They walked over there, Malene talking the whole time.

"We're looking for a profile of a sexual assault perpetrator. The assailant used an anesthetic that appears to be from a vet clinic."

"By any chance, have you been missing any anesthesia?" Ben chimed in.

The doctor thought about it, and gave his honest answer, "I don't know."

"We noticed your pharmacy area is more or less accessible to anyone who would want to go in there and take some."

"You mean, we're not like Fort Knox?"

"Correct."

"Perhaps I should be."

"Well, I'll leave that up to you, Doctor. I'm not sure what the rules and regulations are from the veterinary license board as far as safeguarding pharmaceuticals. But, as you can see, Ben was able to walk back there, unassisted, with nobody in that area. He could've taken any drug he wanted."

The doctor was concerned.

"Maybe we need to do something about that."

"Let me ask you something, Doctor. Is that typical for a vet clinic?"

"I've worked at four. They all have the same kind of layout."

"Are you aware of any vet clinic that actually locks up the pharmacy area?"

"I'm sure there's one somewhere, but not around here. I think people figure nobody's going to steal pet pharmaceuticals."

"We have a profiler on this case," Malene continued.

"A profiler?"

"Yes. Someone who looks at all the evidence and tries to come up with theories about the type of person who may be the perpetrator."

"I see."

"So we'd like to ask you some questions about the profile we have obtained to date to see if maybe you have anyone on staff that qualifies."

"Okay, shoot."

"First of all, we think the person would be extremely clean-shaven, a neatnik, and borderline obsessive compulsive about it."

One look at the doctor's bloody smock, slightly unshaven face, and fairly long hair would remove him from the list of likely suspects. The doctor laughed.

"Not around here. We're too damn busy to be clean."

"I see."

"Listen, we have a pretty busy practice here. Dogs and cats are coming in here all day long. There's really not the kind of time -- maybe there should be, but there just isn't. We definitely change smocks and gloves on every surgery. We throw the gloves away, the smocks go into the laundry bin, I put on a new one. The smocks are taken out to a dry cleaning service. I think you saw the state of the lobby; it's relatively neat, but we are not neatniks. Nobody here is."

"Okay. Next thing: by any chance do you have any people here that are formerly of the military?"

"I am. I served in the Air Force. I flew a helicopter.."

Ben looked at the doctor's hands and noticed that he was not wearing a ring and did not have any kind of tan line where a ring might have been.

"You don't by any chance have a class ring or anything?" Malene had to ask.

"A class ring? No. I never bought one. I was pretty poor when I graduated from vet school; left me about enough money to take a bus home. No class ring for me."

"I see. Anybody else here by chance attend any college or university and actually buy a class ring?"

"We're not much on rings around here. We're surgeons. Rings get in the way of surgery, so I'm not aware of anybody wearing a ring here other than a wedding band. I might add, that's going to be typical in any vet clinic. Think about it, Detective: how do you get surgical gloves over a bulky class ring?"

Ben thought about it.

"You take it off."

"Sure. You take it off and you put it back on. You take it off and you put it back on. What a hassle. And for what? Our clients never really ask where we went to vet school."

"Where did you go, Doctor?"

"The only vet school in the business around here, UC Davis. My undergrad is in biology from UC Santa Barbara."

"I see."

"You are the first person that has asked me that in, gosh, twenty years, so I don't need to show it off, I don't need to show a ring, and I don't. And I don't think anyone else here does either."

Ben saw that the vet staff theory of the case would likely not pan out. They went to plan B.

"Let's talk about the clients coming in here," Detective Malene said. "You've heard our concept of a profile here: former military, wearing a class ring, probably a graduate of a military academy, a neatnik, short hair, obsessive compulsive tendencies, somebody like that."

"Are you asking me if I have any clients like that?"

"Sure."

"Well, first of all, if you're obsessive compulsive about being clean, you probably shouldn't have a pet. Pets are notoriously messy. You ever heard of a clean dog? You ever heard of a clean cat? Anybody that wants to be really super clean really should not have a dog or a cat. It'll drive you crazy."

Ben smiled. How true was that. He looked and saw the owners bringing their pets in. One of them had a Volvo station wagon. The rug on the back part had dog hair all over it. The dog came out and was slobbering. It was a lovely Irish Setter. The owner put a leash on the neck and wiped the slobber off with his hand.

"Oh yeah, right. Obsessive-compulsive guy is going to wipe mouth doodoo off with his hand, right?"

The doctor saw Ben looking at that and smiled.

"Typical customer. They love their animals, the animals are part of the family, the animals are messy, and they deal with it."

Malene figured out the vet staff angle probably wouldn't work. The client angle, plan B, likely wouldn't work either. The odds of finding an obsessive compulsive, super clean, military background person that also happens to own some kind of pet were rather low.

So what was plan C?

CHAPTER 11

CHEERLEADER TURNED PHARMACEUTICAL SALES REP

Just then, a blonde, youngish woman pulled up in a Mercedes SUV. The first thing Ben noticed about the car is that it didn't have a pet in it. The doctor saw Ben's eyes go to the cutey pie driving the car.

"Oh, that's not a client. That's Sheila. She's the pharmaceutical rep."

"Oh."

Malene looked over.

"That's a pharmaceutical rep?"

"Not a pharmacist, never went to med school, doesn't have a doctorate, doesn't look like she would," Ben thought out loud.

"You know, it's kind of funny," the doctor explained. "These pharmaceutical companies are smart at marketing. They specifically hire former cheerleaders to help woo doctors."

Malene thought that to be rather odd.

"To me, it really doesn't matter. I'm looking at medicine, not a date," the doctor continued.

Sheila came out with a large black briefcase filled with drugs. She was quite the A personality, all smiles and able to stand at the top of a human pyramid.

"Dr. Boyce, good afternoon!"

"Hello, Sheila. Just go on in. Mark will deal with you."

"Thank you, Doctor."

Sheila bounced by, exaggerating her walk to ensure the doctor took notice. Malene was astonished at anyone who would use their sexuality as such an obvious marketing ploy. Malene just shook her head and turned to the doctor.

"I think we're done here, Doctor. I want to thank you for your cooperation. Here is my card. If anything comes to mind, please don't hesitate to call me."

Ben shook the doctor's hand.

"We really appreciate your time, Doctor. Good luck with Sheila."

The doctor laughed.

"Oh, I don't deal with her at all."

They got into Detective Malene's car. As they drove to the next vet clinic, they both realized they would likely receive the same kinds of answers. Ben asked,

"Think about it," Ben said. "We're probably going to run up on a dry hole on staff members. If you are a neatnik, it's one thing to say you wouldn't want to own a pet, but at the same time, would you want to work at a pet hospital? What's messier than that?"

"Yeah, that's true."

"But then we've got the likes of Sheila. You see how neat she was? She doesn't have to haul around pets. She just has her little box of medicine."

Malene thought about it.

"The pharmaceutical sales rep would obviously have easy access to all pharmaceuticals."

Malene slammed on the brakes. They came to a screeching halt. Several cars right behind her blared their horns, until she flashed her badge at them.

"Oops, never mind, Officer."

They drove around her. She pealed it into reverse and traveled about one hundred yards on the shoulder side of the road, to the amazement of others on the road, and backed into the vet clinic's parking lot. Just as they were parking, Sheila came out with a big smile on her face. Apparently she got yet another order. Good for her. Malene stopped her.

"Sheila?"

"How do you know my name?"

"We were just here when you said hello to the doctor. He told us about you."

"Okay."

Malene showed Sheila her badge.

"I'm a detective with the San Diego Police Department."

"Okay."

"We are investigating a crime, and believe the perpetrator to be somehow connected to pet pharmaceuticals."

Sheila got defensive and looked down at the ground. Ben relaxed her.

"Don't worry, the perpetrator is most definitely a male."

She looked up.

"Oh."

"So here's our question," Malene continued. "First of all, how many salespeople work for your company?"

"You mean in the San Diego area?"

"Correct."

"We have nine."

"Nine salespeople? There's only seventeen vet clinics around here."

"Oh, we don't just sell vet pharmaceuticals. We sell a full line of pharmaceuticals to doctor's offices, hospitals, the works."

"Oh."

"The vet side is actually a very small side."

"I see. The doctor tells me the pharmaceutical companies are hiring former cheerleaders as marketing reps. Is that true?"

"It is."

"Any exceptions?"

"Of course. Some of the best salespeople we have are male."

Ben thought about it for a second. When he was at Berkeley, he remembered that there were female cheerleaders and male cheerleaders. They called the male ones "yell leaders." Indeed, not to make a catchall profile, but they tended to be cute, gayish guys. In other words, neatniks.

"By any chance, are the male marketing reps also former cheerleaders or yell leaders?" Ben had to ask.

"Yes and no. Some of them are just old school people who've been around quite awhile. The younger set tends to be very presentable. We emphasize a good, healthy look. After all, we're in the medical profession."

Ben, having just seen the likes of Dr. Boyce, couldn't quite catch what Sheila's point was, but ignored it.

"How many other pharmaceutical companies are there doing business around here?" Malene continued.

"You mean how many competitors do I have?"

"Yeah, something like that."

"There are four."

"You ever arrive at a doctor's office, only to find one of your competitors in the lobby?" Ben asked.

"Oh yeah, it happens all the time."

Malene and Ben simultaneously started the next question:

"Have you ever seen a guy-- "

Ben then stopped and deferred to Malene. She started the question over.

"Have you ever seen a guy, either from your company or another pharmaceutical company, and one that calls on vet clinics, who had super-short hair, perhaps even a shaved head, and at the same time just happened to be wearing some kind of military school ring?"

Sheila thought about it. Now wouldn't it be nice if forensic investigations were so easy that Sheila actually knew of such a person that perfectly fit the profile and could say, "Yes, his name is so and so, he works for this company, and you can go pick him up right now"? Well, nothing's that easy in the world.

Sheila shook her head.

"I don't. Sorry about that."

Malene's sail had just lost its air. The search for the perpetrator would have to continue.

CHAPTER 12

GOOGLE: MILITARY CLASS RING

By the end of the day, Malene and Ben had gone to the other three vet clinics, with roughly the same results. The staff were used to getting their hands dirty, filled with animal guts and blood, long hours, and commonly disheveled appearances. If you're looking for a model, you don't want to go to vet clinics. These people are devoted to the safety and care of animals, and probably use up any devotion to their appearances.

Malene dropped Ben off at the police department headquarters, where Ben's lovely Corvair was parked.

"Nice car. Get a lot of chicks with that?" she joked.

Malene was trying to be funny, but didn't see the inappropriateness of making fun about the fact that Ben was now without a woman. Ben shrugged it off silently and left.

That night at home, Ben was busy on the internet. He typed in a Google search for "military class rings." He looked at the Naval Academy, Annapolis, and West Point. These rings were all for sale, to graduates of these fine military institutions, but did not have any kind of eagle diagram on them. Instead, they had the name of the academy on them. There were no letters left on the markings on Erica's face, so it just didn't make sense that it would be a ring from one of these institutions.

Ben went to the West Point Military Academy website, and saw that they had a link to a page of past rings. Now, that was an interesting concept. He was looking at current rings; perhaps there were rings in the past that had an eagle and stars and stripes. He anxiously went to that page. It took a few moments for it to load the rings from 1890 through the present. He studied them like a scientist, increasing the size of each one to see if any of them had appropriate markings of an eagle, stars, and stripes. Amazingly, he found one. It was the class of 1942. There it was, in plain sight. For some reason, during that year, and that year alone, the West Point class ring had a nice American bald eagle and stars and stripes.

Ben printed that page and studied it. Was this the clue to get to the culprit? He immediately called Malene.

"Yes?"

"Detective, Ben here."

"Oh hi, Ben. Listen, I meant to tell you, I'm really sorry about that comment I made to you about finding girls. I really didn't mean to --"

"Detective, don't worry about it. I understand. I'm glad to see that men aren't the only ones who make stupid remarks every now and then."

The detective was not the least bit upset over Ben's blunt choice of words.

"Listen, Malene. Let's put that aside. I have news for you: I think I found something. Do you have a computer at home?"

"I do."

"Please go online."

"Okay."

Ben proceeded to direct her to the West Point Military Academy website, and then to the class ring section, and then to the past class ring sections, and then directed her to 1942. She pulled it up. There was silence.

"Aha!"

Malene could see right away they were on to something. But lest there be too much excitement over this, Malene pointed something out.

"You understand, of course, that the person who graduated in 1942 would now be, what, a hundred years old?"

Ben had already considered that.

"It goes like this, Detective. What do you do with a class ring from West Point when you die?"

Malene thought about it.

"Okay, I see where you're going. You give it to a member of your family."

"Yes. And stick with that. Which member of your family do you give it to? Suppose, for example, you've got more than one child, and let's suppose one of them is a girl. You're probably not going to give it to the girl."

"Sounds rather sexist, but you're probably right."

"Now let's suppose the boy is, shall we say, not deserving of such an honor."

"Oh, okay, so we've got a misfit son."

"Keep in mind the son would be in his sixties, so we're probably not looking at the next generation. We're looking for grandkids here."

"Oh, I see."

"Grandkids could be in their 20s to 30s to 40s, depending."

"So who would the deserving grandson be?"

"He's the son of a son of a misfit of a West Point grad."

"Hmm. Now there's something we can go on. How do you find that?"

CHAPTER 13

THE JOURNALIST

There are times when journalists can get more information than anybody. If you walked in the front door of West Point Military Academy showing a police badge and explained that you are undertaking an investigation of a sexual crime that involved the offspring of a West Point alum, you could well expect to get that door slammed in your face. Ben explained these facts of life to Malene, and had another approach.

"Watch me."

He called up West Point. A school operator answered.

"West Point Military Academy, may I help you?"

"Hi there. This is Ben Nightingale. I'm with the *San Diego Chronicle*. We're doing an article about some of your older alumni, such as those that would have served in World War II."

"I see. Where would you like me to direct your call?"

"For what I'm doing, I think I need somebody involved in alumni affairs or something like that."

"One moment, please."

Within seconds, the phone rang again.

"Alumni Affairs, may I help you?"

"Good morning. This is Ben Nightingale. I'm with the *San Diego Chronicle*. I'd like to know if I could get some help on doing an article I'm writing about some of your older alumni, specifically those that served in World War II."

"Oh, that sounds fascinating. It could be a wonderful article. I don't know how many such folks are out there in California."

"Boy, I'll tell you, I don't have much of a travel allowance. My paper is super cheap and it would just be so wonderful if you happened to have an alum out here in San Diego. Any chance of that?"

"Just a minute, let me check it out."

Ben could hear the sound of the Alumni Affairs person on the computer. She was bringing up some kind of data files of alumni.

"Let's see now, San Diego, and I guess we should punch in the years of, say, 1925 to 1945. That ought to cover it."

"Sure, that sounds perfect."

"Okay, let's see. Here's something. Is Carlsbad close to San Diego?"

"Oh yeah, that's a hop, skip and a jump. I can at least get a gallon of gas and get there."

"Well, we've got a Henry Emerson who was a 1909 grad --"

"I'm sure he's passed on."

"But he had a son, Henry Emerson II, and this gentleman is a 1942 grad. According to our records, he's still alive. We have him in Carlsbad."

Ben just shook his head as he looked at Malene, and asked the million dollar question of the morning.

"By any chance could you give me Mr. Emerson's address?"

"Certainly. 84 Milltower Road, Carlsbad, California."

"One more question before I go."

"Sure."

"By any chance was there a Henry Emerson III that attended West Point?"

"No, that appears to be the end of the line with us."

"Well, it sounds pretty impressive to me. Listen, I want to thank you for your help on this. I'll show you a copy of my article when it's done. I can assure you it will be extremely complimentary of the heroes that attend your military institution."

"Why, thank you. I would love to see the article. Please stay in touch."

"Bye-bye."

Ben turned to Malene.

"That's got to be the guy. I mean, come on. What are the odds of finding a 1942 alum right here? I'm sure he had a class ring. We've got to go see him!"

"Let's do it."

"Wait a minute."

"What?"

"I want to make a suggestion, Detective. I believe it would be better if I interviewed him alone."

"No, this is police business."

"Yeah, but think about it. You think he's going to really want to talk to a cop about what very well could involve his own family member in some kind of horrible crime?"

Malene hated to admit that he was one hundred percent right.

"Okay, I'll tell you what. I will be back at headquarters looking through police archives. I want to see if we've got any reports about Henry Emerson II, III, or whomever the IV was."

"Excellent. You do that. Meanwhile, I'm off to Carlsbad."

Ben's car was low on gas, so he had to make a quick pit stop. He pumped the cheapest gas for the cheapest car on the planet. While there, a pickup truck pulled up to the side of him. It was one of those fully decked out Ford F-250s, with holes on the side, creating a metal box in the truck. There was a silver tool truck. On the side was a sign: "Marvelous Construction, Inc. of San Diego."

Ben looked at the burly driver of the truck, and then studied the turning of the gas pump. In an uncharacteristic splurge, he filled it all the way.

CHAPTER 14

THE EMERSON RANCHETTE

The ranchette was white adobe with red tile roof, faux Spanish style. It was the home of a wealthy man, no question about that. In the front was a circular driveway with a fountain in the middle, complete with birds drinking right out of it. The mailbox read "Emerson Ranch," but would more accurately be described as a ranchette. There were only four acres to this home, hardly qualifying for ranch status. There was another driveway to the right of the home, leading straight back to another white adobe red tile roof structure.

The first thing that caught Ben's eye was the truck parked in this back area. It was a white pickup truck with a black iron frame in the back, several hundred fresh two by fours loaded in the back. The tailgate was down and a red flag dangled off of one of the two by fours. The person that lived in the back, well, we know what he did for a living.

Ben rang the doorbell. A crusty octogenarian with hairy caterpillar eyebrows answered.

"May I help you?"

This was none other than Henry Emerson II, holder of a near ancient West Point Academy graduation ring. Ben immediately glanced down to the elderly man's hands, and saw that conspicuously missing was the ring.

"May I help you?"

Henry was the kind of guy that no matter how much he'd already been through in his colorful life, he was always ready for more. He had a smile, and incorrectly sensed that Ben was a friend.

"I am Ben. I have a question for you. It's about your West Point class ring."

Henry rubbed his hand where the ring should have been. Ben saw that.

"Yes? What do you want to know about my ring?"

"Well, first of all, I would like to congratulate you on being a member of the class of 1942."

"Thank you."

"I am a journalist. I'm doing an article about the locals here that graduated from the Academy."

"Well, I don't think that's going to be a long article. There's probably four of us around here."

"Oh? Do you know the others?"

"Not too well. They weren't in my class, but I know they're around. Here, please come in."

Henry was gracious and stepped out of the way as Ben walked into the high ceilinged home. The home was decorated in a way that a man without a woman would decorate a home. Indeed, the way a military man would decorate the home. Henry's wife passed away long ago, leaving only a shrine of photographic memories placed on the wall near one of the seven fireplaces. Ben's eyes quickly went to those photos. She was a beautiful woman, darkish. The photo was taken during the time when they would place color on a black and white photo, which gave it an eerie aura, like putting makeup on a doll. There were six of these photos, one of which was left intact as a black and white.

"Your wife?" Ben had to ask.

"Yes. Can you believe this? I made it through World War II. I made it through D-Day. I was one of the few that lived and survived the Normandy beach invasion. I went on to help the Allied attack on the Germans, to bring about the end of World War II. Bombs, grenades, bullets going off all around me. Not one of them touches me. I come home and she's dead."

Ben saw the sadness that came over Henry as he spoke of his long past wife. Ever the journalist, he had to know how.

"What happened?"

"Must have been the loneliness that surrounded her. There was no one here for her. I don't know. She took to drinking. One night…"

His voice trembled off. His hands began to shake. His eyes began to tear. Ben did not want to take him to this memory.

"I'm sorry. I don't mean to bring up this sad memory. Please, let's change the subject."

Henry looked up with relief. He sat down on a high backed chair next to the shrine, a place he had sat for many lonely nights. There was a table maid next to the chair. Ben noticed something very interesting about that table. Along the edges were a series of countersunk nails. These were little pin nails, the size you would use to hang up a painting. A series of them were carefully hammered into the corners of this table, pushed in about a sixteenth of an inch. Putty was then placed over the nail head and carefully sanded down and then slacked over. It was the same technique used at the South County Vet Center. Ben looked over at Henry.

Henry saw Ben's interest in the table.

"My grandson built that."

Finally, Henry was lightening up and getting away from his sad memory.

"Your grandson?"

"Yes. He lives out back. He's a carpenter and a damn good one."

"I see. What kind of carpentry does he do? Furniture?"

"No. This was a special project he did for me. He's what they call a finish carpenter. He will make the interior of a home look absolutely perfect."

Ben smiled.

"I see. Did he do any of the work in this house?"

"A few odds and ends. This place was pretty much built way before he was born. He did the cabinets in the kitchen. He did some cabinets upstairs, stuff like that."

"So you've lived here quite awhile?"

"Oh yeah. I got this house from my parents. We've been here for over 120 years. That would make them one of the oldest white residents of California."

"Is your grandson here now? I'd like to meet him."

"Yes. He's out back. He's probably doing some project in his workshop. Here, I'll take you back there."

Henry got up out of his comfortable chair. It disturbed Ben to once again cause this nice man any discomfort, but Ben was on a mission and would not be deterred. Henry was a fairly quick walker. He seemed to be in a hurry to get out of this living room shrine area, and into the sunnier parts of the house. They walked through an entryway, into a kitchen/dining room area, through a kitchen having beautiful windows overlooking a large, grassy backyard. There was no swimming pool; instead, there was the Pacific Ocean. It was a gorgeous view of lawn, sand, and ocean.

To the right of this view was the separate residence where Henry's grandson lived.

"Your grandson lives here. How about your son? Where's he?" Ben couldn't help asking.

Henry stopped right in his tracks, catching Ben off guard. Henry turned to Ben with the same sad face he had just had when talking about his wife.

"He passed on some time ago."

"Oh. I'm sorry."

Ben could sense there was some connection between the two deaths, but what?

"He had the same mental problem as his mom. The doctors called it bipolar."

"Oh."

Ben started to understand there was a genetic passing of a psychological disorder that made these people prone to doing extreme things. He looked over to where the grandson lived and knew that nature in her odd way of working would never miss her mark; like grandmother, like father, like son. They would all have the bipolar disorder. Ben did not need to know how Henry's son died, but Henry wanted him to know.

"Damnedest thing I ever saw. He killed his wife, Henry's mom --"

"Henry?"

"My grandson's name. He's named after me. He's Henry Emerson III. After my son killed his wife, he took his pistol and shot his brains out. Thank God it didn't happen in this home. I'd have to move."

"Where did it occur?"

"On a military base. He was stationed overseas in Okinawa. With all the medical testing they do before you get into the military, you'd think something like this would have popped up on their radar, but it didn't."

Ben started to speculate about the time period of Henry's father in Okinawa.

"That would have been around 1960 or so, right?"

"1987. He was there for two years. He had some kind of major problem there. He was in a heap of trouble. He took out his wife and then he took out himself, and he left poor Henry here to me, but I raised him like my own son. He's all I got."

Ben thought. Great, here's this wonderful man. A hero to our nation, a patriot, a great guy who only has a grandson and Ben is there to take him away. But Ben was on a mission. Nothing would deter him.

As they were approaching the house, Ben heard the unmistakable sound of a talented musician. There was an acoustic guitar coming from the wood shop. He was playing to a CD, to the song called "Suite Madame Blue," by Styx. The guitar was perfect; the voice needed a little work. The singing was real, was soulful; the guitar was professional level.

The minute Henry opened the door to the woodshop area, the guitar came to a crashing halt. Henry III put the guitar down and pretended to be back at work on his cabinet job.

"He built that guitar himself," Henry II pointed out to Ben.

Ben was impressed that this rapist could do such a thing.

CHAPTER 15

HENRY WILBUR EMERSON III

He was in his wood shop -- a handheld skill saw in his hand the size of a power drill. He was cutting a series of one by one boards, used for the interior of a majestic cabinet system that was in the framing stage. The mahogany fronts were tilted up against the wall. The reddish tint of these perfect boards would make a gorgeous cabinet. Henry looked up at his grandfather and smiled.

"Henry, there's somebody here I want you to meet. This is Ben."

"Hello."

Henry III looked up. The second he saw Ben, he did something that he would never do in a million years. He nicked the one by one, leaving a small, barely perceptible three-eighths inch gash on it. Ben did not see Henry III that night at the Tasterilla, but Henry saw Ben and knew that Ben was there looking for him. He was thinking of running, but then it occurred to him maybe Ben didn't know it was him. He touched the gash made into the one by one, shook his head and put it down. He put his power saw down. There was a towel near by. He took that to clean his hands. There was another towel he used to clean the sweat off his forehead and his cleanly shaved head. He put the towels down, walked over to Ben and put his hand out.

"Nice to meet you. I'm Henry."

Ben realized right then and there, without any doubt about it, he was shaking the hand of the man who had raped his fiancée. The question now was how to prove it. Ben noticed that Henry was not wearing any ring. There was a missing piece of the puzzle that was soon filled. Henry walked over to the side of the wall where the mahogany cabinet faces were propped up. There was a window next to them, and on the windowsill was a ring. Ben's eye spotted the antique ring and knew right away what it was -- West Point, class of 1942.

"Is that your ring?" he asked Henry II.

Henry went over and looked at it.

"Yes, it is. But I gave it to my grandson here. Isn't that right, Henry?"

"That's right. I take it off whenever I'm using the tools."

He put it back on his finger and there it was, in full view: the bipolar clean-shaven West Point ring-wearing rapist.

CHAPTER 16

HOW TO CATCH A SERIAL RAPIST

The first thing to know and understand is that a serial rapist has some kind of deep-seated psychiatric disorder. If he didn't, he wouldn't be a serial rapist.

The second thing to understand is that the nature of the psychiatric disorder is one that produces a kind of abnormal sex drive. Unfortunately for the women of San Diego and for the series of victims of his father in Okinawa, the bipolar disorder creates, during a manic session, a heightened sexual drive.

There is also a misinformation process, whereby the person stricken with the bipolar disorder has misunderstood that their victim actually wants to be raped. It will sound completely ridiculous to a sane person, but to the bipolar impacted, it makes perfect sense.

"A thing of beauty must be destroyed," as Henry's dad said.

Ben first went online back at his home and did a search for Okinawa news back in the 1987 period. Sure enough, front page of the old newspapers, there were a series of articles of Okinawan girls getting raped by a US serviceman. They didn't know who it was, they didn't know why or how, but they knew it was a serviceman because one of the girls was found with his hat. He was a US Army Ranger, Special Forces, but could not be found.

Ben also found the article about Henry's son. His name was Adolph, and sure enough, he was a member of the US Army Rangers. In a case that would never make it to the complaint stage, would never get to trial, Henry's son found himself guilty and irreparable. He did something that he knew needed to be done. He wanted there to be no more victims. During his non-manic periods of relative sanity, when he was not in a bipolar episode, he came to grips with the animal that was unleashed inside of him, and knew that there was only one way to stop this demon. He took his own life. He did this, though, in a ridiculous way, as suicide always is, as in a double suicide in which he decided to take his wife's life as well. He had learned in the Rangers how to snap a person's neck by a quick, forceful twisting of their head, placing both hands on their jawbones and snapping it.

He spoke his selfish words moments before, "Honey, I love you and I never want to leave you."

He realized in taking his own life, he would be lonely and he wanted to be with his wife. This was his deranged side; kill her, then himself and live forever with her. After he snapped her neck, she went limp in his arms. He danced with her. One, two, three, one, two, three -- and thought about how she and he would live forever in the afterlife. The music played for more than an hour. He danced with her in his own living room, to a waltz. He held her back, held her up, twisted her around, arched her back backwards, her limp body flailing about. She had that blank look in her eyes of a person without any life left in them.

This beautiful woman, who had absolutely no psychiatric disorder, had been terminated by one of the craziest humans on the planet. The waltz was over. He sat her down on a chair.

He sat next to her, holding her, crying.

"I love you. I love you. I can't live without you."

He took his pistol out, put it to his temple and blew his brains out -- and that was how they were found. Husband and wife dead, the only question being whether they would truly be united in eternity.

Ben read the news from Okinawa and realized the inescapable truth that Henry III was absolutely the crazy ass son of a bitch that raped his fiancée.

How to catch him? How about this method?

Step one -- realize that the serial rapist has some kind of generationally handed down psychiatric disorder, one that was absolutely proven by the series of articles.

Step two -- find the articles, which Ben had just found.

Step three -- download and print.

He printed out a series of four articles about rapes in Okinawa; rapes of young Japanese women that had gone unsolved for over 40 years. He printed the article about Adolph's bizarre murder suicide pact with his beautiful wife. The article explained how there was a record player still spinning silently when the Army military police arrived. One of them quietly turned it off. It spun for several seconds more before coming to a complete stop.

The next day, Ben would return to the Emerson ranchette with those articles. This time, he would go with backup.

He called Detective Malene.

"I've got him."

"What do you mean, you've got him?"

"I found him."

"You found who?"

"The rapist."

"No."

"Yes."

"Whaddya got?"

"Listen, there's not much time to explain. Will you please follow me? I'm driving to him right now."

"Hey, don't do anything stupid here. You're going to get yourself killed -- or worse yet, you're going to make it so that a perfectly guilty man gets off scot-free."

"Oh, I'm not going to screw up because you're going to be there with me."

"Okay. Where you going?"

"Let me give you the address. 84 Milltower Road, Carlsbad, California."

"Out in Carlsbad? That's ranch country."

"It is. Come on out."

Malene got into her car with Detective Olson, a large male detective having no patience for any kind of rapist. He didn't give a rat's ass about the psychiatric disorders that led to this behavior. If he found a rapist, he would crack his neck.

Malene turned to him with a finger.

"Remember, right by the book; no bones broken, no faces smashed in. Got it?"

Like an angry boy, he nodded his head.

"Yes, dear."

They took off and headed up the highway toward Carlsbad. They pulled off on an exit, made a left and then a right and saw Ben's Corvair parked just down the road from Henry's house. He waved them down.

Malene got out first.

"Okay, Ben. Whaddya got?"

Ben looked over to Olson.

"Haven't seen him before."

"Oh, this is Detective Olson. He's in the sex crimes unit. This is Ben. His fiancée --"

"Oh, I know. I know the whole story. You don't have to tell me. Ben, I'm sorry for what happened, but we're going to get this guy."

"Oh, Detective Olson, I got news for ya. I've got him. He lives right down the street. I got him. It's the guy."

"Okay, wait a minute."

Malene was understandably confused.

"What do you have? What did you do? Tell me the evidence. WHAT DO YOU HAVE?"

"Okay. We know, forensically speaking, that there was some kind of ring with some kind of eagle on it that scratched her face, correct?"

"Yes."

"We understood that perhaps the ring was some kind of a military class ring."

"Right."

"We looked up all the military institutes and their class rings, and amazingly, we found out that they don't have an eagle on the side. Well, guess what? I found one that does. The class of 1942, West Point Academy, had an eagle on it."

Olson looked in dismay. He himself was a military man and could not understand how that would have anything to do with this.

"You're talking about an octogenarian? He's the rapist?"

"No. His grandson is and he lives right down the street. Amazingly enough, the guy's name is Henry Emerson III. His grandfather, Henry Emerson II, is a graduate of West Point Academy, class of 1942 and has an antique ring which was handed down by him to his grandson. Now get this."

He put the news articles on the hood of their unmarked detective's car. Of course, it was a Crown Victoria, olive green. The first article discussed a series of rapes in Okinawa.

"Okay, so some girls got raped in Okinawa. How's that connected to Carlsbad?"

"Hold on."

The second article talked about the murder suicide of a man named Adolph Emerson of Carlsbad, California.

"That would be Henry II's son. That would be the father to Henry III, and note what he did."

They read about it and saw there was a bizarre killing, a bizarre suicide. The guy was psycho.

"Oh yeah, and let me tell you how. He was bipolar."

"How do you know he was bipolar?"

"Because his father told me."

"You went here and interviewed the suspect?"

"I went here and spoke with the grandfather. The grandfather, Henry II, explained to me how his wife had the bipolar disorder and how his son also had the bipolar disorder."

"And you can just bet on it, the grandson has it also," Olson chimed in. "Oh yeah. So what do we have? An intrafamily psychiatric condition --"

"Let me show you this article about bipolar disorder," Ben broke in. "Look at the highlighted part. Enhanced sexual drive during manic episodes. Geesh. Look at that. So you've got a psychopath, you've got an intergenerational issue -- it's all connecting up to a group of rapes that happened in Okinawa and now we've got a group of unsolved rapes right here in Carlsbad and you've got a kid here that happens to own his grandfather's class ring from West Point. I'm telling you, this is the guy."

Malene burst the balloon.

"You'll never prove it with this."

But Ben had plans.

"Oh, I got news for you. I'm not done yet. Let me tell you what we need to do."

They spoke for about five minutes about a plan of action. Malene and Olson looked at each other and nodded.

"Let's do it."

They drove another quarter mile to the Emerson ranchette. Mr. Emerson again opened the door.

"Ben. Good to see you again. I was going to call you."

"Ah, Henry, I have with me a couple of detectives. This is Detective Malene and Detective Olson of the San Diego County Sheriff's Department."

"Oh? Is there some problem?"

"Yes, I'm afraid there is. We need to speak with your grandson. Is he here?"

"Yes, he's out back. You want me to get him?"

"Actually, if you don't mind, we'll go to him, but you can come if you'd like."

"Certainly."

Henry showed them the way and the four of them walked to Henry III's place. The first time Henry saw Ben, he figured Ben did not recognize him from that night -- and he figured right. Ben had not seen him. Ben had only pieced this all together, in a weird jigsaw puzzle that was adding all up to Henry III being the guy. But he certainly wasn't 100% sure, and without a doubt, had nothing to prove it. The first time Henry III saw Ben, he didn't run, he didn't show guilt, he remained cool as a cucumber.

But the stress of that first meeting set something off in Henry III. There was a generally unknown process whereby a bipolar person can have months and even years of fairly normal behavior -- then they go into an episode. What sets off an episode is not exactly known in the psychiatric field. There is one concept though, that there can be a stressor that pushes a button that sets it off. This theory would be in part proved today.

Ben and the detectives heard the sound of Henry playing another song on his handmade guitar, called "I am the Highway" by Audioslave.

The first meeting that Ben had, just yesterday, had set Henry III off into the process of a manic episode. He was hyper, he was agitated, he was angry, he was violent, he was ready for action. When he saw the two detectives coming in, their badges exposed on their belt buckle, ready to read him his Miranda Rights, he knew right away that the game was over. His heart started pounding. His adrenaline was flowing. There was no way he could even closely hold any kind of a tool, but he was. He was holding the same power drill. He was putting larger gashes into the one by ones. He had broken one in half.

He had to put the power tool down. They walked in. He didn't use the towels to clean off his hands or his skinhead. Instead, he walked up.

"Hello, detectives."

They were a little bit surprised.

"How do you know we're detectives?"

"Well, your badges are right there."

He was hypervigilant. His eyesight was gleaming. There was a power that was going on that made every piece of light ten times as light and any kind of shiny object would come out a thousand times brighter. Those badges were lit up by the light coming in from above the ocean, through the windowsill onto their badges.

Ben looked right over to the ring and pointed.

"There it is."

Detective Malene walked over. She had a Ziploc bag, carefully put on a surgical glove, picked it up and dropped it in. She held it up to Henry's face.

"This yours?"

"No. It's not mine. It's my grandfather's."

"Okay. Let me try it this way."

"Just a minute," Olson interrupted her. "You're Henry Emerson III?"

"I am."

"I want you to know right now, you have the right to remain silent. Anything you say can and will be used against you in a court of law. You have the right to an attorney. If you cannot afford an attorney, one will be appointed to you by the court. Now having these rights in mind, you can choose right now to waive them and to speak with us or to remain silent. What do you want to do?"

Henry's grandfather was astounded by his grandson's decision.

"I invoke my right to counsel and my right to remain silent."

Ben smiled, turned over to Malene and said the obvious remark, "I told you he was the guy."

Olson looked at him. "Okay," he said. "Let me show you something. You go ahead and remain silent. Don't say a word. We don't have a lawyer for you, so just remain silent. But I just want to show you what we have."

They placed the news articles in front of him.

"This is your dad. He killed your mom. Do you know why he killed himself? Do you understand that he had the same beast inside him that you have and he was trying to get rid of that beast? Look at these articles about the girls in Okinawa. Six girls got raped. We never found out who did it. Your dad knew. He killed himself over it. He realized in his moment of sanity that these rapes would go on and on and on and that he had to stop them. He did the right thing to stop them.

"I want to explain something to you. You don't need to kill yourself. Back then in the 1980s, they didn't have any kind of program to help people with these psychiatric problems. They didn't know what to do about it. Nowadays, there are sex offender therapy regimens. I don't know if you've ever heard about them. I don't know if you know anything about them, but let me just tell you, you don't have to kill yourself. You just put yourself through the sexual offender therapy program and you will get rid of this beast."

"I don't think you want to continue your whole life raping innocent women. I don't think you want to do that. I think you want to stop doing that. I think you're a good Christian. I think that inside you is a good man who is begging us to somehow help you to stop him, and we are here today to help you stop. Now I don't want to play any games with you. You're going to have to go to prison, probably for a long time, but while you're in prison, you are going to get an extensive therapy program that is going to get that beast out of your stomach."

Olson's very large index finger pointed at Henry's gut. Henry stood before the truth. He saw the articles about his dad, about his mom, about his father's victims. Henry knew what he had done. He knew what his father had done. He knew what his grandmother had done. He knew that there was something inside of him that would not let go. He knew that whatever this beast was, he was born with it. He couldn't solve it on his own.

Malene chimed in,

"Listen. You have a disorder. It needs to be treated. You aren't getting treatment. It's not your fault that you have that disorder, but it is your fault that you're not seeking treatment. That's the part where you've gone wrong. Come with us. We will fix this problem."

Henry looked to his grandfather, a man that he would always trust. The grandfather was crying. He knew and felt guilty. It was his choice of a wife, a bipolar wife, that had set all of these events into action.

He started crying.

"It's my fault. It's my fault."

Ben turned over to Henry. Ben respected Henry and immediately corrected him.

"You haven't done anything."

"I did. I selected the wrong wife. She was defective."

"Oh, come on. How can you know that when you fall in love with somebody? You couldn't have known that she had that problem. Hell, the doctors didn't even know it back then. How would you know about it? It was just your own bad luck."

"But I did know later. I saw it. I knew there was something wrong. She was doing things that women just don't do."

"Okay, and then you left, right?"

Ben knew the answer.

"Yes."

"But did you have a choice in leaving? No. There was a war to fight. You were a military officer, a West Point grad."

"I could have told somebody to watch her."

"Well, I don't know who that would've been. Who was out here? Who did you have?"

"I had people. I was just too embarrassed. You have to understand --"

"Oh, I know," Malene chimed in.

"Back then, even as now, these kind of mental conditions are shameful. Nobody wants to talk about it. Nobody wants to admit it. Nobody wants to treat it. They just want it to go its own course, but unfortunately the course is often tragic."

Olson had some ideas to share.

"Listen. The course is tragic. We already know that. We see the pattern. We see whatever your grandmother did. We see whatever your father did, and now you know inside you what you have done. Now you can go ahead and invoke your right to silence. You have that right. I'll respect that right, but I want to tell you right now we're here to help you. We're here to help you solve your problem, get these demons out of your system once and for all and live a regular life."

Ben looked over at the one by ones, several of which were cracked in half. This master craftsman had gotten sloppy in a matter of one day, a day since his visit. Ben grabbed one of the one by ones.

"Look here. Look at that uneven cut. Look how you cracked this. It's broken, just like your life. Time to fix it."

CHAPTER 17

THE ARREST OF HENRY EMERSON III

Henry III didn't say yes or no. Instead, he looked to his grandfather, who communicated the answer through his knowing eyes.

Detectives Malene and Olson looked over to the grandfather and then looked back to Henry III. They sensed there was some kind of unspoken agreement, yes, take me away.

Detective Malene only knew one thing for certain.

"He's not denying it. Detective, cuff him."

Olson took out his handcuffs, and placed one of them on one wrist, turned Henry III around, and placed the other on the other wrist. They made that metallic clicking sound that Henry and his grandfather would never in a million years forget. CLICK.

Detective Malene did the honors.

"Henry Emerson III, I'm placing you under arrest for the rape of Erica Lazarus. You will come with us."

They walked him out to the circular driveway. The birds were no longer drinking out of the fountain. Sensing something wrong, they had flown away. They placed him in the back of their Crown Victoria, carefully pushing his head down to make sure he did not hit the ceiling of the car. Their next stop: San Diego County Jail for booking.

En route, Malene radioed in to dispatch.

"Detective Malene leaving Emerson Carlsbad ranch, transporting prisoner to county jail."

Dispatch responded.

"What's the charge?"

Malene responded without hesitation.

"Rape."

There are those that, due to some weird desire to keep up with the darkest corners of our civilization, have a police radio and listen to whatever is transmitted on the police radio band. This dispatch was heard by no fewer than 16 radio buffs, three of which were freelance journalists. As a result, the entrance to the county jail facility was populated by a group of jail paparazzi, folks that don't chase after movie stars, but instead chase after criminals.

As the Crown Victoria passed into the secure area, no fewer than 600 photos were taken of Mr. Emerson. He did not try to hide himself. When you have 600 pictures taken, chances are pretty good that one of them will come out just perfect. The perfect one showed a bewildered Emerson, skinhead, neat and tight, looking out the window bug-eyed like a deer in the line of an oncoming night traveler. It was a perfect psychotic photo of a psycho, and made for a sickish scintillating headline, PSYCHO RAPIST ARRESTED AT LAST.

Henry proceeded through the booking process. He was fingerprinted, his mug shot taken, his street clothes were removed. They did the typical full body search, and a somewhat weak body cavity search. Contrary to popular belief, the jail personnel do not enjoy that process, and tend to do it in a perfunctory manner so they can tell their boss, yes, I did it. They placed their fingers through his hair, and confirmed that he was weapons, narcotics and contraband-free. They gave him a special color of inmate clothing, red for sex offender. It wasn't because they were going to have him stick out like a sore appendage, but rather this was his ticket into a much-needed protective custody.

There was a rule among inmates that if you were a rapist, you were going to be raped, and likely killed. This is a well-known rule by jail staff, which has a simple prophylactic: protective custody, one person per cell, and everyone knows why. Oddly enough, Emerson's protective custody cell was probably the safest place on Earth for him. If he were to go outside, he would be mobbed and lynched. If he were to go into general population, he would be raped and murdered. Here in PC, he had the semblance of security, which would be his home base during the pretrial proceedings that were about to commence.

CHAPTER 18

MEANWHILE, BACK AT THE MENTAL INSTITUTION

It was not pleasant business, but Ben felt the need to go report this development to Erica. Even if she was catatonic, there may have been some communicative ability remaining. He would take the chance. He would tell her.

He pulled up to the county-operated asylum. The entrance process was not that different than getting into the jail. He was checked for weapons, drugs, went through a metal detector, had his hair rubbed through, just like Mr. Emerson had done. The one item they didn't do was a cavity search. The security in these mental institutions is quite high, as you never know what one of these patients might do. We certainly wouldn't want them receiving a weapon or items of self-medication from a friend or relative.

Ben was cleared and escorted by Dr. Salisbury, an expert in the field of schizophrenia and its more extreme form, leading to a catatonic state. One needed little description of it; to see is to understand.

She stared blankly out an iron mesh window. Not a word would be spoken. She was in a wheelchair; the only time she ever moved was when one of the staff moved her. They would keep her in front of the window during the day and lift her and place her in bed during the evening. She had to be fed intravenously. She had a catheter to urinate and was placed upon a bedpan to evacuate her bowels. By her appearance and her lack of mobility, you would have thought she was a war vet that had been shot in the spine at the neck. This was not purely a psychological trauma for her.

"In part," as Dr. Salisbury explained. "That drug cocktail that she received, on top of her preexisting psychiatric condition and on top of the trauma of her rape has placed her into this state."

"But can she hear? Can she listen? Can she think? Does she know what's going on around her?"

The doctor clearly didn't know but gave hope,

"I think it's possible. There are many in my profession that say no, but the reality is, we don't really know. If you want to communicate with her, be my guest."

He put his arm out, extending it in the direction of Erica's wheelchair.

Ben, without hesitation, went over, kissed her on the cheek. It was like kissing a mannequin made of soft instead of hard plastic.

She may have been screaming out at the top of her lungs, "Help me. Save me. Come to me. Stay with me. Don't ever leave me. I need you. I love you. I'm lonely. Can you please help me through this terrible time? If you stay with me, I promise I'll come out of -- I'll get better. You gotta know. You gotta believe."

But not a word of that was spoken. Instead, it was a blank stare.

Ben stood in front of her, got on his knees as though he was proposing.

"We caught the son of a bitch," he explained. "He's in jail right now. We know who did it. He's confessed, sort of. He's going to pay for what he did to you."

She did not flinch. There was no change in her expression, not even the slightest millimeter vibration on her lips. Her neck did not quiver. Her forehead muscles did not move. Her cheek muscles did not move. None of the thousands of tiny nerve endings and muscle that make up facial contortions, most of which are involuntary, were impacted. She remained blank, stared right through Ben, as though he weren't there at all.

But inside, there was turmoil. There was an echo of what Ben had said. It echoed off the inner sides of her body cavity, it reverberated, the vibrations hit her bones, going into the marrow, traveling up and down her thighbone, through and up her pelvic bone, her backbone, her sternum, her ribcage, up to her neck, and vibrating throughout her jawbone, her cheekbone and her cranium. Ben's words had had their impact. It just couldn't be seen.

Ben remained with her for one hour. He explained to her the whole process of how he had caught this guy. He went on about how they had figured out based on her scar, the appearance of a remnant of an eagle wing, the fact that it could have been a West Point Academy ring, the fact that there were just a few of those in the San Diego area, how they looked into veterinarian clinics, how they initially thought it might be a staff member, then perhaps a vendor, and then of all things coming down to a carpenter that had countersunk some nails neatly into the South County Vet Clinic.

He explained how they found this man's history, beginning with his grandmother who had a bipolar disorder and had her own unfortunate tragedy, with the man's father, who had victimized several women in Okinawa, and in a feeling of guilt, took his own life and that of his wife. Then leading down to the grandson, her assailant, who when faced with the reality of his intergenerational passing of a demon, at last came to his senses and realized there was only one good thing to do, to fess up, and to begin the process of exorcising that demon and making all that he had done right.

Ben explained all this to her, hoping on hope that his voice was somehow getting to her. He couldn't tell by looking at her, but inside her, there was turmoil.

CHAPTER 19

PEOPLE VERSUS HENRY EMERSON III

The following day was the arraignment of Henry Emerson III. Though Henry's grandfather was a wealthy man, Henry III actually had nothing -- no land, no home. He lived rent-free. He had a small business as a finish carpenter, lived off his own income, had minimal savings and lacked the $50,000 to $100,000 required to pay a private criminal defense attorney to take his case.

Henry's grandfather figured if they were going to fight the case and try to prove his grandson's innocence, that he would go out, refinance his home, get a big fat loan and hire the best attorney money could buy. But in a jailhouse agreement made between the grandfather and Henry III, it was understood that there was no reason to spend that kind of money.

"Grandfather, just don't. I'm not going to fight this thing. I'm going to fix this thing. Keep your money. We'll hire the public defender."

At 9 AM in the morning, public defender Dana Fuerenstein was duly appointed by Judge Harold Ransom. Judge Ransom was one of many former prosecutors that had become a judge. He was tough on crime, but would still follow the letter of the law.

"Mr. Fuerenstein, do you waive further reading of the complaint?"

"Yes, Your Honor. We waive. We make a general appearance on behalf of the defendant, who is personally present. We waive further reading of the complaint. We enter a plea of not guilty to all counts.

"Does the prosecutor have discovery?"

"No, Your Honor. We're still preparing it at this point. It'll be done in three days."

The clerk handed Mr. Fuerenstein the complaint. It had two counts. Count one, felony rape by sodomy. Count two, assault with a deadly weapon, to whit a hypodermic needle with a drug cocktail infused into Erica Lazarus.

Henry read the complaint and of course knew exactly what had happened, exactly what he had done, and exactly what needed to be done. He hardly needed a 28 page detailed report of the process of determining that he was the guy. He knew. There was no question about it. He was about to say something about it when Fuerenstein interfered.

"Your Honor, we don't need --" Henry spoke out.

Fuerenstein quickly put his hand to Henry's mouth. Fuerenstein was a large man, the kind that could kick the crap out of most of the sheriff deputies in the courthouse. The deputies were there to protect the judge, the DA and other courtroom staff. They were not there to protect the defendant from being assaulted by his own attorney. What turned out to be an actual slap on Henry's mouth had the good impact of shutting him up.

"Do not say a word. Do not say a word," Fuerenstein scolded Henry.

The shaved-head Henry looked with great surprise at Fuerenstein.

"But I thought --"

Again, Fuerenstein slapped his mouth, cupped it and shut him down.

"Your Honor, I request that my client be immediately taken out of the courtroom before he says something he's going to regret."

"Very well. Why don't we just set some court dates?"

"Your Honor, I request the setting of a hearing on a motion to exclude evidence under Penal Code 1538.5."

"Oh?"

The prosecutor was quite surprised, as word on the street was that there would definitely be a plea bargain in this matter.

"What kind of evidence do you seek to exclude, counsel?"

"Your Honor, if I may, I would prefer putting all that out in my motion. I would also prefer to wait to obtain discovery from the prosecutor, to see exactly what evidence was obtained when they made a warrantless search of my client's residence; a search, I might add, that was done at a time when there was absolutely no exigent circumstances or other circumstances justifying a warrantless search. I want to know what, if any, statements were made that they are holding against him, especially those statements that were made following his expressed statement to invoke his right to silence. I don't know exactly what they obtained in the warrantless search. I don't know exactly what statements were obtained after he invoked his right to remain silent, but whatever they are, we will seek to exclude them."

The judge knew he had no choice but to set a hearing date.

"Alright. Let's see now. If you take three days to get the discovery, why don't we give you two weeks to file the motion, we'll set it on for a hearing about two weeks after that. How about September 14th? Does that work for everybody?"

"Works for me."

The DA nodded.

"Sure."

And there it was. The first showdown in this case would be September 14th, motion to exclude evidence.

Henry's grandfather was dumbfounded by this process. He went over to the public defender and scolded him.

"What are you doing? We're not doing this. We're not fighting this."

The public defender turned on him.

"Listen. I'm in charge here, not you. It's my decision what happens, not your decision. My job is to make sure that all constitutional rights were obeyed, that whatever evidence they have against your grandson was legally obtained, and that any illegal evidence against him be excluded. Now if, after I exclude all that evidence, there is still other evidence against him, they may or may not obtain a conviction based on that other evidence. But I will tell you right now, the only evidence coming into this case is legal evidence. It is my job to make sure that happens."

The court announced the next case, People Versus Powers, a drug case. Fuerenstein, without missing a beat, turned to the judge.

"Dana Fuerenstein on that one as well, Your Honor. We waive further reading of the complaint, enter a plea of not guilty and request a hearing date on a motion to exclude evidence."

Grandfather Emerson looked at this process and shook his head. He could see the public defender's job was to take purely guilty people, to do everything he could to knock out the real but perhaps illegally obtained evidence, and set them free back out on the street.

Ben shared Henry's grief over this process, but already knew about it. Indeed, he himself had asserted the benefit of the Constitution to keep evidence away from the court. It was a rather odd state of affairs, that the truth would somehow not come shining through due to the mandates of the United State Constitution, and in this case, the Fourth Amendment prohibition on unreasonable searches and seizures, and a Fifth Amendment right to be free from compelled self incrimination.

The good news for the prosecutor, the good news for Ben and all involved was that Judge Harold Ransom would bend over backwards to find some way to allow this evidence.

CHAPTER 20

BEN'S FATHER LENDS A HAND

Sam Nightingale, Ben's father, was one of San Diego's more prosperous attorneys. He practiced in the area of corporate law, but was a veteran civil litigator. He knew his way around a courtroom, and knew how the truth rarely mattered in a court of law. What mattered was the truth that was allowed into evidence, which at times could be a small fraction of the actual truth.

"So Ben, the search was illegal. There was no warrant. What were these guys thinking? They just walked in? They knew that you had this suspect there. They knew he was in his home and they just walked in there without a warrant?"

"Well, dad, I invited them."

"Well, you can't invite them in. You don't live there. The suspect has to invite them in. Did he invite them in?"

"No."

"Did they ask his permission to come in?"

"No. His grandfather let them in."

"Now, wait a minute. The grandfather lives at the main house, right?"

"Yes."

"And this is the separate home of the suspect?"

"Right."

"So that's not the grandfather's home. That's this guy's home. Did he ever say words to the effect, come on in?"

"No. Nobody asked."

"They just walked in."

"Yep."

"So tell me, what evidence -- what items of physical evidence were bagged and sealed on that day?"

Ben knew the quick answer.

"A West Point Academy graduation ring."

"Anything else?"

"That was it."

"Okay, and I know what that's for. That matches up to the scar on her face, right?"

"Yes."

"By the way, has anybody from forensics taken it down to the mental institution to compare it?"

Indeed, Detective Malene was doing that right then. They photographed it right next to the scar. It was a perfect match. The photo was rather compelling. You put the wing on the side of the ring, right next to the scar on Erica's cheek and it was unmistakable that that wing was from that ring. The photo was perfect. It showed that whomever was wearing that ring was the person who struck Erica in the cheek and whomever struck Erica in the cheek, of course, was the culprit of her rape.

The question is whether the ring would be admissible into evidence.

"What confession was obtained?"

"I don't think he really confessed, dad."

"What did he say?"

"He didn't say anything."

"You guys make this big speech to him about being a good Christian, about doing the right thing, about getting rid of his demons, all this stuff -- and what, he just stands there?"

"Pretty much."

"He said nothing."

"Right."

"He didn't say you're right or okay or let's do it?"

"No."

"Any body language along those lines?"

"No."

"So I don't know how the public defender moves to exclude a non-confession."

Ben rolled his eyes.

"Stick around. You'll see."

CHAPTER 21

HEARING ON MOTION TO EXCLUDE ILLEGALLY OBTAINED EVIDENCE

"Good morning, Your Honor. Dana Fuerenstein here on behalf of the defendant, Henry Emerson III, who is personally present."

"Good morning, Your Honor. Assistant District Attorney Ed Sinclair on behalf of the people."

Judge Ransom nodded at the attorneys' presence. In the audience was Ben, his father Sam, and Henry's grandfather Henry II. At the district attorney's table were Officers Malene and Olson. The judge knew Ben's father and nodded at him.

Sam nodded back.

"Nice to see you, Your Honor."

"Haven't seen you in awhile, Sam. How's everything?"

"Not good. Don't want to be here."

"Well, let us proceed. Alright, ladies and gentlemen, we are here on the defendant's motion to exclude evidence under Penal Code section 1538.5. Since the defendant is the moving party and has a burden of proof to show illegally obtained evidence, Mr. Fuerenstein, I will turn the tables over to you. You may call your first witness."

"Very well. We call as a first witness, Detective Malene of the San Diego Police Department."

Malene approached the witness stand, put her hand up in the air and was sworn in by the clerk.

"Do you swear to tell the truth, the whole truth and nothing but the truth, so help you God?"

"I do."

"State your name and spell it for the record."

"Detective Alice Malene. M-a-l-e-n-e."

"You may be seated. Okay, counsel, you may proceed."

"You are a detective with the San Diego Police Department?"

"Yes."

"You work in the sex crimes unit?"

"Yes."

"You were part of the team investigating the rape of Erica Lazarus?"

"Yes."

"You were also part of the team that arrested my client, Mr. Henry Emerson III, on August 11th, correct?"

"I was."

"And this discovery packet I'm holding in my hand, the police report, the investigation, the photographs, everything I see here, as I understand it, you put all this together?"

"I did."

"Your Honor, we mark as defendant's exhibit A, a copy of the investigative report."

"So marked."

"Is this the investigative report that you prepared?"

"It is."

"I note there's a signature line here that you signed it."

"I did."

"Your Honor, we move exhibit A into evidence."

The judge turned to the prosecutor.

"No objection. It'll be admitted."

"And I see the following photographs marked as defendant's exhibit B, C and D. Did you take these photos?"

"I did."

"What does the first one show?"

"It shows a photograph of a ring."

"And where did you obtain that ring?"

"We obtained the ring from Mr. Emerson's home."

"The suspect's home?"

"Well, actually, it's part of the home owned by his grandfather, who is present today."

"Okay, but I believe this is a separate residence. Am I right?"

"It is."

"Not connected to the main house?"

"Correct."

"But on the property?"

"Yes."

"Would you agree that that was a separate residence, having a separate walkway, a separate door, a separate set of four walls and a roof, not connected physically to the main house?"

"Yes."

"And can you tell me approximately how many feet are between the main house and that residence?"

"It must be 150 feet. It's a rather large piece of land."

"Very well. On the day that you went there, did you have any idea that there was some kind of pending emergency? Someone's life was at stake? Someone was about to flee? Evidence was about to be destroyed? Or anything of that nature?"

"No."

"Before you went into the house, did you see this ring in plain view?"

"No, I did not."

"Did you have any idea it was there?"

"I did."

"Oh, you knew going into it that the ring might be there somewhere?"

"Yes."

"How did you know that?"

"Ben Nightingale told me."

"Is he in court today?"

"He is."

"Where is he?"

"Right there."

"And I understand he is the fiance of the victim?"

"Yes."

"He undertook his own investigation into this crime?"

"Yes."

"And he led you to this evidence?"

"He did."

"But it was you that actually went in and got it. Am I right?"

"Yes."

"And when you did so, did you have a search warrant?"

There was silence in the courtroom. There was a disappointment among everybody on the prosecution side. They knew there was only one truthful answer.

"No, I did not."

"Detective, I appreciate your honesty on this point. Let me make sure I got this clear though. It wasn't in plain view."

"Correct."

"You knew you were looking for it going in there."

"Yes."

"You knew you didn't have a search warrant."

"Correct."

"Did you ask my client for permission to enter into his residence?"

"No."

"So you didn't have consent?"

"I had the consent of his grandfather. He owns the home there."

"Okay. Let me have this clarified for the record. The grandfather is Henry Emerson II."

"He is."

"Is he in court today?"

"Yes."

"Can you please point him out?"

"He's the silver-haired gentleman with the plaid shirt sitting next to Ben Nightingale."

Henry II raised his hand up.

"The court will note that Mr. Emerson II has been identified."

"You understood that the suspect's grandfather owned the 4.5 acre parcel making up this ranchette?"

"Correct."

Henry was offended by the word ranchette. "It's a ranch."

Ben looked at him. "Whatever."

"Did you also understand though, that his grandson had a separate residence on this place?"

"I did."

"So you knew there may have been evidence that would lead to incriminating my client, right?"

"I did."

"You knew it was inside my client's residence."

"Correct."

"You didn't have any information that my client was going to destroy it, throw it away or anything like that, right?"

"I did not."

"So here's a simple question. I was taught in law school to never ask why, but I want to know why. Why did you not get a search warrant?"

Malene realized, of course, that she should have -- would've, should've, could've isn't going to get her anything today. The truth was, she got a phone call that morning from Ben, who said, come on up and she listened. What she should've done was fully interview Ben on the phone first, used the information obtained from that interview to obtain a search warrant and then proceed to the Emerson ranch or ranchette or whatever it is. But she didn't do it and she realized right then and there she should have -- and what a mistake. If this rapist gets off because of that... what a mistake!

"Actually, I changed my mind. I withdraw that question. If your people want to get into that, I'll allow them to. I'm going to move on to another issue. While you were there, it is my understanding that you read my client his rights. I see it in your report -- read his rights. Yes?"

"Yes."

"And who did that?"

"Detective Olson did."

"Were you present when he did it?"

"I was."

"Did you hear him do it?"

"I did."

"And as far as you could tell, did he do it in a proper manner?"

"He did."

"You put down here in your report, he was read his rights. He was read his right to remain silent?"

"Yes."

"And that anything he said could be used against him in a court of law?"

"Yes."

"And that he had a right to counsel."

"Yes."

"Now, Detective Malene --"

Attorney Fuerenstein took his glasses off. This was not for dramatic effect; he was just getting closer to her and couldn't see her close up. "It is my understanding, based on what is in your report, that my client did not waive his right to remain silent, and did not waive his right to counsel. In fact, did he not expressly state, as you say on page four of your report, that he invoked his right to remain silent?"

"He did."

"And that he wanted an attorney."

"He did."

"Okay. Let me be clear about this. There was no waiver."

"No waiver."

"Well, you know the rule, Detective. Once the suspect invokes those rights, what is your understanding of what you're supposed to do?"

Detective Malene closed her eyes. She knew the answer. It was a horrible answer.

"Stop the interrogation."

"Stop it on a dime -- isn't that right?"

"Yes."

"Not another question, not another peep. If you're going to arrest him, arrest him, take him into custody, do what you gotta do -- but your interrogation of him is over, right?"

"Right."

"They teach you that in detective school?"

"They do."

"They teach you that at the Academy?"

"They do."

"They teach you that in your post-cert classes?"

"They do."

"And you know that rule?"

"Yes."

"And you knew that rule when you were at the suspect's home that day, when he invoked his right to remain silent and his requested counsel. You knew that rule then."

"I did."

"Detective, it says in your report that you continued then to have a discussion with him."

"Yes, I did."

"I'm not going to ask why. I just want to know what. What did you tell him?"

"We explained to him that we were in possession of several news reports --"

"Okay, now just a minute. Now that you're mentioning those, those are listed in your investigative report at page six and I believe you attached the newspaper reports to it, correct?"

"I did."

"And let's mark those, please, as exhibits E, F and G."

"So marked."

"Are these the news reports?"

"Yes."

"Okay. Now this is Okinawa."

"Yes."

"In the year 1987."

"Yes."

"About a guy named Adolph."

"Yes."

"Who committed suicide."

"Right."

"And killed his wife."

"Yes."

"And this Adolph is the suspect's father."

"Correct."

"And the other reports are about some unsolved rapes of Okinawan women."

"Yes."

"Where did you get those reports?"

"From Ben Nightingale."

"He gave them to you."

"Right."

"Wasn't it your investigation?"

"Well, it was my investigation. Ben got the reports, gave them to me -- so I got them. You want to know how I got them? That's how I got them."

"What did you do that day after my client invoked his right to remain silent and invoked his right to counsel with these news reports?"

"I placed them in front of him."

"You did."

"Yes."

"Now I can imagine all kinds of reasons why you did that, so I'm not going to get into the why of it, but let me do this. Tell me what did you say to him with these reports sitting in front of him?"

"I explained to him that he did not have to do what his father did. His father had the same demon in him as he had, and Detective Olson --"

"Whoa, whoa, whoa, whoa. Hold on. I'm going to get to him later. I want to know what you did. Let's split it up."

"Well, I explained to him he didn't have to do what his father did, that there was a way to fix this problem."

"And that fix was what?"

"That he would fess up to what he had done, he would go to prison, he would obtain sexual offender therapy and upon release, he would be solved of his psychiatric disorder, which has brought him into his current state of being a serial rapist."

"Serial rapist? Where did that come from? You got another victim out there somewhere that you're not telling us about? I don't see anywhere in your report where you discuss any other victim."

"Oh, come on, counsel. You know there's other victims out there."

"Oh, I know that? Let me tell you, I know of no such thing. I only know of one case going on here. That's the case of Erica Lazarus. I don't know of any other victim in there. I haven't seen one, haven't heard of one, don't know about one -- so if you've got one, it's your duty to come forward with it."

The public defender turned to the judge.

"Your Honor, I request the prosecutor be admonished that if he has evidence of another victim, he must come forward with it."

"Counsel, I'm sure the prosecutor is aware of his duty."

The DA spoke, "Your Honor, we do not have any evidence of another victim."

Fuerenstein looked at Malene eye to eye.

"So can we not use the word serial rapist?"

"Okay, counsel. How about rapist with a psychiatric disorder which makes him prone to repeating his conduct over and over again, until the end of time? Can I use that phrase?"

"Objection -- argumentative. Nonresponsive, move to strike."

"Sustained, granted. Detective, let's not get into a battle of words here. I think we know what's going on. The bottom line is, we don't have a serial rapist -- at least none is being brought forward and because of that, we will use the equally offensive phrase rapist," Attorney Fuerenstein continued. "Now you were saying a little while ago that Detective Olson also made some kind of a statement to the suspect."

"He did."

"I'm going to ask Detective Olson what he said, but just to hear it right away, you were present when he said it."

"Yes."

"You heard it."

"Yes."

"Tell me what he said."

"Objection -- hearsay."

"Your Honor, the evidence that we're really trying to get at concerns whether there was a confession made and what, if anything, prompted that confession. That's where I'm going with it. So it's not for the truth of the matter. It's for what occurred prior to any confession being given."

"Overruled. Detective, you may answer the question."

"He said, 'you're a good Christian' or something like that. 'You're a good Christian. You want to do the right thing. You want to get these demons out of you. We got a way for you to do it. You can get the treatment you need in prison. They have sexual offender therapy. We will help fix this so that you don't ever do it again.'"

"Detective, I don't see any part of your report where you describe that statement."

"That's because it's not in the report."

"You left that out?"

"Yes."

"Now let's see. Why did you leave it out? Let me think about that for a second. Oh, I know. Because you realized it was a completely illegal statement and of course you did not want to fess up yourself to some kind of illegal police misconduct. Is that it?"

"Objection -- argumentative."

"Sustained."

"Well, Detective, why don't you tell me? Why did you leave it out?" Fuerenstein asked.

"We don't put in every nut and bolt of what happened. We don't put in every line item, every statement, every sentence, every word. We put in the important stuff. That's what goes in."

"Oh, you don't think you're a good Christian, do the right thing, fess up, we'll get you the help you need -- you don't think that's important stuff?"

"Well, counselor, in light of the fact that he didn't confess, I would say it's not important."

"Oh, so had he confessed, you would have put it in?"

"Had he confessed, I probably would've put it in."

"Okay. Well, let me ask you this: did he confess?"

"No."

"Did he make any outwardly statement 'I did it, you're right' or 'okay, get me the help you're talking about'? Did he verbalize that in any way, shape or form?"

"No."

"He remained silent?"

"He did. Like I said counselor, he invoked his right to silence."

"He did, and you did not honor that, did you?"

"Well, I wasn't asking questions. We were just talking. Just because he wants to be silent, doesn't mean we have to be."

"Oh, Detective, yes it does. You're supposed to --"

The judge intervened, "Counsel, don't argue with the witness. Just ask a question, okay?"

"Yes, Your Honor."

"Move it along here. Come on. I get the idea."

"Okay. In the face of these statements that you made, you note in your police report that there was no denial."

"Yes."

"You say it here on page six. The suspect did not deny that he committed these crimes."

"Correct."

"Well, Your Honor, that may be the one and only statement we have to move to exclude. The fact that there was no denial."

The DA stood.

"Your Honor, you can't move to exclude a confession if no confession ever occurred."

"Yes, I see the issue clearly now. Let me try it this way. If you don't mind, counsel, I have a couple of questions. Was there any body language that the defendant engaged in that led you to believe that he was responsible for the rape of Erica Lazarus?"

"Body language?"

"Yeah. I don't know. He might've looked down at his feet. He might've looked sullen. He might've put his hand on his forehead. He may have sighed. He may have groaned. He may have made some kind of utterance, though not a word, that when coupled with body language, and when further coupled by a generalized lack of denial of the serious allegations, could be reasonably inferred by a fact finder to indicate an agreement with guilt. Was there anything like that?"

"This guy was stone cold."

"Okay. So I take it you're not going to have stone cold evidence at trial."

"Right."

"Counsel, it appears the only issue you have to exclude is a lack of a confession, and I don't see how you exclude the lack of a confession. I would agree with you that had he confessed, that there would've been grounds to exclude his confession. I don't have any quibble about that," the judge said. "Once he invoked his right to silence, the detective, with all due respect -- and I realize you're just trying to do your job -- I realize you're anxious to catch this guy -- but the bottom line is, as you acknowledge yourself, your interrogation of him is to stop on a dime. But there's no confession. How do I exclude a confession when there's no confession? Counsel, you can say it however you want. I'm not excluding the absence of a confession. I will say as a general rule that the fact that a suspect remains silent is inadmissible. That's just a rule no matter what happens. That comes, as we all know, under the Fifth Amendment jurisprudence. So I'm sure the DA is not going to seek to admit his silence as evidence -- or let me say it this way: if the DA is going to try to do that, that much would be excludable. Now let me hear from the People on that."

"Your Honor, we would not seek to admit into evidence his silence before this discussion. It would not be something we would do. We understand the rule that a suspect has a right to remain silent and that the fact that he remains silent may not be used against him in any way, shape or form, thus we will not be using that evidence."

"Well, counsel, I'm afraid to tell you as to your motion to exclude a non-confession based on an illegal interrogation after he'd invoked his right to silence and his right to counsel, that motion is denied. Now as to your motion to exclude the ring, why don't we get back to that? First of all, can somebody help me out there? The relevance of the ring?"

"Oh, good point. Detective, you took these photos of Erica Lazarus?"

"Yes."

"Exhibit B, C and D?"

"Yes."

"Exhibit B is the ring?"

"Yes."

"Exhibit C is what?"

"It is a scar on Miss Lazarus's face from the night of the incident."

"Who took that photo?"

"I did."

"Okay. Then there's another photo. What does that show?"

"This shows about two weeks later a photo of that same scar, which thankfully was still there. What I did was held the ring right next to it, and you can see here it's a perfect match.

The defense counsel showed the photos to the judge.

"You see, Your Honor, there's the match. They're trying to show that the eagle wing that is outlined on the side of the ring actually came up as a kind of scar on the victim's face."

The judge looked at it.

"Indeed, it does. It appears to be a perfect match."

"Well, it is a perfect match. That's why the ring is relevant to these proceedings, and that's why we're moving to exclude it."

"I see. Okay. Counsel, do you have any questions on the ring issue of Detective Malene?"

"I just have one more question of the detective -- and really, it's one that goes more to the DA. Do you intend on introducing this ring and these photos during the trial of this case?"

The detective was about to answer when the judge interrupted, "Wait a minute. It's not up to her to figure out what evidence is going to be used or not used. That's up to the DA.

"Oh, I would agree, Your Honor. Just to show standing to assert this motion though, I think the DA should have to state on the record whether they do intend to use that evidence."

"Okay, very well. Mr. Prosecutor, what say you?"

"Yes, of course we intend to use evidence of the ring and the photographic evidence of a perfect match between the ring and the scars on the victim's face."

"Very well. So noted. Any further questions, counselor?"

"No. That'll do it."

"Alright. Prosecution?"

Assistant District Attorney Ed Sinclair stood, and would now take over the questioning.

"When you went there that day to seek entry into the residence where the suspect lived, did anybody let you in?"

"Yes."

"And who was that?"

"The suspect's grandfather, Henry Emerson II."

"The gentleman sitting right there?"

"Yes."

"He let you in."

"Yes."

"Did you have to ask him for permission?"

"Objection -- relevance."

"Overruled."

"Did you ask him permission?"

"No."

"Did you ask him anything?"

"We asked him if we could go see his grandson."

"And what did he say?"

"Yes."

"Did he show you the way?"

"Yes."

"Did he walk with you out to the other house?"

"Yes."

"Did he tell you who owned the house?"

"No."

"Who did you understand owned the house?"

"Objection -- relevance, hearsay."

"Goes to good faith or lack of bad faith."

"Overruled."

"I was told by Ben that the grandfather owned the entire ranchette and that it had been in their family for over 100 years."

"Okay, and based on that, did you reasonably believe that the grandfather had authority to consent to your entry into the residence?"

"Objection -- leading."

"Yes, it is leading," the judge agreed.

"Okay, let me rephrase it. When you entered into the residence that day, on what legal basis did you proceed?"

"The grandfather had consented and based on that consent, we entered the home."

"Very well. No further questions."

"Any redirect?"

Public Defender Fuerenstein stood.

"Yes, Your Honor. Thank you. You yourself did not ask the grandfather if he owned the place?"

"I did not."

"Did you ask if the other home was somehow separately owned?"

"No."

"Did you ask if it was a separate apartment that involved any kind of lease arrangements, rental payments or anything of the sort?"

"No."

"Did you do any investigation into who owned what, who leased what, who lived where or anything of the sort?"

"I did not."

"Instead, you relied on the information given to you by Ben."

"Yes."

"You would agree that was all hearsay, correct?"

"Yes."

"Why did you not take steps to confirm it? I mean, you could've just asked him."

Detective Malene was about to answer when the criminal defense attorney withdrew it.

"Actually, never mind. I don't want to know why. What's important is that you didn't. You didn't, did you? You didn't inquire into it."

"No, I didn't."

"Would you agree in failing to inquire that you have violated police procedure?"

"Objection -- relevance."

"It's not irrelevant, Your Honor. Police procedures are what guide the police into obeying the law."

"Overruled."

"I did not violate police procedure. I had a reasonable basis on which to believe that the grandfather Emerson was the owner of the ranchette and possessed legal authority to consent to my entry into those premises and based on that consent, I entered and obtained the ring."

"That's it?"

"That's it."

"Well, Your Honor, there you have it. Pure legal issue. Issue of law, not a fact. It's up to you to rule on it."

"Actually, before I rule, I want to hear from the grandfather. Mr. Henry Emerson II, the court is calling you as its own witness."

Mr. Emerson took the stand.

"State your name please."

"Henry Emerson II."

"Spell it for the record."

"H-e-n-r-y Emerson, capital I-I after that."

"Very well. Mr. Emerson, are you the owner of a ranchette located at --"

"Excuse me, Your Honor. It's a ranch."

"Very well. Of the ranch located on Milltower Road, Carlsbad, California?"

"I am."

"And is it true, as we've heard here, that this ranch has been in your family for something like -- well, over 100 years?"

"Yes."

"That would make you one of the longest-owning landowners around here, right?"

"Well, if I may say it in perhaps an impolite way, one of the longest landowning white families."

"Yes, of course. I think there were native peoples here perhaps for 20,000 years before us."

"Indeed."

"Very well. Now, did you give permission to Detective Malene to enter into your grandson's residence?"

"I did."

"And did you do so freely, voluntarily, without being forced to do it or threatened to do it or in any way improperly spoken to?"

"Oh, it was not a problem. I am pro-law enforcement. I am a Republican. I am a conservative. I would be the last guy to stand in the way of a police investigation. I freely gave them permission."

"Okay, and the place where your grandson lives -- is there a written lease?"

"No."

"Is there a verbal lease?"

"No."

"Is there any kind of lease?"

"No."

"Does he pay rent?"

"No."

"You just let him stay there?"

"Right."

"How long has he been there?"

"Oh gosh, 11 years."

"Okay, and before that, where did he live?"

There was a long silence.

"He lived in Okinawa."

"With his father?"

"Yes."

"And his mother?"

"Yes."

"He was there back in 1987?"

"Yes."

"I see."

"He was 10 at the time."

"I see. It doesn't really matter, but please tell me he was not present at the time when his father killed his mother and at the time when his father took his own life."

"I'm afraid, Your Honor, he was in the house at the time. He saw it."

"I see. I'm sorry to hear that."

There was a sullen silence in the courtroom over this revelation. It was easy to see how a kid who had gone through that could become a monster.

"So you would not describe him as a tenant, would you?"

"Oh, no. He's family. We don't call a family member a tenant. We call them family."

"And he's your guest?"

"He is family."

"And he can stay there on what sounds like an indefinite term."

"He can stay there as long as he wants. In fact, just so you understand, he goes to prison on this case, when he gets out, provided the law will allow it, I'll have him back."

"Okay. So he's in the category of an indefinite family guest into a family residence owned by the grandfather that gave consent to enter the premises on that day."

"Correct."

"Very well. Mr. Fuerenstein, do you have any questions you'd like to ask the witness?"

Mr. Fuerenstein stood.

"Mr. Emerson, you from time to time go and see him at his residence?"

"I do."

"Before you walked in the door, do you knock?"

"Yes, I do. I respect people's privacy."

"You would agree that that's a private place?"

"Yes."

"It's his place."

"Correct."

"Separate and apart from the home."

"Yes."

"Not connected physically."

"Correct."

"And you honor his right of privacy."

"Right."

"You knock on the door."

"Correct."

"Did you knock on the door the day that Detective Malene was there?"

"I believe we did. That's just my normal way. Knock on the door. It's me."

"Has he ever not let you in there?"

"Oh, no. That's just me being polite. He always lets me in."

"Okay, but that's the procedure?"

"Yes."

"Is there a doorbell?"

"There is, but I never use it. I just knock on the door."

"Did you explain to Detective Malene why you knock on the door?"

"No."

"Did you knock on the door in front of Detective Malene on the day that your grandson was arrested?"

"Oh, yes. I was at the door first. I knocked on it. My grandson answered. The door was opened."

"Did anybody ask your grandson for permission to come in?"

"Not exactly."

"What do you mean, not exactly?"

"Well, no."

"So you guys just walked in."

"We did."

"Did he do anything to stop you?"

"No."

"Did he protest?"

"No."

"Did he object?"

"No. He saw me first. So really, what he was doing was letting me in. He didn't quite understand that behind me were two detectives."

"I see. So he consented to you coming in, but he never really consented to the detectives coming in, did he?"

"No, I don't think he ever did. No. But I consented to them coming in."

"I understand. I have no further questions, Your Honor."

"Okay. Do the people have questions?"

"No questions, Your Honor."

"Okay. I will hear brief argument, starting with the defense."

Mr. Fuerenstein stood.

"Thank you, Your Honor. I think you have the issues well in hand. As to the confession --"

"Let me just stop you right there, counsel. We're not going to talk about that. That's already been ruled upon. The motion to exclude a non-confession is denied as moot. The prosecutor has made it clear he's not seeking to introduce your client's silence before his allegations, and in light of that, the motion is denied. Let's talk about the ring."

"And the photographs showing the ring next to the cheek of my client. Yes. First of all, let me clarify something" Fuerenstein responded.

The judge held the exhibits.

"This one right here, exhibit C. This is a picture taken on the night of the incident of the victim. You can't exclude this, right?"

"Oh, no. we're not seeking to exclude that one," Fuerenstein responded. "We're seeking to exclude the one taken afterwards, exhibit D, showing the ring next to her cheek."

"Very well. That's what I understood. I just wanted to clarify."

"Let's talk about the ring," Fuerenstein continued. "We know the plain view doctrine does not apply. The prosecution witness made it very clear that the ring was not in plain view, thus the exception to the search warrant does not apply. We know the exigent circumstances doctrine does not apply. The prosecution witness confirmed there was no emergency or exigency. There was no life and limb or the disposal of evidence or the flight of the suspect at hand, thus that exception to the warrant requirement does not apply."

The judge was impatient.

"Counsel, let's just get to it. Obviously what applies is the consent rule, and it's very simple. If you consent to a search, you can't complain about the lack of a warrant. Let's get to that."

"Quite simply, Your Honor, the grandfather did not have authority to consent to this search of the separate unit occupied by my client."

"Well, I don't think it's that simple, Counsel. It's the grandfather's house, it's his property. Your client is not a tenant. There's no lease agreement. There's no rent being paid. He's in the status of a guest. I just don't see how a guest has some kind of property right to a place over the property right of the owner. If the owner says you can go in, then you can go in. I'm not so sure that this separate residence theory is going to work for you. Keep in mind the US Supreme Court case in *Randolph v. Georgia*. There, the court ruled where you have two spouses, each owning half of a house, and one spouse gives consent and the other does not, that in such case, because of the joint ownership, an entry without a warrant would lack legal consent. In that case however, the husband who did not give consent vocalized an objection to a search. Here, the evidence is that the grandson, the defendant, a non-co-owner, did not verbalize any sense of an objection whatsoever. We've heard that from the prosecution witness and from the defendant's grandfather. We haven't heard any evidence to the contrary. I'm going to find that to be a fact, that there was no objection by the suspect to the search."

"Your Honor, he doesn't have an affirmative duty to object. They have an affirmative duty to get the warrant, unless there's an applicable exception."

"Well, Counsel, here's the problem. The exception is, his grandfather consented. If he believed he had some kind of property right to the premises, whether it be a leasehold, a guest status, an invitee or whatever, it did become his burden to vocalize an objection in the face of a consent by the actual owner. Had he objected, it may be that the consent of the grandfather would have been vitiated, provided your client could prove up some type of actual property right. But the way I see it, what's his property right? I think we would all agree the grandfather could, whenever he wanted, toss this guy out. He's a guest. Just like if I have someone over for dinner, I can ask them to leave."

"Oh, I'm not so sure you could get rid of him, Your Honor. You'd probably have to do an unlawful detainer."

"Well, you could do it, but I don't know what his defense would be. Let's suppose the grandfather asked him to leave, and he opposed it and forced the grandfather into making an unlawful detainer. What would his defense be at the trial of the unlawful detainer as to how he would be entitled to remain there? I'm an invited guest and I get to be there as long as I feel like it? I don't think so. I don't think he has any property rights on the premises. I just can't think of any kind of leasehold right, tenant right -- anything other than an invited guest, and that invitation could be withdrawn at the whim and will of his grandfather at any time, and there's nothing he could do about it. In that kind of situation, I believe the grandfather's consent had legal authority and permitted the search of the premises without a warrant.

"I've heard the evidence, thought about the law. It gets down to a real property issue. It gets down to an issue of what rights, if any, does this suspect have in his separate unit? And I find, based on the testimony of his grandfather, that he had no rights whatsoever in that unit, and that the grandfather's consent was legal and gave the detective full authority to enter and search the premises without a warrant, and that once inside, they legally saw and obtained the ring. The motion to exclude the ring and the photograph of the ring next to the cheek is accordingly DENIED."

CHAPTER 22

THE AD

The court further set a date for a preliminary hearing in 10 days.

"Mr. Emerson, you are ordered to appear back here on October 2 for a preliminary hearing in this matter. At that time, the prosecutor will be putting on evidence to show that a crime was committed and that there is satisfactory evidence to show that you were the one who committed that crime."

"But Your Honor, there's no question!" Emerson said.

The quick-witted public defender again placed his hand physically on Emerson' mouth, shutting him up instantaneously.

"Your Honor, my client will not speak any further. I request that he be taken out of court forthwith. We will be back here on October 2. Thank you."

The judge was impressed with how quickly Fuerenstein could muzzle his client and agreed to the request.

"Very well. We are out of session. See you on October 2."

Ben and his father Sam left the courtroom somewhat bewildered.

"It's good news, Ben. The evidence is coming in."

"What's the bad news?" Ben had to ask.

Sam looked up into the courthouse hallway ceiling. The hallway had wood on either side and photos of judges that have long since passed. There was a lovely chandelier. It was a formal environment, built to evoke tranquility, seriousness and the process of getting at the truth. He turned back to his son.

"The bad news is, there's a solid chance that it will get overturned on appeal."

They continued to walk down to the elevator.

"What can we do?"

"At this point, the matter is in the DA's hands. Let them do their job, Ben. You don't really need to do anything."

"I don't want to just stand back and do nothing. There's got to be something we can do. What?"

Sam thought about it and smiled. Ben saw that smirk and knew his dad had some idea.

"What? What is it?"

"There is something we can do."

"Okay. Tell me."

"Just a second."

The elevator was filled with others. Sam did not want to give up his trade secret among the others in the elevator. Ben was fidgeting. It upset him that the elevator stopped at every single floor. At last, they got out of the elevator and walked outside the courthouse. Ben turned to his dad.

"Okay. Tell me. What's your idea?"

"We could place an ad in the newspaper."

"An ad?"

"Yeah."

"For what?"

"The ad would read something like this: Imagine the mug shot photo of Mr. Emerson."

"Can we get that?"

"Oh, yeah. It's a public document."

"Okay."

Ben took over from there.

"I got it. Do you know this man?"

"Right."

"Has he harmed you?"

"Right."

"Has he raped you?"

"Right."

"Has he injected you?"

"Right."

"And then we get other victims."

"Yep."

"And then they come forward."

"Yep."

"Is that admissible?"

"It can be. The evidence code allows for the admissibility of other wrongful acts, if they have substantial similarities to the act at issue in the case. So you find another victim that got injected at a restaurant and was then raped and specifically sodomized -- that'll come into evidence. And you know what'll happen? The jury gets two of those, it's all over."

Ben thought about it.

"What if the jury got 10 of those?"

"Well, then it would really be all over. I'm sure that would never go to trial. Under the pressure of all those other victims, the whole case, I'm sure, would resolve and your man would be placed into prison, where he obviously belongs."

They probably should have warned the DA about this track that they were taking. In their excitement, they either forgot to, or subconsciously just didn't want to. After all, the DA might say no.

Ben, as a reporter, obviously knew his way around the newspaper, and knew a special ad program they had called "remnant" ad. These remnant ads are cheap, cheap, cheap. What happens is just before the paper goes to print, there are often unsold spaces in the paper, which go for extremely low prices, as much as one-fourth of the regular price of an ad. By way of example, a quarter page ad in a major newspaper can easily cost $6,000. A remnant ad for a quarter page can cost $2,000. That's $2,000 per day. Ben talked to his dad about it.

"Yes, of course I'll pay for it Ben, don't worry about it."

"Okay. How many days should we do?"

"Well, what's the deal you can get us?"

"I talked to the ad people. They told me $2,000 for a quarter page."

"That ought to do it."

"How about five days? Let's start with that and see what happens."

"Step one, get the mugshot," his dad reminded him.

"Okay. Well, how do we do that?"

"Simple. Let's go to the jail and ask for it."

"Just like that?"

"Just like that."

"Okay."

They walked out to the parking lot. There was Ben's Corvair, a funny enough looking car, and Sam's beautiful S-series Mercedes. Hard to believe these cars belonged to related people, but that's how it was.

"Let's take my car," Ben offered as a joke.

Sam looked at his car, looked at Ben's car and laughed.

"How about let's walk?"

"Oh?"

"The jail's right over there."

Indeed, it was right across the street from the courthouse.

"Okay, great. Let's go."

They walked over, came into the lobby of the jail and asked for the desk sergeant. The desk sergeant arrived shortly, a notably skinny geekish looking man. The typical story of a beefcake, former military rugby player jail guard went right out the window with this guy.

"I'm Sergeant Neeley. Can I help you?"

"Yes. I'm Sam Nightingale. This is my son, Ben. Hello. I'm an attorney."

"I know. I can tell the way you're dressed."

"Well, let me show you my bar card."

"Don't need to see it. Who's this, your client?"

"No, this is actually my son."

"I see. So what can I do for you?"

"My son's fiancée is Erica Lazarus. She was the victim of the rape by one of your inmates here --"

The sergeant finished the sentence, "Mr. Emerson."

"Yes."

"I see. Do you want to see him?"

"No. We do not want to see him."

"What do you want?"

"We'd like a color printout of his mug shot."

"Oh, I see. Do you mind if I ask what for? I mean, I don't want to get into attorney/client privilege stuff here."

"Oh, it's okay. It's not a secret. You'll see it. We are trying to find other victims."

"You think there are other victims?"

"We believe so. We've learned his father was a serial rapist."

"Oh. Like father, like son kind of thing?"

"I'm afraid so."

"Oh gosh. Well, just a second. I'll be happy to help you on this. There is a form you have to fill out."

"I'll be happy to do so."

"Just a minute. I'll be right back."

The sergeant went back to his office, picked up the phone, made a call to someone over at booking. That staff attendant complied with the sergeant's request, opened up a computer, went to the file with all the mug shots, found the JPEG of Mr. Emerson, and hit the print button.

They actually had a color printer down there, which produced a fairly good printout of the recently taken photograph of Mr. Henry Emerson III. The booking attendant walked the mug shot down to the sergeant's desk.

"Here you go, Sarge."

"Thanks Alan. Appreciate it."

The sergeant took out a notebook, and took out a form for a mug shot. They do indeed have a form for everything, and amazingly enough, there is a special form to request a mug shot. They do this all the time for journalists, who love to place the photo of some movie star who got busted on a DUI. In this case, this still unknown defendant was about to become quite famous.

Sam filled out the form, put his name and address down, occupation: attorney, purpose for photo: to assist in the process of locating other victims of this man.

"How's that?"

"Works for me."

Sarge was happy to help. Sam signed the form and they did an exchange, one form for one photo. Sam took the photo, handed it to Ben.

"Okay, Ben. This is now a newspaper issue. Do your thing."

Ben and Sam proceeded to the newspaper and placed the ad. The print ad folks were rather amazed at the drama behind the ad, and had different ideas of what to say in it.

"You have to put a contact. Who do they contact? Where? How?"

"Yeah, that's true. Contact who?"

"How about contact you, dad? You are the victim's attorney."

"Okay. Put down my name and law office."

"Then the question is, what are you asking for? We don't want to be too graphic about it."

"Okay, let's not spell it out," Ben said.

"Right. That's what I'm saying. You don't need to. If someone is a victim, they're going to know this guy. So what do you want to say?"

"Have you been a victim of this man? If so, contact Sam Nightingale, attorney at law, telephone and email. How about that?"

They looked at each other.

"Works for me. Let's do it."

The newspaper had an interesting decision to make about placing an ad like this. It's not your typical buy one, get one free ad. They could place it way at the back of a section that will hardly ever be read, which would produce zero results -- or they could strategize over it and place it into an area where they know it will get results. Because of the good purpose of the ad, that of truth, justice, and the American way, and because the likely target of the ad would be female women, and probably all things being equal, fairly attractive female women, it was decided that the ad should be placed in the fashion section of the newspaper.

The editor was not consulted about this. Perhaps he should've been. Normally the ad department doesn't worry about the editorial staff. Their ads have nothing to do with editorial content. But this ad kind of crossed over the line, and put the newspaper into a status of assisting the investigation of a crime.

Ben had no problem with that. That's what investigative journalism is all about, but to be sure, investigative journalism normally doesn't use an ad to get at the truth. But in this kind of situation, you had to do whatever works. So the ad would come out front page of the fashion section, lower right hand corner -- a perfect eye spot. It would come out tomorrow.

CHAPTER 23

THE FIRST CALL

The first call was not a victim of Mr. Emerson. It was, instead, the prosecutor, who was quite irate.

"Who the fuck died and made you king?"

"Oh, hi. This is Sam."

"Oh, I know who it is. You know who this is."

"Oh, yes. Hello."

"You put that ad in there?"

"I did."

"Without my permission?"

"I don't need your permission."

"You sure as fuck do."

"No, I don't. I have a right --"

"Don't tell me about your rights. Don't tell me about your right as counsel for a victim, to go out and collect up evidence. You are fucking up my case."

"No, I'm not. Your case actually doesn't even exist, except for what my son has done. So let's make sure you're clear about that. You've got nothing without him."

"Okay, let me tell you what we're going to do. I want you to withdraw that ad immediately."

"Or what? You're going to dismiss the case just to get back at us?"

"No, I'm not going to dismiss the case. I'm going to go in and seek injunctive relief. I do not want you to screw up my case."

"How is an ad getting more victims to come forward going to possibly screw up your case?"

"You don't get it. The public defender will be all over this."

Indeed by the end of the day, before one victim had called in, the public defender filed a motion entitled: "Notice of Motion and Motion to Transfer Venue of Action Due to Prejudicial Pre-Trial Publicity." The motion was set for the same date as the preliminary hearing.

The DA received a copy of the motion and faxed it over to Sam with a handwritten note on it.

"I told you so."

CHAPTER 24

THE SECOND CALL

Meanwhile, there was a different kind of response to the ad at the San Diego Zoo. Inside the zoo, there was a vet hospital. Although Ben and Detective Malene were quite exhaustive in their search for vet hospitals, and did indeed interviewed every single one of them, there was one they left out. It is normally the case that a large scale zoo will have its own in-house veterinary hospital. After all, where on Earth would you bring a sick elephant or giraffe?

Inside this hospital, was a veterinary doctor by the name of Paula Router, DVM. She was an animal lover through and through, and had developed such an affinity for animals that you might say she replaced human relationships in her life with animal relationships. There is a reason for that -- as in her life, there was one particular human, none other than Mr. Emerson, who shattered her world, and convinced her that the human race was so despicable that she wanted nothing to do with any of them. She wore zoo fatigues, olive green, camping boots, short-sleeved shirt and for all her anti-human work, was actually quite an attractive member of the species. She was darkish with blue eyes, small mouth, small nose, and had lovely cheekbones. Her selection of the veterinary field as a career was already mid-path when she came across the tracks of Mr. Emerson.

Indeed, in a telltale sign of Mr. Emerson's unfortunate presence at her place of business, the cabinets to the medicine drawers and other vet supplies were beautifully and perfectly built, with countersunk tiny nails holding them all together. He had been here, had spotted her, had spied on her, had tracked her, followed her to her car, drove behind her, knew where she lived, knew where she ate, knew where she went. He didn't attack her right away. He waited, like a boa constrictor will wait up to hours to finally catch and strangle a rabbit.

It was here that he had learned about the vet-used anesthesia, especially the stronger ones literally needed to knock out an elephant or a hippo. You put that kind of drug into a human, they'll be laid out, possibly dead. He figured if you need 20 milliliters for an elephant, two milliliters mixed with saline water and another barbiturate would be plenty for a human. He was able to access the drugs. He was literally building the safe for them. He got the syringes, he got

94

the elephant tranquilizer, everything together. They never searched him going in or out of the zoo. It wasn't a prison -- at least not for the humans there. He was able to walk out without any problem at all with this deadly concoction. He waited in the zoo parking lot for her.

Paula had no idea. He followed her. She had no idea. He drove behind her. She drove quite slowly. She lived with her parents. He wouldn't do it there. Her parents would take her out, the three of them. It was a lovely family. He would follow far enough behind that they would have no idea. Her father was extremely unsuspecting. Her mother didn't have a clue, and Paula was more focused on the country road path showing horses and cows and an occasional sheep. She loved the view, and wished she could live out there.

There was finally the opportunity. They stopped to get gasoline. Paula went in to get the bathroom key to use the ladies' room. Emerson parked his car at a store next to the gas station and walked to the gas station. He pretended to be waiting at the men's room. When Paula came out of the restroom, she was holding the key in her hand, her purse in the other hand. He put on a knit ski mask like the ones bank robbers use. As she opened the door, he slammed it all the way open, quickly snuck inside and closed the door and locked it. He took the key, threw it down on the ground and faced her.

"What are you doing here?"

He quickly put his hand to her mouth, not unlike the way his public defender had done just a couple days ago. She screamed, but it was muffled by his hand. He took out the syringe, stuck it right into her neck, and filled her with this elephant tranquilizer. She went limp, and while limp, she was his to do with as he pleased. He did to her the same thing he did to Erica, in a sadistic, despicable but thorough manner, and in the same antiseptic way, with a condom, later to be flushed down the toilet. Not one pubic hair of his was left on her. There was not one fingerprint. There was zero semen, zero blood, zero saliva. Everything was flushed in the toilet. He left her there, in the stall, bleeding, bewildered, drugged and completely incapacitated.

Since she couldn't identify him, there was no case. She figured he was just gone forever. That day that she was at her desk in the vet hospital with a nearby Siberian tiger on his back. The poor thing had a gall stone problem that she was fixing. On that day, as she was reading, of all things, the fashion section of the *San Diego Gazette*, she saw her assailant one more time. She put the paper down.

She picked up a pair of scissors. She walked over to what looked like a small jail, inside of which there was a sleeping gorilla. He had just had surgery to remove a bursting appendix. He had a bandage on his abdomen area. He was going to be just fine. She reached through the iron bars and with the scissors, clipped several locks of hair off of the arm of the gorilla. She collected up these locks and placed them on a piece of paper. She then walked back to her desk area, took those locks of hair and put them on the photograph of Mr. Emerson. She placed them on the area of his shaved head, to see what this person would look like with a full head of hair. She knew it was him. He had long hair then. Now he had a shaved head, but he was the same man, no doubt about it.

She had a cup of coffee. Her hands trembled. It would seem like the last thing you want to take when your hands are trembling would be another sip of coffee. In this world of opposites, it is the case that hyper people can actually get calmed by caffeine -- just like a hyperactive student can be calmed by Ritalin. She sipped the coffee. She put the cup down. She took out her cell phone and called Sam.

CHAPTER 25

ERICA GETS A VISITOR

The first thing Ben wanted to do, he did.

"Paula, I want you to do me a huge favor. Will you please come with me and meet Erica, my fiancée?"

"Okay."

Paula was fully aware of what had happened to Erica, and as a fellow victim was, of course, sympathetic.

"But where is she?"

"I'm afraid to say she's in the mental asylum. She has not come out of a trance state since the day of the incident."

Paula was somber and could completely understand how the female psyche in a post-traumatic stress reaction could put you into a catatonic trance-like state. Whatever would get you out of it would remain to be seen, but could involve, among other things, the passage of at least several years. She had gone into such a trance-like state herself that lasted about 67 days. For her parents, it seemed like an eternity. With her, it was the same reaction. There were too many drugs in the cocktail: elephant tranquilizer, an added barbiturate, the saline fluid, an overdose and on top of that, the trauma of the brutal sodomy. With all that put together, it should not surprise anyone that the woman would go into a protective preservative self-securitizing trance.

There are some things that are just too much for the human to take in, so the body takes action and literally puts you out for a space of time until you can wake up and actually handle it. It is a form of self-inflicted involuntary therapy regimen that nature has found to be the most appropriate course right after the event. Later, other human-given therapy would hopefully round off the edges and make the person if not near-whole, at least half of what they used to be.

"I don't know how long she'll be in this trance," Ben explained to Paula. "It may be if you go there and you share with her your situation, that somehow -- I don't know -- somehow --"

Ben trailed off and started to cry.

Paula saw his pain and had only one response, "Let's go."

Sam would go on this trip as well. Instead of taking the Corvair, they went in Sam's Mercedes. It took about a half hour to get there, during which not a word was spoken. Sam played some soft country music, a song about a man who had lost everything because he lost the woman that he loved. It was background music that everybody was ignoring, but had to pay attention to in the face of such silence.

They entered into the mental asylum, and were taken down several shiny corridors into Erica's room. Erica was in the same way that she had been for each of Ben's visits; in a wheelchair, connected to an IV, catheter in place to a pee bag, looking out a window. Her view was interrupted by iron bars that would assure she would never escape. Oddly, the victim was the prisoner.

Paula stood before her fellow victim and cried. Not a word needed to be said. They connected in some type of female sixth sense telepathic journey. Paula's perfect visualization of what she had gone through was passed off like a video MPEG off to Erica. For the first time in the 58 days since the date of her incident, Erica actually had what could easily be described as a very real, human reaction. Tears came down her eyes. Her blank expression on her face turned into sadness. Even as a sad reaction, any reaction was good news. Ben's idea was working. There was a transference of experience from one victim to another. It didn't bring Erica out of her shell. That would take longer. But the process had truly started. They stayed together for an hour in this silent way. Paula then looked up and Sam understood.

"Time to go."

They left, got back into Sam's car, turned on the same country western radio station and proceeded back to Sam's office. As they pulled into the parking lot of Sam's office building, Paula's zebra striped zoo issued SUV could be seen. The license plate read ZOODOC. She thanked Sam. Sam had to correct her.

"No, thank you. What you're doing for Erica is better than anything I had ever imagined would come of our ad. I'm so happy you called."

"Sam, if there's anything else I can do just call me. You know where to reach me."

"Well, actually, there is something you can do. October 2nd, 9 AM, department six, preliminary hearing in the case of *People v. Henry Emerson*. Be there."

She looked at him right in the eye. She looked at Ben and with the firmness of a man, stated without hesitation, "Count on it."

CHAPTER 26

CONSOLIDATED HEARING ON MOTION TO CHANGE VENUE AND PRELIMINARY HEARING

Emerson was in his red jail outfit and seated at the defense table. Public Defender Fuerenstein was seated next to him. Assistant District Attorney Sinclair was at a separate table, where Detective Malene sat. In the audience was Ben, his father Sam and Henry's grandfather Henry II.

Just then, the judge came out.

"Good morning, counsel. State your appearances, please."

"Dana Fuerenstein for the defendant, Henry Emerson III, who is personally present."

"Assistant District Attorney Ed Sinclair for the people."

"Very well. Today we have two matters to address. The first is a motion to change venue. The second is the preliminary hearing in this matter. Let's begin with the motion to change venue. The public defender may now present his arguments."

"Your Honor, we have attached as exhibit A to our moving papers, a copy of an advertisement that was placed in the --"

"I'm fully aware of the ad. I saw it myself. My wife saw it, commented on it. My staff saw it. The whole country obviously saw it."

Just then, Paula walked in the door. She was wearing her work outfit, zoo greens, with the sewn-in name, PAULA ROUTER, DVM. As she walked in, she proclaimed, "And I saw it."

At that point, Emerson turned and faced yet another accuser. There was a trembling that can go through the spinal cord of a defendant when they at last see their victim in court.

"Oh shit."

Indeed, Emerson knew he had been had. He knew the purpose of the ad. He knew that Ben was in the newspaper business. He knew Ben's father was a lawyer. They knew how to do these kind of things. They had the money to do it, and sure enough, the ad had fished out of the many skeletons of Emerson' unkempt and extremely messy life, none other than Paula Router.

The public defender made his typical knee-jerk reaction.

"Objection."

"Objection to what?" The judge was confused. "There's no question pending, Counsel."

"I object to her presence here."

"We don't even know who she is. And Counsel, let me admonish you, we're in the United States of America, where we have public court proceedings. If you want to bar the public from these proceedings, if you want to seal these proceedings, you'll have a heavy burden of convincing me that due process for your client requires that the public somehow be shielded from the truth of what he did and the evidence against him. Objection is overruled. Ma'am, may I ask you to please identify yourself?"

"I am Doctor Paula Router. I'm a veterinarian with the San Diego Zoo and that man right there brutally sodomized me, just like he did to Erica Lazarus. I'm here to help the prosecutor in any way possible."

The courtroom was filled with silence. Her statement was like a tsunami, and knocked everybody over. The judge did the proper thing.

"Counsel, in my chambers."

And then he looked to Sam.

"Sam, you too."

The judge's chambers were quite elegant, and showed the photos of his illustrious career. Interestingly, he used to be a boxer, Golden Gloves champion, and was quite good. He learned all that growing up poor, joining the Boys' Club. Boxing lessons shot him to statewide fame as he took the Golden Gloves championship three years in a row. His trophies and his championship belts were hung up next to his San Diego University School of Law diploma. You could tell right away that the judge, though proud of his accomplishments in the legal profession, was most proud of the fact that he had escaped his neighborhood, rose up into championship mode, and never looked back.

Sam had known the judge for many years, but today was a little bit uncomfortable.

"Okay, so Sam, I take it your ad worked."

"In a simple response, Your Honor, yes, it worked."

"So what do we have here, gentlemen? I think the defendant has a big problem."

The public defender knew a quick answer.

"Inadmissible evidence of other wrongful conduct. We object under the Evidence Code, section --"

"Stop right there. Just stop. We're not making a record here. I'll let you say all that on the record, but let me just tell you, I'm going to hear from her. We're going to have her tell her whole story. And what I'm going to be looking for is evidence of similarity. As you know the rule, it needs to be similar to what the accused is being accused of. I remember the example my law professor gave."

Sam was in the same class.

"You mean the bank robber in a gorilla suit?"

The judge pointed at Sam.

"That one. So if I find another bank robbery, another guy in a gorilla suit and that turns out to be the accused, that other bank robbery is admissible into evidence here on the issue of identity. Same guy, same weird gorilla suit, same situation. So Sam, why don't you enlighten us? Are there similarities?"

"Oh, yeah."

"Is there an injection?"

"Yes."

"Some kind of animal tranquilizer?"

"Yeah."

"Was it done at a restaurant?"

"Oh, Your Honor, ask me if it was done in a bathroom."

"Okay, I guess it was."

"It was."

The public defender was quick.

"But not in a restaurant."

"No, this was at a gas station."

The public defender was pleased with this huge difference.

"Completely different."

"Okay, that's like the guy in a gorilla outfit -- instead of robbing a bank in the gorilla outfit, he robs a savings and loan -- so I don't think it's that different. This woman was at a bathroom, is that right?"

"Yep."

"We got the injection, you got animal tranquilizer --one question. Was this sodomy with a condom and absolutely no evidence left?"

"Exactly."

There was silence. The public defender knew it was way too similar not to be admitted into evidence.

"Counsel, I'll of course let you put on your record, put on your objection, but I don't think it takes a psychic to know how I'm going to rule on this. You got to know it's coming in, and you also have to know that when a jury hears about two remarkably similar issues and one can positively ID this person, then your guy's going down, like it or not."

He turned to the DA.

"Is there an offer?"

"Uh, no, Your Honor. It's the policy of the DA's office to permit these matters to first go to a preliminary hearing, have the defendant bound over to a felony arraignment, have the matter set for trial, and then at a pretrial before the trial, it is at that point we would make an offer."

"Yes, I'm aware of that policy. I want to ask you to break it today. Make your offer."

Sam realized at this point he could not speak. It was up to the DA to come up with some type of proposal that the defendant would take. The public defender would not speak right now either. The offer had to come from the prosecutor. The prosecutor turned.

"Plead to the sheet --" That's a code word to plead guilty to everything that's charged. "Take the midterm on all counts. We'll stay the enhancement, on one year on the assault with a deadly weapon. You'll get the midterm of eight years on the rape, you'll get the midterm of three years on the assault with a deadly weapon -- total sentence 11 years. Parole thereafter, while in prison to complete a program for sexually deviant behavior --"

The judge interrupted the DA.

"I believe the proper phrase is sexual offender therapy."

The DA continued, "Okay. We'll go with that."

"One question." The public defender would still protect his client, no matter how guilty. "The other woman, what do we do about her?"

The judge had a quick solution.

"Has it been more than five years?"

Sam looked up.

"Yes."

"It's outside the statute of limitations. He's going to get to walk on that one."

The judge pointed his nose and finger at the public defender.

"I want your client to look at this as basically a sentence for two rapes and two injections. He is quite literally getting a two for one special, and he ought to take it. Go talk to him."

Fuerenstein left the judge's chambers and walked back out in the courtroom. The bailiff knew the drill. He unlocked the defendant from his chair and escorted the defendant back into a door where there was a holding cell. They would speak right there.

Fuerenstein explained the deal.

"So you know this other girl?"

Emerson said nothing, which meant yes.

"Well, she's come forward now."

CHAPTER 27

THE NON-PLEA BARGAIN

The phrase "plead to the sheet" is criminal law parlance for "NO DEAL." It means plead guilty to everything the DA charges and submit yourself to the court for sentencing. Prosecutors will do this when they do not want to allow a defendant to have any kind of a compromised or mitigated sentence. It is a rather daunting process to convince a defendant to take such a plea.

As Public Defender Fuerenstein had to explain to defendant Emerson, "The deal is, there is no deal. You plead guilty to everything. The court will do what the court will do."

"Oh, that's wonderful. Any other negotiations?"

"Well, there is a commitment that you'll get the midterm of each count."

"The midterm?"

"Yes. On a rape case, that's eight years. On an assault with a deadly weapon, you'll get three years. Total, 11."

"Swell."

"There is one small compromise the DA has made."

"Oh?"

"The complaint also alleges that you caused great bodily injury. There is a one year enhancement for that. On top of the three years, you would normally get one more year. They're willing to stay that."

"Oh, so I don't get 12 years."

"You get 11."

"11 years."

"Yes. The DA and the judge explained it like this. This is basically a two for one deal. The other victim out there, she did not come forward in time to allow prosecution. There's a five year statute of limitations. So the way they're looking at it, rather than give you a compromise on this, they're going to give you the full boat. You'll pay for hers as well in this one, unofficially."

"I see."

"They will use her event to justify the sentencing, but there really won't be a problem. As long as they seek and get the midterm, the sentence will be basically unappealable."

"I see."

"So here's the question: You want to do it?"

"I wanted to plead guilty at the beginning of this. I don't deny that I did what I did. I am trying to do the right thing here. Remember, you're the one that filed all these motions."

"I know. So you say yes?"

"I say yes."

"Here's how it's going to go. The judge will read you a series of constitutional rights that you have. He will ask you, with these rights in mind, do you waive them? You will say, yes, I waive them. He will then put on the record the basic terms of our plea, as I just described. You will then be set out for a sentencing hearing, to happen in about a month. Between now and then, you will meet with a probation officer who will do a background check on you, will ask you questions about your offense and will then make findings and recommendations to be submitted to the court. Then, at sentencing day, you will be sentenced to state prison for 11 years. Are you sure you're ready to do all that?"

"I'm ready. One question."

"Yes."

"Detective Olson told me that once I'm in prison, they're going to give me some kind of program to help me. I hope that's true."

"They will. There's a sexual offender program. It's mandatory for all sex crimes."

"But the program, does it work?"

Fuerenstein rolled his eyes.

"I've seen many cases where it doesn't, but it's up to you to make it work. If you have the right attitude walking into it, if you want to solve your problem, if you want to get rid of the demons inside you that are making you do this, it can work. Are you ready to do that?"

"I am."

"Okay, let's go."

Fuerenstein nodded over to the guard. He opened the small holding cell door and escorted the defendant and Mr. Fuerenstein back into the courtroom. Mr. Fuerenstein nodded to the DA. The DA turned back, looked at Ben and Emerson's other victim and nodded. Ben acknowledged, looked over at Emerson's grandfather and nodded. Emerson's grandfather realized this was the right thing to do. Ben's father Sam was not happy, but realized this was the best thing.

The clerk picked up the phone and called the judge, who was in his chambers. Within a couple of moments, the court reporter came back out and the bailiff spoke.

"All rise. Court is now in session. The Honorable Harold Ransom presiding."

The judge took the bench.

"Alright, call the case of *People v. Henry Emerson III*. Counsel, state your appearances."

"Ed Sinclair, Assistant District Attorney for the people."

"Dana Fuerenstein for the defendant, who is personally present."

"I understand that we have reached a disposition of this matter. Counsel, is that correct?"

All eyes turned to Public Defender Fuerenstein.

"Your Honor, it is correct. This will confirm that we discussed this matter in chambers. My client will be pleading guilty to all charges in the complaint, namely one count of felony rape, one count of assault with a deadly weapon and will admit the enhancement of causing great bodily injury. The indicated sentence will be the midterm on counts one and two. The prosecutor has stated that they will stay the enhancement, so that the total sentence will be 11 years."

The judge turned to the prosecutor.

"Is that your understanding?"

"Yes. We will accept that sentence range, subject only to anything that might pop up during the course of the probation department investigation and preparation of a pre-sentencing report."

"Very well, and of course, if anything does pop up that changes this result, the defendant will be free to undo his plea, if he so desires. Mr. Emerson, I'm now going to recite a series of constitutional rights that you have. You will indicate to the court if you are agreeing to waive those rights. In entering into this agreement, I need to be assured that you aren't being forced into this, that nobody's made any type of promises or other threats to you, other than the description of the sentencing range as just described. Mr. Emerson, is that the case?"

"Yes, Your Honor."

"Very well. You have a right to a jury trial to determine your guilt or innocence. This right is secured by the Sixth Amendment to United States and guarantees each criminal defendant a right to a speedy and fair jury trial. Having that right in mind, do you agree to voluntarily waive and give up that right?"

"Yes."

"You have a right to counsel. I see you've invoked that right. You have counsel and I take it that that right will not waived."

"Your Honor, I appreciate the services of the public defender's office and do certainly request that they stay on through sentencing in this matter."

"Very well. That right will not be waived. You have a right during the trial to issue subpoenas to compel the attendance of any witness. Having that right in mind, do you wish to voluntarily waive that right?"

"I do," Emerson replied.

"During the jury trial, you have a right not to testify, and a right to be free of compulsory self-incrimination. Having that right in mind, do you wish to waive it voluntarily?"

"I do, Your Honor."

"I also wish to inform you that the conviction could impact your immigration status. If you were not born here --"

The public defender interrupted.

"Your Honor, he was born here, so I don't think this applies."

"Well, if it's all the same, let me just give the notice to the defendant. A felony conviction like this could very well cause the immigration authorities with the United States government to revoke any grant of either a permanent residence card, a citizenship status or other immigration status, and could result in deportation proceedings. Now Mr. Emerson, with all these rights in mind, do you wish to change your previously entered plea of not guilty to the charges?"

"Yes, Your Honor."

"To the charge of count one, felony rape, what is your plea?"

"Guilty, Your Honor."

"To the charge of count two, assault with a deadly weapon, what is your plea?"

"Guilty, Your Honor."

"To the enhancement charge of having caused great bodily injury, what is your plea?"

"I admit the enhancement."

"Counsel, do you agree there's a factual basis for the plea?"

"I do, Your Honor."

"Very well. The court finds a knowing and voluntary waiver of the constitutional rights described. The court accepts the change of plea and directs the clerk to enter the pleas of guilty as just stated. This matter is referred to probation for a pre-sentencing report and is set for sentencing on November 2. Anything further?"

The court looked in the audience to see if there was any comment to be made by anybody. Everyone was silent.

"Very well."

"Your Honor, I just have one question," Mr. Emerson said. "I was told by Detective Olson that when I'm in prison, I'm going to receive some type of beneficial sexual offender therapy. Is that right, Mr. Olson? You told me that?"

Mr. Olson nodded his head.

"This is done through the California Department of Corrections and Rehabilitation," the judge replied. "They do have programs in prison. Those programs are mandatory for sex offenders. They will put you through that program. How well you do on those programs is up to you. You get out of it what you put into it. I want to encourage you to give it your all. There is a way to solve your problem, but it will not happen unless you go into the program with a fixed desire to solve it. I hope you will go in that way."

"I can assure this court I will do just that. Thank you, Your Honor."

"Very well. Court is adjourned."

CHAPTER 28

THE SEED IS PLANTED

Paula invited Ben to come see her place of work. Ben was happy to see just about anything other than a courtroom at this point. He was able to enter the zoo for free as Paula's guest, and a couple walks up a hill later, found himself at the front door of the highly secure vet hospital [inaudible].

"Welcome to the number one vet hospital in the world."

"I guess so."

"This is the place where we drain excess fluid from an elephant's knee, take out an infected appendix from a gorilla, and solve the gall bladder problems of a Siberian tiger."

As she spoke, Ben saw a sleeping gorilla in the small cage and a healing Siberian tiger. The gorilla cage was interesting to Ben. It had iron bars, not unlike a county jail cell. In one corner was a rather docile gorilla, still healing. Ben walked over and looked at the sleeping gorilla.

"Watch out. Don't get too close. He could wake up quickly, tear an arm off," Paula warned him.

The gorilla's eyes opened, which scared the crap out of Ben. He backed up.

"Oh shit."

"See? Watch out. These gorillas are very strong, even one missing an appendix."

He walked away from the cage, over to another cage with a Siberian tiger that was sound asleep.

"Nice kitty."

He knew not to get close to that cage.

"No doubt this could rip off your face in one swoop."

Ben looked at the massive paws on the Siberian tiger.

"Wow. I would not want to mess with this dude."

"Actually, it's a she."

"Okay, either way."

Paula walked Ben over to her desk. Ben sat down. He noticed a rather odd sight. It was the mug shot of Emerson.

"I see you have that out."

"It should be remembered. To forget, I first need to remember."

Ben noticed the gorilla hair taped onto the picture.

"What did you do?"

"It was a rather odd science project, to see this bald man with fairly long gorilla hair. This is how I recognized him. When he attacked me, he had long hair."

"Long hair?"

"Yeah, long like a girl's."

"Really?"

Ben studied the picture. He saw a shaved man with long, black hair. He thought about something that hadn't yet registered in his conscious mind, but was very much fermenting in the subliminal crevices of his brain.

CHAPTER 29

THE SENTENCING

The mental ward of the hospital agreed that they would allow Erica to attend the sentencing of Mr. Emerson. Ben and Paula greeted her at the asylum, and assisted as the men placed her into a wheelchair, wheeled her down the shiny antiseptic corridor, through a group of security doors and out into the ramp leading down to an open van. The van had one of those elevators that collected her chair and brought her inside the vehicle. Ben and Paula would ride with her to the courthouse. Sam drove behind them as an escort.

Ben held her hand during the entire trip to the courthouse. Paula sat in front of Erica and didn't say a word. She didn't need to say a word.

On arrival at the courthouse, the hospital staff put her back on the elevator and down to the pavement level. They took the courthouse elevator up to Judge Ransom's courtroom. Emerson was already seated at the defense table, next to Public Defender Fuerenstein. The DA had just arrived, and was in the process of putting a briefcase down. The door opened, and in came two of Emerson' victims, Erica and Paula, accompanied by the hospital staff. Ben, and Sam followed.

The court reporter came out and sat down. That's how you know court's about to go into session. The judge soon followed.

"All rise," the bailiff announced. "Department six of the California Superior Court for San Diego county is now is session, the Honorable Harold Ransom presiding."

"Good morning," the judge announced from the bench. "Call the case of *People v. Henry Emerson*. Counsel, state your appearances."

"Dana Fuerenstein, public defender's office, on behalf of the defendant, who is personally present."

"Ed Sinclair, Assistant District Attorney on behalf of the people."

"Today we're on for sentencing in this case. Counsel, is there any reason that sentencing should not go forward?"

"None, Your Honor."

"Very well. Before we pass sentencing, I'd like to know if there are any victims' statements. I see Erica Lazarus is here."

Ben stood.

"Yes, Your Honor. She's here. She's present, but I'm afraid in her state she cannot speak."

Paula stepped forward.

"Your Honor, if I may. I believe I can speak for her."

The judge did not like this idea.

"Paula Router, please step forward and be sworn in."

The clerk requested her to raise her right hand, which she did.

"Do you swear to tell the truth, the whole truth and nothing but the truth?"

"I do."

"Be seated, please."

She sat at the witness table.

"Miss Router, I would prefer that you speak on behalf of yourself and not on behalf of the victim. I'm only saying that because I don't believe the victim has spoken with you and I don't believe you're in a position to make any statement on her behalf. I fully respect the fact --"

Paula interrupted the judge -- something you're not supposed to do, but victims can pretty much do almost anything in a court.

"Your Honor, she has spoken to me."

"I thought she couldn't speak."

"She spoke to me in a way that did not require actual words. I got it -- a full and complete description from her of what she's going through."

The public defender, of course, would have to object to telepathic hearsay, but realized there was no such objection in the evidence code. Before he spoke, the judge stopped him with an open palm.

"Counsel, I understand you probably don't agree that this constitutes any kind of proper evidence in a court of law. Let's first hear it. If it's completely off base, I'll strike it from the record. Let me just state, defense has an objection to this evidence based on -- what? Lack of foundation?"

"Hearsay, lack of foundation."

"Very well. Miss Router, please tell us what you have learned from what I believe to be -- what, telepathic communications between you and Erica Lazarus?"

"Your Honor, I do not feel I have any kind of telepathic powers. I do not have any kind of mystical ways. I'm a doctor. I'm a person of science, but I can tell you that standing in the room with Erica Lazarus back at the asylum, where she stares blankly out the window, that there has been some form of communication between the two of us. These were not spoken words, but I got a full and complete description from her about the impact of this crime on her, about what it's done to her and about what she's currently going through, and I would like to share that, if I may, with the court."

There was a moment of silence. The judge realized the only thing to do would be to let her speak.

"Very well. Proceed."

"First of all, I want you to understand that inside this shell of an empty woman, there is a very much alive woman. She has a full range of emotions, of capabilities, of communicative abilities. She can be happy, she can be sad, she can cry, she can laugh, she can love, she can hate, she can accept, she can object. She can do everything mentally that we can all do. The only problem is, she's frozen. It's a type of psychological paralysis whereby she cannot explain it, she cannot move, and I might add, there is no corresponding orthopedic or nerve damage to physically or biologically stop her from regular human movements. This is purely 100% a psych-induced paralysis of her entire body, but her brain -- let me just say it. It's completely alive. She senses everything.

"She knows where she is right now. She knows who that man is. She remembers exactly what he did to her. She realizes that this is the man that put her into her permanent state. Your Honor, at this point in her life, I can tell you what she wants to do. She wants to forgive. She wants to come out of her state. She wants to move on from where she is. Before this event happened, she was engaged to Ben Nightingale right here. They were going to have a wonderful life together. That life has been completely derailed. She wants to get it back on track. This is what she wants. Now how to get there? What can we do to do that? Well, she's explained it to me.

"This man that did it to her, first of all, he needs to do the right thing himself. She doesn't want the court to force it on him. She doesn't want the prosecutor to force it on him. She doesn't want to force it on him herself. She wants him to do it on his own, by his own choosing, by his own efforts, by his own attitude. He needs to do it. The first question she has to Mr. Emerson, will he do this?"

She stared down Mr. Emerson. He was scared to death; trembling, shaking. His face was ghost-white. He stood.

"Your Honor, may I speak?"

"Mr. Emerson, you've been asked a direct question by this victim -- a question that she has given you that comes from Erica Lazarus, and I will tell you to please turn to Miss Lazarus and answer that question."

He turned around. He was in tears. His grandfather was in tears, was reliving everything he'd already been through with his first wife, with his son and his wife, and now with his own grandson. It was repetitive, it was generational, and it had to stop.

Emerson spoke to Erica.

"First of all -- and I know this is going to sound like nothing to you, but let me just say it. I'm sorry. I'm sorry a million times. Let me say it again. Unconditionally, without a doubt, I am sorry. I don't want to blame anybody or anything for what I have done. I did it, I am responsible for doing it, I take full and complete responsibility for it, and I stand before this court today to be held accountable for what I have done. And I'm sure I'll never make up for it. I'm sure I can never undo what I did. I'm sure I will never pay the debt I have to you.

"But I do want you to know -- number one, I pled guilty to this. Number two, there was no plea bargain. It was plead guilty, receive a full sentence, go to prison, and here's the part that I want to tell you. While in prison, I will be attending a sexual offender's program. With God's help and with as much strength as I can find in every molecule and cell of my body, I will do -- and this is my promise to you -- I will do everything in my power that I can possibly do and then I will double that power, and I will find a way to release the demons inside of me, and to become a good and proper person, and to never do this again, ever. That is my promise."

Emerson cried. Erica cried. She put her head down. Ben held her hand. The two male nurses were nearby. The grandfather came over and stood next to her. He put his hand on her shoulder. She received it. She knew who he was.

The defendant turned back to Paula.

"Does that answer your question?"

Paula looked over to Erica as though receiving a form of communication from her. Paula smiled.

"Your Honor, that does answer the question and I'd like you to know, Erica has two words in response. Thank you."

The judge looked to Paula for any further statement.

"Anything further?"

"I think that pretty much tells it all."

"Well, Paula, one thing we should do though, for the record, is just explain your background and connection to this case. If you don't mind, and without giving us a million details, could you do so?"

Paula took a deep breath. She looked over at Erica. Erica gave her a kind of signal.

"Do it. Do it for me. Do it for him. Do it for justice. It will help."

Paula opened up her purse and took out the mug shot that she had changed by taping gorilla hair onto it. She pulled it out of her purse and showed it to the judge.

"Your Honor, this is how he looked when he did what he did to Erica Lazarus, to me. He had long hair then, black hair -- but everything that's been described to me about Erica's case, he did to me."

The judge held out his hand for the altered mug shot.

"Let's make this as the court's sentencing exhibit A."

The clerk put a yellow sticky on it and wrote "exhibit A" on the sticky and handed it back to Paula. She continued.

"I have vowed not to be a permanent lifetime victim of this man. I have vowed to get over it. I do not know how I will do it, but I can tell you that coming forward in this case somehow seems to be a step in the right direction. Somehow this is a healing process for me. I will continue on this, but I'd like the court to know Erica was not his only victim. I was also a victim."

"Are there others? Sam?" the judge wondered out loud.

Sam Nightingale rose.

"Your Honor, I can tell you that in response to our ad, we received several phone calls, but only one victim materialized. Paula Router, who is now before the court."

"Very well. Now Paula, do you wish to say anything else to the court? If you do, now is your chance."

She looked at Mr. Emerson.

"Mr. Emerson, do exactly as you said you would do. Just do it."

Emerson stood to direct his attention to Paula.

"I promise you I will."

"Very well, Your Honor. I have nothing further to say."

"Any questioning by the people?"

"None, Your Honor."

"By the defense?"

"None, Your Honor."

"Very well. Ms. Router, you may step down. Ben, you wish to make a statement?"

Ben came forward.

"Thank you, Your Honor."

The clerk swore him in.

"Do you swear to tell the truth, the whole truth and nothing but the truth so help you God?"

"I do."

"Please be seated."

"Please begin by telling us your connection to this case."

"My name is Ben Nightingale. The victim, Erica Lazarus, was my fiancée --" He corrected himself. "Is still my fiancée. She is the one for me. I love her more than anything in the world. I do not understand the planet Earth without her. I do not understand life without her. I am without direction, without a path and remain in an entirely confused state without her at my side, without her in my life. I beg of the medical community to take care of her and to bring her back to me. If what the defendant said today is going to help her on that path, then oddly, I must join her and tell this defendant the same thing she told him. Thank you.

"I do not forgive him for what he has done. I will try to do so. If he comes forward and does what he says he will do, if this causes Erica to forgive him as well and to heal herself and to come out of her own paralysis and to return to me so that we can be married and have the family that we dreamed of and to have the life that we dreamed of -- if all these things can happen, I will find a way in my own heart to forgive this man for what he has done.

"I also want to thank his grandfather, who has been courageous in his cooperative efforts. It's not easy to bring your own family into a court of law and to persuade and convince him to plead guilty to very serious charges. I thank you, Mr. Emerson, for what you've done.

"I have not had this ability, like Ms. Router, to communicate at all with Erica. I wish I could. I only know the woman that was very much alive, a writer of books, a woman of many emotions, of many insights, a huge brain -- a brain strong enough to do all the things she was able to do and strong enough to shut her down. I wish for that brain to turn back on, to come out, to fill her with life again and to give her the path toward love, toward family, toward everything that we had discussed before. Honey, I love you. I miss you. I want to marry you. Please come back to me. Come back to us. Do what you need to do, but get it done and come back."

He trailed off in silence. There was not much to be said about what he said.

The judge turned to the prosecutor. He didn't have to ask the question. The DA shook his head no; same with the public defender. There would be no questions, no further comment.

"Very well. You may now step down. The court will now pronounce judgement. The defendant will rise."

The public defender rose with Mr. Emerson.

"You are hereby sentenced to the midterm of eight years on the first count of felony rape. You are hereby sentenced to the midterm of three years on the second count of assault with a deadly weapon -- to whit, a hypodermic needle filled with a psychotropic concoction that you prepared and administered. You are hereby sentenced to a one year enhancement for causing great bodily harm; however, the court stays that enhancement. The total sentence is 11 years. While in prison, you'll be subject to mandatory sexual offender therapy.

"I encourage you to apply yourself to that program as you have promised to do so previously. The defendant is remanded into custody of the California Department of Corrections and Rehabilitation. Good luck to you, Mr. Emerson. And Paula, good luck to you. And Erica, good luck to you. And Ben, good luck to you. This court is now adjourned."

On the long bus ride to the California Department of Corrections and Rehabilitation reception facility at Chino, California, the song "Turn the Page" ran through Emerson's mind.

CHAPTER 30

THE ANGEL RETURNS

There are some people who are put on Earth with a mission, as though an angel from heaven. It can fill us with anger, disappointment and a full range of negative emotions when we begin to question the design, the intent and the purpose of these angels. They can be so perfect in every way, they can accomplish their good deeds, do it all beautifully with perfect presence and then sadly and seemingly tragically, become removed from us, taken away forever.

We can take in the sunset before the rivers, and notice how large the moon is in its orange way as it comes up the horizon, and look at all of Mother Nature's goodness. We can learn not to live in disappointment and anger, and realize that everything has its time and place, everything has its purpose. When that purpose is done, there are new lives to be lived and lives to be undone.

In this strange way, Paula was taken from us. A couple days later at work, while attending to the gorilla, this docile creature turned momentarily evil, grabbed through those iron bars with his superstrong hands, took her neck and in a second, cracked it, killing her instantly.

Among those that would attend the sunny California funeral were Ben, Sam and Erica.

While everyone else looked down into the casket, Erica looked up into the sky.

CHAPTER 31

SEXUAL OFFENDER THERAPY: DAY ONE

She was a surprisingly gentle-looking therapist. Her name: Abigail Miller, Ph.D.

"You may refer to me as Dr. Miller."

One sentence out of her petite mouth told everyone that this bitch was in charge. The men were seated in a circle around her. The cast of characters was rather daunting, and perhaps the last group of men that any woman, even this petite Ph.D, would ever want to find herself surrounded by. But not to worry, they were all handcuffed to their chairs. A group of four correctional officers sat in the room, assuring that nobody would do anything stupid.

There were six of them. There was French Hayes, a black man from south central LA. He looked like a professional basketball player, shaved head, tall, lanky, strong, no tattoos and had made the terrible decision of raping his probation officer. When introduced, he showed his progress in the program.

"I am French Hayes. I'm a rapist. I'm a sexual offender. I raped my probation officer. I did it. It was wrong and I'm here to fix myself."

Dr. Miller smiled and then it turned into a frown.

"Okay class, how many of you think that was real?"

Nobody raised their hand. She turned to him.

"I think it was almost real. Don't worry. We're not done yet."

She turned to the next member. This was Stephen Lipsig, a white guy from Riverside. It had taken Stephen years to get to the point where he would finally admit what he had done.

"I am Stephen Lipsig. I am a sexual offender."

He paused. Dr. Miller looked at him. She was encouraging him.

"Say it."

He paused a little longer. Frenchie shook his head.

"Man, you just can't do it."

"Hey, I'm in the middle of a paragraph here, okay? Now back off. I exposed myself to a girl," Steve finally admitted.

Frenchie helped him along. "A girl? She was 11 years old."

"Well, that's a girl."

"Okay."

Dr. Miller coached him on.

"And what else did you do, Stephen? Did you touch her?"

"No, I didn't touch her."

Dr. Miller shook her head.

"Well, we'll get there."

Frenchie laughed and shook his head. Dr. Miller scolded him.

"Hey, do not respond negatively to his disclosure. We'll bring it all out day by day. We'll get another bit with each session. You watch."

Next up was Brian Tsaupolis.

"Hello. I am Brian Tsaupolis and I have been convicted as a sex offender."

"Hold on, hold on, Brian. I want to hear you say you are a sex offender."

Dr. Miller was right. Just saying the conviction was like some other person did something.

"This is bullshit. You've got to come clean about what YOU did."

"Well, I didn't do it."

Everyone shook their head.

"Oh, come on, man. Would you get off this shit?"

"Class, everybody quiet."

Dr. Miller was angry. The idea was to keep everyone else silent while everyone made their disclosure.

"If he doesn't make the disclosure today, don't worry. We're going to just keep asking him every single day. And I got news for ya, Brian. You're not getting out of here until you fess up to what you did. Are you clear on that?"

"Are you clear on this, Dr. Miller -- I fucking didn't do it. I'm never going to fess up to it. The jury was wrong. The judge was wrong, and you are wrong."

A correctional officer walked over to him and stood next to him. He looked up at the towering officer.

"I'm not doing anything. I'm sitting here handcuffed."

"I don't like your tone."

"Sorry, sir."

"Okay, just keep it down. Maybe I'll just sit right here next to you throughout the class."

"Pull up a chair. Why don't we listen to what you've got?"

"Hey, asshole, I'm the one guarding the slimebags like you that found their way here. I'm not the guy that does this stuff. You are."

Dr. Miller could not order the correctional officer to stand down. The class remained silent.

Next up was a rather dubious sight, suspicious to say the least -- a man in a wheelchair by the name of Kevin Chambers.

"I am Kevin. I'm an accused sexual offender."

"Whoa, whoa, whoa, whoa, whoa. We're way past accused here."

"Accused, hell, jury trial, convicted, appeal reversed on a stupid ass technicality, tried again, convicted again. Man, you've had 24 motherfucking jurors say that you're one guilty motherfucker. Let's get off this accused bullshit," Frenchie laughed.

Dr. Miller looked over to Frenchie and shook her head.

"You're just incorrigible. I want to teach you to be silent while others are making their disclosure. Officer, take him away."

This was bad news for Frenchie. He wouldn't just be taken away. He would be placed in the hole. He pleaded with her.

"Oh, come on doctor, I'm just trying to help you here."

"I don't need your help. I told you to be silent. I've told you several times. You aren't listening. Take him away."

He shrugged his shoulders, shook his head, rolled up his eyeballs and knew exactly where he would go -- the hole. This was a security housing designation where he would be placed in 30 days' solitary confinement -- no therapy, no human relationship or communication of any sort and maybe when he came back, just maybe, he would learn how to shut up during the disclosure process.

The officers took him out. As he stood, it was rather amazing how tall he was. Everyone looked up at him and thought, 'Wow.' They also couldn't help but think, 'Why would such a tall, well-built, handsome man stoop down to the level of a rapist?'

More on that later. For now, it was Kevin's turn.

"I'm Kevin Chambers. I am an accused sexual offender."

Dr. Miller rolled her eyes.

"I'm just going to listen. I'm not going to judge you. Why don't we go like this -- tell the class what you've been accused of."

"I was at a church --"

"Okay now, Kevin, let's be a little more specific. You weren't just at a church."

"Okay. I worked at a church."

"Yes. Go ahead."

"A little girl hurt herself."

"How did she hurt herself, Kevin?"

"She fell down."

"How did she fall down?"

"They say I pushed her."

"Well, did you?"

"No. I didn't push her."

"What happened after she fell down?"

"I tried to pick her up."

"But what happened?"

"I couldn't."

"How come you couldn't?"

"Because I'm in a wheelchair."

"So what did you do?"

"I got off of my wheelchair."

"Why did you do that?"

"I was trying to pick her up."

"But you can't pick her up."

"But I tried."

"And then what did you do?"

"I was on the floor with her. She couldn't move. She was crying. I didn't like the sound of her crying. I put my hand over her mouth. She started crying more. I tried to make her quiet. I told her, 'Stop. Stop the crying. Someone's going to think something's wrong.' Then she looked at me with this look."

"Oh, come on, Kevin, don't start blaming her again."

"She did though. She looked at me right in the eye."

"Well, just because she looked at you in the eye doesn't mean she's ordering you to do something that you shouldn't be doing."

"It was my interpretation."

"Well, your interpretation ended up destroying that woman's life, destroying your own life and causing a huge problem for everybody involved, didn't it?"

He was quiet. He knew she was right.

"Okay."

"Okay, what?"

"Okay, my interpretation, yes, like you said. It made a big problem."

"Oh, yeah. It made a big problem alright. Tell us about the problem. What did you do, based on your misinterpretation?"

He was quiet. This is the part of the day he just absolutely hated.

"She did it."

"Kevin --"

"She did."

"She did what?"

"She lifted up her dress."

"Oh, come on, Kevin. You expect me to believe that? The girl's 13 years old. You're a man in a wheelchair. Why on Earth would she lift her dress up?"

"I don't know why she did it. Why don't you ask her?"

"Okay. Kevin, go ahead. After she lifted up her dress, what did you do?"

"I kissed her."

"Oh, you kissed her. Let's talk about that kiss. You know, when you tell me kissing, I always think a man kisses a woman on the lips, kisses her on the cheek, kisses her on the neck. Tell us, Kevin, where did you kiss her?"

He was quiet. The men were quiet. They all knew the answer.

"Down there."

"Down there? Down where, Kevin?"

"In her, you know, private parts."

"You mean her vagina?"

Kevin hated that word, but he knew that was the right word.

"Yes, her vagina."

"You did that?"

"Yes."

"What happened after you did that?"

"They came in. They caught us."

"They didn't catch *us*, Kevin. They caught you. You were the one doing something wrong. That little girl didn't do anything wrong. You knocked her down, you knocked her unconscious, you grabbed her, you pulled her dress up and you orally copulated her while she was unconscious. Isn't that exactly what you did?"

Kevin put his head down.

"I didn't do it. I didn't go it. I'll go to my grave with that."

"You'll go to your grave inside these walls with that attitude. Look, everybody understand something. It's easy enough to take the copout here and just to deny you did it. I don't have a problem. I didn't do anything wrong. It was the girl's fault. It was my mother's fault. It was my father's fault. It was the police's fault. It was the governor's fault, the president's fault. It's always somebody else's fault. You can just go ahead your whole life, blame others. You can talk to me about how it's not a big deal what you did. You can say it wasn't wrong. You can say she asked for it. Just go ahead and keep thinking like that, and I'll tell you what you're going to get out of that. You're going to get a permanent stay in these walls. You're never going to get out of here. I don't know if I have your attention about this, but if you ever hope to get out, this is what I need. Are you listening?"

Everyone looked up. She had their attention.

"Number one, I need a complete and full confession out of all of you. I need you to say it honestly, truthfully, in great detail. Don't leave out anything. Number two, I'll need to hear an acknowledgement. I did something very wrong. How many of you believe what you did was wrong?"

The only person that raised his hand was Emerson, the new guy.

"Well, look at this. A breath of fresh air. Here's our newcomer. You are?"

"Henry Emerson, from Carlsbad."

"I see. Welcome to the group. Why don't you tell us what you didn't do?"

"Well, ma'am, I'll actually tell you exactly what I did do."

"Well, that would be refreshing. Let's see. Let me look at your rap sheet here. Conviction, one count rape, one count assault with a deadly weapon. What was the deadly weapon?"

"Hypodermic needle."

"Oh. And I'm afraid to ask, what was in the needle?"

"Combination of things."

"Like what?"

"An anesthetic, a barbiturate and some saline."

"An anesthetic? Where the heck did you get that?"

"I got it from a vet's office."

"How did you have access to that?"

"I'm a carpenter."

"Okay, and a carpenter and a vet's office have what connection?"

"I was doing some construction work at a vet's office."

"Oh, I see. And what, you found some animal tranquilizers?"

"Yeah."

"And you took those?"

"I did."

"And you put that into a hypodermic needle."

"Yes."

"And then what?"

"I stuck it into my victim's neck and put that concoction into her."

"Oh boy. So that knocked her right out?"

"Yeah."

"This woman -- can you tell us please, how old was she?"

"I'm not sure."

"I mean, was she a little girl?"

"Oh no. She was an adult. She was probably in her late 20s."

"Okay. How's she doing now?"

"Terribly."

"Oh?"

"Somehow my drug concoction and the event put her into a disabled state."

"Disabled?"

"Yes."

"How so?"

"She has some kind of psychiatric response. She's now in a mental institution. She doesn't speak. She doesn't do anything. She's like a vegetable. The doctors explained it. It was a type of psychological paralysis. I'm not sure what's ever going to bring her out of it. All I know is, I'm the person responsible for putting her into it."

"You know that?"

"I do."

"You understand that?"

"I do."

"Now class, here's something we all have to understand. The impact of what you have done is huge. You need to understand the impact of what you have done. Sounds like Mr. Emerson has the beginning of an understanding. Is that right, Mr. Emerson?"

"Yes."

"Did you do it?"

"I did."

"You're guilty?"

"Yes."

"Did you plead guilty?"

"I did."

"Interesting. So today we have our first person that actually fessed up to it, made a confession, is willing to say what he did, understands that it had a huge impact on the victim. And what? Let me ask you, are you here to try to fix yourself?"

"I am."

"Wow. I finally got one."

The correctional officers rolled their eyes. They didn't believe a word of it.

CHAPTER 32

MEANWHILE, BACK AT THE NEWSPAPER

Ben was busy at his job as an investigative journalist. He was trying to put this tragedy behind him. What happened happened, justice was done, the culprit was in prison. However long it would take Erica to become medically solved, who knew? There was not much he could do about that. He would visit her. He would tell her he loved her. He would do everything in his power to comfort her. But today, he would work.

Ben poured into his job. He began a process of herculean investigative journalism. He was driven not by a desire for the truth, but by a desire to forget the truth. His specialty was political corruption. His current article had to do with a bit of a scam done inside the real estate planning department at the county level.

They received public funds for what is known as redevelopment. The idea is that these funds are to go toward funding various low income housing projects and similar 'help the poor' projects. The mayor, in his inestimable wisdom, had decided that what the city really needed was a downtown shopping center. So instead of using that money to build low income tenement style housing, he had instead authorized its use to fund the creation of a downtown mall. The folks that would benefit from this were corporate giants, such as Macy's, Forever 21, JC Penney's, and other retail giants.

Ben figured it all out. He had interviewed over 40 people about it. There was a group of poor people who were wondering, "How come we don't get any new low income housing around here?"

There was a group of rich people that were wondering, "How come we're helping corporations with taxpayer dollars?"

This was a very Republican area. They did not believe in welfare, and they certainly did not believe in corporate welfare. He also interviewed, or attempted to interview, the corporate retail giants.

Their comment: "No comment."

Then he interviewed the mayor.

"What you have to understand is that economic development has a ripple effect that will impact everybody in this community, including the poor," the mayor told him.

"Okay, so let me get this straight. We help the rich people get richer and somehow that helps the poor people."

"No, that's not what I'm saying."

"Isn't this what has been known as trickle-down theory? Hasn't that been proven to be a bunch of hogwash?"

"No, it's not hogwash. It will completely work."

"Okay, so if there is a very poor person -- he's homeless, he has no money, no way to get a home, he's got tattered clothes, he's unkempt, he hasn't taken a shower in weeks -- is he going to get a job at this mall?"

"Oh, I don't know. That's not up to me."

"Well, you're giving out free money. Why don't you make a condition that the retail giants must hire homeless people, get them shipshape, cleaned up, put clothing on -- hey, they know where to get the clothes. How about that? Make a condition. You want our free money, you got to hire these people. There you go. There's your trickle-down. Why don't you do that?"

"Oh no, we would not micromanage their hiring process."

"Okay. You will just take money meant for poor people, give it to rich people without any conditions and let them, in the goodness of their heart, decide whether they'll take care of the poor people. Is that your position?"

The mayor was silent. The article came out: Mayor Admits Reverse Robin Hood, Steal from the Poor, Give to the Rich.

Ben's father Sam was enjoying his morning coffee on the veranda of his beautiful home. It was another lovely day. He chuckled at his son's excellent article. The phone rang.

"Sam here."

"Hey, dad. Did you --"

"I got it right here."

"How did you like it?"

"Amazing. Absolutely wonderful. Loved every word of it."

"What else can be done about it?"

"Oh, I don't know. You want to fight this fight, you go ahead. This is not my fight, Ben."

"Maybe you should do something about it."

"Like what?"

"Like try to stop it. Isn't there some kind of legal procedure you can use?"

"Oh, I don't know what it would be."

"How about a RICO case?"

"RICO?"

"Yeah. This is corruption. This is a scam. There's an enterprise."

"The enterprise? What would that be?"

"The city."

"Okay, you got the city, the mayor, multiple victims, doing things that are fraudulent, improper, using interstate commerce, wire fraud. Hmm. Gee Ben, maybe you're onto something there."

"Yeah. How about an injunction? Let's stop it. Let's make it so that these funds are used in a proper way and that the poor people don't get screwed for the benefit of the rich people. How about that?"

"But I'll need a client."

"Oh, I got 'em. I got 10 easily."

"They have to have proper standing."

"These are poor people that were supposed to get low income housing funds to improve their neighborhood, and instead have been deprived of those funds because they've gone over to Macy's and other corporate giants. Is that good enough for you?"

"You got 'em?"

"I got 'em."

"Sign them up."

And there would be born a great battle, taken off the pages of the newspaper and into the courthouse. A battle of poor versus rich, a battle of what one person can do to bring down a mayor and a corrupt city. A battle that Ben would start, and his father would finish.

CHAPTER 33

THE PENILE PLETHYSMOGRAPH

The following description of the penile plethysmograph is from Rudy Flora, Joseph T. Duehl, Wanda Fisher, Sandra Halsey, Michael Keohane, Barbara L. Maberry, Jeffrey A. McCorkindale, Leroy C. Parson -- *Sex-Offender Therapy, a "How-to" Workbook for Therapists Treating Sexually Aggressive Adults, Adolescents, and Children* (The Hayworth Press 2008, at page 101):

"THE PENILE PLETHYSMOGRAPH:

Phallometry can be utilized with the sexual-offending population in several areas of intervention. The use of a phallometric measurement can be a portion of the initial assessment; a confrontational tool to assist the client in facing denial; help in determining progress prior to the completion of a treatment program; and as a means of condition therapy to control deviant thoughts. There are currently two forms of phallometric measures, including the penile plethysmograph (PPG) and photoplethysmography. As part of gaining a physiological arousal assessment, these testing methods provide vital insight into the secret deviant sexual arousal and preferences of sex-offending patients. Specialized training is required to administer and interpret the results of these measures. The information is combined with other assessment tools in order to predict deviance and possibly likelihood of recidivism. The ultimate goal of phallometric measure is to locate clinically significant scores, which notate a client's deviant sexual arousal.

According to Byrne (1998), history indicates the first phallometric method was designed by Kurt Freund in the 1950s as a means to measure sexuality. The military utilized the PPG to locate potential homosexuals or sexual deviants in order to keep them from entering the service. Later, a group known as Behavioral Technology, Inc. (BTI) in Utah, took Freund's concept and developed more standardized procedures, ethical non-pornographic stimulus, event markers to locate and attempt fake results, measure attention spans and process information, while assisting in locating the non-responders to the test. The PPG now provides valid research while using the devices on patients and has proven to be a forerunner in the field.

Phallometric devices record three physical components, including sexual arousal, galvanic skin response (GSR), heart rate and respiration (RESP) readings as both the brain and body are used to process arousal. The clinician is trained to look for abnormalities and extreme scores, which dictate the outcome of the test. Originally, the stimulus was pornographic and leading, as the clients watched pornographic movies while being measured, which produced less reliable results. Other manufacturers believe the client should read scripts, hear stories over earphones and then attempt to imagine themselves in the same sexual situations. In recent years, designers have created audio recordings and used photographs (visuals), stimuli of minor children with no nude depictions, while the only nude photos are of adult males and females. Having arousal to no actual physical movement or obvious sexual acts proves the client has the same amount of deviant thought regardless of the type stimuli, thus demonstrating that deviance is not motivated by pornographic image alone. The BTI and PPG is approved by the Food and Drug Administration (FDA) in order to be considered a medical device and gain acceptance as a useful assessment tool. It is the only known FDA approved PPG in the United States. The researchers note that only approximately 10% of all males will not register a GSR reading, which may be due to having calluses or rough, thick skin on the fingertips or there are some people who do not produce these bodily responses. Should a technician detect these readings, the information is highlighted and the clinician includes this in the report. This type of research has proven beneficial to sex offender treatment agencies across the nation, as they can rely on the validity of the results and standardization of the stimuli for consistent, accurate measurement of deviant sexual arousal."

Flora, et al in *Sexual-Offender Therapy* describe the devices at page 102-103:

"PHOTOPLETHYSMOGRAPHY:

Female sex offenders have become more visible in recent years; however, these offenders have been in existence just as long as the males. According to Carich and Mussack (2001), manufacturers designed a device, much the same design and size of a tampon, which measures the sexual arousal by recording changes of vaginal vasoconstriction. Research presents that female arousal is not computed as easily as male reactions. A male arousal is more physically based, and the female arouses to more emotionally based stimuli. Thus, for the technician performing the test and the interpretive clinician, it is more difficult to decipher the accurate level of female deviant sexual arousal toward stimulus of specific gender or age groups. This information is then processed by a computer, scored, and given to a clinician for interpretation.

PENILE PLETHYSMOGRAPHY:

Male offenders have been proverbial guinea pigs used for phallometric research studies for many years. The first designs for the PPG included styles of measuring devices. Carich and Mussack (2001) stated technicians used an adjustable rubber-band style gauge or transducer, which contains mercury, named Barlow for the designer. Currently, there have been other models created to offer a more accurate measurement for the circumcised penis and using the Barlow for those clients who are not circumcised or are obese. The PPG is used to assess a client's arousal levels and specific focus of gender and age preference..."

Dr. Miller's second session with Henry was one on one.

"In this session, Mr. Emerson, we are going to determine the core areas of your sexual erotica. Here's what we do."

Henry looked at the device. It looked like a kind of condom with wires attached to it.

"Jesus, is that going to shock me?"

"Oh no. Don't worry. There will be zero electricity transmitted into you. Instead, this measures your vibrations, your pulse and your reactions to various erotica."

Miller put the device onto Henry's penis. This required some cooperation from Henry. He had to pull his pants down, pull his dick out and watch in amazement as this fairly cute girl put on a kind of condom, connected with a group of wires to a recording device. That device would then store data about Henry's reaction to a book of pictures.

The first picture showed, disgustingly enough, a young boy naked, laying down, butt up. Henry looked at the picture and shook his head. He was not turned on.

Dr. Miller showed him a second one with the boy turned over to the other side, with a frontal view of his prepubescent genitalia exposed. Henry shook his head. There was no registration of any erotic response. Good for Henry on that.

The next photos were similar, except of young girls. Once again, Henry simply proved himself to not be a pedophile. The girls did not excite him in any way. She was a very young girl, prepubescent. They showed her laying down with her butt exposed, they showed her laying on her back with her prepubescent genitalia exposed. Henry was nonplussed, did not react at all and got a zero on her. That was a good zero.

Next there was a teen girl. She was about 16, 17, small sized breasts, looked like a delinquent. I don't know where they got that photo. She had a tattoo, was kind of rough and had freckles. She was shown naked, in a posed photo taken where she was laying on a bed. She had super white skin. Her hands were stretched out above her head. This registered a small mark on the machine. Henry was a little bit turned on. Dr. Miller wrote a note down: Picture four, slightly positive.

Picture five was kind of a trick shot. It was the same girl in the same pose, but in this one she was wrapped up in belts, her hands were tied, her ankles were tied and there was some odd device around her mouth. It was leather, it had a ball that went in her mouth. The question Dr. Miller was trying to get an answer to was whether this kind of restrained woman was somehow more interesting to Henry. Well, she hit the Bullseye on that one. The erectile meter went up. Henry got excited on that one. Dr. Miller noted: Picture five, moderate excitement.

Picture six was the same girl, except they rolled her over. They had her tied up, her butt was up, they'd taken a pillow, put it under her stomach to prop her ass up. They showed two views -- a side view and one directly behind. This, of course, got Henry really excited. The erectile meter went up and up. He was actually getting a hard-on. Dr. Miller noted that: Hard-on, pictures seven and eight.

She saw it was getting a little too hot, and decided that this session should end.

"Okay, Henry, I get an idea that you're getting a little too excited about these. I want to terminate this for right now. I have more pictures to show you. We will continue this tomorrow. Fair enough?"

"Whatever you say, doc."

Henry looked down at his hard cock and looked at the doctor as though she were going to take this condom machine off of him.

She smiled.

"No, Henry. You do it."

Henry smiled back, realized his plight would be to take care of his own dick that day. He removed the sheath and put it on the table. He buttoned up his pants again. The correctional officers then escorted him back into his cell.

CHAPTER 34

RELAPSE PREVENTION PLAN

Another day in prison, another day of sexual offender therapy. The therapist, Dr. Miller, was present with a handout. There were six men there, including Henry. They reviewed the handout, which she described. It had a title: Relapse Prevention Plan [note: this plan is from Flora et al *Sexual-Offender Therapy*, exercise 18.1 at page 126]:

Name:

Probation Officer's Name:

Therapist's Name:

Date:

Your relapse-prevention plan is a work in progress. The plan focuses on particular thoughts, feelings and behaviors that were part of your offense chain and how you can avoid falling back into the same patterns and having the same distorted views before your offense. Spend time working on this plan inside and outside of the group to insure that you have the best opportunity at success in your recovery.

1. Acknowledgement (discuss what you did to your victim):
2. Responsibility (discuss your responsibility in your offense and to your victim):
3. Triggers are anything (i.e., issues, events and/or feelings) that cause you to give up and potentially lead to having a victim through sexual offending. Look at your life and identify the biggest triggers that you are dealing with at this time.
4. Stressors are the thoughts, feelings, and behaviors that you have allowed, making you more prone to committing your offense. These are not excuses for you, but can be risk factors that add to why you sexually offended another person. Name at least five stressors that you were experiencing at the time of your offense.
5. What stressors are you dealing with at this time? Name at least five.

6. Grooming behaviors are those behaviors that you used to get you closer to your victim. Oftentimes you befriended the victim and his or her family in some way in order to gain their trust and make it easier to have access to your victim. Briefly discuss what you did to groom your victim.

7. Describe the events that led up to your offense.

8. How long in advance had you planned your offense?

9. In what ways did you try to get close to your victim before the offense?

10. Explain the specific types of feelings that you had toward your victim before your offense.

11. What specific types of feelings did you have toward your victim after your offense?

12. Did you know your victim before the offense?

13. What was it about your victim that drew you to him or her (physical features, age range, personality type, etc.)?

14. What were the reasons that you chose your victim (e.g., easy access)?

15. Did you have fantasies about your victim before your offense?

16. Did your fantasies about your victim end with masturbation?

17. Do you still have fantasies about your victim? Explain your answer.

18. What feelings are you currently having about what you have done mentally, emotionally and spiritually to your victim?

19. In what ways are you making amends for the harm that you have caused your victim?

20. If you have the impulse to offend again, what are some positive ways that you can stop these desires (e.g., stop and think before you act)?

21. What are some appropriate ways that you can reduce your stress?

22. In what ways has your offense changed your relationship with your family and friends?

23. High-risk situations -- Just as a recovered alcoholic should not order dinner in a bar, you should not attend places or see people that are likely to cause additional stress and/ or be a trigger for you, which will lead to a situation that is considered high risk for you. Being in a high-risk situation does not automatically mean that you will reoffend; however, your risk goes up considerably. It's important that you view your high-risk situations as warning signals that are there to alert you of the danger. It's critical that you remember the risks that surrounded your offense.

    a. Where did your offense occur (e.g., at a local department store, playground, or in your home)?

    b. What was your thought process like at the time of your offense (e.g., fantasies of your victim)?

    c.   Explain what type of relationship (if any) that you had at the time of your offense (e.g., single, happily married, or you had broken up with your girlfriend or boyfriend).

    d.   What was your emotional well-being like at the time of your offense (e.g., confident, happy, depressed, feeling sorry for yourself, or angry)?

    e.   What stresses were you dealing with (or not dealing with) at the time of your offense (e.g., financial difficulties, relationship difficulties, or work difficulties)?

    f.   What are your plans to change these thoughts, feelings, and conditions to avoid (as much as possible) high-risk situations in the future?

    g.   How did you convince yourself that what you were doing was OK (e.g., it happened to me or she or he agreed to it)?

24. It is important that you have a plan in place for what you will do in the likelihood that you end up in a high-risk situation unintentionally. What are your plans if you find yourself in a situation that is considered high-risk for you?

25. Your life has been without a positive direction since you allowed yourself to harm another person. It is important that you have goals for your life. Briefly write three goals that you hope to accomplish the next year in treatment. These goals can focus on anything in your life that will take you in a positive direction.

26. How will you accomplish these goals?

27. How will you know when you have reached your goals?

28. Who in your life can you use as a support to help you when you are having difficulties (i.e., friends, church leader, and/or the group)?

29. In what ways are you willing and/or motivated to make positive steps to avoid reoffending?

30. By the time that you have finished treatment what do you hope will be different about your life?

I realize that before this relapse-prevention plan or my recovery can work in my life, I must be willing to be honest with myself and look at all of the unmanageability in my life. I must show personal responsibility, honesty, and strive to live my life without sexual misconduct. I must admit to what I did and express genuine victim empathy and remorse. I understand that there will be consequences if I reoffend. I also realize that if I reoffend, I will create another generation of victims. I pledge that I will have no more victims. I make this promise to the group members, the community that I live in, the victims that I have created, and to myself, one day at a time, for the rest of my life.

Client Signature   Date Signed

Therapist Signature   Date Signed

Probation or Parole Officer Signature   Date Signed

"The first step for you to do is to simply read all of the questions on this form," Dr. Miller explained. "Let's take a moment to do that. If you have any questions, please hold off on asking them until you've read the entire form. Proceed."

The men looked at the multi-page form. None of them liked it, especially the first question: "Acknowledgement (discuss what you did to your victim)." They had to stand up and say this in the past. Many of them did not like admitting what they did, but on this form they would have to write it out, and if they didn't write it out, there would be hell to pay.

"By the way, for those of you who would like to not fill this form out, let me explain something. Under California law, if the District Attorney's office obtains two opinions of licensed psychologists that you are likely to re-offend, they are allowed to start a proceeding after you get out of your prison sentence. That proceeding can cause you to be placed in a mental institution, for up to two years at a time, during which you will receive further sexual offender therapy. If you cannot complete this form and convince me that you are on the way to healing, to solving your issues, and will make yourself a relapse prevention plan towards the overall goal that you never do this again; if you cannot do that, I will assist the district attorney by giving them one doctor's opinion that you will relapse. I will also assist them in finding the second doctor, and you will never see the light of day. Now do I have your attention?"

The men looked up. One of them, Mr. Chambers shook his head.

"Fucking bullshit."

"What was that?"

"I said, I'm on it."

"Good. Okay, the questions are pretty straightforward. If you have any questions though, about the questions, let me know. I'll be happy to answer them."

"I don't understand item three, about triggers," Henry asked. "I don't know what a trigger is. I don't know what causes me or gets me into the mode of wanting to do this. Can you help me on that?"

"Triggers are defined as how you choose your victim and how you create an environment for offending. Triggers can be things like stress, loneliness, fear, anger, losing a job, false beliefs, infidelity and a host of other issues. [Flora et al, *Sexual-Offender Therapy*, page 89] Let me read to you from a book I have on sexual offender therapy Flora et al, *Sexual-Offender Therapy*, page 89]:

"When these difficulties occur, the offender who is not always psychologically equipped to address the problem appropriately, may resort to self-soothing methods that have worked in the past (e.g., masturbation, viewing pornography, or engaging in inappropriate sexual acts). The desire is to feel better, unfortunately at the expense of someone else."

"Class, I would like to give you a case study on triggers.

"Mr. Mansion was the stepfather of three; his wife worked the midnight shift as a registered nurse. He worked in a minimum-wage job and they had one vehicle. As Mr. Mansion revealed the story of his offense, it became apparent that his inability to cope with anger, frustration and hurt lead him to commit his crime of fondling his fourteen-year-old stepdaughter.

"According to him, eighteen months prior to his offense he was the primary caregiver of the children. He cooked, cleaned, and cared for the children. His wife, when not asleep, went out with her girlfriends. This initially did not bother him because he felt that due to his wife's stressful job, she needed time to relax.

"As once a week turned into three or four days a week out with the girls, their time together was compromised. When he complained, she stalled him and promised that they would spend more time together, but that never happened. This created feelings of hurt within himself. He believed his wife's need to be with her friends was more important than being with him. He also suspected she was having an affair. His anger began to manifest itself in continuous arguments and accusations of infidelity, which further decreased their time together.

"Their sex life, which according to Mr. Mansion was a once daily event, now was reduced to two or three times a month. A month prior to his crime, it was reduced to once a month. This convinced him that she was having an affair. Instead of finding a peer to share his problems with, he turned to his fourteen-year-old stepdaughter who was having her own difficulties with her mother.

"She became his confidant, sharing all of his suspicions and concerns about his wife with her, including his lack of sexual satisfaction. As the sexual frustration grew, he shared his frustration with his stepdaughter/victim and she would ask questions about their sex life. At first he was reluctant to talk about the things he and his wife did sexually, then he thought, 'Whom else could I talk to?' Feeling justified, he answered every question she had about sex and those conversations became the fuel for his fantasies.

"He reported masturbating as many as six times a day prior to his offense. Using his stepdaughter as the primary stimulus for his masturbatory behavior, he stated that on the rare occasions when he made love with his wife he thought about his stepdaughter. When asked, 'Why did he share such a private matter with her?' his response was, 'She was the only one that understood the problems in the house. Besides, when my wife took the car, I was miles from anyone I could talk to and she was right there. Because the stepdaughter's response to him was 'sympathetic,' they created an alliance against his wife. Whenever Mrs. Mansion tried to discipline or censor her child, Mr. Mansion usurped his wife's authority by telling his stepdaughter that she didn't have to do whatever her mother said. This lead to several huge arguments where the stepdaughter sided with Mr. Mansion, causing the wife to mention the possibility of divorcing him.

"This possibility greatly concerned him, fearing that his stepdaughter would be taken from him. To ensure that his wife would stop talking about divorce, he stopped his complaining and allowed her to come and go at her leisure. Oftentimes, he would encourage her to go out, giving him more time with his stepdaughter/victim. By now Mr. Mansion had elevated his stepdaughter to peer status in his mind; he was using her physically developing body as the source for his fantasy. He reported using those images to masturbate several times a day and thought of marrying her when she became of age. He became so comfortable with the way things were going he encouraged her to wear her mother's 'baby doll' nightgowns, stating that she filled them out better than her mother. To maintain the aura of secrecy, he told her not to wear her mother's gowns until her siblings were in bed, fearing that they would tell her mother and she'd forbid her from wearing them. They fell into a routine of waiting until the younger children went to sleep and the stepdaughter would parade around in the gowns. These actions went on for weeks. He had asked her not to wear panties on a few occasions, but she refused and he never pushed the issue.

"One summer night she complained of it being hot. He suggested that she sleep in the living room where the fan was. While going to the restroom later that night, he passed by the living room and saw her bare bottom out from under the gown. He slipped into the living room and watched her bottom for a while and then he began to masturbate. Prior to ejaculation he started fondling her bottom and vaginal area. She woke up, screamed, and ran into her siblings' room where her mother was sleeping and told her what happened."

Dr. Miller then turned to Mr. Emerson.

"Does that answer your question? Does that help you to understand your triggers?"

"Oh yes."

He nodded affirmatively. He knew and filled out item three.

"Loneliness, sadness, miss my mother, miss my father, worry about my future, worry about my past, worry about myself. I have huge levels of anxiety."

"Are there any other questions?"

Nobody had a question.

"Okay. I want everybody to take their time. We've got plenty of that around here. Go ahead and fill it out and remember, do a good job. If you can come up with a proper relapse prevention plan, it is going to give you a path to your own personal freedom. If you can't do it, it is going to give you a path to permanent imprisonment."

The men proceeded busily to fill out the questionnaire.

CHAPTER 35

HEARING ON MOTION TO DISMISS THE RICO CASE

Naturally, the mayor wasn't going to take this RICO case sitting down. He hired one of the most powerful law firms in San Diego, a group famous for bringing massive class action cases against corporations. He figured it would be a good idea to have one of these plaintiff's asshole attorneys as a defendant asshole attorney.

Their main partner had had his own bout with the law, owing to some improper use of back pay by the lawyers to the clients in class actions. Oops, you're not supposed to do that. There is always a search and a need for a client in these huge class action cases, and sometimes the law firms cross the line by literally buying a client. The law firm did that, something they became quite infamous for. Their main front show ended up doing a stint in federal prison over it. This would be, of course, the perfect law firm to represent the mayor against a charge of violation of the racketeers' influence corrupt organizations (RICO) act.

The first response by the law firm is something known as a motion to dismiss for failure to state a claim. The case ended up before Judge Alan Wickenberg of the United States District Court for the southern district of California.

Ben was in the audience section and watched his father as he listened to the judge describe the standards on a motion to dismiss.

"Gentlemen, as you are both aware, my function on a motion to dismiss is to examine the pleadings and to determine if the facts alleged in the plaintiff's complaint are sufficient to state a claim for relief under the RICO act. I do not look into the truth of the allegations, I do not look into what proof the plaintiff has in the allegations. Instead, I look solely to the allegations themselves, and make a determination if there is indeed a claim under the RICO act.

"The plaintiff has alleged that the mayor has used the city as an unlawful enterprise. One of the requirements under the RICO act is an allegation of some type of enterprise, whether it be a legally recognized enterprise, or an unofficial or nonregistered illegal organization, such as the mafia. In this case, the city is alleged to be the enterprise.

"The main point on the motion to dismiss is that a city cannot be the kind of enterprise that can result in a legal claim. This pure legal issue is one that the court can rule on as a matter of law. At this juncture, I rule that the city is a proper enterprise.

"The complaint alleges that the mayor committed a series of what we refer to as predicate offenses, in the form of wire fraud and mail fraud, in inducing the federal government to part with federally subsidized redevelopment monies, and did so with a series of deceptive written statements, that the funds would be used for low income housing as required under the redevelopment funds program, when in fact the mayor's true intent was to earmark those funds for allocation to corporate retail giants, and indeed in doing so was paying back those corporate giants for their generous funding of his mayoral campaign.

"To this allegation, the mayor claims immunity, that under the RICO act he is immune from prosecution due to his status as mayor. I find this position to be utterly without merit.

"The last claim asserted by the mayor is that the claim does not adequately plead the RICO claim, in that the plaintiffs do not have direct standing to assert the claim, as they are not directly impacted by the redevelopment program. This I put in the category of pure chutzpah.

"The whole point is that the plaintiffs, who are a collection of low income residents of San Diego, indeed several of them are homeless, were supposed to be the very beneficiaries from the program that, but for the mayor's improper conduct, would have been the happy recipients of low income housing. For the mayor to step into court and say they weren't ever going to get anything anyway, shows that he misses the whole point of these redevelopment funds. They are not to help his corporate buddies. They are to help the homeless, the poor, the downtrodden. They are to assist them in the process of getting off the homeless ranks and into the apartment dwelling ranks. Perhaps this mayor will never get it.

"For now, it is enough for me to state that the court denies the motion to dismiss, and directs the defendant to file an answer to the complaint within 10 days of this order. SO ORDERED."

This is one of those court appearances where the parties weren't allowed to say a word, where there was nothing to say. The judge had reviewed and read all of the complex legal briefs and was prepared to rule. He really did not need to hear from anybody. Indeed, to call it a hearing is a little bit of a misnomer. It was more like a day to listen to the judge make his decision, which is exactly what happened.

Ben, of course, was taking copious notes of everything the judge said. After the hearing was over, he congratulated his dad.

"You were brilliant."

"Oh yeah, my oral advocacy skills were really tested today, right?"

"Well, the bottom line is you won, they lost."

Ben looked over at the mayor's attorneys.

"I've noticed the mayor didn't quite make it down to court today."

"No, he's busy running the city."

"Into the ground?"

Counsel was not happy with that statement.

"It's not over yet, by a long shot."

Sam reacted:

"Oh, I know. There'll be pretrial discovery, there'll be subpoenas, there'll be depositions, there'll be requests to produce, we'll have to get all the writing given to the federal government, we'll have to compare those to the conduct of the mayor in actually giving these funds out to the corporate giants. We'll have to do subpoenas to the corporate giants to see all the monies they got. We'll have to get all the letters written between the corporate giants and the campaign funding arrangements made. Gosh, you're right. It's not over yet by any means."

The defense attorney listened to Sam rattle off all these discovery techniques.

"Sam, you seem reasonable enough."

"Yes, I am the definition of a reasonable man."

"We should talk."

"I'm all ears. You want to talk right now?"

"Not here."

He looked over to see a group of no fewer than 15 newspaper reporters, with Ben at the front of the pack. They were salivating for the story. They wanted the comment. They wanted the dirt. They wanted to know what the mayor was going to do about these charges, and they wanted to know right then and there.

"Very well."

They walked past the journalists, into the court hallway. The journalists were following them, asking questions throughout the corridor.

"Will the mayor be resigning?"

"No."

"Is the mayor guilty of these charges?"

"Absolutely not."

"Is the mayor going to fight these all the way to trial?"

The attorney stopped.

"Absolutely, yes."

Nothing, of course, could be further from the truth.

CHAPTER 36

HENRY'S RELAPSE PREVENTION PLAN

Back at the prison, the group therapy session continued. Some of the men looked up with empty stares, unable to write really anything of substance. The man in the wheelchair was one of these. He did not believe in relapse. He did not believe in his first lapse. It's hard to describe how you will take steps to assure that nothing will happen again, when you don't believe your incident ever happened in the first place. He would never get out of prison.

Henry, on the other hand, was busy as a little bee, writing away, crossing out, rewriting, erasing and got to the point where he had to make a special request.

"Sorry doctor, but do you have another eraser?"

The doctor smiled. She appreciated his effort. She knew he was trying. She grabbed another pencil and handed it to him.

"Can I see what you have so far?"

He looked up as though he was trying to hide it.

"If you don't mind, I would prefer finishing it all."

She looked at his handwriting.

"It's so messy."

"I know. I have all this to say."

Henry was the ultimate in a finish carpenter, capable of doing such beautifully inlaid nailing. When it came to handwriting, however, he could barely write. An odd juxtaposition of wildly divergent personality traits. Perhaps we should not be surprised at such internal contradictions.

The doctor had an idea.

"Henry, do you know how to type?"

He looked up.

"As a matter of fact, I do."

"Excellent. I'll tell you what. I think you could really do a good job on this profile and I want to make sure that happens. I want to do whatever I can to help make that happen, so I'll tell you what I'm going to do. I'm going to excuse you. I request that the correctional officer take you down to the law library right now. There's a typewriter in there. I want you to take this form. I want you to type up your responses. Officer, is that okay?"

The officer shrugged his shoulders.

"Anything you want, we'll do."

"Very well. I want to tell everybody else, I'm not going to give Henry special treatment here. If any of you would like to type up your responses, just let me know and we will do so."

None of the others wanted to do that. They were happy not writing in any way, shape or form.

Henry got up.

"May I?"

She nodded. The correctional officers then escorted Henry out of the therapy room, down the hallway, through a few more corridors, to a place called the prison law library. Inside, there were quite a few prisoners busily preparing documents to further their agenda of "I am not guilty; let me out of here." The good news, 99.99% of these petitions, habeas corpus or appellate briefs, would absolutely fail.

These prisoners did not understand that the best method of getting out of prison wasn't to remain in denial; in fact, the best way is to admit the wrongdoing, deal with what you have done, and seek appropriate treatment to correct yourself. Once upon this path, these inmates could find a way to leave. For some reason, nobody was telling them that -- or at least, nobody that they would listen to.

Henry sat at the typewriter and began typing away. It was impressive typing. He could jam. He quickly filled out the first page, and within an hour, had all four pages completed.

Here are Henry's answers and preparation of what would become known as "Henry's Relapse Prevention Plan":

Name: Henry Emerson III

Probation Officer's Name: Not applicable; still in prison

Therapist's Name: Dr. Abigail Miller

Date: December 5, 2012

Your relapse-prevention plan is a work in progress. The plan focuses on particular thoughts, feelings and behaviors that were part of your offense chain and how you can avoid falling back into the same patterns and having the same distorted views before your offense. Spend time working on this plan inside and outside of the group to insure that you have the best opportunity at success in your recovery.

1. Acknowledgement (discuss what you did to your victim): **I applied a hypodermic needle into her neck, rendering her semi-unconscious and then anally raped her.**

2. Responsibility (discuss your responsibility in your offense and to your victim): **I am 100% responsible for the entire event. I did it, I did it to the victim and I understand that it harmed the victim.**

3. Triggers are anything (i.e., issues, events and/or feelings) that cause you to give up and potentially lead to having a victim through sexual offending. Look at your life and identify the biggest triggers that you are dealing with at this time: **My triggers include a feeling of shame and trauma over the suicide by my father, his murder of my mother and his conduct in committing a series of rapes of other women while he was in the military. I don't understand why, but I am somehow reliving what he did. I feel terrible about my upbringing, about my parents, about who I am, and I seek for sex a method of obtaining some type of release from this plight.**

4. Stressors are the thoughts, feelings, and behaviors that you have allowed, making you more prone to committing your offense. These are not excuses for you, but can be risk factors that add to why you sexually offended another person. Name at least five stressors that you were experiencing at the time of your offense: **Feeling bad, feeling ashamed, feeling traumatized, feeling exploited, feeling betrayed, feeling awful.**

5. What stressors are you dealing with at this time? Name at least five: **Feeling bad, feeling ashamed, feeling traumatized, feeling exploited, feeling betrayed, feeling awful.**

6. Grooming behaviors are those behaviors that you used to get you closer to your victim. Oftentimes you befriended the victim and his or her family in some way in order to gain their trust and make it easier to have access to your victim. Briefly discuss what you did to groom your victim: **I placed a hypodermic needle in her neck and shot her with a drug cocktail that rendered her semi-unconscious.**

7. Describe the events that led up to your offense: **I was in the bar area of a restaurant. I was looking for a new victim. I had the hypodermic needle in my coat pocket, ready to go. I looked at various and decided on my victim. I followed her into the bathroom. I came in behind her and then attacked her.**

8. How long in advance had you planned your offense?: **I planned this offense from my home. I had to prepare a drug cocktail, place it into a hypodermic needle, put that into an envelope, stuff that into my coat pocket, go to a restaurant where I knew women would be there, and then sat at a bar and waited until the right woman arrived.**

9. In what ways did you try to get close to your victim before the offense?: **I followed her into the bathroom.**

10. Explain the specific types of feelings that you had toward your victim before your offense: **I don't know what kind of feelings I had towards my victim. Lust, for one. She is hot. I also saw her as a fellow traumatized woman. I could see there was some kind of psych issue that she had, one that I wished to explore.**

11. What specific types of feelings did you have toward your victim after your offense?: **After the offense, I left her there. She looked so beautiful in her spent way, exhausted, abused, delirious. I felt a kind of love for her.**

12. Did you know your victim before the offense?: **No.**

13. What was it about your victim that drew you to him or her (physical features, age range, personality type, etc.)?: **She's very beautiful. She has contradictory elements; dark and light. She was very sad, I could tell; emotionally traumatized, having some kind of psych problem. She was the perfect match for me.**

14. What were the reasons that you chose your victim (e.g., easy access)?: **I liked the way she walked. I liked her sadness. I liked her trauma. I liked her psych state.**

15. Did you have fantasies about your victim before your offense?: **While following her into the bathroom, I noticed the way she walked and shook her ass. It made me very excited.**

16. Did your fantasies about your victim end with masturbation?: **My fantasy was to anally rape her, not to masturbate. I did not have to masturbate. My cock was completely hard the minute I pulled down her pants.**

17. Do you still have fantasies about your victim? Explain your answer: **I do have fantasies about her. I don't know; maybe I'm in love with her.**

18. What feelings are you currently having about what you have done mentally, emotionally and spiritually to your victim?: **I know I hurt her very badly. I feel terrible about that, but I want her. I need her. I don't know how to live without her.**

19. In what ways are you making amends for the harm that you have caused your victim?: **I'm not allowed to contact her, so I don't know how to make amends to her. I'm willing to do anything I can. For starters, I pled guilty to the crime and I'm here doing this program.**

20. If you have the impulse to offend again, what are some positive ways that you can stop these desires (e.g., stop and think before you act)?: **I need to get over what happened to my father and my mother. I'm not sure how to do that. I feel so utterly lost in what happened to them. If somebody can help me find a way to get over that incredible loss, I think I can find a way to stop my desires, to get a relief from that trauma.**

21. What are some appropriate ways that you can reduce your stress?: **I know I need some kind of medication for my bipolar disorder. Lithium does not seem to work so well. I need something else. I also need some kind of anxiety drug. I don't want to push a bunch of drugs onto me right now, but I'm not sure that therapy can eliminate the stress I feel over what happened with my parents.**

22. In what ways has your offense changed your relationship with your family and friends?: **My family is my grandfather. I am not sure that he will ever speak with me again. I believe he will forgive me. I hope he does.**

23. High-risk situations -- Just as a recovered alcoholic should not order dinner in a bar, you should not attend places or see people that are likely to cause additional stress and/ or be a trigger for you, which will lead to a situation that is considered high risk for you. Being in a high-risk situation does not automatically mean that you will reoffend; however, your risk goes up considerably. It's important that you view your high-risk situations as warning signals that are there to alert you of the danger. It's critical that you remember the risks that surrounded your offense.

    a. Where did your offense occur (e.g., at a local department store, playground, or in your home)?: **The offense occurred at a bar, in a restroom. I need to stay away from places where victims mingle in a public area, and then retreat to a private area.**

    b. What was your thought process like at the time of your offense (e.g., fantasies of your victim)?: **My thought process included fantasies of releasing myself and my world. I knew exactly what I would do. I had a movie of it played before I did it. I saw myself injecting her with the hypodermic needle, I saw myself pulling her pants down, I saw myself anally raping her.**

    c. Explain what type of relationship (if any) that you had at the time of your offense (e.g., single, happily married, or you had broken up with your girlfriend or boyfriend): **I did not have a girlfriend before the offense. The only relationship I had was with my grandfather. I hope he will forgive me.**

    d. What was your emotional well-being like at the time of your offense (e.g., confident, happy, depressed, feeling sorry for yourself, or angry)?: **My emotional well-being is way off normal. I am bipolar, and am deeply traumatized about what my father did to my mother, and what my father did to himself, and what my father did to many other girls.**

    e. What stresses were you dealing with (or not dealing with) at the time of your offense (e.g., financial difficulties, relationship difficulties, or work difficulties)?: **I did not have work or financial problems. I did not have a relationship difficulty. I have a problem with my father and my mother and my bipolar disorder.**

f. What are your plans to change these thoughts, feelings, and conditions to avoid (as much as possible) high-risk situations in the future?: **My plans are to seek appropriate therapy to get over what happened with my father and mother, to deal with my bipolar disorder, to take steps to control my sexual urges that occur when I'm in a manic state, and to somehow find another method to release my pain.**

g. How did you convince yourself that what you were doing was OK (e.g., it happened to me or she or he agreed to it)?: **I did not convince myself even for a second that what I was doing was okay, but I will say this. I convinced myself, and even still believe, that I have a true love for the victim. I do not have any crazy fantasies that she is in love with me.**

24. It is important that you have a plan in place for what you will do in the likelihood that you end up in a high-risk situation unintentionally. What are your plans if you find yourself in a situation that is considered high-risk for you?: **My plan to avoid this kind of conduct in the future: Please help me develop this plan. I'm not sure how to deal with my problems. I need help. Please help me.**

25. Your life has been without a positive direction since you allowed yourself to harm another person. It is important that you have goals for your life. Briefly write three goals that you hope to accomplish the next year in treatment. These goals can focus on anything in your life that will take you in a positive direction: **Goal 1: To find a way to get over what happened to my parents. Please help me in this. Goal 2: To find another way to release my pain. I have an answer to this: I love music, I love to play guitar, I love to write songs, I love to sing. This is a wonderful outlet for my anxiety. Goal 3: I need to mend my relationship with my grandfather. I know he is deeply disappointed in me. I want his respect back.**

26. How will you accomplish these goals?: **I need treatment for my bipolar disorder and to get over the problems with my parents. I hope you will help me in this and I will need further help when I get out. I will probably need lifelong therapy for these issues. As for my music, just give me my guitar. I'll take it from there. As for mending my relationship with my grandfather, I would like to start by writing him a letter telling him how sorry I am about all that I did.**

27. How will you know when you have reached your goals?: **I do not know if I will ever reach my goals. I will try to solve my issues, but I have a feeling they will never go**

away. I can reach a higher level of music. I have never been recognized for what I can do and how I can play. Maybe someday I will get that recognition. As for my relationship with my grandfather, when he sees me, when he looks into my eye and smiles the same way he has before, I will know that I have achieved that goal. I believe I can achieve my goals concerning my music and my grandfather. I do not believe I can achieve my goal in getting over my bipolar disorder and in getting over what happened to my parents, but I am certainly willing to give that a huge try.

28. Who in your life can you use as a support to help you when you are having difficulties (i.e., friends, church leader, and/or the group)?: **The only person in my life that I can rely on in any way, shape or form is my grandfather. He is a wonderful man. If there's any issue, I will go to him. I do not have a therapist on the outside. When I get out of here, I hope you will help me find one. I will also have that therapist hopefully on my side and will turn to that therapist anytime I am in a danger zone.**

29. In what ways are you willing and/or motivated to make positive steps to avoid reoffending?: **I am extremely motivated to stop offending. I will take the current therapy program that you are providing me very seriously. I hope you see this in me right now. I will also continue in therapy when I get out of here.**

30. By the time that you have finished treatment what do you hope will be different about your life?: **I do not ever expect to finish treatment. My expectation is to continue in treatment after I get out of here. I hope treatment helps me in understanding and dealing with the trauma of what happened to my parents, and helps me live with my bipolar disorder, and helps me mend my relationship with my grandfather.**

I realize that before this relapse-prevention plan or my recovery can work in my life, I must be willing to be honest with myself and look at all of the unmanageability in my life. I must show personal responsibility, honesty, and strive to live my life without sexual misconduct. I must admit to what I did and express genuine victim empathy and remorse. I understand that there will be consequences if I reoffend. I also realize that if I reoffend, I will create another generation of victims. I pledge that I will have no more victims. I make this promise to the group members, the community that I live in, the victims that I have created, and to myself, one day at a time, for the rest of my life.

Client Signature   Date Signed
Henry Emerson III   12-05-2012
Therapist Signature   Date Signed
Probation or Parole Officer Signature   Date Signed

Henry then prepared the "personal safety plan."

1. My triggers are as follows: **Anxiety/trauma, depression, anger, shame, feeling lost, needing a release from all the pain that I'm suffering because of what happened to my parents.**
2. My high-risk situations are: **When I am in a manic episode, I have heightened sexual arousal and seek anonymous nonconsensual sex as a method of releasing myself and my inner pain.**
3. My interventions are as follows: **Call my grandfather, call my therapist, call somebody to help me.**
4. My support persons are as follows: **My grandfather, my therapist.**

Henry took the pages out and neatly piled them together. There were no staples or paperclips in the law library. These could obviously be used as a weapon. He turned to the correctional officer present.

"I would like to be escorted back to group now."

The officer understood.

"Are you done?"

"I'm done."

"Did you answer all the questions?"

"I really did. I think I did a good job."

Unlike the therapist, the correctional officer was not the least bit impressed with Henry's progress through therapy. He shook his head in disgust.

"Let's go."

Henry proceeded down the corridor, back to the area where Dr. Miller was giving her group therapy/sexual offender treatment. Henry was escorted back into his seat. The other men were still writing. Henry proudly presented his pages to the therapist.

"There they are."

She looked at it, reviewed it very carefully and then at the end of the form, where it says "Therapist Signature," she signed it and dated it.

"Henry, I'm proud of you."

CHAPTER 37

THE APPEAL

Unbeknownst to Henry, Ben, Ben's father Sam, Erica and anyone else, the public defender's office had filed a notice of appeal of the judgement of conviction against Henry. The case was then passed on to the public defender appellate counsel, who had prepared an opening brief challenging the issues surrounding the alleged unlawful entry in Henry's home, the search without a search warrant, and the non-confession/confession of Henry.

Normally, the DA would inform the victim's family of such an appeal, but for some reason this one fell through the cracks. Perhaps it was because the direct victim, Erica, was still in a catatonic state, and they had not thought to advise a technically non-family member, Ben, about it. The bottom line, not only did Ben not know about it, Erica didn't know about it, Sam didn't know about it, and most surprisingly of all, even Henry didn't know about it.

The public defender saw legal issues, and had a kneejerk reaction of a public defender; appeal, object, argue, exclude, suppress and evade the truth of what the client had done.

The question remained whether this appeal would be the one in one thousand that would actually result in a reversal.

CHAPTER 38

THE POLYGRAPH

Henry was in Dr. Miller's office inside the prison. It was time for a polygraph test.

"Henry, this is all about full disclosure," she explained. "What I want to make sure is that you have completely and fully told us everything you did, how you did it in its full and complete way."

"I understand."

"You've made several standup disclosures in group therapy."

"Yes."

"You've explained two incidents."

"Yes."

"What we're going to do today is have you go live on the polygraph and I'm going to have you explain the two incidents. I want to make sure there aren't any more. Henry, I'm concerned about you. You're making great progress, but I have this idea that there are more out there. Today we're going to find out the truth."

Henry had this look on his face. *Oh God, will the truth come out?*

"Okay. Before we start, I want to get some what we call pretest information from you. This is just some basic data. Are you ready?"

"I'm ready."

"Okay. Let's start with this."

She had a clipboard out and on the clipboard was a form entitled "Pretest Interview." It had a series of questions and blank spots for the answer.

Polygraph Pretest Interview {From Flora, Duehl, Fisher, Halsey, Keohane, Maberry, McCorkindale, and Parson, *Sex-Offender Therapy*: A "How-to" Workbook for Therapists Treating Sexually Aggressive Adults, Adolescents and Children (Hayworth Press 2008)}:

1. What is your residence address?
2. Do you rent or own the house where you are living? Or do you live with someone else, like parents or friends? Does anyone live in the house with you? Any minors? Who are they? What are their ages?
3. What is your weight, height, date of birth, and present age?
4. What is your social security number?
5. What are your home and work telephone numbers?
6. How far have you gone in school?
7. Are you employed, and if so, what is the name of your employer, employer's address, length of employment, and job title?
8. What are your criminal convictions, both felonies and misdemeanors?
9. Have you ever had a polygraph test before? Did you pass that test? If no, why not?
10. How is your general health? Do you have any sexually transmitted diseases? Are you taking any medication? If so, what dosage, and for what health problems? Pulse and blood pressure?
11. Have you had any heart problems?
12. Have you had any emotional or nerve problems?
13. Have you had any pills, drugs, marijuana or alcohol in the past 12 hours?
14. Have you ever been an alcoholic? What is your history of using illegal drugs?
15. Are you experiencing any pain or discomfort now?

HISTORY OF SEXUAL CONTACTS

Date of Contact   Your Age Then   First Name of Contact   Age of Person   Sexual Activities Number of Times

_____

_____

_____

_____

_____

_____

_____

She handed Henry the clipboard with the form.

"Please fill this out."

Henry studied the form.

Henry's first question was on number one.

"Do you want my house address back home or my prison address?"

"Well, let's give your address before you went to prison."

Henry proceeded to fill out the form.

1. What is your residence address? **84 Milltower Road, Carlsbad, California.**

2. Do you rent or own the house where you are living? Or do you live with someone else, like parents or friends? Does anyone live in the house with you? Any minors? Who are they? What are their ages? **My grandfather owns the home I live in. I do not pay rent. I live in a unit by myself. My grandfather lives in the main house. He is 71 years old.**

3. What is your weight, height, date of birth, and present age? **I weigh 155 pounds. I am 5'11". I was born April 12, 1988. I am 26 years old.**

4. What is your social security number? **527-44-1605.**

5. What are your home and work telephone numbers? **760-555-1400.**

6. How far have you gone in school? **High school graduate; attended two years of junior college in San Diego.**

7. Are you employed, and if so, what is the name of your employer, employer's address, length of employment, and job title? **I am a self-employed carpenter. I own my own carpentry company. I have been doing that since the age of 17.**

8. What are your criminal convictions, both felonies and misdemeanors? **I was convinced for felony rape and assault with a deadly weapon. I have no other criminal convictions.**

9. Have you ever had a polygraph test before? Did you pass that test? If no, why not? **I have not ever had a polygraph before.**

10. How is your general health? Do you have any sexually transmitted diseases? Are you taking any medication? If so, what dosage, and for what health problems? Pulse and blood pressure? **My physical health is perfect. I do not have any sexually transmitted disease. I do not take any medication. I have a psych disorder which was diagnosed as bipolar disorder.**

11. Have you had any heart problems? **No heart problems.**

12. Have you had any emotional or nerve problems? **I have a psych disorder diagnosed as bipolar disorder. I have many emotional and nerve problems.**

13. Have you had any pills, drugs, marijuana or alcohol in the past 12 hours? **No.**

14. Have you ever been an alcoholic? What is your history of using illegal drugs? **No. I have taken illegal drugs in the past; marijuana, cocaine, stuff like that.**

15. Are you experiencing any pain or discomfort now? **I am experiencing the discomfort of being forced to confront what I did.**

HISTORY OF SEXUAL CONTACTS

Date of Contact	Your Age Then	First Name of Contact	Age of Person	Sexual Activities	Number of Times
1998	10	Kim	9	played with her	many times
1999	11	Laura	11	played with her	many times
2000	12	Yoshuda	12	played with her	many times
2001	13	Kiko	12	playing around; oral sex	many times
2002	14	Taiko	14	playing around; oral sex	many times
2003	15	Reika	14	playing around; oral sex	many times
2008	25	Paula	unknown	forced anal sex	1
2009	26	Erica	unknown	forced anal sex	1

Henry studied the chart, as though he had just finished a painting. Perhaps he had, a painting of his unfortunate life. He handed the chart back to Dr. Miller.

She scanned it quickly, and got to the page about his sexual experiences. She reviewed it silently, put the clipboard down and then turned to Henry.

"You ready to go live?"

Henry nodded affirmatively.

"Very well."

She put a series of straps around his chest and arm, calibrated the machine and started a couple baseline questions.

"Please state your name."

"Henry Emerson III."

"Your birthdate?"

"April 2, 1988."

"And your address?"

"84 Milltower Road, Carlsbad, California."

She looked at the baseline movement of the needle. It showed a beautiful, perfect horizontal line; not a single bump.

"Henry, you have prepared a pretest survey. Is that right?"

"Yes."

"And is this a copy of it?"

She held the clipboard in the air.

"It is."

"The information you put in here, is it true and accurate?"

"Yes."

"Have you completed the form completely and thoroughly?"

"Yes."

"I want to bring to your attention this last page here, about your sexual experiences. You see these?"

"Yes."

"Are these complete?"

"Yes."

"Henry, I see that the sexual experiences you describe go up until the age of 15. Let's talk about those for a second. Were those all consensual sexual relations? In other words, the girls you were with, they agreed to let you touch them in the way you touched them?"

"Yes."

"It was consensual?"

"Yes."

The needles were perfectly still. The lines coming out were perfectly silent. This was the truth.

"And the girls were all kinds of ages, if not exactly your age."

"Yes."

"Were they pretty?"

Henry smiled. He remembered all of them.

"Oh, yes. Every one of them was very pretty."

"You say you played with them and I think they played with you?"

"Yes."

"I believe I know what you mean by that. You touched their private parts?"

"Yes."

"And they touched yours."

"Yes."

"Was there any oral sex?"

"Yes --"

The line started to squiggle a little bit.

"Well, let me split that up. Some of the girls, there was no oral sex."

"Correct."

"And some of them had oral sex with you."

"Correct."

"You list two here where you had oral sex."

"Yes."

"Now did you perform oral sex on them?"

"Yes."

"Did they perform oral sex on you?"

The line started to squiggle.

"One yes, one no."

It was a mixed answer. He clarified it.

"Very well."

She made a note of that.

"Now Henry, all of a sudden it all stopped. It sounds like each year you're finding a new girlfriend somewhere where you live. I noticed the names go from American girls to Japanese girls."

"Yes."

"How did that happen?"

"I moved to Okinawa, where my father was based."

"Okay."

She of course knew the whole terrible story of Henry's father and of Henry's mother, and of what happened there. She'd seen the newspaper articles. This was something she did not need to go into, but of course therapists loved to get into it. That's what they do. They should be called "delvassists."

"Now Henry, I know what happened there with your father. Let me ask you, when the sex experiences you describe -- when it stops, is that at the time when your father killed your mother?"

The line started to squiggle all out of control. Henry hadn't given an answer and yet the machine was saying he was lying. How can a non-answer be a lie? She understood that he was having a very understandable reaction to this very difficult question. A lot of people would've backed off of it, but not Dr. Miller.

"Henry, answer the questions. Is that when you stopped having sex with other girls?"

"Yes."

"Why, Henry? What made you stop? Did you feel bad about what your dad did? Did you feel ashamed?"

"Yes, I felt terrible."

"But Henry, you didn't do that. Your dad did it. He's not the same person as you."

"YES HE IS. DON'T YOU GET IT?" Henry screamed out.

Dr. Miller tried to calm him down. The polygraph from this point forward would be effectively useless. It was all over the place. It was the kind of graph you would see with a patient having seven heart attacks at once; it flatlines and then starts up again, flatlines again, goes up again and the whole thing remains something the doctor would look at and say, "I don't know what to do with this guy."

She had to calm him down.

"Okay, wait a minute. We'll have to continue this later. You're way off the charts right now."

She turned off the machine. She unstrapped Henry.

"Henry, we will deal with this issue. I think we have focused in on your trigger. We're going to explore it fully and completely. Please trust me. I am here to help you.

Henry looked at her with these broken puppy eyes. He did trust her. He was near tears.

"Please help me," he pleaded, with the saddest tone you could ever imagine.

She looked at him. She looked at the polygraph, the zigzags all over it. It told a pretty obvious story of a man in great turmoil. She nodded her head.

"I will."

CHAPTER 39

SUMMIT AT THE MAYOR'S OFFICE

There is a law called the Brown Act. It is an open meeting act, under which our state government offices and local offices are required to hold meetings in the public. The idea is there should be no secret back room deals. There is a small exception to this rule; when the government is discussing the settlement of a lawsuit. In this setting, they are allowed to have a back room deal, in which they discuss openly behind closed doors.

Later, if a settlement is reached, it will be placed in the public view. But the discussions, deliberations, admissions, analysis which precedes any decision to settle, remains confidential and away from public view.

There was such a discussion about Sam's case against the mayor. The question from the mayor and his top level people was whether to resolve the case or fight it to the bitter end. The mayor was present, the vice mayor was present, the second vice mayor was present, the mayor's attorney was present, the city attorney was present and appropriately, a representative from the redevelopment agency was present.

The city attorney spoke first,

"We're in deep shit."

Mayor Jack Cowens shook his head.

"Jack, listen to me."

The mayor continued shaking his head. Guys like this -- triple A personality, got their way often in life, either by hook or crook -- they don't say settle. They say fight to the bitter end. But guys like city attorney Bill Sazevich, they find that the greatest thing in the world is the art of compromise.

"Look, Jack, here's the deal."

"No deal."

The mayor was angry.

His vice mayor, equally guilty in every regard, agreed with the mayor.

"We can't settle this case. It's like a full admission, an indictment of his whole character, of what he is, who he is."

"This is a part of stealing from the poor and giving to the rich. What could be worse than that?"

The city attorney had a quick answer to that one.

"To be actually convicted of it. How about that? What could be worse than that, in presenting the entire case to a jury in federal court and having them come out and say, you are 100% guilty so sayeth we all? You want to do that, Jack?"

There are few other people that would call the mayor by his first name, but Bill had known the mayor for many years. It was in this way that he found himself in the position, riding on his coattails as city attorney.

The vice mayor spoke up, but Jack had to stop her.

"Don't you see --"

"No, wait. Let's hear Bill out. Bill, what are we looking at if we go down on this?"

"Well, first of all, you're not looking at any time. The US attorney hasn't gotten on the bandwagon yet, but you got to know if a civil jury convicts you of this, there could easily be a grand jury indictment, like, three days later. It's one thing to want to fight for your principles, to fight for your character, to fight for your life, but it's another thing to be looking at prison time. Federal prison time on a RICO count, it could easily be five years, ten years, fifteen years -- the way it works depends on the number of zeros at the end of the take. If there's one million, you get five years. If it's ten million, you're looking at ten. Unfortunately for the mayor, the amount was a staggering $27 million. You want to screw around with that or do you want to just bury this thing in a settlement agreement?"

Jack looked at the attorney.

"We settle this thing -- what, it goes away?"

"It doesn't exactly go away."

"Well, what's the settlement agreement going to say? I'm guilty, therefore I'm going to pay?"

"The settlement agreement will have a provision in it that says, nothing herein shall be construed as an admission of liability."

The vice mayor pounded on the desk.

"Don't you get it, you idiots? When you give them the check, that's a confession. Twice they're going to know you're guilty. Who pays $27 million who isn't guilty? Hello?"

The city attorney looked out the window. There was a very peaceful scene. There were some palm trees. There was the ocean. It was quite lovely. He looked into the turmoil of the mayor's office.

"Look, perhaps you'll seek some solace in the following. A -- the settlement agreement will contain the provision, 'there will be no admission of liability.' B -- the money that's paid, it's not your money," he said.

"Well, whose money is it?"

"It's the people's money."

"So what, are we stealing from the poor again to pay the poor back the money we stole from the poor and gave to the rich? This is almost like a bad joke.

"We've got insurance for it," Bill explained. "I've already worked it out. They're going to pay some money on it. The city's going to pay some money."

The mayor stood up to that one.

"How much do I got to pay?"

"That's the beauty, Jack -- zero. All you got to do is say yes."

He looked over to his vice mayor. He looked over at the redevelopment agency head. This guy was one of these midlevel bureaucrats who didn't give a shit about his mandate to help the poor. He only cared about doing whatever it was the mayor who put him there wanted him to do.

"Take the money back, okay?"

"Now exactly how am I going to do that?"

"You call the son of a bitch up that we gave it to, and you tell him to give it back."

"Okay, small problem on that. We gave it to him, they got it, they put it into a little thing called a shopping mall. It's sitting in the shopping mall, so we really can't get it back from them now can we?"

"Well, can't we say it was a loan?"

The mayor was exploring ideas.

"It wasn't a loan. You think there's a little bit of paperwork on this thing? It was $27 and a half million, for crying out loud. It was a giveaway, clear and simple. You gave that money away, and they got it free and clear and there's no way in hell they're going to bring it back. Come on."

The mayor was thinking.

"If I can get it back from the rich and give back to the poor, wouldn't that actually make me look kind of sort of good?"

The city attorney responded, "Well, not really. It's sort of like a bank robber just giving the money back. You're still a bank robber. You just gave the money back. That doesn't get you much. It's a matter of mitigation. It might keep you out of 10 years of prison. The judge might give you five, but it doesn't show you're being good."

The mayor was upset. "Well, if that's not going to work and it's not going to turn me into a good guy anyway, then fuck it. Let's just make the people pay."

The city attorney explained,"Right. Let's make the people pay after we stole from the people and we're going to pay the people back by stealing from them again. Isn't that a great idea?"

This is the great thing about American justice. This very solution could very well occur, if the mayor would just say yes. There was a long period of silence.

Back at Sam's office, it was in the late afternoon. Sam was in the middle of discussing an issue with a different client on a completely different case. He was trying to explain to the client that, like it or not, he had to answer all the stupid questions that the other side was asking him to answer.

"It's not a question of what you want to do. It's not a question of what you might want to answer. It's not a question of what information you might want to give. You've got to answer them. You've got to give them all the information or you just got to dismiss your case. So it's your choice. You either fully answer this stuff or back out of the case. What's it going to be?"

Just then, the phone rang.

"Excuse me."

Sam was pissed off. His client was not answering the questions, was not cooperating and was bothering him. He then took the call.

"Sam here. Oh hey, Bill."

"Sam, we want to settle."

Sam was intrigued.

"Really?"

"We do."

This would be one of the crowning moments for Sam -- to resolve a huge corruption case, which in the same stroke, would give a bunch of poor people low income housing and a good place to live.

At the same time, it would give his son, who he loved dearly, the path towards one of the greatest and most prestigious awards in journalism, the Pulitzer. Ben was the one that figured it out, that wrote it all up, that found out all the information, that found the aggrieved poor people, that delivered them to Sam, that signed them up for a case, that brought the case forward. He was the engineer, he was the architect, he was the mastermind. It brought about a real world event. It brought about a wonderful solution.

The mayor would go down. The vice mayor would go down. The head of the redevelopment agency would go down. The only guy left standing in the city's ranks on this issue would be Bill himself, the city attorney.

Bill asked, "So, what's the deal?"

Sam answered a question with a question, "You tell me."

"$27.5 million back to the redevelopment agency -- a commitment that they'll spend it as they're supposed to on low income housing."

Sam smiled, "That's what we want."

"That's what you're going to get."

"What do I get for attorney's fees?"

"How far are you into this? What have you done? You filed a complaint. You pulled some --"

"Don't give me this crap. I'm getting $27 and a half million back where it belongs. You better give me at least $3 mil."

"We'll give you $1 mil."

"How about $2?"

"How about $1.5?"

"How about $1.9?"

"How about $1.8?"

"Done."

Oh, would the press have a field day with this one! Of course, Ben got a phone call from his dad explaining the whole settlement and Ben had it in the paper on the front page before the mayor even knew the deal was accepted.

There was a letter written from the city attorney's office to Sam.

"This will confirm our intent to settle the above referenced matter on the following terms:

The sum of $27.5 million will be replenished into the redevelopment fund, and specifically earmarked for low income housing.

We agree to pay you an attorney's fee equal to $1.8 million.

The settlement agreement will contain a provision in which all sides agree that the settlement does not constitute an admission of liability.

You will dismiss the case with prejudice. You will sign a typical general release and waiver of all claims.

The settlement will be subject to approval by the city council.

The settlement will be further subject to approval by the United States Court District Judge.

Please indicate your agreement with the above terms on behalf of your clients, the plaintiffs herein, by signing where indicated below."

After Sam signed that agreement, there were two faxes. The first was to Bill, his good buddy in the city attorney's office confirming it. The second was to Ben so he would have the opportunity of writing the article of his life. Two careers, two goals, father and son, total successes, home run -- all done in one piece of paper. It was beautiful.

CHAPTER 40

PARALLEL LIVES

Sam's beautiful home in La Jolla was a gorgeous estate -- Mediterranean, overlooking the ocean, secured gates at the front, a beautiful lawn, driveway, perfectly manicured, a gorgeous front entering into this huge interior area -- chandeliers, marble floors, huge paintings of ancestors, a black grand piano, a bust of Caesar. Tragically, after the settlement was signed, sealed and delivered, Sam was hunched over in his favorite chair, dead of a heart attack.

It would be Ben's solemn job to find his father in this way. He was so excited to walk into the house with a copy of the letter from the Pulitzer organization. He hadn't won it, but he was on the nominee list. This is kind of like being a nominee for the Academy Awards. Even if you don't get it, just being a nominee itself is a major success.

This was not Ben's first time on the nominee list -- which meant he had an even higher chance of winning it. He was so excited to come in to show his father this letter. When he walked in, he suddenly saw the shock of his life -- his father humped over in this dead way. He knew in two seconds what it was. His dad was dead.

Ben dropped to his knees. The letter fell to the ground. Just a second ago, it was the greatest thing in his life. Now it was an irrelevant piece of paper. His father, the last of his family. His mom had passed on before, he had no brothers, he had no sisters. He was the only child, the perfect child. A great child -- inquisitive, precocious, out of the box thinking, needing nothing from his parents, needing nothing but his own wit, his own desire and drive to do good things, to do the right thing.

His father had been forever proud of him. Who needs another lawyer in the family? An investigative journalist who got to the truth of corruption? An investigative journalist who knew how to find things that no one else would even have the inkling to find? He was a detective. He was a lawyer. He was a writer. He was relentless.

But on this day, he was turned into a sobbing, broken man, down on his knees crying before his dead father. The tears would flow into a river of despair.

Suddenly, there was a kind of awakening in Ben. He looked up and he realized that this house, this majestic mansion, this kingdom, would now be his. This is the kind of home, for those of you who aren't familiar with California real estate prices, that would sell for $7 million. It had nine bedrooms, five bathrooms, two kitchens, fireplaces all over, a gorgeous backyard, huge swimming pool. It had a separate guest home at the other end of the house. It was so different than what Ben was used to.

He drove up in his little Corvair. He would now turn it in for his father's $100,000 Mercedes.

He would give up his apartment and those nice Mexican guys making their barbecues and their muscle top t-shirts. He would give all that up. He would now move into the house his father built. He would take it over. It would now be his. This was the new Ben.

Grandpa Emerson, the parallel life. Two lives, both going forward, seemingly disconnected, having nothing to do with each other. Two men, great men -- a war hero, a champion, a sports star on the one hand -- Grandpa Emerson. What he did, he did in a great way, no question about it. He was a bicyclist in the Olympics. He had fought in World War I, heroically. He had attained the rank of General during World War II. He retired with more ribbons, medal and honors than you could fit in a small toolbox. It never went to his head.

He loved his country. He loved his head. He loved everything about his day. The day his wife killed herself was the last day on Earth for Henry, but he remained on Earth nevertheless -- toiling in his house and watching over the last remnants of his life, his cherished grandson.

After the passing of his son and his son's wife, he had this constant harrowing dream. He was plagued with horrible thoughts,

"It's all my fault. It's all my fault. I'm the one that chose my wife. She was the one that had this terrible seed in her, this genetic disorder. This psychological problem that nobody really understands and nobody can fix. It was in her. She was gorgeous, she was beautiful, she was a sexual animal -- and she created offspring in the same way.

"His son was absolutely handsome beyond words, sexually provocative at a young age and filled with the same genetic disorder that his mother had -- the misunderstood, misdiagnosed, misaligned and forever impossible to solve problem called bipolar disorder.

"It's all my fault. I selected her. I married her. I made it with her. I created offspring with her. I made these people. They are the ones, the very monsters that I created."

It was his harrowing demise. It was a thought that came to him every single day. He would look out the front of his door. He saw the fountain with the birds in it. It was so peaceful. There was water flowing from the top. The birds would come in and drink from it. They were his friends. They could fly away whenever they wanted. They were not his prisoners and came there every day for water.

Flowing over in the distance was the American flag on a flagpole, majestic, flapping in the wind. Henry would look at it as though he was still on a military base. He would salute it. It was his country. It was his nation. It was his freedom. It was something that he gave his life for, that he fought for and he would do it in a second if ever called upon any member of the armed forces. Go and attack -- he would be there. When and where would be his only question. He was always at the ready, ready to fight, ready to roll, ready to go to war for anything the United States needed him for.

On this day, he went out to the front area and had his last harrowing dream of his own participation in the crimes of his son. He replayed the whole thing in his head for the ten millionth time. His son dancing with his beautiful wife, holding her dead body limp in his hands and then putting her down so elegantly and taking his gun, putting it to his head and blowing his brains out.

He then thought about his grandson Henry, now in prison on the same path. He was going crazy with rage, crazy with fault, crazy with thought.

"It's all me, because of me. Why did I pick her? What was it about her that I needed so bad?"

Then he realized. It was the woman in her that wanted him so much, that loved him so much that he could not resist, no matter how dangerous, no matter how sick, no matter how troublesome. He needed that strong love. It was an animal love, a primal love, a love that salivated at the mouth, drooled down into a pile of spit and looked up at him and said, "Give me. Give me. Feed me. I want you."

He could never resist that. He had to have that. He knew that there was something sick behind it, but he couldn't resist that sickness. It was too alluring, too provocative. It was too mesmerizing. *My God, I could never get enough of her.* Henry knew in choosing her, he was choosing the devil. He was choosing someone who would steal his soul in exchange for sexual favors. He was a psych whore. He traded the tranquility of a family for sexual favors, in a way though that you couldn't even write about. What his wife had done to him was a climax that no man could ever resist.

He was filled with a sense of fault. He did it. He chose her. He knew what he was getting into. He did it anyway. He realized in having a baby with her that he would create another monster just like her. He knew that when she killed herself that he had created a son that would probably someday do the same. Of course he would. It always repeats itself. These psychotic disorders pass down from generation to generation. Whatever the father does, the son does. Whatever the mother does, the son does, the grandson does. It'll never stop. It'll never end.

Why, then, is this put out there? Why on Earth does Mother Nature in her own desire to create species protective mechanisms -- things that make us a better species -- why did she create the bipolar disorder? Not only is it completely indecipherable by the top medical doctors, but it has a built-in sexual component that assures its regeneration and repetition generation to generation. These people are out to have sex and they're going to have it whether you like it or not, whether you want it or not, whether you say yes, no or maybe -- they're going to get you. What is it with that?

The answer? You can study the annals of history and find the greatest people on the planet, the ones that created new histories, they created new nations, they created new books, new subjects, new disciplines, new science -- the ones that advanced us to the next level. Who are these people? Take a look at them. Joan of Arc, bipolar. Napoleon, bipolar. Abraham Lincoln, bipolar. Winston Churchill, bipolar.

Why do we need these people? Because they are the very people that make our society, our civilization -- they make it all. And we need to make sure, apparently -- at least Mother Nature thinks so -- that they procreate.

So bipolar comes with this other little amp to it. It's the amp of a sexual provocativeness -- a relentless, unstoppable demand for sexual activity. Mark it as a fact -- they will get what they want.

Henry knew it. He was a victim to it himself. No question about it. The greatest sex he ever had was with his wife when she was in a manic phase. Nothing even close to it. Mouth-watering, mouth open, all juiced up -- she would take him down like he was a little girl. When she was done with him, all he could do was look up at those pretty blue eyes, smile and say, "When are we going to do that again?"

He knew it. He fell for it. He was a victim of it, a victim to it. He couldn't get enough. He could never say no. He could never remove himself from that, and could never in a million years ever have another woman. Who else would ever compare to that? How could you possibly match such a woman? He couldn't and he never did. He never remarried.

He had his one son, a son that absolutely followed the path of his mother. The same terrible sexual provocativeness plied out on a group of innocent young Japanese girls in Okinawa. They may have said yes, but he didn't wait for an answer. He took them down and did them. He may have left them with a smile, but at some point they woke back up and they weren't smiling anymore, because they went down to the police and they reported him. He raped them repeatedly, serially.

At first, the police didn't want to believe it. A serviceman? A guy like that? Impossible. After awhile, there just were too many of them. The evidence started to rack up. They could point to him. They could identify him. He was going down and he knew it. He was madly and hopelessly in love with his wife. Unfortunately, she did not share the same sex drive he had. It just wasn't the same.

Bipolar people never get with fellow bipolar people. That would be dynamite on dynamite, gasoline on napalm. God knows what would happen with that. It didn't happen with Adolph. He was with a very dry woman. He had to force himself on her, and she sort of let him do it. She gritted her teeth. Her mouth was dry. It was the whole idea of taking it, of not asking for it, of just forcing it on them. They might have closed fists, they might have open fists. They could have a closed mouth or an open mouth. Some of them would spit and drool. Some of them would just scream. All of them were so exciting for him, there was no way he could ever stop. Once he did one, he had to do another; and once he did another, he could never stop. He would not have ever stopped had it not been for his own courageous decision -- perhaps it was the wrong thing to do, but he solved a lot of problems by taking his own life.

In the process, he took his wife. He shouldn't have done that. She was the victim of circumstance. She went down, limp into his arms. He danced with her, he sang to her, limp in his arms, dead as can be. And then he took his gun, put it to his head, pulled the trigger and went limp himself. And maybe it's true, as he planned, that the two of them, lovers in love, mismatched on Earth, were a perfect match in Heaven.

Grandfather Emerson looked at the water fountain. He would not have this bad dream ever again. He was sick of it. He couldn't handle anymore. He was of this constitution that would live probably well into his 90s. He was well into his 70s, and was not about to die. He was not about to live with all of these nightmares. It had to end and it was going to end now.

He saluted the flag. He was in full dress uniform, medals, jacket, pants, shiny shoes, name tag, two stars.

"Ten-hut!"

He turned to the flag, turned to the birds in the water fountain, lifted up the gun to his head. He counted, "One, two, three."

Methodically, without fear, he pulled the trigger that would end the nightmares, end the dreams. He would not be at fault anymore.

CHAPTER 41

THE AFTERMATH

Henry III was in the middle of group therapy when the news came. A correctional officer interrupted. At this time, that guy in the wheelchair was fully confessing, at long last, to what he had done. Henry had his hand on his arm. He supported him. He persuaded him. He convinced him to get real and say the truth, say what really happened. What he did to that little girl when he knocked her down, fell off of his chair, took her down and pulled her dress up. He explained it all.

"I know I did it. I know I said I didn't do it. I know I denied it. Let me now say, I did it, and I want to thank Henry for bringing me there. I would not have been able to do this on my own."

He stopped, and Dr. Miller started something that she normally would never do. She clapped once and then twice and kept clapping. The other members of the class had refused a real disclosure. They joined in the clapping. They clapped for him. They clapped at his example of standing up there and admitting what he had done. There was a freedom in the truth. If you tell the truth, you can never be criticized. You said what you did. You owned up to it. You were accountable for it. You realized you're the guilty one. Once you finally do that, you're on the path to free the demon. You could now release it and start your new life.

Every man there had done that, thanks to Henry. They were on a path, but last to go was this guy in a wheelchair. He cried like a baby. The other men came over, held him, encouraged him.

"Way to go, man. You're on your way."

They all shook their heads, knowing that in this truth was a path to salvation, to rehabilitation and to freedom from life in prison.

It was during this hug fest that the warden showed up. It was very rare that the warden would ever show up to group therapy.

"Doctor."

"Yes, warden."

The men got back into their chairs.

"I need to see you and Henry right now."

This was a rather odd state of affairs. They followed the warden. They went to a nearby office. It was empty. The warden sat down.

The correctional officers walked in, but the warden shooed them out. They knew Henry. They had heard from the doctor of Henry's excellent progress. They knew they could trust him. They knew that he was a model prisoner, a model participant in sexual offender therapy. They knew that the warden could sit in an unguarded room with this felon, knowing that there was no way he would ever get hurt.

"Henry, it's about your grandfather."

"Yes? What happened?"

Henry could tell right away that there was terrible news. The look in the warden's face was not congratulatory. It was ashen.

"Henry, I'm afraid your grandfather was found dead this morning."

"Dead?"

The therapist closed her eyes. Oh, my God. This was all Henry had. This was Henry's own salvation, dissipating into thin air. She looked at Henry. She was scared for him. Would they lose all the progress he had made? Would he regress back into the demon monster he was?

Henry put his head into his hands.

"No, no, no."

He started crying.

The warden came over and put his arm around Henry.

"I'm sorry, Henry."

Henry looked up, his blue eyes filled and now red.

"How did it happen?"

The warden hated to answer that question. This warden was a good man and one thing about good men -- they don't tell lies. He wasn't going to lie to Henry.

"Henry, your grandfather shot himself."

Henry was expecting that answer. He knew his grandfather was of incredible health. There was no other way, unless there was a fire or tornado or something crazy like that -- and they don't have tornadoes in San Diego.

"He shot himself."

The therapist now wanted to intervene and get the warden out of the picture.

"Warden, if I may -- can I please now deal with this? I mean, we've got a patient situation here, and I'm not sure if your delivering this news in, shall we say, the most therapeutic way."

The warden deferred to the good doctor.

"Let me allow you to carry on, but before we do that, I feel duty-bound to give you something."

The warden reached into his pocket and pulled out a piece of paper.

Henry recognized it right away. It was his grandfather's personal stationery. It had right on it "Henry Waldorf Emerson" and the address. It was fine parchment paper.

"Oh, God. Is this --?"

The warden nodded.

The therapist wanted to grab it first. She was going to review it and determine whether it would be delivered to Henry. But the warden knew better.

"No, he has to have it. Your grandfather wrote it. He didn't write it by accident. Henry, I have a simple idea here. The last words of your grandfather are words that we should listen to, words that we should read. We don't have to agree with them, but by God, we should listen to them. Don't you agree?"

The warden turned to the therapist.

"Don't you agree?"

The therapist closed her eyes. She lifted her hands up. He was her best student, the best participant by a million miles, and this whole thing was going to come crashing down over a piece of paper that the warden was now going to hand him.

"No, I do not agree. Do not give him that piece of paper."

She was bossing around the warden. In the pecking order of the prison, the psychologist is several pay grades below the warden. The warden respectfully disagreed, and handed Henry the note written by his grandfather on the day he committed suicide.

Henry held it in closed form. He looked at the therapist. Henry was under the rule of the therapist and would defer to her.

"Doctor, I am going to obey you. The warden may not, but I will. Now you tell me right now, am I supposed to read this? These are the last words of my grandfather. I don't know what he said. I don't know what he was thinking. I don't know what caused him to take his perfect life. I think I should know, but I'll tell you what. If you tell me I'm not ready, I'm going to give this to you. I'm going to let you hold onto it. I'm going to let you figure out when I'm ready to know and then you're going to give it to me. Now you tell me, what are we going to do?"

The warden was very impressed with Henry's sense of doing the right thing. He looked over at the therapist, though, and telepathically informed her to give that letter right now to Henry. *You tell him to read it. I want him to know right now.*

The therapist was frustrated. There was a therapy issue, and there was a demon issue. Of course Henry should know now. Of course he shouldn't wait a month, a week, a year or whatever. And how do we know he would ever be ready for this? The therapist looked up and gave her judgement,

"Henry, read it."

The clock ticked slowly. The parchment paper was thick. It was almost like cardboard. He opened it, and there were the words of his grandfather. In big letters, "IT'S ALL MY FAULT."

Henry put the letter down right on the table, and flipped it around so the therapist could read it. The doctor read it, got up out of her seat, walked over to a sobbing Henry, and hugged him. She cried. He cried. God, even the warden cried.

A correctional officer heard the sobbing. He was right outside the door. He opened it a crack, looked inside. The warden shooed him away. The correctional officer closed the door, and allowed them to remain, crying, sobbing and hugging over who was at fault for all the terrible things that Henry had done.

CHAPTER 42

APPELLANT'S OPENING BRIEF

It was one of the many unfortunate consequences of the untimely death of Henry's grandfather, but Henry was unable to read his mail. Had he been able to do so, he would have found a rather sizable document entitled, "Appellant's Opening Brief," filed by the appellate public defender, the legal brief meticulously reviewed the trial court's order denying Henry's motion to suppress evidence based on Fourth Amendment grounds, and denying the motion to suppress the non-confession of Henry based on Fifth Amendment grounds.

Henry wasn't reading anything. He took his pile of mail and tossed it into an ever-growing pile. He couldn't read, couldn't pay attention. He had depression, honestly and thoroughly, over the fact that his grandfather had killed himself because his grandfather felt that he was at fault for the things that Henry had done. Guilt on guilt.

Had he seen the brief, he may very well have called the appellate attorney and informed her, Rebecca Woods, to withdraw it and to dismiss the appeal. He was satisfied that his conviction was just and proper, he was doing extremely well in his sexual offender therapy, he was doing exactly what he needed to do. He knew he was at fault. He knew he had a long way to go. He was doing well, but he was just scratching the surface. The last thing he wanted, the last thing he needed, was some kind of bizarre technical wind that would release him from the prison.

The brief came in, unread by Henry. It had been filed with the court. It would now require an opposition from the California State Attorney General's office.

CHAPTER 43

IS THERE ANYTHING I CAN DO FOR YOU?

From that day forward, the warden would make a point of visiting Henry in his cell every day. A friendship grew between them, not uncommon in the penological world, where the executive officer of a prison takes a special note of the ultimate top model prisoner, and gives him an appropriate acknowledgement.

Henry had risen up above the tragedy of what he had done, the tragedy of his grandfather's death, and did not regress back into some demonic state. Instead, he continued in his group therapy courageously, methodically and relentlessly.

Inside his cell, there were four binders filled with copious notes of all the lectures of Dr. Miller. He would write the notes in class, neatly place them into a binder, and would then type them into a second binder. He had two sets -- a handwritten set and a typewritten set.

When the warden came to his cell that day, he was busy typing away the notes about self-esteem. There was a lesson about how when things bring us down, we can do things to make us feel better, and sometimes the things we do can make us feel better about very bad things. When we're feeling down, we need to do something to bring us up, something to make us feel better.

The warden interrupted the typing. It was a welcome interruption. Henry had plenty of time to type.

"Good to see you, warden."

"Hello, Henry."

The cell door opened. As the correctional officers all knew, they did not need to guard it, and walked away. The warden took a chair. Henry had a cell by himself. He was in ultra-protective custody. Not only was he a rapist, which made him marked for danger, but also as a model prisoner, he became marked for death by the many other prisoners that believed you should not be a model prisoner. It was sort of like you are kow-towing to the man. For that, they would kill him.

"Henry, what are you typing?"

"This is about self-esteem."

"Tell me. I want to know as much as you know."

"According to the good doctor, in the studies of many people, many sexual offenders have a huge issue with self-esteem."

"Go figure."

"Here's how it goes. We have a downward spiral of negative events in our lives. Our families are dysfunctional, maybe we were molested as kids -- which, by the way, I wasn't."

"Okay."

"Something happened. In my case, my father's suicide and murder of my mother. It puts me into a mood of feeling shameful, feeling terrible, of having a complete lack of self-esteem."

The warden listened.

"And?"

"So we try to do something to feel better. We want to feel better. We want to feel above it. We want to feel somehow better than somebody else. How do we do that? How do we get there? What do we do? We use our hands, we use our feet, we use our cunning, we become like a wild wolf. We hunt somebody down, we put them down -- and in doing that, we feel better, we feel above somebody. Our self-esteem rises, but then there's a break. There's kind of a reaction. Serotonin is released. We become happy. We get a high out of someone else's low."

The warden thought, *Wow, that's scary shit.*

"So what to do? That lesson tells you the problem. It tells you what the consequences of the problem. Here's what I want to know, Henry. What the fuck is the solution to that?"

Henry looked up and smiled.

"Warden, don't worry. I've got a solution."

"What is it?"

"You've got to find some other way to lift your spirits. You got to do something else, something that's not going to hurt somebody."

"But what should that be?"

"Depends on the person. Depends on your interests. Depends on what you want. For some, it could be, get a dog. For others, it could be unfortunately, and often is, alcohol and drugs -- not a good thing. For others, it could be get a good job, just work, make money, take care of your family. You know, if you just have some kind of modicum of success, however modest, you can get beyond the self-esteem problem."

"Well, Henry, let's talk about you. What did you do for self-esteem? What have you done in the past?"

Henry looked up.

"Oh, I've got an answer to that."

"Tell me. What is it?"

"Music."

"You play music? I didn't know."

"That's because I don't have an instrument, warden."

"You don't have an instrument?"

"No."

"What do you play?"

"I play the guitar."

"Well, I can get you a guitar."

"I want my guitar!"

"Just name it, it's done."

"Warden, you see these hands? These are the very hands that raped two women, but these very hands also can do good things. You want to hear about it?"

"Absolutely, Henry, I want to hear all of that."

"I'm a carpenter by trade. I build cabinets, all kinds of furniture, that's what I do, but there's something else I do. I'm a musician. You know, warden, the thing about being bipolar -- it usually comes with something else. Something else with me was music. I want you to know what I did with these hands."

"Go on."

"I took a piece of wood. I took it apart. I carved it. I honed it perfectly. I made the most beautiful, perfect rosewood acoustical guitar that you could ever imagine. I made the strings myself. I put these little ivory tips -- I made the tips. I connected it all up. I built that with my own hands from scratch with a couple tools and my workshop. It was the most perfect guitar that makes the most perfect music that you could ever imagine. That's the guitar I want."

"Where's that guitar now?"

"Oh, I know exactly where it is. It's at my grandfather's house."

The warden put his hand to his head, kind of shaking it.

"I mean, my house."

Of course, his grandfather willed the entire estate to Henry. Even as an imprisoned man, he'd turned into a rich man. Henry inherited $9 million in municipal bonds and a home in Carlsbad worth about $4 million. It was on 4.5 acres with a beautiful ranch estate and the house that Henry used to live in. In that house there was a small workshop, and in that workshop, hanging on the wall, there was the most perfect, beautiful rosewood guitar that this planet had ever seen.

On that day, the warden dispatched two correctional officers to go to Henry's house, to go to that workshop, to enter to find that guitar, to very carefully put it in the back of their car and to deliver it back to the warden. The warden got that guitar and proudly walked down the series of hallways to Henry's protective custody cell. He arrived holding it as though it were a cross.

"Henry, your self-esteem shall be lifted in a proper way."

He handed Henry the guitar. Henry wept tears of joy. It was like a long lost son that he hadn't seen.

"Thank you, warden."

He studied it, looked at it, recognized it, knew every single millimeter of it. The warden remained, as though expecting something. Henry looked up.

"Was there something else?"

"Oh, yeah. There's something else."

"What's that, warden?"

"You got to play me something. I got you your guitar, sent a couple guys out on a mission that I might add wasn't, shall we say, completely by the book. They got the guitar, brought it to you, and you don't think I'm going to leave here without you playing me a song?"

Henry smiled.

"I got a song for you, warden."

It took him a second to tune the guitar. He adjusted the tips. It was professionally done. Within a couple minutes, it was ready to go.

"Here's a song, warden. Please listen."

He strummed the guitar beautifully, perfectly and sang the song, "Suite Madame Blue."

The warden and several nearby correctional officers were mesmerized by Henry's beautiful music.

CHAPTER 44

VIDEOCAM FUNERAL

Henry's grandfather would not be buried in California. Instead, as a war hero, a retired general, he would be buried at Arlington National Cemetery in Virginia with full honors.

Despite the warden's attempts at doing a major favor for Henry, it was impossible to make arrangements to fly Henry there. He had the money to fund it, with multiple millions in inheritance coming his way. He quickly offered to pay for the airfare for all the correctional staff that would have to go, full room and lodging, and for any and all expenses incurred on the way. Unfortunately, California law would simply not allow it, Virginia law would not allow it. He was given an order by the governor of Virginia, thanks but no thanks. We don't want your rapist in our state, even under heavy guard, and even if only for a matter of one day.

The United States Army was a bit more sympathetic to the grandson of this war hero. Four star General Malcolm Speagel issued an edict to the commander of Arlington Cemetery:

"You will please make arrangements so that the sole surviving heir of General Emerson will be able to watch his grandfather's funeral via videocam.

Regards, General Malcolm Speagel."

The following Saturday, at 10 AM, a funeral with full honors commenced. It was agreed by Dr. Miller that the funeral would provide a strange type of therapeutic assistance to not only Henry, but all of the men in the sexual offender program. The warden agreed. The men should know as low as they may feel about themselves, being convicted rapists, being in prison for indefinite periods of time, having nothing, no freedom, no money, no nothing -- the reality was, they all came from somewhere.

"These men need to know that they are not the nothings that everyone else will tell them they are," the warden said. "They may feel like garbage, but they aren't garbage. Show them Henry's grandfather. Show them who he was and let them understand that, like Henry, we are all somebodies."

Dr. Miller agreed and smiled with the wisdom of the warden.

That day, at 7 AM California time, there was a videocam set up in the therapy room. Henry was in the front seat, and sat in awe as he saw the military procession carrying his grandfather's body via horse-drawn cart. It was full military dress uniform. There must have been 2,000 of them there. There were Admirals from the Navy, Generals from the Marine Corps, Generals from the Army, and the top brass of the Air Force. When a general passes, the generals come out to send him off.

The horse-drawn cart was followed by no fewer than 28 military vehicles, all carrying these impressive generals, today's current war heroes. As they got out of the automobiles, there were salutes all around. General to general, saluting each other, realizing that their own importance would always date back to those who had come before them.

At the place of General Emerson's burial, General Speagel addressed the impressive collection of military brass.

"Gentlemen, we lay to rest here General Henry Emerson, a two-star general who fought in World War I and led the troops to battle in World War II. He is the holder of no fewer than six medals of honor for valor, for bravery, for excellence in combat action and for exuding all of those character traits that we would hope all of us would have and cherish, and would fight to the death to retain. He was there in Normandy. He landed on the beach on D-Day. He led those troops without fear, in front of enemy fire. That day, we lost many, many good men, but we did not lose General Emerson. He got to the end of that beach, and carried his men forward to overtake the German stronghold, and replaced it with the Allied invasion, and the end of World War II.

"We owe to our fallen general our freedom. We owe to our fallen general the American way. All that we enjoy here today is because of this man, and the many others who have fallen before him, and the many others who will take his example, and carry it forward. We loved him in life. We cherished what he did. We honored him and today, we lay him to rest. We bid him farewell and we let him know, you have touched our hearts. You have moved us. We have listened. We have watched. We are following. We are you."

The commander then brought everyone to attention.

"TEN HUT!"

All generals went to attention. Four jets flew by at just below supersonic speeds. One of them veered away, showing the fallen general.

The commander belted out another command, "Sergeant-at-arms!"

The sergeant came forward and saluted the commander, saluted the other generals and then faced a group of 21 men. He gave the command that commenced a 21-gun salute, firing away into the sky.

One, two, three, four, five, six, seven, eight, nine, ten, eleven, twelve, thirteen, fourteen, fifteen, sixteen, seventeen, eighteen, nineteen, twenty, twenty-one.

21 shots, the road to freedom, the way to respect, to honor, and to show that this man made a difference.

Henry watched from the prison in complete awe of the respect that these men were giving his grandfather. The warden stood next to Henry, put his hand on his shoulder. During the 21-gun salute, the warden, a former military man himself, saluted Henry's grandfather and bid him farewell.

CHAPTER 45

A LETTER TO HENRY'S FATHER

Later that day, there would be a further group session at the prison. Dr. Miller headed it up. The men had come to respect Henry for his courage in facing his demons, for his willingness to stand and disclose, honestly and thoroughly, what he had done, and for his willingness to explore what it was inside of him that made him do the things he did. This was creating a wonderful ripple effect of other men giving similar disclosures.

"Today the subject we are going to explore is about the cost of sexual offenses. What are the costs? Let's talk about that."

The doctor passed out a worksheet. It had a table of various cost items that the men would have to look at, think and wonder about.

"I want you to look at this worksheet, understand that these are categories of costs that have occurred as a result of what you did. Some of these costs are costs to yourself. Some of the costs are obvious -- you're taken out of the job market, you're taken out of the free world, you're locked up here, you can't earn a living, you can't have a family, you can't really do anything except deal with me here.

"Some of the other costs are costs to the victim. Some of them are rather obvious. Some of your victims will be permanently scarred as a result of what you did. Some of them will be disabled. Some of them may be dead. Some of them may commit suicide. Some of them may never have families. Some of them may never be able to take a husband. Some of them may not ever have children. They may not ever have a regular sexual relationship with a man. They may have lost complete trust in a man. They may never get over what you did to them.

"So I want you to think about those costs and I want you to write it out. I want you to try to put numbers by those costs. In other words, what number would you put for a woman who, because of what you did to her, can never have a husband, can never have a regular, loving relationship and will never have children? I want you to think about that. I want you to think about how a woman has a natural desire, just like you do, to have children -- that having children can be, more or less, the most important thing in a woman's life -- and you have taken that away from her. She will never be able to do that. What is that worth, in dollars and cents? What would you put on that? Would you put $10,000 on it or would you put $10 million on it? I want you to think about that. Use your own numbers, use your own assessment, use your own values.

"I want you to think about some of the other costs. Check out the form. There's a cost of running this prison. Think about it. Look around you. You've got a whole building here devoted just to sexual offenders. You've got correctional officers. They have to be paid. You've got people like me in here, trying to help you get treated. You've got the warden running the whole prison. So what are the costs of operating a prison? What does this cost? A place to house you, to treat you and to attempt to change you so that we can release you back to society.

"Let's go back a bit to the day of your arrest. How many police officers were involved? We have to pay all those police officers. How many cars did they drive? We have to buy all those cars. How many uniforms did they have to have? We have to buy all those uniforms.

"Let's go to the court process. You were held in county jail before court, most of you. So how much did that cost? What do we need for that? We need a county jail, we need a whole jail operation, we need correctional officers at the jail. We need everything that is needed to run a jail. You need a bus to get you over to the court. Let's go to the court. What do we need for that? We need a judge, court reporters, court clerks, big file room, big building, you need court bailiffs at the court, there's a jail at the court, there's a holding cell at the court -- all that costs money.

"All these costs and expenses are given to you as categories on this form. I want you to fill them out. I want you to make an estimate of what it is that you have done as far as the cost -- not only to yourself in terms of the direct losses to yourself, but also the cost to the victim and the public cost to society at large. What does it all add up to?"

Henry raised his hand.

"Yes, Henry?"

"When we talk about the cost to ourselves, you have these categories of the fact that we're now in prison, we can't work, we can't make money, we don't have our freedom -- all that is rather obvious to me, but I got a question. What about the impact of what we have done on our other family members? What about the cost to them?"

"Yeah, what about that?" the doctor agreed. "Look at that. Think about it. How many of you have parents that are still alive?"

Everybody but Henry raised his hand. The therapist was a little saddened that she'd even asked the question. She looked at every one of them.

"Tell me something. What cost have your parents suffered as a result of what you did? Are they shamed? Are they humiliated? Do they cry for you? Do they cry for your victim? Are they proud of you? Do they wish you had never been born? Do they blame themselves for what you did? Are they suffering from pangs of guilt, of sorrow? How do they feel? What do they feel?

"Henry, thank you for your question. I think it's an excellent idea, and I want to start with that part. Let us start there. Let us start by, all of you, writing a letter -- a letter to your parents. Henry, I realize your parents are not alive. I want you to write a letter to them anyway. I want you to write a letter to them where you explain that you recognize and understand the cost to them and where you acknowledge it and where you do something about it. Let me explain to everybody here -- the point is, first, to just recognize the costs, but the second point is, let's do something about it."

Kevin, the man in the wheelchair, had a question.

"Yes?"

"What can we do about it?"

"What can we do about it?" Dr. Miller reiterated.

"Yeah."

"What can you do about all these costs that your conduct has imposed on yourself, on your victim, on your family and on society at large? Is that your question?"

"Yeah."

"Good question. Anybody got an answer on that?"

Everybody was quiet. It seemed like a rather daunting exploration. The cost was staggering. It could be billions from one rape, multiple billions from multiple rapes. The room had eight men in it. That's a cost of easily $8 billion. These men didn't work, made no money, had no money -- how could they ever do anything about that?

"Henry, you got any ideas?"

"Yeah, I got an idea."

"Okay, let's hear it."

The men all turned to Henry to listen.

"We can get better. We can find a way to get better. This is what we owe to everybody."

Dr. Miller smiled.

"I like that. Anybody else like that?"

Everybody nodded. They all liked that. But how? They also realized that right there, right then in that room, there was an answer and the answer was to listen, to participate, to be honest, to have courage and to do what Dr. Miller said to do, and to do it every single day. To do it methodically, regimentally and never give up, to never say die and to do it until the end of their lives. They needed it, their victims needed it, their families needed it, society needed it. They knew right then and there, facing these staggering costs, that what they could do, they would do.

"Let's start, gentlemen, with a letter to your family. We're going to write a couple letters here. I'm going to have you write a letter to your victim. Don't worry, she's never going to get it. I'm going to have you write a letter to the public. Don't worry, they're never going to get it. I want you to address the costs. I want you to explain what it is you're going to do about it. I want you to be honest. I want you to be courageous. I want you to be heroes. Let's begin it with a letter to your parents. You've got your notebooks, you've got your pencils. Please begin."

The men were not used to writing letters to their parents, other than to say, let me have this, send me that, I need, I need. This would be a new letter where they would acknowledge the huge cost to their parents and would offer up a method to help. Leave it to Henry to be a little bass ackwards about the whole thing. He was still fixated on the recent loss of his grandfather, and couldn't help but think about what his father had done to his mother and to himself. He did something that he never had done before, which was to confront his father about what he had done.

Sergeant-Major Adolph Adams Emerson II
United States Army
Okinawa Military Base, Okinawa Japan

Dear Dad,

You didn't have to do that. There was another way. I'm not sure exactly what that way was, but I know there was another way. You could've faced what you did. You could've seen that inside of you, there was something -- something that is also inside of me. That monster, that demon must be released and must come out.

Had you faced what you had done -- I don't know. It would have been different. It would have been different for all of us. Mom would still be alive. She would've taken care of me. Mom would've known how serious our problem was. She wouldn't have ignored it. She would understand that a brain problem can be a million times worse than a broken arm or a bad kidney.

She would have taken it seriously. She would have brought me, somehow, to treatment. I don't know if it would've worked. I may still be the way I am now, but I would've had a chance. Instead, like you, and like your mother, we went untreated. We refused to see doctors. We refused to do anything. We never explored it. We never studied it. We never attempted to understand it. Instead, we just let that monster grow inside of us, let that monster do whatever it wanted. It was a hungry monster, wasn't it, dad? I know what you had in you, because I got the same thing. It's hungry. It must be fed.

And you let yours eat. Oh God, what did you do? Look what you did. It could've been different. You shouldn't have done it. There was another way. I don't know what it is, but I'm going to find out. I'm doing it myself. I'm going to do it every day. I'm never going to give up. I'm going to try, try, try. I'm going to find that monster. I'm going to kill him. I'm going to get rid of him. I'm going to be okay.

I am you.

Your son,

Henry

CHAPTER 46

SAM'S PRIZE

Whether our deceased parents can really look down on us from Heaven and smile at our accomplishments remains a mystery, a hope, an idea. There is nothing more important to a parent than to know that their child has done a great thing.

For a child, receiving the recognition from their parents can remain one of the greatest things in their life.

But on this day, on the day of the Pulitzer Prize Award ceremony in Washington DC, Sam was looking down on his son Ben with an ear-to-ear grin.

"For excellence in journalistic reporting, for looking into something that nobody else touched, that nobody else saw, you dug, you dug deeper, you found answers. You found human answers. You found a truth that nobody really wanted to know -- a truth that showed corruption at the highest level, damaging real people at the lowest level. And it didn't stop there. You brought about a real world result. You brought in the law. You brought in your father, who brought this to justice, who caused a correction of this terrible injustice. None of it would have happened without you, Ben. You're the one that put all those wheels into motion and for you, on this night, we give you the highest award in journalism, the Pulitzer Prize. We honor you, we congratulate you."

Ben felt awkward to receive such a standing ovation in a room of more than 3,000 fellow journalists. He walked to the stage as though he was receiving an Academy Award. He's not the kind of man to want the public spotlight, but on this night, whether he liked it or not, wearing his rented tuxedo, wearing black polished shoes that he had just purchased, uncomfortable as they were, he walked proudly to the podium, accepted his award and faced his fellow peers, the top ranking journalists in the United States. He looked upward and held his award to the sky.

"Thanks, dad."

He faced the journalists.

"I wish I could do more. I will do more. I am only starting. You will see me again. This is my promise. This award tonight has given me great encouragement to keep doing what I'm doing. Thank you. And dad -- I love you. Thank you."

Ben bowed, shook the hand of the presenter and left the stage. There was work to be done.

CHAPTER 47

ERICA

Ben was once again in Erica's room at the asylum. Unfortunately, she just wasn't getting better.

"I don't know, Ben," the doctor explained. "Someday there's going to be a trigger that brings her out of this. We're not giving her drugs --"

"Oh, please don't. Drugs are what got her here."

"I know. I got that. We're not going to do it. We talk to her. We touch her. She just stares like that, out the window."

Ben looked over and saw the beautiful Erica, those gorgeous blue eyes looking at the window. What does she see? What was she looking for? What was she thinking? What was she feeling? She didn't look sad. She didn't look happy. She just looked like nothing. Ben didn't know what to do.

"Honey, can I show you?"

He put his award down next to her. She would've known, as a fellow writer, what a big deal the award was. It had zero impact on her. Then he pulled something else out. Ben is the last to be a showoff, but he decided maybe it would be good for her to see that there was hope, that there was goodness, that there was something to look forward to.

"Honey, please see."

It was a photo album of his home, of his father's home -- the home he now lived in. It was really quite an impressive house -- 4,500 square feet, two floors, six bedrooms, fireplaces in three of them, four bathrooms, gorgeous entryway, an impressive outward look and all of this right next to the water. Begonias surrounded the front of the house. Ice plants were in the back, leading down to a beach into the Pacific Ocean.

"Honey, this is my home. This is our home. When you're better, please come here. See me. Be my wife. Live with me. Please find a way to come back."

The doctor saw the pain in Ben and realized his loss. He put his arm around him.

"Trust me, Ben. There will be a day when she comes back."

CHAPTER 48

I AM YOU

The process of writing a song goes like this: it comes to you, takes you over, possesses you, and you must write it. It happened to Henry. He was in his cell. The song came, and he had to write it. He sang, he played, he strummed. It took awhile; at first, disjointed, sounding like noise, but it slowly began to gel and became a song called "I Am You."

I AM YOU

By Henry Adams Emerson III

Dad, I'm calling you down to tell you something
That someone should've told you long ago
That what you did, you shouldn't have done
What you did was wrong
There was another way
I'm not sure what
But if you told me,
We could've seen
And found it together.
Whatever it is
Inside of you
Is also inside of me
That same monster
We could work together
And learn how to kick him out
Whatever you have, whatever you know, whatever you are
Whatever you'll be
However far you'll see
However close you'll look
You must know
I will see the same
I will be the same
You and I are one and two
I will forever know
I am you

CHAPTER 49

ORAL ARGUMENTS IN THE COURT OF APPEALS

The three justices had white hair, a learned look, and were grumpy. The clerk called the case of *People v. Henry Emerson III.*

Counsel for the people, from the state Attorney General's office, announced his appearance, "Michael Angelforth, on behalf of the people."

The justices nodded. The appellate public defender announced her appearance.

"Sonja Kingsberry, on behalf of the defendant and appellant."

"Very well. Miss Kingsberry, you may proceed."

"If it may please the court, we are here on an appeal from a judgement of conviction following a plea of guilty. The issues on appeal concern whether the entry into Mr. Emerson's residence without a search warrant and without consent violated his Fourth Amendment rights; whether the subsequent and ensuing search of his premises violated his Fourth Amendment rights; whether the seizure of a ring in the residence constituted an unlawful seizure of evidence; and whether the ensuing discussion following the reading of the defendant's Miranda Rights and the defendant's request for [unreadable] violated his protection against compulsory self-incrimination, as guaranteed by the Fifth Amendment.

"If I may, I would like to begin with the issue of the entry into the residence, to keep the issues as presented in roughly chronological order as they occurred."

"Very well, counsel. Proceed," Justice Baines responded. He was inviting the argument. This was a bad sign for the people.

"Quite simply, it's a residence. It's separate from the main house; separate by about 100 yards. It is occupied by the defendant. Nobody asked him for permission to enter. There's no question they didn't have a search warrant. There were no exigent or emergency circumstances. There's no good faith exception to the search warrant rule. Basically, there was no exception at all. The theory the trial court accepted was that my client's grandfather walking them out to his residence somehow constituted a valid consent."

"Well, now wait a minute," Justice Morris interrupted. The grandfather, of course, was the owner of the entire premises. He was the owner of the main house. He testified quite clearly that his grandson resided there -- not as a tenant, not as a co-owner, but basically as a family member living for free."

Miss Kingsberry followed up.

"These are more or less undisputed facts. The question today is a purely legal one, ripe for this appeal of applying Fourth Amendment jurisprudence to those facts. We submit under the court's *de novo* standard of review, its independent review, that it may apply its legal analysis to these undisputed facts, and can and should rule that my client's residence, as a separate physical structure, set apart from the home, consisted a residence separate and apart from the home for which either a search warrant or permission or other exigent circumstances were required. The entry into the home was accordingly a violation of my client's Fourth Amendment rights.

"There you have it. Your Honors, I will let you apply the laws as you deem fit to those basic undisputed facts, but I will leave you with one thought. The Fourth Amendment is not determined on whether a person makes rental payments.

"Let me give you an example. Suppose there was a landlord/tenant relationship and my client was somehow in default under his lease and had not paid rent in three or four months. He would still have Fourth Amendment rights. The Fourth Amendment does not depend on money, does not depend on finances, does not depend on property rights other than the very concept asserted here -- that a man's home is his castle, even if he doesn't pay rent or own it. If that's where he lives, the full force and effect of the Fourth Amendment applies. A search warrant was needed. None was obtained. The judgement should accordingly be reversed."

She paused and looked for the facial expressions of the justices. They were stoic.

"If you have no questions on that issue, I will proceed to the next issue of the search and seizure of a ring in the home. Of course we all know the rule -- the fruit of the poisonous tree. You cannot use the fruit of an illegal entry into a home or search of a home. Anything obtained during the course of that search should be excluded from evidence in any subsequent proceedings.

"My client made an appropriate motion to have the ring excluded from evidence. That motion was denied by the trial court; denied on the same faulty basis as his denial on the issue of the illegal search and for the same reasons as stated. The seizure of the ring should be declared as illegal. Its use against my client is the sole piece of physical evidence, was improper and violated my client's Fourth Amendment rights. Accordingly, the judgment of the trial court should be reversed and the case should be remanded."

"Counsel, let me stop you right there. As far as what we should do with this case should we agree with your position -- you want a remand. What would then be left to try? I mean, if that's the only evidence against your client, how is the prosecutor to go forward?"

"Your Honor, I'm not prepared to provide a strategy for the prosecutor to go forward on. That'll be their problem. All I can say is that ring was illegally obtained and should've been excluded. The chips must fall where they may, and if it means there is no evidence, then there is no evidence."

The three justices looked at each other and realized, once again, the seeming unfairness of the Fourth Amendment rule. The basic idea was, if evidence is obtained illegally, it is excluded, no matter how devastating it may be to the prosecution's case. That's the law. That's how it works.

"Very well. Why don't you move into your next issue about the confession -- and counsel, let me have you focus on this. The motion to exclude the confession was denied on the basis that there was no confession. Please focus on that issue because quite frankly, we don't see a confession either. I'd like to see your issue on that."

"The issue before the trial court, and on which the trial court based its denial, was that, as you observed, there was no confession and if there is no confession, how can it possibly be excluded?

"There was a confession of sorts. It was a body language confession. There was no overt statement -- yes, I did it, yes, I'm guilty or something along those lines. Instead, there was a statement made by the detective -- do the Christian thing, do the right thing, come with us, we're going to help you. Well, we know about the Christian burial case."

The justices all nodded their heads. Oh, yes.

"In the Christian burial case, detectives told a suspect to do the right thing and give a murdered girl a Christian burial. He finally confessed, and showed them where the body was. The US Supreme Court agreed that that confession was a violation of his Fifth Amendment rights and excluded the evidence.

"We have a dramatically similar situation here. They explained to my client that the Christian thing for him to do would be to give himself up and to go in. At that point, they were probably of a view that they did not have probable cause to obtain an arrest warrant. Defendant/appellant agreed to go with him. His body moved with them. They took him out of there. They brought him to jail. He agreed and consented to an arrest. That arrest, without an arrest warrant, was a consensual arrest that gives the court the confession it is looking for. That's what I have to say about that. Any questions?"

"Counsel, suppose they did have probable cause to arrest him, and they just arrested him without any further discussion by him. He wouldn't have to agree or disagree to his arrest. He just let it happen. You got a confession there?"

"In that hypothetical as stated, I would agree with the tone of your questioning -- that there is no confession in that scenario. We don't have that here. I want you to consider this. Did the officers have any kind of legitimate basis to determine my client was guilty at that point?"

"Well, let's look, counsel. Come on. I mean, we've got newspaper articles --"

"I'm sorry to interrupt you, Mr. Justice, but those newspaper articles, though scandalous, amazing and frightful, all had to do with my client's father, not my client, number one. Number two, where is the rule that a newspaper article is admissible in evidence? It isn't evidence. It's pure hearsay. Some writer in Okinawa, Japan penned an article about something that happened to my client's father long ago. That is not evidence against my client."

"Well, Counsel, you may think it's not evidence, but it sure led the detectives to the right person, now didn't it?"

"There's a big difference between information that may be validly used as an investigative tool on the one hand and actual admissible evidence. I don't have any complaints that someone went on the net, did a Google, found articles, printed them and connected up dots. That's what investigations are all about, but to call that admissible and evidence? Imagine in a court of law, I move to admit these articles into evidence. On what basis? They're pure hearsay. We don't know what the truth is that happened in Okinawa."

"Counsel, would there not have been another objection; that of relevance? I mean, basically we're dealing with wrongful conduct committed by another person. How is that relevant against your client?"

"It is the ancient question of the sins of the father becoming the sins of the son. I would find it quite worrisome if we were to allow that into evidence, that a father robbed a bank makes a son a thief, that a father committed a rape makes his son a rapist. That is the ultimate slippery slope."

Another justice chimed in,

"And yet as we have read in the people's brief, expert opinion testimony can be offered to show that certain psychological traits are very much handed down on an intergenerational basis -- that in this case, unfortunately the father had been diagnosed as having bipolar disorder, as had the son. Indeed, even the grandmother. You do have a basis -- not of a crime or a propensity of a crime, but rather of a genetically transmitted psychological disorder, which unfortunately creates the premise for a personality trait that evolves into a sexual offender. So there is a kind of relevancy to that evidence if you can get by the hearsay rule."

"An expert, duly qualified, who takes the stand may base their opinion on hearsay evidence," the justice chimed in.

Everyone was quiet as the judge announced the well-known rule about expert witnesses.

"Everyone else is supposed to base their information on whatever it is they have seen or done or smelled or felt directly in front of them -- not so for expert witnesses. They can read treatises, reports, other information and of note to today's case, newspaper articles."

"That the evidence illegally obtained is powerful, is compelling, is fundamental to the prosecution's case to secure a judgment -- actually, does not go into the court's consideration at all," the able public defender said. "What should go into the court's consideration is whether the evidence obtained was obtained illegally. If you find that it was illegal evidence, no matter how dramatic, no matter how important, no matter how critical it may be to the prosecution's case, your job, as you know, under well-settled principles of Fourth Amendment and Fifth Amendment jurisprudence is to exclude that evidence, and to realize the bigger picture and the public good of enforcing a criminal justice system that is grounded in fundamental constitutional rights to protect the accused at all stages of the criminal justice process.

"I ask that the three of you today, that this court invoke its duty and obligations under the Federal Constitution, under the California state constitution, that you invoke these important fundamental individual rights secured by our constitutions, and that you agree and determine that the entry, search and seizure and that the interrogation and body language confession that was obtained by the detectives in this case were illegal, should be excluded and that the judgement obtained thereby should be reversed. Thank you."

She sat down. The justices then turned to the state's attorney, who had unfortunately a bit of an uphill battle.

"May it please the court, I'd like to begin --"

"Mr. Angelforth, I want to first get you to make a couple clarifications for the record. Number one -- and I think this is clear from the evidence put before the trial court, it's clear in the record -- but I'd just like to have you acknowledge it verbally today and I want you to reflect on it and to consider. Question number one, there was no search warrant, correct?"

"Correct. There was no search warrant."

"Question number two, the residence in which Mr. Emerson, the accused, resided in -- it is physically detached from the main home. Correct?"

"Correct."

"It is separated by a distance of approximately 150 feet."

"Yes."

"And it is a full residence. It has a bathroom, a bedroom, a living room. It has a kitchen area -- all of the things we would expect to see in a residence."

"Yes."

"At no time did the detectives obtain the consent of the accused to enter the premises. Correct?"

"Correct."

"And they entered without any kind of theory or concept of an emergency or exigent circumstance."

"Correct."

"Nobody was about to get hurt, no evidence was about to be flushed down the toilet, there was no impending bodily injury. There were no exigencies, there were no emergencies of any sort. Correct?"

"Correct."

"There's no good faith exception to the warrant requirement here that I can see. Do you see one?"

"There's a good faith belief of consent."

"But you can't have consent from person A that lives in house A to enter the home of person B that lives in house B, can you?"

"Yes, when person A owns both homes."

"Oh, now wait a minute. This gets us to what, a landlord/tenant case that we have? A landlord cannot allow someone to go search in his home. They don't have authority to do that."

"Your Honors, he's not a tenant. Well, he is a guest. That's what we would classify him as, a guest."

The public defender did something she wasn't really supposed to do and stood.

"It should be pointed out that he is also an heir and the grandfather has since passed on and he is now an owner."

It's rare that the justices would let anybody interrupt the oral argument of the other side, but this was allowed.

"Yes, that's an interesting point. We see that in the evidence. We see the certificate of death given. We previously granted a motion to take further evidence on appeal, to allow that in. We were not deciding the merits of that claim. We see the death certificate, the will in probate and the fact that post illegal search, the accused has become the owner in fee simple absolute of the entire premises."

"But that shouldn't matter," the state attorney responded. "I mean, this is all after the fact. The point is, what was his interest in the land and the house and the residence on the day of the search?"

"Well, I suppose this is not like a dinner guest. This is a family member who's resided there on a long term basis, who makes this place his residence -- he lives there, he works out of there, he has his business there -- everything he does is there. How is that not his separate residence?"

The state attorney saw he was going down in flames.

"Well, let's try it this way." He would not give up. "If the grandfather owns the property, he can go into any room in the property."

"Let me just interrupt you right there, Counsel. I understand your idea about that, and I would certainly agree with you if he lived in the house. In that example, sure, the grandfather could let him in, but he doesn't live in the main house. He lives in a separate dwelling. This is where we are hung up today. We believe, and we will find, that that is his separate dwelling. Factually, it's undisputed. That's just what it is. How could we find any other way? It's detached physically and spatially. It is a separate stand-alone dwelling. It's almost like a neighboring home. What difference would it make? Suppose there's a property line that separated it into a separate parcel. Then you probably wouldn't be able to make this argument at all, correct?"

"I'm not prepared to respond to that hypothetical, Your Honors."

"Very well. Why don't you move on to your next argument. How is the seizure of the ring somehow legal? Can you please explain that?"

"First of all, we take the position that the entry into the home was legal and that any subsequent search would thereby be legal and anything found in the course of that search could be seized if it constituted evidence of a crime."

"Okay, stop right there. You agree then, that your case hinges on the legality of the entry into this home without a search warrant?"

He hated to agree, but he had to.

"Yes, we do."

"Let's go to the confession issue. We don't see a confession. She states it's a body language confession. Let me think about that. Did your office have a right to arrest him on the spot? Did they have probable cause? Did they not need his consent? Could they just walk him right out? Or was there zero admissible evidence, as being argued by the defendant's counsel? Proceed."

"First of all, there's no confession. That's just a fact, and it is among the undisputed facts of this case that this court can apply its own *de novo* or independent review. The trial court found there was no confession. Of course, Counsel can't point to one. The defendant was basically silent."

"You would agree, Counsel, that had he spoken and he had given a confession, that that confession would be inadmissible? He was in a custodial situation. He invoked his right to counsel. Rather than stopping the interrogation, they gave him the Christian burial speech -- dramatically similar. A confession would've been excluded had it occurred. Would you agree with that?"

"No, I would not agree that such a hypothetical is relevant to our analysis today."

"Oh, wait a minute. Let me stop you right there. I'll figure out what's relevant or not and I want to know if you agree basically that there was a violation of the Fifth Amendment right and privilege against self incrimination. Do you agree that that occurred here?"

"No, because there was no confession."

There was a moment of silence.

"Very well. Proceed."

"This body language confession argument -- it doesn't fit the definition of confession."

"Let me just stop you right there. Haven't you ever heard the phrase body language? Somebody asks the question, did you do it? You look down at your feet, you shake your head, you nod affirmatively. You don't say a word. I would call that a body language confession, wouldn't you? It's a confession through body language, so it would constitute a confession under that circumstance. I'm not saying that's what happened here, but I am saying and suggesting to you, Counsel, to grapple with the concept that this could be a silent confession. Whether or not --"

Another justice chimed in.

"Indeed, we have a jury instruction -- implied adoptive admission. Where a party is accused of a wrongdoing, where a person who is innocent of that wrongdoing would reasonably be expected to deny it and the party does not deny it -- such can be considered an implied adoptive admission and can be used in evidence against the accused. So there is such a thing grounded in the law as a silent confession. That jury instruction is an oldie but a goodie. As you know, Counsel, prosecutors use it all the time."

The state attorney general rolled his eyes. He saw that this was not going well.

"Well, let me suggest this then. They told him to do the right thing, do the Christian thing -- solve the evil demons in you, release them, we can help you do that, we will solve your problem, just come with us. How is that not coaxing him, interrogating him and getting him to agree? Of course that's what happened. It was just a statement though. It's not a question. It was a statement."

"I don't think the Fifth Amendment is going to be determined on the basis of punctuation," another justice remarked. "If a question ends with a question mark or a period, you're saying the whole Fifth Amendment turns on that? Well, that wouldn't be. From now on, all you have to do is not ask a question. Just put a statement to an accused. No, counsel, I'm afraid that's not the law. You're going to have to do better than that."

The other justice pointed out, "They had probable cause to arrest him. There was no evidence that they didn't have probable cause to arrest him. There were no findings made by the trial court to that effect."

"We're looking at that right now. What constitutes probable cause is a legal issue for a court to decide. We can look at all the facts and circumstances, what was presented to the officers on the day in question and we can review it and ask ourselves, was there sufficient evidence to give rise to a substantial belief that this accused has committed a crime? Was there articulable, specific evidence? Was there evidence that would've been admissible in a court of law."

"What do you have? You've got a ring that does have matches to scars on the victim's face."

"The only problem being that the ring was obtained illegally."

"Then they've got a bunch of newspaper articles connecting up the accused's father with a series of rapes and psychological disorders that occurred in Japan. So what do you call that? You call that evidence?"

"It is evidence. It is admissible. We would have had a psychiatric expert witness testify that the father's plight, his psychological breakdown, his bipolar disorder, his sexual offender status, his serial rapes were all unfortunate chemical biological issues that were handed down to his son with the same result. You've got --"

"Hold on right there, Counsel. Like father, like son."

He hated to say it, but it was so true.

"Exactly."

"But that's illegal. We don't do blood crimes. The sins of the father will not be passed down to the son. We don't allow them to be."

There was a cold silence. The prosecutor had little else to say on the issue.

"Your Honors, we submit to you that there was probable cause to get an arrest, that they arrested them, that they did not ask his permission, they did not need his permission or consent to that arrest, that they did arrest him, that his conduct in walking out of his place --"

"Oh, you don't need to say place. Let's just call it what it is -- his home."

"Very well. Walking out of his home did not constitute a verbal or body language confession, a judgment to be affirmed as is. Thank you."

"Very well. This court ends in recess. So ordered."

The gavel went down. The case had been duly argued. What was left was the written opinion of the justices.

CHAPTER 50

HENRY'S LAST DAY IN PRISON

Henry was in another session of sexual offenders therapy when the warden came in. One of the other inmates was giving a speech about the terrible things that he had done.

Henry was coaxing him forward.

"More detail, more detail."

"Man, I told you what happened."

"No, you didn't tell us what happened. We want to hear the details. Tell us where your hands were. Tell us how many times she said no, how many times did she hit you, how many times did she scratch you? What did she scream? What did you do to get her to do and submit to you? Tell it all."

The warden came over to Henry, put the piece of paper down in front of him, and turned to the therapist.

"You're not going to believe this."

"What?"

"Henry, check it out."

On the top page, it said: Court of Appeals of California, For the Fourth Appellate District. In big letters: TO BE PUBLISHED -- this means it was a significant decision to become part of the legal landscape of California.

The decision began with some ominous words:

"We are mindful of the impact of our decision. We have seen many cases where an illegal search will allow somebody that is guilty to go free. This can be upsetting, but we remind everyone that we are a nation of laws, that under our criminal justice system, we have at the highest level a series of fundamental rights set forth in our national constitution and in our state constitution.

Where those fundamental rights are violated, there is no other remedy we have found to be appropriate other than an exclusion order to exclude the evidence from trial. No matter what impact that might have on the prosecution's case -- it can gut the case, it can cause the guilty to walk free. This is our only remedy. We will enforce it. We will invoke it, and we do so today.

As we have set forth below, we hold that the search into Henry Adams Emerson III's home was illegal, and a violation of the Fourth Amendment prohibition against unreasonable searches and seizures; that the subsequent search and ensuing seizure of physical evidence, a ring, was likewise illegal.

We further uphold that the speech to Henry about doing the right thing, the Christian thing, constituted an illegal interrogation and violation of the Fifth Amendment prohibition against compulsory self incrimination, and that when Henry agreed and consented to his arrest and walked out of there with the detectives, that this constituted a body confession. We hold that the trial court's decision to deny the defendant's exclusionary motion to exclude evidence of the ring and evidence of this confession, was in error.

We accordingly reverse the judgment, and remand this case for further proceedings below."

Henry was paralyzed.

"There was no error."

"Apparently there was."

"I didn't authorize this."

"Well, it happened. You're going to be released."

Dr. Miller couldn't believe it.

"Warden, he's not ready. He's got years to go and he knows it."

He was hardly finished. Henry had travelled perhaps 10 miles on a 1,000 mile journey.

"Henry, all I can tell you is this decision right here orders us to release you. You're going to be bussed back to the county jail," the warden explained.

"Henry, you can't go," Dr. Miller reacted. "There's just no way. You're not ready."

He turned to her.

"I'm scared to death."

He didn't want to go. This was a prisoner being released involuntarily.

"Help me. What can I do?"

"Henry, take this."

She scrawled out a phone number.

"This is Dr. Sara Wainwight. When you get out, you call her. You talk to her. You tell her I referred you to her. She will help you continue in your program. Agreed?"

He looked at her.

"Agreed."

The warden and several correctional officers walked Henry down the hall, to his cell.

Henry packed up all his belongings, organized all his papers, carefully placed them into three boxes. He was assisted by three correctional officers as he put on street clothing, walked down the corridor one last time of the protective housing unit, down a series of corridors, out a series of gates to processing, to administration and into a courtyard area where a bus awaited. It was a sheriff's deputy bus, en route to the county jail, where he would be held pending further proceedings before the San Diego County Superior Court.

CHAPTER 51

RAPIST FREED

The headline was obnoxious and troubling, and hit Ben like a ton of steel. He was at the very newspaper that published it, which made it all the worse. Of course they wouldn't let him write a thing about it. He was way too close to the story.

He stormed into the editor's desk.

"What the hell is this?" He was screaming, he was crying, he was shaking. He was salivating. He was majorly pissed off.

"I'm sorry, Ben. We're reporting the news."

"They let this motherfucker go? Are they out of their minds?"

"Ben, it's the system."

"Don't tell me about the system. The system is so screwed up."

"Ben, I don't know what to do."

"Where is this motherfucker going?"

"County jail."

"Is he there right now?"

"He's there right now."

"Can we go see him?"

"I don't know."

Ben was out the door, into his father's Mercedes, and drove like a maniac to the county jail.

He went in, he showed his photo ID and filled out the inmate visitor form. About 10 minutes later, Ben was told that Henry would not accept him as a visitor.

"He has the power to reject a visitor?"

"Oh, yeah. It's optional. He said no."

"When's his next court date?"

CHAPTER 52

DISMISSAL

They appeared before Judge Ransom. He was not happy. Judges don't like to be reversed on appeal. They don't like to be told that they were "in error." When the Court of Appeals rules, the superior court judge must obey.

"Call the case of *People v. Emerson*."

"*People v. Emerson*. Counsel, state your appearances."

The clerk was methodical, almost robot-like in her announcement. The appellate counsel would no longer be involved in this matter. It was now back to the original Assistant District Attorney, Ed Sinclair.

"Assistant District Attorney Ed Sinclair, appearing on behalf of the people."

He turned to look at the audience. Of course Ben was present. Ben looked over to Henry, who was sitting there in his county jail red jumpsuit with two sheriff's deputies right behind him. They protected him as though he were public enemy number one. The irony in the heightened level of protective housing status, one man to a cell, waist chains, leg irons, escort to court with two correctional officers right behind him, sit him a chair, cuff him to a chair, don't let him move, don't let him out of your sight, guard him, he's extremely dangerous status was this: Today, following a couple of announcements about to be heard, Emerson would be released from custody.

The judge probably knew this from the get-go.

"Let me first hear from the people. I'm sure you've had a chance to review the Court of Appeals' decision."

"I have, Your Honor."

"So tell us, tell the court how you wish to proceed."

"Your Honor, it is with great regret that I must inform the court without the ring, we do not have sufficient evidence to make a case against the defendant, Mr. Henry Adams Emerson III. Accordingly, the people move to dismiss based on insufficient evidence."

The able public defender hardly had to say a word.

"No opposition."

The judge was not happy about the order he would have to make. He shook his head. He looked at Henry.

"Mr. Emerson, I've heard nothing but glowing reports about your progress in prison."

"Thank you, Your Honor."

"I'm worried about you though. Those same reports told me you're not done yet."

"Your Honor, I'm not even near done."

"I wish I didn't have to do what I'm about to do, but I'm afraid the Court of Appeals' decision does leave us with no choice. In light of the Court of Appeals' decision, barring the physical evidence that came from the search of a home and other orders and findings stated therein; in light of the district attorney's motion to dismiss based on insufficiency of the evidence, the court hereby GRANTS the motion to dismiss, and deems that this matter be and is hereby dismissed. Bailiff, you are hereby ordered to process him out of custody to be released to the general public. So ordered."

The judge slammed the gavel down and left the bench.

CHAPTER 53

BEN'S REACTION

There is an emotion called revenge. Before this day, Ben did not have this emotion. This feeling had been eliminated by the fact that Henry had been convicted of a crime and sentenced to a lengthy prison term. Whatever anger and desire for revenge that Ben had was dissipated by Henry's acknowledgement of the crime, guilty plea to the crime and sentence to prison.

Today that all changed. Henry now got off way too light -- a couple of years in prison for destroying Erica? No way. On the way out of the court room, Ben became absolutely batty and started talking to himself out loud.

"I can't fucking believe it -- unbelievable, ridiculous."

He turned to a bailiff. "What the fuck is the matter with you?"

The bailiff was taken aback by this. Lucky for the bailiff, Assistant District Attorney Sinclair was right behind him. He waved the bailiff off and whispered to him, "Something terrible just happened. Let it go."

The bailiff had seen plenty of crazy people at the courthouse and let Ben walk right by. Ben walked outside the courthouse and crossed the street into his car, seething with anger. This will not stand.

His first reaction was simple enough. He drove straight to Henry's house. He knew the way. He'd been there before. It was about a 20 minute drive. He was on the road. The entire way there he was thinking, *This guy thinks he's no longer a prisoner. The state won't take him as a prisoner. The county won't take him as a prisoner. Well, somebody's got to take him as a prisoner. That somebody is me.* He started thinking about all the rooms of his house. There were many. Which one would make the best cell? Which one locked the best? Which one had no windows? Which one could you scream in and not be heard?

He was met with a big surprise when he arrived at Henry's home. Somebody had beat him to the punch. It seemed like the good doctor, the therapist, was well aware of victim hostility and especially a victim's lover/fiance/husband.

She'd notified the authorities, "Watch out for Ben Nightingale. He will seek revenge."

Sheriff's deputies waited at the front gate of the Emerson residence. There were two parked on either side. There was one parked at the door, preparing for the arrival. They knew. It was a rather obvious idea. The rapist that gets away with rape is in danger and oddly enough, it would be the job of law enforcement to protect this man, this rapist from Ben.

Ben saw the sheriff's deputies. They had been given a description of Ben and his likely car. The minute he drove off, two of them tore after him, lights on. Ben drove right by the driveway. He had not committed a crime. Just driving there in anger didn't constitute a crime -- not yet.

The deputies pulled him over. One of them was quite large. One of them was quite short. They looked a little bit funny together. The short one did the talking.

"Are you Ben Nightingale?"

"Yes."

"Can I see some ID, please?"

Ben pulled out his wallet and handed his driver's license.

"Is this your current address?"

"No. I filed a change of address though. I now live in La Jolla."

"Okay. So Ben, you live in La Jolla. What brings you out here?"

"Just going on a drive."

"Don't bullshit me, Ben. You know damn well where you're going. You going to do something, Ben? Something you're going to regret?"

"No."

"Well, Ben, let me explain it to you. We know you. We have been alerted about you. We know all about revenge. We know what you're thinking. Let me just tell you, we understand but we can't let it happen. We're going to be here. We're going to be here on 24 hour alert. Our job is to protect this man from one person -- you, and we will succeed. So how about you just forget about this street, this house and this man? You go find a different way to deal with your anger. How about it, Ben?"

Ben was quiet. His hands were on the wheel of his father's Mercedes. He was obviously angry, but he didn't want to show it. His knuckles were quiet. His grip was tight. The deputy looked inside.

"Relax, Ben. Breathe. Chill."

Ben shook his head. He tried to smile, but it was so fake. He looked at the large deputy, the small deputy. He looked at his rearview mirror. He saw four more deputies behind him.

"All you guys working for this piece of garbage?"

"We don't work for him. We work for the county. Our job is to keep the peace. We're going to do our jobs."

"Deputies, can I go now?"

"I want to hear it from you, Ben. You are not going to drive here again."

Ben looked back. He saw all the deputies in front of the driveway. He smiled. He looked at the deputy. He had just given him a great idea.

"Okay, deputy. I'm going to make you a promise. I will not drive by here again."

CHAPTER 54

HENRY IS HOME

Judging by the entourage of sheriff's deputy cars, you would think Henry was a movie star that just got released from jail. No fewer than nine sheriff deputy patrol cars escorted a jail transport van from the county jail to Henry's home. They pulled up to the driveway and Henry saw something he wasn't expecting to see for a long time -- a place called home. They drove him right into the front of the house. He was wearing street clothes, no handcuffs, no leg irons.

He walked out of the van a free man. A deputy opened the door and couldn't help but say, "Welcome home, Henry."

Henry acknowledged the deputy and thanked him.

"Thanks, deputy."

He walked in to his grandfather's very large home. Now it was his home. He walked through a large living room to the kitchen area, back to the sliding glass door area -- a beautiful view of the Pacific Ocean. It was gorgeous. He walked out to the garden, a lawn, a pool and a pathway. The deputies followed him on the pathway, all the way to the door of his other home. It was locked. There was police tape around it, left over from the night of his arrest. It had been previously removed and put back by the team of correctional officers sent by the warden to retrieve Henry's guitar. Henry could see this by the fact that the tape that affixed the plastic yellow ribbon to the wall had been broken and new tape had been placed over it. He thought nothing of it. He removed it and put it in a nearby garbage can.

He walked in and saw his home. In his pants he had a key to the house. He opened the door and walked in to see his home, his residence, his castle. A deputy had followed him.

"Mr. Emerson, I request permission to enter."

Henry turned back and smiled.

"Sure, come on in."

The deputy entered with another deputy.

"How does it feel to be back home?"

"Weird. I'm not really ready."

"Well, you know what to do."

"I do."

Henry pulled out the piece of paper that Dr. Miller gave him. There was the number of the therapist that he would call. The deputy looked over to the phone.

"Let's see if it works."

They picked it up. Unfortunately, the bill hadn't been paid in quite awhile and the phone was dead. Henry didn't have a phone. The deputy pulled out a cell phone. He wanted to help.

"Here, use mine."

"Thank you."

Henry looked out the window at the beauty of the Pacific Ocean and called the doctor. The phone rang several times and then she answered. This was Dr. Laura Doris; she went by Dr. Do for short.

"Doctor's office. May I help you?" the receptionist answered.

"This is Henry Emerson."

"Oh, Mr. Emerson. We've been expecting your call. Just a minute. Dr. Do will be here in just a second."

He was on hold for only a second.

"This is Dr. Laura Doris. May I help you?"

"Doctor, this is Henry Emerson."

"Oh, Mr. Emerson. Thank you for getting to me. How long have you been out?"

"I just got out."

"I mean, exactly how long?"

"I got out an hour ago. I made the drive to my home. I got into my home and a nice sheriff's deputy, who is right here with me, let me borrow his cell phone to call you."

"So you did as you were told. You called me right when you got out."

"I did."

"Excellent. Are you going to do everything else I tell you to do?"

"I have learned how to follow directions quite well. You tell me what to do, I will do it."

"Okay. Here's what I want you to do. Tomorrow morning, 9 AM, my office."

"Yes."

"You're going to be here?"

"I will be there."

"You got a car?"

"If I have to ride a horse there, I'll be here."

Actually, the fact of the matter was, Henry's driver's license had expired. His grandfather's car, a Cadillac El Dorado, had not been driven in quite some time. Because of that, its battery was dead. So he actually didn't have a way to get down there. He turned to the sheriff's deputy for advice without really asking for it.

"Henry, don't worry. We're going to be here. We'll take you there."

"Doctor, I got a ride."

"Okay. Nine o'clock. Bring a binder with blank paper."

Henry smiled. He knew about these binders.

"I'll be there with a binder."

CHAPTER 55

BEN HAS A PLAN

Ben did not go home. Instead, he traveled to the address on his driver's license; his former home, the apartment. He looked very out of place pulling up in his father's $100,000 plus Mercedes into this rather rough apartment complex.

Sure enough, as he knew it would be, there were four nice Mexican men at the barbecue, wearing those predictable tank tops, cooking burgers for their families. He knew the men. They were always down at the corner apartment.

He parked by his old apartment, which was occupied by a new family. He walked by, looked inside, smiled, kept walking. He proceeded to the corner apartment. He knocked on the door. Nobody answered.

The men at the barbecue looked up, were really surprised to see Ben down there. They all knew what had happened.

He knocked again. This time the door opened. A man not in a tank top with a gun appeared, grabbed Ben by the neck, threw him into the living room, down on the ground, and put the gun up against his head right behind his ear.

"What do you want, motherfucker?"

"Whoa, take it easy, take it easy. I'm here for something."

"Talk."

"I need some drugs."

"Bullshit. You don't need any drugs. You need to get the fuck outta here."

"Look, it's what I've come for."

The man let Ben up.

"I know you."

"Yeah, I used to live here."

"Yeah. What are you living here for, whitey? You don't belong here."

"Well, you'll be happy to know I left. There goes the neighborhood."

"So what's up? I remember you. You're the one with the girl that got raped."

"Yep."

"I'm sorry about that, man."

This drug dealer had a bit of a heart.

"I wouldn't want that on anybody. Man, if somebody raped my girl, I tell you --"

He held the gun out.

"What would you do?"

The man looked at Ben, realizing Ben was up to something.

"I'd shoot the motherfucker."

"Okay, hold on though. Think about it. What happens then?"

"What do you mean what happens? Motherfucker's dead."

"Yeah, what happens to you?"

The man thought about it.

"I go to prison for the rest of my life."

"Great. Some revenge. There must be a better way."

"Is that what this is about?"

Ben shook his head yes, but stated, "I'm not saying anything."

The drug dealer smiled.

"What do you need?"

"I need something that'll bring a man down. I don't want to shoot anybody. I don't want to beat anybody. I just want him down, out, cold -- and I want him to stay out cold for awhile. Then I want him to continue to be so out of it he can't fight me off, he can't do a damn thing."

"Okay. How about liquid Valium? That's an easy one."

"How do I give it to him?"

The man pulled out a bag of syringes.

"Don't reuse them. It's not sanitary."

He opened the bag and gave him 10 vials of liquid Valium.

"How much to knock him out?"

"Well, first of all, use about a quarter of a vial -- see how that does. Later, he'll work up a resistance. You'll have to go to half a vial."

"How much?"

The big-hearted drug dealer smiled.

"Man, this one's on the house. Next time though, you pay."

Ben shook his head.

"No, no. Let me pay now. I've got cash."

"Nope. This one's on me. Consider it something to help my karma."

Ben put his hand out. The man shook it. Ben was going to walk out with a clear plastic bag of syringes and several vials of Valium. The guy saw how clueless Ben was.

"Whoa, whoa, whoa. Homie, stop."

He went over to the corner. He had a backpack. He emptied it out. He put the syringes and the Valium in the backpack and handed over the backpack.

"Do me a favor? Bring this back next time you see me."

Ben took the backpack, put it on.

"I will be back."

He walked out of the apartment, down the hall by his old place, around the stairs, and walked by the men at the barbecue. They studied the backpack. They didn't say a thing. They didn't judge him.

Ben got in his car and drove away.

CHAPTER 56

HOME DE-PROVEMENT

The 12 year sentence Henry received struck Ben as roughly equivalent of proper justice. Sure, he would have liked to have seen a longer sentence and sure, Henry's public defender would have like to have seen a shorter one, but 12 years was no small chunk of change. More than a decade of a man's life in exchange for his evil deed plus a five year parole period, during which Henry would have been under extremely strict monitoring and a further regimen of ongoing sexual offender therapy.

But now that was all out the window. It did not sit well with Ben at all. Rage? Anger? Bitterness? A feeling of betrayal by the system? All of the above. His anger left him to one bitter, dark conclusion: If the state wasn't going to make a prisoner out of this guy, he would.

He was back at his father's home. He walked through the rooms and tried to see which one would make the best prison cell. This was an elegant home, with every room having gorgeous windows, French windows, paned glass, gorgeous curtains -- not the kind of adornments you would expect in a prison cell. None of them were very secure. Although he had wonderful alarm systems and an iron gate at the driveway, this was all designed to keep people from outside getting in.

Ben now had a new challenge -- how to find the proper room for keeping someone in from getting out. The master bedroom? No. The other three bedrooms? No. Every one of them had these gorgeous windows. They would be so easy to break. He'd have to board them up, and then once he did that, it would look rather obvious from the outside that something odd was going on. You're not allowed to have boarded up windows in La Jolla. Neighbors would know. Neighbors would call. Something would happen.

There was one room, though, that Ben thought would work. His father's den. This was a darkish office; walnut walls, photos of his grandfather, even his great-grandfather. There was a mahogany desk. There was a computer. There were various certificates and diplomas, photos of Sam, photos of Ben. There was only one window, and it looked out the backyard -- so if it were boarded up somehow, nobody from the public view could ever see.

Ben studied the den and realized the simple reality. It would have to be this place. These California homes are built without basements, so there was no concrete downstairs. There was no shed. There was no out second home like Henry had. There was really no other candidate other than this den.

He imagined it as a jail cell. It would be a pretty nice one. The wood-panelled walls, the darkish light, an emerald green rug -- it was a pretty nice room. How to turn that room into a jail cell?

Ben chuckled with the thought. He couldn't hire a contractor to do this job. It would be a giveaway to tell some contractor, "Please create a jail for me."

It'd be one of those jobs that after he completed it, he'd have to kill the guy.

So Ben had an idea. The prisoner himself would be the contractor. All Ben had to do was take a trip to Home Depot to get whatever materials were needed.

So let's see now. What do we need?

He looked at the door leading into the den. He looked at it on the way out. He closed that door. He noticed the wall, the wall framing, the footings on the wall. The idea was, he would make an extension of the wall to cover the door area. This way, you would walk right by that room and wouldn't even know it was a room.

The materials needed? Pretty simple. Drywall, hammer and a crowbar -- maybe some nails, a little bit of putty, some tape -- you're good to go.

He looked at the wall on the inside and could see right away a great opportunity. It led to the back of a bathroom and adjoining next bedroom. It walled off with his shower.

He left the den room and walked around to that shower room. This was a walk-in stand up shower that could have a fake door placed. This was a room that Ben really didn't use. For now, he would place a door in the bathroom shower that would open into the den and Henry would build it.

Seal off one door, make another door and cover up that window. What to cover the window with? The good news, it wasn't very large. How about some iron bars? Iron bars would actually fit in with some of the existing motif. There were iron bars in front of the house. There was an iron gate -- so iron bars around that window would fit in.

That would be a job he could actually hire an outsider contractor to do. He would do that first -- put the bars up and have that window sealed. That part would be a legitimate job. Nobody would ask any questions about it.

Ben called the contractor up and had some iron bars placed up within a day. The window wouldn't be sealed off. Instead, it would be made so that the bars were right up to the window. If the window got broken, say, by a fist or head crashing through it, it would just crack the glass. The glass would come flying down to the patio below, it would crack into many pieces -- but those bars would remain. There's no way you could get out from those bars. It would work. It wasn't quite perfect, but it would work at least for a couple months.

Ben went off to Home Depot and bought four pieces of plywood, four pieces of drywall. He would pay cash. There would be zero paper trail of this transaction. He threw the receipt away into a Home Depot garbage can on the way out.

The cashier had a funny question.

"So, what are you building?"

"Oh, a little something at the house. Nothing big."

"Well, with this plywood and this drywall, you can build something very big."

"Well, we'll see."

"Need any books on this?"

"Probably, but let me try it without."

"You got any tools?"

"Yeah, I got some tools. I think I'm covered."

"What about putty?"

"Oh, good point. I need some putty."

The cashier called on the speaker system, "Can of putty, cash register four, please."

A man was quickly dispatched. He got a small can of putty and brought it to cash register four, where Ben was waiting.

"Thank you."

For this job, Ben had to use his convertible Corvair. It had the top down. He put the plywood and the drywall in the back seat, where it would hang out, and make his trip home. He drove it right into the garage and closed the door.

He brought each piece upstairs and into the den. He stacked them against the wall. He brought the putty in, a putty knife, a hammer, some nails and a small toolkit. Hopefully his prisoner would be able to take it from there.

CHAPTER 57

STEALING A PRISONER RIGHT OUT FROM UNDER THE SHERIFF'S NOSE

It was late in the afternoon. Though Ben was a fish out of water when it came to construction projects, his next project would not be so.

He took his father's Mercedes and took a drive down to the marina. He punched in the secret code to gain access into the marina, walked down the planks. In his hand, he held a key that had a flotation device on it. He proceeded down the wood ramp into the marina area where there were thousands of impressive boats, one of which had the name *Justice* on the back. It was an apt name for tonight's activity.

Ben knew where it was. He'd been on it many times. He walked cheerfully by several owners who waved at him.

"Hey, Ben."

"Hello, Mr. Struthers."

"Sorry about your dad."

"Thank you."

"How it's going?"

"Fine."

Ben just kept walking. There were three other greetings by other boat owners. They knew Ben well. He walked by as though he were not up to no good. Putting on a good face when you're about to commit a horrendous crime is a skill that certain people have and though Ben was not experienced in this game, he did a masterful job of presenting himself in a professional good kid manner, as he had done on many other occasions when he'd walk down the wood plank, taking a right turn, a left turn until he reached a majestic yacht by the name of *Justice*.

This was no ordinary boat -- not the kind you'd just take out to catch a fish. This was a 49 foot Glasspar, with double inboard engines, the kind of boat that you could actually take out to the open ocean and do some serious deep sea diving.

For Sam and Ben, this was the boat that they had gone out in many times. The photos on the boat showed them scuba diving. Several of them showed Ben at the side of the boat with his silver aluminum tank, neoprene wet suit, yellow bordered face mask, snorkel out of his mouth and Jacques Cousteau Calypso regulator in his mouth. He had gloves on his hands, an undersea hunting knife on his ankle, flippers. The photo showed him waving just before he did a back flip and splashed into the water. The next photos show him in the water, swimming away.

On the side of the boat, there was a Zodiac raft with a small Johnson nine horsepower engine. This baby would be put to use tonight.

Ben went into the cabin of the boat. It was gorgeous. It had a high ceiling, a fan in it, wood tables, a leather couch, an impressive kitchen. He sat at the table and took out the goods he had gotten before, from his former neighbor.

He had three syringes and three vials. He looked at the vials, not knowing how much to put in; he figured one vial per syringe and three syringes because you never know how screwed up a caper might get. He carefully filled up the syringes, measuring them as though he were a doctor. He pushed the syringe down. Some of the Valium squirted out. He had a plastic syringe tip, which he put on to each of the syringes. He carefully wrapped them together with a couple rubber bands. He had a fanny pack, which he unzipped, and put the syringes in, and then closed. He put the fanny pack on, and was ready for business.

He put the key into the ignition. It started up with a rumble. He let it warm up. It was a small job to go outside, untie the knots to each of the hookups to the dock. He'd done this many times before, and knew exactly how to do it. There were three ropes. He brought the ropes in, went back to the helm and slowly powered the boat away from its dock. He proceeded in reverse into an exit lane. He traveled past the five mile per hour speed limit sign on a buoy, and made his way out to the open sea. He turned on the boat's GPS system and its depth sonar system. It gave him a wonderful map of not only where he was going, but the channel, its depth and the exit path out the marina channel, out to the sea, up the coast north to a place called Carlsbad.

He pulled up a Google map to find the location on a computer. Ben was pretty smart about computers. He actually had bought a new one, a laptop. The good news about laptops -- they only cost $600. The bad news -- whatever you do can be searched and found by others. Ben knew this all too well. He did a Google search for a map to Carlsbad, to the address to Henry's home. That gave him the driving directions to the home. He would then use his GPS system to get there by sea.

CHAPTER 58

MEANWHILE, BACK AT THE RANCH

The warden paid Henry a visit and brought something that he knew Henry would very much want: his guitar. Unfortunately, the county jail would not allow Henry's guitar. It stayed with the warden in his office until the warden knew Henry had arrived safe and sound at home.

The warden brought it to him personally and had a kind of paternal discussion with him. They were in the main living room of Henry's gorgeous home. The warden couldn't help but be impressed with Henry's new escalation in status.

"Not long ago, you were a prisoner with nothing and now look at you. You're a multimillionaire living in this castle."

Henry was nonplussed.

"I had nothing to do with this. I didn't earn it, didn't build it, didn't make it -- the only part of this house I did were the cabinets and the kitchen."

The warden nodded.

"Henry, I got something for you though -- something you did build."

He pulled out the guitar. Henry was so pleased to have it. He strummed it, played some chords and put it down.

"Thank you, warden. You're a good man."

"Henry, I want you to be safe here. I'll tell you something. I see many guys get out and go right back in. I'd like to see you not do that."

Henry showed the warden a piece of paper.

"I think this is my ticket right here."

The warden look at it. There was a phone number of Dr. Doris, the therapist.

"I'm seeing her tomorrow, 10 o'clock."

"Okay, and what are you going to do there?"

"I'm going to do whatever she tells me to do. I'm going to do the whole program. I'm never going to quit. I'm going to just keep going, probably until the day I die."

The warden nodded in appreciation. "Henry, you're on the right path. You just keep doing that every day. Now, whaddya got all these sheriff's guys out here for?"

There were two by the front door, there were two by the gate -- a total of four.

"The county can't afford this," the warden said.

"I'm paying. These guys are all off duty."

"Oh, I see. Private guards?"

"Yep."

"What are you worried about?"

"Oh, come on. I'm a rapist. I just got freed from prison, way too early. Everybody know it. It's been on the front page. You know how it is. Someone's going to try to kill me or something."

"Somebody? As in, just some guy from a member of the public or somebody in particular?"

"Could be both. I don't know. All I know is, I don't feel safe. I want protection."

"Yeah, so you got some protection."

"Yep. I got four guys. That ought to do it."

"And you got the money to pay them?"

Henry shrugged his shoulders, put his hands out, showed the warden the spacious skies in his own new living room. The warden saw the obvious.

"I guess you do. Well, Henry, you know I'm not going to leave here until --"

Henry stopped the warden.

"I know." He picked up his guitar. "Until I sing you a song."

"Exactly."

Henry thought about the song and thought of a perfect one -- "Bridge of Sighs," by Robin Trower. It was a sad song of emptiness following sin, of an attempt to cleanse oneself when one could not be clean, of an attempt at getting forgiveness when none would ever be granted, of an attempt at making good of the bad that he had done.

He sang it to the warden.

Bridge of Sighs
By Robin Trower
[Used with permission]

The sun don't shine
The moon don't move the tides
to wash me clean
Sun don't shine
The moon don't move the tides
to wash me clean
Why so unforgiving and why so cold
Been a long time crossing Bridge of Sighs
Cold wind blows
The Gods look down in anger
on this poor child
Cold wind blows
And Gods look down in anger
on this poor child
Why so unforgiving and why so cold
Been a long time crossing Bridge of Sighs

CHAPTER 59

BOAT TRIP

Ben's boat moved through the night seas. The half moon reflected off the water. He went out about half a mile from the shoreline, where the water was a little deeper. He pierced across the water, smashing into waves on the way, watching as the water splattered to the left and right. He made his way to a date with destiny, a date of revenge, a date to start a new kind of existence for Ben -- one where he would leave the realm of victim and enter the realm of perpetrator. Perhaps there is a thin line between the two, a line that Ben would crash through tonight.

It took him about 45 minutes to get to the point where his GPS showed him he was at a parallel with the Google map showing the way to Henry's home. He stopped the boat, put the anchor down, got to the front of the boat, brought his binoculars out and searched. The boat had a telescope in the main quarters that was far more powerful than the binoculars. Ben quickly saw that the binoculars were not visualizing enough. He walked back into the living room of the boat and pointed the telescope toward the homes.

At last, he saw it. The second home where Henry used to live, the main house where Henry was now living. He scanned it left to right. He couldn't see the front parts of the house, but he knew what was out there -- sheriff's deputies parked in front, guarding the front. Nobody was guarding the back.

He waited until it was late, until Henry was asleep, his guards were off guard -- maybe watching TV, maybe playing video games, maybe talking to their girlfriends or doing something other than guarding. He waited until 11 o'clock at night.

He took the Zodiac boat out. He double-checked the Valium-loaded fanny pack. He put on a neoprene wet suit, all black, lowered the Zodiac into the water, pulled on that small Johnson motor, got it started and proceeded to fly across the water into Henry's backyard.

His first thought was to look into that second house to see if perhaps Henry was there. That had a door that was open. He very quietly opened that door, tiptoed in to an empty space, walked into another room that led to the living area, went by a small kitchen area, a dining room table area and back to where the single bedroom was. There was nobody there. He explored the other rooms of this place and determined Henry was now living in the main house.

He very quietly walked back to the wood shop area, out that door and tiptoed across a walkway -- next to the swimming pool, around it, onto the backyard lawn area and up to the wall of the back of the house. He stood behind it with his back to it. A light was creating a shadow. He looked up at that light. He wanted to curse at it. He needed that light out. The shadow was darting right across a patio area in full view of a sliding glass door leading into the family room area. He could see in that room were two sheriff's deputies. One was watching TV. The other was talking on his cell phone, sitting at a kitchen bar. They both had guns ready to go.

Okay, now, Ben thought to himself. *How am I going to do this? These guys are trained fighters, combat style. They both look beefy -- former military. They both have guns.*

Ben was a skinny ass journalist with zero fight training. His only weapons were three hypodermic needles, one of which he definitely needed for Henry.

The other problem was that one of these guys was sitting at a bar table in the kitchen looking right out the sliding glass door. If Ben went in that door, he would immediately be in full view of this guy. He could quickly alert the other guy and all hell would break out, so that wasn't going to work.

Ben thought, *There's got to be another way.*

He noticed that the lights in the back patio area only went up to the pool and not beyond the other side of the pool, so he traversed back out the patio area to the other side of the pool and then, in the dark, crawled across the back lawn to the other side of the house.

When he got to the other side of the house, he found something that could work out quite well -- a set of garbage cans. Could he climb up on the garbage cans, traverse up the wall and somehow magically Spiderman-style make his way into the bedroom or living room and attack Henry? No, Ben was not even near that good.

Instead, he did something very simple. He picked up one garbage can and threw it on the other, making a crashing sound that sent the two sheriff's deputies into action mode. Ben hid behind another garbage can.

As the sheriff's deputies came out, he saw the two flashlights on. They both had their guns drawn. Ben would have a very short window of opportunity here. The deputies looked over and saw the garbage can knocked over.

One of them concluded, "Probably a raccoon."

They both turned around and made their way back into the interior of the home. Ben would now take this opportunity to get them. He had in his right hand a syringe, in his left hand another syringe.

He tiptoed in his little neoprene moccasin shoes behind the two sheriff's deputies. He lifted both his hands up at once, matador-style and plunged the syringe into each of their necks, quickly filling them with more Valium than a sane person should ever take.

The men both tried to yell, but Ben put his hands around both their heads. They were both far stronger than Ben and shook him off like a bull would if he got the matador on his head. Ben hung on like an amateur rodeo star, holding their mouths so they couldn't scream, slopping around backwards and forwards. They swung him in a complete somersault. He landed right on his ass in front of them.

Just as they were about to shoot him, cuff him, taser him, mace him, kick him and plug him, things got a little foggy. They teetered, their views got fuzzy, they collapsed. Boom, onto the ground. The giants were out.

Ben kicked one of them to make sure he was out out. He took a set of handcuffs out of the deputy's pocket and cuffed the man to a nearby pole. He cuffed the other to the wrist of the secured one. He carefully placed the key to the handcuffs about 15 feet away from the deputies. Somebody would come by later to unlock them.

Now Ben had a clear entryway into the house. The other two deputies were guarding the front gateway. They didn't hear a thing. Ben returned to the backyard patio area. That door had been left open by the deputies. It was previously locked. So in one smashing of a garbage can, Ben figured out a pretty good way to neutralize the two deputies, unlock a door and gain easy access into the kitchen, past the living room and up a stairway.

There were quite a few rooms in this house. Ben figured Henry would not stay in the master bedroom. There was probably another bedroom. He looked into the first one; nobody was there. The second one; nobody was there. The third one; there was a sleeping Henry.

Next to Henry's bed was his beautiful rosewood guitar. Ben tiptoed into the room. There was a night light on. He had a syringe in his hand. Henry was sound asleep. Ben looked over Henry. There was a pause. There was something about the hunter and his prey that makes the hunter want to stop, just for a second, before he pulls the trigger. He studied his prey. Henry looked so peaceful there.

But unfortunately in this process, the pause can often prove fatal for the hunter. Some of the seawater that had collected on Ben's wet suit managed to come off of it. Several drops of seawater went right on to Henry's face.

Suddenly, unexpectedly, Henry woke up. His bright blue eyes were filled with rage as he saw hovering over him, some kind of masked man in a black neoprene rubber suit. It could be none other than Ben.

Ben wasn't quite ready for Henry's quick awakening. Before Ben could plunge the needle into him, Henry managed to grab Ben by the shoulders, jump on top of him and with his full weight on Ben's torso, brought him crashing backward to the wall.

In the process, Ben landed on Henry's guitar, smashing it into a thousand pieces.

Ben was on his back on top of the guitar. Henry took a look at the guitar. It was a distraction that would prove fatal. Ben took the opportunity to cram and shove the needle into the base of Henry's neck, injecting him with the Valium. He held onto Henry, giving him as much of a bear hug as a skinny little geek could. He held onto him until Henry's grip loosened, he collapsed and fell backwards. Henry was out.

Ben pushed him to the side and got up. There were several pieces of guitar wood in his neoprene suit, one of which went in like a needle. He had to pull it out. It hurt. He kept it, and placed it in his fanny pack. He would not leave any blood evidence.

Ben looked out the window and saw the two other sheriff's deputies cars, parked in front of the gateway into the home. The two deputies were in the car, not imagining in their wildest dreams what was going on inside the house. Ben realized there might not be much time. He went into action mode.

He dragged Henry down the stairs to the first floor area, across the rug, across the linoleum floor, out to the still open patio window. This would've been a good time to have a wagon or wheelbarrow or something, but unfortunately Ben did not have either. He picked Henry up and slopped him over his shoulder. Luckily, Henry did not weigh very much. He was also a lanky guy. Prison food hardly fattened him, so he was a bit on the skinny side.

Ben's adrenaline was going at full speed. He closed the door behind him and made his way across the patio, the lawn area, the pool area, down the path by the second house and continued down the path to the beach area. He put Henry down on the sandy beach area and rested a bit. He had to check again, but Henry was out. He then dragged Henry across the sand to the part of the sand that became wet from the sea, which was tougher, stronger and easier to traverse. He got down to where the Zodiac boat was. He put Henry onto that boat, backed the boat out into the water. He paddled it out a bit. It would be too noisy to just start up right there.

Ben started the engine and made his way back out to the ocean, to where the boat by the name of *Justice* sat and waited.

After getting to the boat, he parked the Zodiac to the back of the boat. They had a small loading plank there where, after scuba diving, they could pop themselves up, take off their scuba tanks and get back in the boat. Today, instead of taking a scuba tank off, he would be putting a prisoner on. He lifted Henry up with his shoulder, over the edge of the boat and made Henry do a somersault into the inside of the boat. Plop! Henry fell down into the boat.

Ben then traversed up the small ladder at the back of the boat and found his prey still unconscious. Ben brought Henry into the inside of the boat. He took some rope and tied Henry's legs and wrists together.

He started up the boat engine, and made his way back to La Jolla. This time, he would not go to the marina. There was no way he could take Henry out of there without one of his friendly neighbors seeing him. Instead, he went to the beach of his father's home, and reversed the process.

He parked about half a mile out at sea, put the anchor down, put Henry back into the Zodiac boat, started up that boat engine and went straight to his home. He got to the beach right behind his home, took Henry out of the Zodiac and did the hard job of dragging him up the sand, up a small path, across a garden, a pool and into his back patio door. He brought Henry up the stairs -- thump, thump, thump -- down the hall and into the awaiting den. He opened the den door, put Henry inside still tied up, locked the den door from the outside and put the key into his fanny pack.

Ben had now taken Henry as his prisoner.

CHAPTER 60

WHAT NOW?

The next morning, Ben checked on Henry. He was still groggy from the Valium, but conscious. He was tied up. Ben made his way in, quickly closed the door behind him and felt secure by the fact that Henry was all tied up.

"Good morning."

"What the fuck are you doing, asshole?"

"Okay, I see we have a little attitude problem."

"Get this fucking rope off me right now."

"Okay. Tell me, it's morning time. You got to pee?"

"Yeah."

"Okay, let's start with that."

Ben brought in a bucket and put it at the foot of the bed.

"So pee."

He was able to use his hands to put his zipper down, pull his dick out and pee into the bucket. It took awhile, but it was done. Ben then took the bucket into the nearby bathroom and poured it all out, flushed the toilet, left the bucket in the bathroom and came back to Henry.

"You know who I am?"

"I know who you are."

"Then you know what's going on."

"What?"

"You are my prisoner."

"Okay. How long?"

"Well, let's see now. You were given a 12 year sentence?"

"Yes."

"How much of that did you do?"

"One year, ten months."

"Not enough."

"I'm sure you're right."

"You're going to do 12 years here."

"You're going to keep me here in this house for 12 years?"

"Yep."

Henry looked out the window and he saw the iron bars.

"I see."

He looked around. He noted the plywood and the drywall stacked up against the wall.

"What's that about?"

"You're going to help me build something."

"What's that?"

"Your jail cell."

"Oh?"

"Yeah."

"And what if I don't?"

Ben laughed.

"Well, I'll tell you right now, I'm not going to tell you I'll kill you because I'm not going to kill you. But if you don't, I'll figure out some appropriate punishment. Why don't you just agree to do it? Don't you have a sense that you probably owe me?"

Henry nodded yes.

"I know I owe you."

"Okay. Now you can sit here all day with those ropes around you or I can let you walk around the room. What would you rather do?"

"I would rather have you take the ropes off me."

"Okay. Now let me show you something else. Before I do that, I got to do something to you."

Ben pulled out another syringe.

"Oh, what is that shit? Keep that the fuck away from me."

"Don't worry. It's Valium. It's not going to make you a psychotic catatonic like you did my fiancée, asshole."

Henry resigned himself to a forced injection, again into his neck. This put him right out again. It would be several hours until the groggy Henry was able to get back up. When he woke up, he noticed a full array of building tools, including spackle, the putty, a hammer, a saw and plywood propped up against the wall. Of course, Ben, the taskmaster was also there.

"You ready for work? Before we start -- sandwiches."

Ben fed him a roast beef sandwich, which Henry, who hadn't eaten in awhile, devoured.

Henry stood, still groggy and explained to Ben, "You know, I don't have a real clear mind right now."

"Look, I got to keep you drugged up," Ben explained. "I don't want to be beating you. I don't want to have to restrain you, so the drugs will be my restraint. Just do the best you can."

Ben watched in amazement as his prisoner began the process of removing a door, of inserting two pieces of plywood where the door used to be, of nailing those into the two by four studs, then covering those with drywall, hammering that in with nails, spackling with putty over those nails and then applying a Navajo white paint over it from the outside hall area.

It took a full day, but by the end of the day, if you walked down that hall, you would have no idea that there used to be a door there.

Ben then took Henry to the adjoining bathroom. He had Henry cut a three foot by six foot opening into the wall that would lead right to the shower on the other side. They placed another piece of plywood there. There was plywood on the other side, but this one would have a hinge on it. They made a seamless wall that, with a double push, one to unlock, a second to open would then open forward into the shower and gain access into that room.

Ben had no plans to use his shower and instead, had a false door that would allow him entry into the jail cell. He then removed all the tools and placed a heavy lock on the bathroom door. Henry would have full access to the bathroom, but once inside, he could not get out.

Henry, according to Ben's plans, would stay in this way for the next 12 years. Ben's only use of force against Henry would be the Valium. He would not beat him, he would not cuff him, he would not electroshock him, taser him, pound him with a billy club or any other use of force. Instead, a daily injection of a little more Valium would keep Henry at bay.

CHAPTER 61

PRISON IS NOT ENOUGH

Ben got to thinking. Keeping Henry in the house as a prisoner just wasn't enough. He wanted more, but what? A lot of terrible crimes develop in stages. First, you have a basic crime in mind. Kidnap the person, take him prisoner. But then after you've done that, it gets to be unfulfilling. You want more.

Ben was looking at Henry, laying there unconscious and was thinking, *There's got to be something more.*

Just as he was making a plan about that something more, there was a knock at the door. Ben quickly left the room, carefully locked it, exited the shower, locked the bathroom door and went to the front door.

There were no fewer than eight sheriff's deputies.

"Ben Nightingale?"

"That's me."

"Step aside. We've got a search warrant."

"Search warrant for what?"

"For Henry Emerson. You got him here?"

They walked right by Ben. This time they didn't need permission. They obtained a warrant. They explained to a judge that there was evidence of somebody coming from the ocean. The trail Ben had left included footprints of neoprene rubber and a drag path of Henry's feet to an area where they could tell by the shape of the indentation, there was a Zodiac boat. This has a triangular front area, but leaves a rather distinct impression in the sand. They also were able to look at boat records and learn that Ben knew his way around boats and indeed, had a boat that also had a Zodiac. They confirmed with the friendly neighbors at the marina that Ben had been down at the dock taking his boat out just on the day when Henry went suspiciously missing.

They prepared an affidavit, setting forth all this information, and presented it to a superior court judge. They also described Ben's motivation in terms of revenge. They described the whole situation of how Ben's fiancée had become catatonic and institutionalized. They described how

Henry managed to escape his lengthy prison term on a technical glitch that they were not about to repeat, that of the unlawful entry and search of a residence without a search warrant. They explained how Ben attempted to visit Henry at the jail upon Henry's release from prison.

The judge agreed there was probable cause, that there was evidence of a crime at Ben's home and issued a search warrant permitting the deputies to do a full scale search of the entire house to locate Henry Emerson III.

Ben realized he had no choice but to allow the deputies to roam through his home. They were there for four hours. They looked up and down and around, in every cranny, every cabinet, every bathroom, every shower. They looked everywhere.

A deputy came back to Ben.

"Alright, Ben, where is he?"

"Where's who?"

"Don't get cute with me."

"Well, tell me, guys. If you want to look for something, why don't you just ask me? Maybe I'll tell you."

"We think you've got Henry Emerson here."

"Why would I want that sack of shit in my house? Don't you understand? He raped my fiancée."

"Oh yeah, we understand exactly that. We understand that you're upset that he got out early. We look at you as the only human on this planet motivated to take this man hostage."

"Oh, I want him as my hostage? What am I going to do with him?"

"I don't know, Ben. You tell us. What are you going to do with him?"

Ben just shook his head.

"Guys, I don't have him. You want to look some more, look some more. You want to arrest me, then arrest me. But right now, looks like you don't have a body."

"We have a missing body. That's what we have now."

"Well, you've looked here. If you want to look some more, come on back. But in the meantime, guys, I think you should be spending your time looking somewhere else. Someone else may have taken him. I hate to tell you, but a lot of people in the public, they don't like rapists. There's a little thing called vigilantism. Could have been someone completely unconnected to the case who just thought it was wrong to let this guy out. Enough is enough, and they decided to take him. All I know is, he's not here."

"Ben, did you take your boat out for a cruise the other night?"

"Yeah, as a matter of fact I did. Is that illegal now? I can't go out on my boat?"

"No, you can go out on your boat. Where'd you go?"

"I just went out to the sea, no big deal."

"Okay."

The sheriff's deputies' next stop would be that boat. They would search it up and down. They wouldn't find the laptop that Ben did the Google map search on because he threw it out. The radar system doesn't record, the GPS system doesn't record -- there was really nothing other than that laptop that had any record of where Ben went that night.

They looked at the neoprene wet suit that Ben used that night. They noticed one piece of evidence, a hole in the suit.

"Hey Ben, how'd you get this hole?"

Ben was brought down to the dock. They showed it to him. He explained it away.

"You ever seen a sea urchin?"

"Oh yeah."

"Those little spines they have?"

"Yeah. They hurt like hell."

"Unfortunately, I brushed up against one. The little bastard got me good."

"I see. When did that happen?"

"Just the other day, when I took the boat out."

"So this is a brand new hole?"

"It is."

"Did it pierce your skin?"

"It did."

"Can I see?"

"Okay. You want me to pull my pants down?"

"Yeah."

Ben took his pants down and showed the puncture wound to his thigh. It had been cleaned away. There was not one molecule of rosewood guitar wood. It was just a puncture wound. Anything could've made that -- anything from an ice pick to a sea urchin to a piece of a guitar. Ben had carefully cleaned his wet suit. There was no wood left on that. He just had remnants of salt water, salt water that could've come from anywhere.

"Do you mind if we keep this?"

"Knock yourselves out."

They took the neoprene away. It'd go back to a lab where a technician would examine every millimeter of it, searching for either Henry's DNA, which as a sex offender, they had a profile of, a splinter or a piece of wood from Henry's guitar or some other evidence, even plant material from Henry's backyard that would somehow connect that wet suit to Henry's disappearance.

Unfortunately for the lab tech, the kind of beach ice plant that grew wild in the back of Henry's home and leading to the beach was the same kind of ice plant that grew wild at Ben's La

Jolla home. So the juices from those plants, which were neatly tucked away into the bubbles of the neoprene rubber, proved absolutely nothing. There was nothing distinctive about the ice plants just up the way in Carlsbad from those down the way in La Jolla. There wasn't even a molecule of a splinter left in that puncture hole.

The tech had to explain to the deputies, "Sorry. Came up negative."

Unfortunately for the sheriff's deputies, their search of the home came up empty, the search of the boat came up empty. All they had was a wet suit with a hole in it. At least for now, Ben would remain a free man, but in the vernacular of law enforcement, "a person of interest." They knew he somehow had done it. They just couldn't prove it.

Ben waved as the four sheriff's deputies and the CSI SUV drove away with empty Ziploc bags.

CHAPTER 62

THE RAPE OF HENRY

A month went by. During this period, Ben watched his prisoner. It got a little on the boring side. Henry would wake up, he would need food, he would take a shower, he would lay in his bed, he would do nothing all day. Ben would check in on him.

After several weeks of this, Ben began to harbor an empty feeling. Simply keeping this man prisoner was not enough. Ben thought about him. He visited Erica. He spoke with Erica about it, even though Erica couldn't speak back.

"Honey, it's just not enough. He's sitting in there. He's doing nothing, just taking up space. I'm sick of it. He's not suffering enough. Something has to happen to this man, something bad, something super bad, something --"

He turned and looked at Erica. It dawned on him what he wanted to do.

"Something like exactly what he did to you."

Ben left the mental asylum and drove right back to his old apartment complex. He went up, greeted the tank top-shirted father with tattoos, once again barbecuing in the parking lot area of the apartment complex. They smiled. At this juncture, Ben was way past the line from victim to perpetrator and was going for the gold.

He walked upstairs by his old apartment and down to the corner unit where he met his new buddy, the drug dealer that went by the fake name of Poncho.

"Hey Poncho, me again."

"You're already out of that shit?"

"No, no. That's not what I'm visiting you about today."

"Okay, what is it, man? Come on in."

He let Ben in his apartment. Inside, there were a bunch of those velvet paintings, fluorescent colors -- one of Elvis, one of Jesus and one of Poncho Villa. These were the heroes of this drug dealer, all displayed in fluorescent velvet. Ben did not want to see what they looked like with the lights turned off and the curtains pulled.

"So what can I do for you, my friend?"

He brought out a Dos Equis beer.

"Thanks."

Ben opened it, took a swig as though it were perfectly normal for him to have a beer at that time of the day -- when in fact, this was the first time in his life that he'd ever done so. He turned to his friend.

"I need a person who will do something for me."

Poncho sat back in the chair.

"Okay. Can you be a little more specific, my friend? Like, what?"

"This project is not so nice."

"Hey, look man, if you want to murder someone, I'm a drug dealer. I'm not into that."

"No, no. Nobody's going to get killed here. No murder."

"Okay, then what?"

"I need you to get me a guy who would be willing to rape a man."

"You want to rape some motherfucker?"

"I don't want to do it. I want someone else to do it."

"Why don't you do it?"

"Not into fucking guys."

"What makes you think I know someone who's into fucking guys?"

"I don't know. I'm just asking. Do you know somebody? Maybe you don't."

Poncho started thinking of his array of colorful friends.

"Hmm. Eddie might do it."

"Eddie?"

"Yeah. He's kind of odd."

"Well, I think I need an odd kind of guy."

"Yes, you do. Tell me about the guy you want raped."

"He's my prisoner."

"The guy doing the Valium?"

"Yep."

"Is he a white dude?"

"Yes."

"Big, fat, ugly, stinky, hairy ass motherfucker?"

"No, not at all. Tall, thin, blue-eyed, shaved head, clean as a whistle, kind of obsessive about cleanliness."

"Oh, one of those."

"Yep. So get me some dirty, greasy, disgusting, tattoo-laden, ugly ass, yellow toothed, bad breath, tobacco smelling, whiskey drinking piece of shit man. Tell him, don't take a shower for three days. Come by my house and fuck this guy in the ass."

"Okay, and I got to ask this stupid question. What are you going to give him for it?"

"Well, I'll pay him I guess. I got money. What's he need, $1,000?"

"Oh, I don't know. For that kind of sex, I think he's going to need more than $1,000."

"Alright. How about $2,000?"

"Yeah, he'll do it for $2,000. I'll talk to him. When do you want it done?"

"How about, like, today?"

"Hold on a sec. Yo, Eddie -- come out."

Amazingly, out of a room comes Eddie. This had to be one of the ugliest motherfuckers on the planet. He had a Mohawk, which on some people looks good -- but this one did not. He had a teardrop on his eye, and several prison tats on his arm. One of them was a butterfly. One of them was a cobra. Somehow those two connected, although it was anything but clear.

Eddie had a perfect set of white teeth -- but this was only because he'd recently got all his teeth smashed out in a fight -- a nice shot with the bottom of a beer bottle. Cosmetic dentistry has developed the common sense to make new teeth look imperfect so that they look real. This guy's dentist didn't quite have that art down. He had this brand spanking new super white perfect set of new teeth. They looked like they were possibly made in prison, along with his prison tats and Mohawk hairdo.

He, of course, wore a tank top shirt, a pair of Levis rolled up and black combat boots. One thing about Eddie -- he was no fat ugly guy. He looked like the kind of guy that lifted weights all the time. He had six pack abs. His face was visited perhaps by shattered meteorites, the same ones that struck the moon during millennia past. In overly hormonal men, with a little more testosterone dose than nature intended, the sweat glands on the face act up and produce volcanic pimples. Of course Eddie, being ever concerned on how beautiful he was, had to scrape them all off with his nails and left a bunch of divots. Unsightly, but pure Eddie. A testosterone-laden, prison tat, brand new white teeth, Mohawk-bearing with six pack abs, perfect shaped Mexican. The perfect man for Henry.

Ben nodded in approval. He turned to Poncho.

"This will do just fine."

Eddie turned to Poncho. He trusted him implicitly.

"What do you want me to do, man?"

"We got a little project for you."

"Okay. First of all, let me ask how much?"

Poncho turned to Ben.

"You tell him."

"$2,000."

"There you go, brother."

"Two thousand bucks?"

"Yeah."

"For what? I hope I'm not going to be killing anybody because I'm not killing nobody. Been there, done that."

Ben smiled.

"No, this will be more of a sexual encounter."

Eddie wondered, "A sexual encounter?"

"Yes."

Eddie continued, "Okay. When you say encounter, I'm thinking ET."

Ben explained, "No, this is an earthling, to be sure -- though some would argue perhaps not."

"What's the catch?"

Poncho smiled. "Man, there is a catch."

Eddie was hesitant. "Okay."

Poncho explained, "I mean, no one's going to pay you two thousand bucks to fuck some hottie."

"Oh God, so she's some ugly ass bitch?"

"No, to the contrary -- not ugly at all."

Eddie questioned, "Well then, what is it? She's got a disease? I ain't putting my dick in no diseased woman."

Ben assured him, "We'll cover you. You're going to wear a condom."

"Okay, but still, if she's got a disease, I don't even want to go there -- not worth it for a million bucks."

Ben explained, "I'm pretty sure this person is disease-free but listen, don't even worry about it. You're going to use a condom."

Eddie was still worried. "Okay. You got to tell me the catch. You're not telling me the full story. I'm absolutely sure of it."

Ben stated, "Okay. I'll come clean with you. The she is not a she."

"Not a she? What do you mean?" Eddie was very uneasy.

"It's a he."

Eddie was angry. "You want me to fuck some dude?"

Poncho persuaded him. "Two thousand bucks, man. Take you an hour, you'll be done with it."

"Oh, come on. Poncho, are you putting me up to this shit?"

"He needs a favor. It's against a man who went against his fiancée. They used to live here down the way."

"Oh, that girl you were with?"

"Yeah."

Eddie went on, "I was wondering what happened to her."

Ben explained, "She's in a hospital, permanently out. She's in a coma. This motherfucker that I'm asking you to do put her there -- shot her with some drugs. He raped her, messed her up forever."

Eddie sounded interested. "You know where he is?"

Ben knew. "Yeah, he's at my house."

"He's at your fucking house?"

"Yeah."

Eddie was about to ask how.

"-- Oh, never mind. I don't need to know. So what do we do?"

"You come to my house."

"And then what?"

"And then you do him."

"Just like that?"

"Just like that."

"Two thousand bucks?"

"Two thousand bucks."

He turned to Poncho. "Do you mind?"

"Do I mind what?"

"If I make a counteroffer."

"Be my guest."

"This is kind of crappy ass work -- pardon the pun. Two thousand bucks, although that may sound like a lot of money to some --"

Ben interrupted him.

"Listen, I got news for ya. I don't give a shit about money. I give a shit about something else. It's called revenge. I want this motherfucker to get what he's got coming. You want more money? I'll give you more money. Let's go like this -- just double it. Four thousand. How about that?"

"Four thousand cash?"

"You want a check? You want a Visa card?"

"Cash please."

"Cash it will be."

"You got it on you right now?"

Ben smiled. He reached into his pocket, pulled out an envelope. He had a stack of hundred dollar bills in there, neatly wrapped into groups of ten. He pulled out four of those wrappings, put them on the table.

"Count it -- four grand right there."

Eddie was about to count it. Poncho stopped him.

"It's not polite to count."

"Oh, a drug dealer with manners."

"Indeed."

Ben looked at Poncho.

"It's all there."

"I know it is, bro."

"Okay. Shall we?"

Eddie put the money in his pocket.

"Just a minute. I want to go get ready for my date."

The first thing he wanted to do was go brush his brand spanking new fake ass teeth. How stupid was this? He bought one of those Crests with Scope in it and brushed his teeth over and over again.

After awhile, Poncho had to stop him.

"Will you quit already? Jesus, this motherfucker -- he's got these new teeth. He lost his old teeth in a bar fight. Some asshole smacked the beer bottle in his mouth, knocked out all his teeth. Now he's got a new set and he thinks he's got to brush them 11 million times a day. Stop it already."

Ben was patient. At last, he came out. He put on a button down shirt over his tank top, looking kind of spiffy for an ex-con.

Ben asked, "Are you going on a date? You trying to look good for this guy?"

Eddie was unapologetic. "No, I'm just -- you know, getting ready. I don't know."

Ben rolled his eyes. "Whatever."

"Okay, one more item."

"Yes?"

Ben didn't know what was missing.

"The condom."

"Oh, guess what? I don't have one."

"You got one, Poncho?"

"Nope."

"Well, I don't have one."

Ben assured him, "Don't worry about it. We'll go get one."

"Let's do it."

Ben asked, "So Poncho, you want to come with us?"

"As thrilling as it sounds, I'll pass."

"Very well. Okay Eddie, you drive with me. Let's go."

This was the first time Eddie had been in a $100,000 Mercedes. In fact, it was the first time Eddie had been in a car that didn't have hydraulic lifts that made it bounce up and down. They stopped on the way at a Walgreen's.

"Come on, Eddie."

This unlikely couple was in line with a handful of condoms. People looked at them as though, *Oh God, are they, like, together?* Ben, the bohemian WASP -- Eddie, the ex-con Hispanic sporting a Mohawk and excessively white teeth. What a beautiful couple. It didn't help that Eddie had to smile all the time. He was so proud of his goddamn teeth. Ben rolled his eyes. He didn't even want to explain.

They got to the front and bought a box of Gold Trojans.

"Wonderful. Let's get the fuck out of here."

They got back in the slate gray non-hydraulic lifting Mercedes and proceeded to a much nicer part of town, the area known as La Jolla Beach.

They entered the front door. Eddie was amazed at the house.

"Wow, man. You live here?"

"Yeah, well, what can I tell ya?"

"This place is intense. You were living in our place before? You really moved up."

"It's a long story."

"I bet. What, did you find some oil or something?"

"Never mind. Are you ready for this?"

Ben's heart was pumping. Adrenaline was flowing. There's a thing that happens to a man before he commits a crime. Even a crime like this, once removed, is like sending someone else to rob a bank. Even if you're sitting back in your house thinking about the bank robbery, you will be pumped up. It might take you days to come down from it all. This one was the same way, even though Ben wouldn't lay a finger on Henry -- knowing that Eddie would created an adrenaline rush.

"Hey Eddie, we're going upstairs."

In the hallway, just before the stairs, he flipped him the box of Trojans. Eddie caught them midair, put them in his pocket. Eddie stopped by a mirror on the way, opened up his mouth -- of course he had to look at his teeth again. Ben almost ran into him. He wasn't expecting Eddie to stop there.

"Okay, here we go."

Eddie turned to Ben.

"Hey man, let me get in the mood here, okay?"

"Alright, take your time. Why don't you go up and meet your date?"

"Sure."

They went upstairs. They walked right by the room with no door into a bathroom, into a shower.

"Where the fuck you taking me?"

"There's a secret entryway."

"Oh."

"Follow me."

He unlocked the hidden door in the shower and walked through. Eddie followed right behind him, and then appeared in the room with Henry, who was asleep. Henry was filled up on Valium. He couldn't do shit and just to make sure of it, Ben took another hypodermic needle and shot Henry with a little more.

"This'll keep him down. Otherwise this guy would probably beat the shit out of you."

"Oh, I don't think so."

Eddie was a pretty damn good fighter. Most guys that have lived through prison know how to fight.

"Okay, so what do we do?"

"What do you mean what do we do? You fuck him."

"Yeah, but I mean, how we gonna do this?"

"Listen, don't ask me how to do this. You know how to do it, don't you?"

"I've never fucked a man."

"Well, just pretend he's a woman."

"But he's not a woman."

"Okay, do you need some help on this?"

"I don't want any help."

"Okay, how about this. I'm going to walk out. You do it. When you're done, knock on the door."

"What door?"

"That door right there, the one we just walked through."

"You gonna be over there?"

"I will be."

Ben wanted to see it, but realized as a voyeur he would be directly participating in it. He liked his status as an indirect participant, so he left. He walked down the hall, looking at the place where Henry had built a wall where there was once a door and proceeded downstairs.

Eddie then was left alone with Henry. Henry was out, wearing boxers and a t-shirt. Eddie walked around the bed a couple times, shaking his head like he was on speed.

"Man, oh man, this is disgusting."

It's hard to get excited looking at a guy. I mean, if you're gay, it would excite you -- but if you're hetero, it really doesn't.

He pulled down Henry's boxer shorts. He did it quickly, not slowly as Henry had done to Erica. He saw that Ben was kind enough to leave some hand cream. He took some hand cream, put it on his hand, he pulled his own pants down. He started to grease up his dick. He wasn't getting hard. It was soft.

He looked at this guy. He decided to put a little cream on Henry's cheeks. It was disgusting. It just wasn't happening. This guy was a guy and Eddie was a guy. His dick wasn't getting hard.

He walked over to the window and looked outside. He had a view of the pool area. Down there, Ben was using the net to clean off insects and small leaves from the pool. Ben looked relaxed walking around the pool, picking up a little here and a little there. He didn't realize Eddie was looking down at him.

Eddie returned. He saw his prey sprawled out. He tried to jack off a little bit more, tried to get a hard dick, but it just wasn't happening.

He returned to the window.

"Yo Ben, come on up."

Ben looked at his watch. It had only been about five minutes. Could it have happened that quickly? No way. He put the net down. He ran upstairs through the hidden door in the shower and then saw an uncompleted sight. He could see Henry had a shiny ass and the hand cream placed on it. He also could see there was no used condom anywhere. There was no condom wrapper.

Eddie was sitting there with his mouth closed, his pants up. He reached into his pocket, pulled out the $4,000 and handed it back to Ben.

"Can't do it, man. Sorry."

"What?"

"Man, the guy's a dude."

"Yeah."

"I can't fuck a dude. You gotta get some kind of gay guy. He'll do it. I mean, come on man, look at him. You want to fuck him? I don't want to fuck him. I'm looking over here. I'm jacking off. I'm trying to get excited. It's not happening and it won't happen. I'm sorry. I can't do it. Get me out of here."

Ben took the $4,000 back, shook his head but realized there was not much he could do about it. I mean, what can you do about human relations? If the guy's not going to get a hard dick with Henry, he's not going to get a hard dick. What are ya gonna do? What was Plan B?

He thought about what Eddie say: Get a gay guy. Maybe that was the answer. Yeah, that is the answer. Get a gay guy.

CHAPTER 63

THE SENSITIVE NON-RAPIST

Back at Poncho's place, Ben discussed his options with Eddie. Poncho was thinking the whole thing was rather humorous.

"Well, hey, the birds and the bees -- how about the birds and the birds or the bees and the bees -- they don't always get together, I guess, huh? Gee, Eddie, what -- you didn't get excited?"

"No, man. It wasn't cool. It wasn't happening."

"Hah. Well, what's next?"

"Listen, Eddie came up with a thought."

"Eddie? A thought? You got to be kidding me. He couldn't get a hard-on but you actually have your brain working? That's a first."

"I told him he needs a gay guy. I mean, I'm sitting here looking at this man, you know, and I'm just not getting excited. I mean, it's a dude. I don't want to do this dude," Eddie said.

"Okay, so yeah, we get a gay guy."

"Alright. So listen, Poncho, you know a gay guy that'll do it?"

"Hey listen, motherfucker. I don't hang out with gays."

"Don't get all rough with me. What are you, racist?"

"Racist? That's nothing to do with race. Fuckin' A, man, I just don't like gay people."

"Oh, it sounds like you're a little insecure about your manhood."

Poncho stood up like he was going to beat the shit out of Ben. Looks like Ben had touched a raw nerve.

"Okay, cool, man, cool. Don't worry. I'll find a gay guy. Chill out. You don't know one, fine. Eddie, how about you?"

Eddie took a similar pose at Ben, like he was going to beat the crap out of him for even suggesting he would know a gay guy.

"Alright, cool, cool. Don't worry. I'll find one. Thanks for trying, guys. I really appreciate it. Listen Poncho, I'll be back next week for some more Valium, okay?"

"No problem, man. Look, sorry I got mad."

"Hey, it's cool. Alright, guys."

Ben took two hundred dollar bills and placed them in Eddie's shirt pocket.

"This is for trying."

Ben drove home. He knew right where to go. You don't drive around looking for some gay hooker. Those days are long over. Instead, you go online. Piece of cake.

"Let's see, craigslist.com -- gay man under adult services."

He pulled up the website. Oh my goodness, there were all kinds of guys and the ads were just so obnoxious. Well-hung, ready for heat, call me for some meat.

"Oh, how about that guy?"

He opened up the picture.

"Yeah, look at him. Nice Hispanic guy, toned. Is that really him?"

It was like a male model turned hooker. You got to wonder with these internet sites whether everyone's full of crap or not -- but that was good enough. He called the guy.

"Hey, this Enrique?"

"It is."

"Got a project for you."

"I bet you do."

"Want to come by?"

"I'll come by. What's your address?"

Ben gave him his La Jolla address.

"Oh, upscale?"

"Certainly. When can you come?"

"I can leave right now. I'm about 20 minutes away."

"Come on by."

The man who went by the name of Enrique showed up 20 minutes later. First of all, he was about 5'1" and not even close to the buff dude that was on his Craigslist photo. That guy was tall, dark, handsome, buff, gorgeous. This guy was stubby, extremely average, not ugly but certainly not handsome. Looks like he hadn't showered that day so his hair was looking a little rough. He wasn't anywhere near as toned as the guy in the picture.

Ben looked at the guy and laughed.

"What's so funny?"

"Oh, I was just thinking, you know, you don't quite look like your photo."

"Oh, that's an old pic."

"Yeah, right. I suppose some years went by and you shrunk?"

"No, no. That's me, just a couple years ago."

"Yeah, like 10 years ago?"

"Hey man --"

"Okay, don't worry, don't worry."

"Okay, you want me or not?"

"Come on in."

He walked in.

"Listen, here's the deal."

They walked by the same mirror where Eddie had to look at his teeth and of course the gay guy had to stop and look at himself. He smiled, tilted his head, did a little modelling maneuver and thought about how gorgeous he once looked.

"Okay, let's go, let's go. Enough with the mirror."

Ben thought, *I'm taking that mirror down.*

They went upstairs.

"Hey, you don't fool around, huh?"

"Look, this isn't for me."

"What do you mean, it's not for you?"

"It's for somebody else."

"Oh?"

"Yeah, a friend of mine."

"Where's your friend?"

"Follow me."

They walked by the hallway where the door used to be into the near bathroom.

"We're going to do, like, a bathroom job here?"

"No, I've just got a little entryway here."

"Entryway?"

"Yeah, follow me."

They went through the shower, found and opened the hidden door.

"Please enter."

Enrique walked through into the den. At this point, Henry, though still on Valium, was conscious. Ben came in.

"This is Henry. Henry, meet Enrique -- your date."

"What do you mean, date, man? Oh man, I feel dizzy."

Enrique looked at Henry.

"Oh."

"Oh, you like this guy?"

"Yeah, he's cute."

"Wonderful, a match made in heaven. Okay, here's the deal. Enrique, you're going to do him."

Henry started to sit up.

"Oh, no, fuck, don't do this. I mean, come on."

"Hey, hey, look. This is the deal, asshole. What you did, you get."

Enrique was trying to understand what was going on here.

"You mean he doesn't want this service?"

Henry yelled out, "Fuck no. This guy's making you do it on me."

"Oh, that's terrible. Why would you do that?"

"Because he did it to my fiancée."

"He did what?"

"I raped his fiancée," Henry offered up.

"You raped his fiancée?"

"Yeah."

"But why aren't you in prison?"

"He was," Ben answered. "Motherfucker got released on a technicality."

"Hey, I didn't ask for that."

"Okay, but listen -- today you're going to get a little feedback from Enrique here."

Enrique had an issue with all this.

"Look, sex is a wonderful thing between two people in love -- or paying for it, whatever. But it's a beautiful thing. When it's forced, it becomes an ugly thing."

Ben rolled his eyes and shook his head.

"Look Enrique, thank you for this extremely interesting philosophical debate, but here's the deal. I'm going to pay you to fuck him, and you're going to do that. You know why you're going to do that? Because I'm going to pay you a whole lot."

"Oh, a whole lot? Like what?"

"Tell me your normal rate. What do you usually charge for this service?"

"Two hundred."

"Two hundred bucks?"

"Yeah."

"How about a thousand?"

"You know, it's not about the money."

"How about two thousand?"

"Hey look, just stop right there. It's not about the money. I mean, if someone wants to hire me I'll do them, no problem. I'll do them for $200 without any complaints. They can fuck me, I'll fuck them -- whatever they want to do, I'm here for that. But that's because they want it and I'm going to give it. It's consensual --"

"And let me guess. Don't say it -- it's beautiful."

"Yeah, it is."

"Okay, so today we're going to do something a little bit on the dark side."

"Yeah, but I don't wanna be dark side guy. I mean, I don't know what kind of fucked up deal you got here. You got this guy in your place. You're -- what? Keeping him here against his will? I mean, what is this shit? And now you want me to fuck him -- you want me to basically rape him. You want me to be your tool of revenge? Isn't that it?"

"Go to the head of the class."

Henry decided he would help things a little bit.

"Look, let me stop everybody right here. You know, Ben, I know what I did was wrong. I'm dealing with that, okay? At least I was until you took me prisoner. I had a therapist --"

"Oh, fuck the therapist shit. I don't go for that therapy bullshit. What you need is a hard dick up your ass."

"I'll do it. I owe Erica. I need to be accountable."

Henry started crying.

Enrique looked at Henry. He saw a crying man, a vulnerable man, a hurt man, a man trying to get rid of his evil demons, a man trying to make good on a crime he had committed, a man who was willing to be raped as part of a process of paying back his debt.

It brought Enrique to tears.

"That's the most beautiful thing I've ever seen."

He walked over and held Henry.

"Here."

He put Henry's head on his shoulder.

"You can cry on my shoulder."

He cried and cried. Enrique cried.

Ben just rolled his eyes. *Oh, great.*

Enrique then stood up.

"You're a very bad man. I don't know who you are or what you think you're doing here, but this is wrong and I'm not going to do it."

Enrique stormed out of the room, walked right to where a door used to be, smashed into the wall and realized it would go to another entryway through the shower.

Ben walked behind Enrique, locked the door behind him.

"Hey, look. Hold on. I got a little problem here."

"What?"

"The problem is, you now know something about me that I don't want anybody to know."

"Well, stupid shit, you shouldn't have brought me here then. I mean, hello. You didn't think I'm going to figure this out in, like, two fucking seconds?"

"So I don't want you to."

"Oh, you're going to hold me prisoner here now? You're going to have two prisoners? What, you going to have six pretty soon? It'll be like having puppies, man -- prisoner puppies. You better get your shit together here, buddy. Look, let me tell you something. I've been a hooker for seven years. I'm an outlaw. I live under the table. So you got shit on me. If I don't rat on you, you don't rat on me. How about that? Because I really don't give a shit. You take care of your issues with this guy, whatever. All I can tell ya is, I'm not going to participate in it. I am not going to be your tool of revenge. You're gonna have to find somebody else."

He walked through the front door.

Ben charged in front of him and blocked the front door.

"Oh, what? Are you going to kill me now?"

"Listen, I'm not going to fight you."

Enrique slapped Ben across the face like a girl.

Ben was not a fighter. The slap stinged him.

"You motherfucker."

Ben imagined for a second sticking the syringe that he had into Enrique's neck, filling him full of Valium, causing him to collapse -- but then what? Put him in the sea? Does he want a murder count now? He didn't want to go from aiding and abetting a rape to murder in the first or second degree, depending on how a psychologist would describe Ben's state of mind. The jury decision between a passion killing and a planned premeditated cold-blooded murder. He realized he really had no choice but to let this guy go.

"Okay, Enrique. I'll let that go. I'm sorry. I'm not going to block you. I'm going to trust you. You're not gonna rat on me. I'm not gonna rat on you. But here's the thing. It's a rather uneven deal because ratting out a hooker over a person keeping somebody as a prisoner and aiding and abetting a rape is like trading a pawn for a queen -- pardon the pun."

But still, as lowly as Enrique's crime was, it was his way of making a living. The good news, information that Ben didn't even know, was that Enrique had three prior convictions for prostitution. A fourth conviction would actually send Enrique to at least a six or nine month county jail term -- and county jail for a gay hooker can be a very unpleasant experience.

Enrique and Ben met eyes. Enrique put his hand up.

"I mean it, man. I'm not telling anybody. Just let me go and walk out of here, we'll be cool."

Ben opened the front door and let Enrique walk out. Enrique got in his car, drove away and left Ben's house, hopefully forever.

CHAPTER 64

NOW WHAT DO I DO?

Ben sat in his living room, puzzled. It simply was not enough to have Henry as a prisoner. He needed to get Henry raped -- and yet, there was no real way to do it. He had heterosexual men with the moral compass to do it who couldn't get a hard dick, he's had a gay guy too sensitive to bring himself down to that rude level.

He started to wonder.

"What I really need is a guy like Eddie into the body of a guy like Enrique." That's when the idea hit him. "Of course, a she-male. Why didn't I think of this before?"

He jumped up, went to his computer, went back to Craigslist, went down to the erotic services page, typed in she-male and up came a group of 12 listings.

These are men who have taken hormones to become women with cocks. They've got breasts. They're missing their facial hair. They've got toned shape. They've got hips. They've got it all. They're not petite. They still have their manly muscles. They weigh up to 175 pounds. Some of them haven't quite bridged the gap between male and female, and look entirely too male to even pass as a she-male. There should be a subcategory of male-shes, not quite a she-male.

But the idea here could possibly fit. A she-male with enough male in him could very well have the moral compass of a bad guy, with the hard dick of a gay guy that would at last do Henry. It was truly a match made in heaven.

CHAPTER 65

HIS NAME WAS CARLITA

He used to be Carl -- now it's Carlita. He thinks he's a woman -- not even close. The guy is a guy. He's got tits. Wonderful. Take some hormones, any guy can grow tits. This guy probably didn't quite understand that he didn't really look like a babe of a girl.

He thought he did when he showed up at Ben's place wearing those black stockings ready to be ripped off, heels -- oh God, even a black dress -- a wig for hair. It was a wig probably purchased at Walgreen's. But on top of everything else, this was a poor male-she, looking 75% male, 25% female -- perfect for Ben.

"Come on in. Carlita, huh?"

Ben hadn't had time to take down that darned mirror in his hallway. Of course, when Carlita walked by it, she had to stop and look at what she perceived to be a totally hot chick. This man trying to be a woman looked simply disgusting, but in a way that was perfect for Ben. After all, the last thing he'd want to do is give Henry the benefit of a totally hot looking female. Let's not give the guy a treat. Let's give him a beast.

"Okay, Carlita. Here's the deal. This is not for me. It's for a guy upstairs."

"Oh, somebody else is here?"

"Yes."

"Listen, if we're going to do two for one, I charge more."

"Oh, don't worry, hun. It'll just be one on one -- and you can go ahead and charge more."

"Oh?"

"What's your usual rate?"

"$200 -- but look, you gotta make a choice. Either you do me or I do you. It's not going to be both."

"Oh, a she-male with rules? We gotta sign a contract about this?"

"No, I'm just telling you if I do you, I just can't be done. It has to do with the way my asshole works."

"Oh. Don't worry, I don't need to know anything about how your asshole works. Let's go like this. Here's the deal. You're gonna do a guy. He's not gonna do you. So we're agreed -- two hundred bucks, you do the guy, right?"

"Yeah."

"I'll tell you what. I've got good news for you. I'm going to double it. I'm going to give you $400. In fact, I'm going to give you $500."

Ben counted the money out.

"One, two, three, four, five -- here you go, Carlita. Now follow me."

On the way up the stairs, Carlita tripped on her own heel. She was quite clumsy. Women have a way of walking so elegantly. This guy was basically a man weighing about 160 pounds -- couldn't quite traverse the stairs in his little heels. It didn't quite work.

Ben wanted to suggest that perhaps she take the heels off, but then again, he didn't want to be too presumptuous. It might upset Carlita's inner bitch. We wouldn't want that.

So Carlita, ever wanting to be the perfect woman, insisted on making the rest of the way up the stairs with her heels. To his/her credit, she made it up the rest of them without slipping. She brought her dress down a little bit, and proceeded to walk like a model would down the runway of Ben's hallway -- toe-heel, toe-heel.

Ben just shook his head. *Puh-leese, there are no cameras here.*

But Carlita was that kind of a man -- wanting to show his inner woman, his inner babe. Inside Carlita was a gorgeous woman. Unfortunately on the outside was a dude with tits.

Carlita followed Ben into his third attempt to get his revenge of Henry. They went by the hallway where there used to be a door, into the bathroom, into the shower, into the hidden door.

"Oh, this is so mysterious."

"Yeah, it is. It's like a mystery. Follow me."

They went in. Henry was lying in bed. Carlita immediately liked him.

"Oh, my."

She grabbed her dick, which was just hard in half a second.

Ben was thinking, *Wow, that's the quickest hard-on I've ever seen.*

"You want to see it?"

"Oh, no, no, no. Don't show it to me. Show it to him. He's the one that wants to see it."

Carlita put on a condom.

Henry watched, put his hand up to his forehead, and shook his head.

"Oh, God."

Carlita walked over.

"Hi, hun. How you doin'?"

Her low voice was not the least bit soothing to Henry. Ben waved Henry goodbye.

At last, Ben would get what he wanted.

Carlita took Henry by his hips, pulled off his shorts, applied some cream to her dick, applied some cream to his asshole, and shoved herself inside him.

Henry gasped out, "Ouch."

She grinned.

"First timer?"

She pumped and pumped until at last, she came.

Henry laid still, crying quietly. Carlita didn't notice. She removed the condom and placed it into a tissue.

She came out, her now-ripped stockings in the waste can and met a smiling Ben who was still in the bathroom -- as close as a voyeur could be without perhaps being a voyeur.

Carlita walked out and smiled without guilt. Carlita handed Ben a tissue with a used condom full of cum. Ben looked at it like a scientist, smiled, and threw it in the toilet.

He walked Carlita out to her car. Carlita put her hand on Ben's chest, which Ben quickly removed.

"Look, thanks for coming by. By the way, I may need you again, so let's stay in touch."

Carlita drove away and Ben smiled.

It was a good day for revenge. At last, Ben got some.

CHAPTER 66

THE EMPTINESS OF REVENGE

The thing about revenge is it turns you into the very monster that you're seeking revenge against.

Ben thought about this. Had he not become a rapist? Think about it for a second. You're angry at a rapist so you get the rapist raped. What does that make you? That makes you a rapist. Ben didn't like that. It angered him -- and in his anger, he became upset. He was upset at Henry for what Ben perceived as Henry's condition which created the circumstances whereby Ben felt the need for revenge. Ben was really pissed off. He had turned himself from a cool, intelligent, bohemian rich boy, top notch, Pulitzer Prize winning investigative journalist, to the lowly position of a rapist. What a decline in Ben's status. According to Ben's own process of rationalizing what he did, it was one thousand percent Henry's fault.

It wasn't enough. In his anger and his bitterness, having the she-male or male-she do Henry wasn't enough. It wasn't forceful. It wasn't by a stranger. It wasn't a taking. It didn't have all the elements of a true rape. It was a contracted rape. Basically, a hooker that did a guy.

He decided he wanted to find a way, a real way, to get Henry raped.

Ben was back online looking at the she-males. He got an idea. Of course, this would be how the crazy plan would play out. A heterosexual male would not rape Henry. A gay guy is too sensitive to do the rape. A she-male would do it, but it just seemed like it didn't count as a rape. So how to make Henry the victim of a rape? It involved combining all three of these near misses into one explosive triumvirate that would create, at last, Henry as a rape victim.

Ben called Carlita.

"I didn't expect to hear from you so soon."

"Carlita, got a question for ya."

"Okay."

"You're taking hormones?"

"I was off them for awhile."

"I see. Is that why you look so -- well, you know --"

253

"Well, I was a little skinnier before. I put on some weight. I got off the hormones. I go through this process because sometimes I really kind of want to be a man again."

"Here's what I want to know. The hormones you take --"

"Yeah?"

"To become a woman --"

"Yeah."

"Where can I get them?"

"You want to do that?"

"No, I don't want to do it. The guy you did --"

"Yeah."

"He's interested in that."

"That beautiful man?"

"Yeah."

"Oh, just leave him exactly how he is."

"No. We're going to change him a little."

"Okay."

"So where do I get them?"

"Oh, you're probably thinking you've got to go to some back alleyway and meet some dangerous man with a hood and hat --"

"Look, Carlita, just tell me where the fuck I can get them. Don't give me the drama here."

"Amazon.com."

"What?"

"Yeah, you can get them right there."

"I can get female hormones on Amazon.com?"

"Just plug in the search engine, female hormones."

"Hold the phone right there."

Ben had his laptop, went to Amazon.com, went to their search engine, plugged in "female hormones" and sure enough, there was a whole group of them for sale right on Amazon.

"Carlita, thank you. That's all I need."

He hung up the phone and typed in his first purchase of a three month supply of female hormones. The hormones were advertised as having the ability to turn a man into a woman.

CHAPTER 67

HENRY'S HORMONE HELL

Henry was still drugged up on his daily dose of Valium. Ben decided he'd keep it a secret. Instead of just telling him, 'I'm going to turn you into a woman,' he hid it from him.

"Hey Henry, I brought you something special today."

"Oh?"

"A milkshake."

Henry looked up and saw a vanilla milkshake. It had been quite awhile since Henry had a milkshake, so he drank it. What he didn't know was inside that milkshake was his first dose of female hormones. They don't take effect in a day or two days or a week or two weeks. It takes awhile.

Ben did something he shouldn't have done. He read the instructions -- one pill per day -- and instead, gave three. Exactly what side effects it would cause would remain to be seen, but it would certainly speed up the process.

Within three weeks, the first thing Henry noticed -- the hair from his leg and chest were all falling off. He didn't understand why. Nobody was telling him that he was taking the hormones. The other thing he noticed -- his dick was getting smaller. That was troubling, but then he thought, *Hey, my dick was what gets me in trouble all the time. If it would get smaller, maybe that's a good thing.*

As a month went by, he noticed in the mirror shapely hips, a rounder butt, woman-like tone, tender skin, smoother skin, absence of facial hair. He grew his hair longer. It used to be a shaved head. Now he had a pixie cut that would soon grow longer.

Ben saw the process of turning Henry into a woman. All told, it took three months. Oh my goodness, Henry was no male-she. She was a full she-male looking hottie -- nice, small breasts, tall, thin, lovely blue eyes, cheekbones, short hair, but looking good. She had a little biddy constricted cock and balls and was ready to walk the walk. Drugged up on Valium, stumbling out of the room, Ben decided to take Henry on her first tour of the town.

He placed one little device in her purse -- an iPhone. Why an iPhone? Because an iPhone has a GPS on it. This would be a way of tracking her if she ever disappeared.

Ben drove her down to a part of town famous for sports bars. Let's see what would happen between Ben, the newly-formed Henry, and a sports bar on a busy Friday night.

CHAPTER 68

THE RAPE OF HAZEL

Ben introduced Henry as Hazel, the involuntary transsexual -- though he left the latter part off the introduction. The men were impressed and so were some of the women. Most of the women in the sports bar were somewhat testosterone-laden or not exactly babes -- thickish, loud, beer-drinking, smoking, raucous and excited about each touchdown.

Hazel was drugged up on Valium. She was wearing sunglasses, a black dress, no stockings, simple heelless shoes. She looked quite nice and simple. She wasn't overdone, trying too hard to look like someone she wasn't. She looked like who she was -- a man who had been turned into a woman.

There was a football game on that she couldn't care less about. Everyone else in the bar was going crazy over it. She was the only one just sitting there, sunglasses on, hand on her head, looking like she was about to get sick.

Several of the men in the bar noticed this, of course. Men are good at finding a victim. These men had a sex offender inside of them just waiting to come out. Two of them in particular took notice. They walked over. They couldn't help themselves.

"Hey girl, you feeling okay?"

Hazel looked up at them.

"Yeah, I just feel tired tonight."

"Oh, okay. Can I get you something? You want a beer?"

They looked over at Ben. It was very impolite for a man to walk over to a man's date and ask to buy the date a drink, but Ben relaxed them.

"Hey guys, go ahead. Not my girlfriend. She's my cousin."

"Oh."

The men were happy to see they would not have a confrontation with Ben.

"But guys, let me tell you something. She doesn't drink so if you don't mind, if you're going to buy her something, get her a Sprite."

The guys were happy to oblige.

"Bartender, a Sprite for the lady."

The bartender was quick to comply. He brought over a Sprite, which Hazel was happy to receive.

One of the remnants of being a male quickly came out as Hazel did not use the straw -- instead, picked the glass up and took a rather impressive three gulps of that Sprite, emptying out all but one-third of the glass. The men watched with some trepidation over how this woman could suck down that Sprite. They were silent for a moment.

Just then, there was a score on the football game. The men ignored it. They were captivated by Hazel. They spoke with her. They talked to her. They bought her another Sprite. They couldn't keep their eyes off of her. They were mesmerized by her.

Hazel hardly had to say a word and hardly could say a word. She looked at the men up and down. In an odd change in her sexual identity, from Henry to Hazel, she became attracted to men. The female hormones in her, primarily estrogen, created a desire for a man, a desire for a cock. There was a new desire inside her, a feminine side that now eclipsed her male side. She did something that women do. She tossed her hair back. She stretched her neck.

Ben saw that this would all work out just fine. He turned to Hazel and explained, "I've got to go to the bathroom."

The men were happy to let Ben do whatever he needed to do to get the hell out of there. He left Hazel alone with these two men.

When Ben came back out of the restroom, Hazel's half-done Sprite was still there, but Hazel was not. Ben walked out and saw the men with Hazel near their pickup truck in the dark parking lot.

The pickup door was open. Hazel was inside. One man was standing on the outside. The other man was inside on the passenger side. Hazel was in between. They were having their way with her.

One was doing her from behind, while Hazel was sucking the other. It was a threesome that, from Ben's perspective, did not exactly look, shall we shall, nonconsensual. The men got a bit of a surprise when they put their hands down her pants to find not a pussy but a little soft dick, all shriveled up, incapable of getting hard. A lot of men might have run or beat the crap out of her or done anything other than stick their dick up her ass. But these two testosterone-laden alcohol-fueled men with sexual offenders resting inside of them -- on this night, they would not change their minds.

They would do her, and they did her for quite awhile, one in the ass, one in the mouth and then switching and doing her over and doing her over and finally ending and leaving her in the parking lot with a broken dress, a missing shoe and smeared lipstick. They drove away in their pickup truck.

Ben walked out, took Hazel into his Mercedes, and drove her back home. On the way back, it was quiet. Ben once again felt the eternal emptiness of a successful revenge.

CHAPTER 69

JEALOUSY

Not a word was spoken between Ben and Hazel on the way back to Ben's home.

He clicked the automatic entry button, which opened the wrought iron gate leading to his driveway, proceeded down to the driveway and parked his car by the front door.

He got out, unlocked her door, opened it like a gentleman. She got out and they proceeded into the house. She walked right by the mirror without glancing, even for a tenth of a second. She proceeded up the stairs, down the hallway, dutifully going into the bathroom through the secret door and into her room.

Ben, ever the jailer, locked the door behind her.

He went down the hall to his room, where he would lay and replay the evening's events.

Envy is about wanting what someone else has. Jealousy is about losing what you have. Ben was feeling doses of both.

Jealousy is a hard emotion. It can hit a person like a ton of bricks. It is a combination of envy, possessiveness and anger. It can often lead to violence, and often does. For some reason, we say green with envy, but filled with jealousy.

Ben was definitely filled with jealousy that night. It was an odd emotion for him because he hated Henry. How could you ever be jealous over someone you hate? Ben concluded he must not hate Hazel. Indeed, it was a predictable attraction to Hazel.

This is the boomerang impact on revenge attempts. People will think somehow that revenge is a good thing. They will make a plan to seek their revenge, but so often that plan will go awry. The revenge will become hollow, or in this case, it will miss its mark.

When revenge works, we can often be left with the guilty feeling of becoming the very monster that we were seeking to punish. The rape victim becomes the perpetrator of a rape. The murder victim's family becomes the next murderer.

When revenge misses its mark and the attempt to get back at a person doesn't work, all kinds of other emotions can flow. In this case, under the particular circumstances of Ben and Hazel, the emotion that flowed through every vein of Ben's body was that of jealousy.

He sat in his bed, looked up at the ceiling, eyes wide open -- angry, mad, bitter, with a cinematic emotion on a permanent replay button. The night's events would not leave his mind. The more he thought about it, the angrier he got.

Consider why our human psyche would produce quite naturally the emotion of jealousy. What good is it? Most people would say jealousy hurts. Let us not be so judgemental on Mother Nature, as she often totally knows what she's doing. Why, in the realm of specie protection, in the realm of the Darwinist theory of evolution, and the concept that we develop certain traits that overall assist the progress and dominance of our species, why would we quite naturally and commonly have the emotion of jealousy?

It may have to do with the benefit to family that arises from an overall possessiveness of one's mate. It is not good for the family to have a mate go off with another. It is better to keep the mate in the grips of a single relationship, and not allow the mate to stray. Because of this, Mother Nature has implanted an extremely strong and close to the surface emotion called jealousy, which can be easily triggered.

A woman's glance at another woman's man can cause incredible fury in that man's mate. That fury may be delivered to the other woman or the man, depending on how the insecure woman delivers her emotion.

But make no mistake about it, the emotion of jealousy is one millimeter below the surface of our psyche and is ready to pounce up and attack any kind of threat to our romantic or sexual relations.

The goodness in this can be seen from the standpoint of family protection and the overall concept that humans, unlike so many animals, were designed to be singularly mated, one on one, which jealousy helps to preserve.

Of course, this is just a theory. There may be other explanations as well. But let us begin any analysis of the emotion of jealousy from the premise that it is a good thing, and not a bad thing. Let us assume for a moment that Mother Nature does know what she's doing, and has given us the psychological tools in an overall effort to assist the development and progress of our species.

Whatever its theory, one thing that cannot be denied is that it exists in a big, bad way, and that evening existed through every corpuscle of Ben's body.

Paradoxically, Hazel didn't have even a gram of this emotion in her. She laid in her bed, looking out the small, barred window, wondering when, if ever, she would complete the sentence that Ben had imposed on her.

CHAPTER 70

WHAT CAN I DO FOR YOU?

The following morning, Ben woke up to a temporary relief. During his sleep, the replay on his memories of the night before had finally turned off. But upon awakening, unfortunately, it came back on.

He shook his head, got up, washed his face off and shaved. After he had completed this process, he decided to see about a more evolved approach toward Hazel.

A jealous man can choose between a Neanderthal approach, in the mode of clubbing the woman over the head, hoisting her over his shoulder and dragging her unconscious comatose body into his cave for a so-called relationship. Obviously the Neanderthal approach is not recommended by relationship experts, at least those that don't have knuckles dragging on the ground.

The other approach, the more evolved approach, is to compete for the affection of the woman. Women, like men, have options. They can have guy A, B or C. If you happen to be guy C and you want the woman, you need to compete for her affection by showing you are the best man for her. So put the club down, forget about dragging her to your cave, and think for a moment, as Ben did, *How can I win her affection?*

The true oddity in Ben's form of jealousy was that he wasn't really competing with anybody. This incident that made him so jealous was one that he had planned and delivered her into. The men that got her that night would not ever see her again, would never call, would never compete for her and were, in the classic sense of the word, a one night not even standing in a pickup truck. So Ben was competing, really, with nothing.

Like a man who was guilty of violence against a woman and would go out and get flowers and chocolates as though that would solve the problem, Ben would do the same -- but in his own special way, with his own special nuance.

He walked into Hazel's room and found her in bed with nothing but a bra and panties on. He could only see a spectacularly beautiful woman. Hazel's hair was near shoulder-length, brunette. Her skin was quite toned. The hormones brought about a very female ass, shapely legs and the kind of small breasts found on teenage girls. She was really quite a sight.

It had been awhile since Ben had been with a woman. He was a hot-blooded man and this sight quite naturally made him aroused. But he wasn't there that day for sex. He was there in an odd way for forgiveness and to attempt to sway Hazel into considering him romantically. Oh please, just say no.

So what do you suppose Ben would say or do to bring that about? As ill-advised as this path may be, like it or not, this was the path he was on.

"Hazel?"

Henry didn't respond.

Ben realized that she was still not used to the name.

"Henry?"

Now she responded, "Oh, yes."

"Listen, about last night --"

Hazel was groggy from the impact of the Valium.

"Yeah?"

"I'm sorry."

"You're sorry? For what?"

"Well, you know, for bringing you into that situation. I'm sorry."

"Oh, okay. Well, listen. You're the boss here. I'm your prisoner. Basically I'm here to submit to whatever you want me to do."

Ben put his hand out and waved it.

"You know, I'm done with that. I, I've decided to turn a leaf here. I'm done with that. You've done enough. You've submitted to enough and I gotta tell ya, I feel really crappy about what I've done."

"Oh? You want to talk about it?"

"I am talking about it."

"Okay, continue. You say you feel bad?"

Hazel was not without knowledge of the therapy of confession and the positive process it could bring about. She also knew full well that men and women would often avoid acknowledging what they've done. Rather than forcing a confession down a person's throat, it required a soft touch to coax it out of them.

"Why do you feel bad?"

Ben didn't even know he was dealing with a therapist. Ben had no idea what Hazel had been through at the prison. He had an image of prisoners out in the weight yard lifting weights and planning escapes or other murderous schemes.

But not so with Hazel. She had become quite an expert at therapy, and the wisdom behind therapy. She knew how to get to people and plied her skills onto Ben.

"What do you feel bad about, Ben?"

Ben looked up. They met eyes. She was quite beautiful, no question about it. She smiled. She was playing with him, but having a little fun.

"Go ahead, Ben. You can tell me. I mean, where am I going? I'm right here. I'm your prisoner."

"I'm angry at myself."

There, he said it. He had anger at himself.

"Good, Ben. Talk to me about your anger. What is it? Anger about what? Are you angry about what I did to Erica?"

"I am, but I have a different kind of anger now. I have an anger --"

He stopped. He looked out the window. He could almost say it.

Hazel decided maybe she could seduce it out of him a little. She saw he was looking out the same window she loved to look out, the window with the bars. She walked over to it in her bikini underwear, slender body looking out. She stretched. She arched her back, sticking those little teenager breasts out. She kicked her leg up.

"Oh, it's a beautiful day, Ben."

Ben was transfixed on this gazelle-like body. His mouth was open.

She turned. She walked to him, got down on her knees before him and told him, "Tell me, what are you angry about?"

She looked up with her blue eyes as he looked down at her.

"I'm angry about what I've done to you. I'm angry at myself for doing that. I'm angry that I would become a perpetrator of violence."

"Violence, Ben? Is that what you call it?"

"I would have become a perpetrator of sexual violence."

"Ben, go ahead and say it. You can say it. Sexual violence -- what is that? What's the word for it?"

Ben knew the word.

"Say it, Ben. You know what it is. Say it."

"I'm angry that I caused a rape on you."

Ben closed his eyes, put his hand to his forehead and looked away. He was so upset. Hazel was in a rewarding mood.

"There now, you said it. You said it."

She placed her hand on his chest, patted him. She brought her hand lower, down to his stomach, patted him some more on his stomach area.

"Do you feel better now, Ben? It's good to say it. Go ahead and come clean. Say what you did. Talk about the anger about what you did, what it does to you, how it fills you with a type of shame and anger. You don't want to be a rapist, do you, Ben?"

"No, I don't want to be a rapist."

He looked down and saw her on her knees with her willing mouth open, inviting him. He smiled.

"I don't want to ever do that again. And I'll tell you right now, that's over. We will never do that again. I'm so sorry for what I've done and I hope --"

"You hope what, Ben?"

Ben's eyes filled up with tears. The idea of asking a rapist for forgiveness seemed so perfectly reasonable at this point.

"I hope you will forgive me."

Hazel showed forgiveness, perhaps improperly, by holding Ben's half-hard cock and massaging it. She cupped his balls, gently tickling and scratching him in the area to the side and behind the balls. She stroked him lightly.

With her new female hormones, she liked cock. Henry didn't have any kind of homosexual tendency in him. Hazel was filled with estrogen, had a lovely body, beautiful skin tone, gorgeous hair and a hungry mouth.

She pulled his underwear down. His cock vibrated as it came out, twitching to and fro. She took it and placed it gently into her mouth. He responded by pumping into her. She remained stationary as he continued to pump. He took his hands around her ears, placed them gently around her head and did what is commonly referred to as a face-fuck -- back and forth, in and out. The sliding of the cock over her lips got her quite excited. That little cock of hers became hard. It had shrunk from its normal size to about one-third of that size, but a hard cock is still a hard cock.

Ben looked down to see the hard-on she had in her panties. It was an unusual sight, woman's bikini underwear and inside, a hard-on. Ben got excited naturally. There's this tendency to appreciate a hermaphrodite, a she-male: part man, part woman. In this case, she was about 90% female, but a very important 10% male.

She started stroking herself as he continued to go in and out of her mouth. It didn't take long. He ejaculated. She took it out of her mouth and let it come onto her palm. She stroked him as every molecule emptied. She stood and walked away from him, into the bathroom. She took the napkin, wiped her hand clean and brushed her teeth.

Ben stood there in the room. His legs were weak, shaking. His cock was wet but no longer hard. He had been taken by Hazel in a way that he had never expected to be taken. Wow, one thing was undeniable: it was good. It was exciting. It was really good, really exciting.

He followed her into the bathroom. She was now washing her face. He allowed her to finish. She turned to him.

"Do you feel better now?"

"Yes, much."

"Good. So what are you doing today?"

"Hazel?"

"Yes?"

"Is there anything I can do for you?"

Hazel walked by him. She didn't know if he meant a sexual thing or a nonsexual thing. He followed her back to the room. She got dressed. She put on a cotton dress, some flat shoes and proceeded to brush her hair.

"Oh, I don't know."

"Well, tell me because whatever it is, I'm going to say yes."

"Ben, you remember the night when you took me away from my house?"

Ben put his head down in shame.

"Yes, I do."

"Do you remember the struggle we had on my bed?"

"Yes."

"Do you remember what you crashed down on?"

"Yeah, I do. It was a guitar."

"That was my guitar. You probably didn't know this, Ben, but I built that guitar from scratch. I found the wood. I carved it. I sanded it. I chipped away at it. I developed a handle. The only part of that that I bought and didn't make were the ivory tips and the strings. Everything else was handmade by me."

Ben didn't know that.

"Oh, God. I had no idea."

He felt the part of his leg where a splinter from that guitar had entered. It had long since healed.

"I'm so sorry to have destroyed your guitar."

Hazel said no more about it, but Ben was not a complete Neanderthal. He understood where she was going.

"Hazel, is that what you want? You want a guitar?"

Hazel quickly flipped around, hair tossing in the moment. She smiled.

"Yes, Ben. I want a guitar."

CHAPTER 71

KNOCK AND TALK

Ben and Hazel were downstairs having a civilized breakfast of strawberries, coffee and croissants, European style. There was a knock at the door. Ben walked out. Hazel walked behind him. He opened the door. There were four deputies there. Oh, great. He noticed they were not carrying any kind of piece of paper.

"No search warrant, guys, no entry. It's that simple."

The deputy responded, "This is a knock and talk. We're not asking for entry. We're just asking to talk to you."

"Okay. Do I have to talk to you?"

"No, you don't. You can just close the door and ignore us."

"Very well."

Ben pushed the door closed, but one of the deputies put his boot in the doorway. Hazel was there. Ben introduced her.

"This is Hazel."

"Hi, Hazel."

Hazel, like so many feminine women, was a little bit goofy in front of a man in a uniform. She smiled, pushed her hair around.

"Good morning, officer," she said it in a tone that was pure flirt. The deputy smiled back and looked at Ben.

"So Ben, I guess you're moving on?"

"Don't start psycho-analyzing me. This is Hazel. She's at my house. Is there any other question you have?"

"Yeah, one question."

"Okay, go ahead. I'll answer it."

"Where's Henry?"

Hazel would not give Ben away. She had a very simple opportunity to do so right then and there. Perhaps it was due to the difficulty that she would have in convincing them that she was Henry. Henry didn't look anything like Hazel.

Ben gave a straightforward, completely false response, "I don't know."

"You don't know?" they asked.

"I don't know."

"Ben, we know you've got him."

"Look, you guys already searched the house before. I don't know whether a judge will give you another search warrant. I'm not letting you go through that again. It was very uncomfortable having you guys go through everything top to bottom here."

"There must be some place we missed. I'm sure he's here."

"Why? Why do you think he's here?"

"Because he's nowhere else."

"Well, maybe he's dead. Someone might've killed him and taken him out somewhere and you guys just haven't found the body."

"Ben, why don't you tell us where the body is? We want to know."

"Guys, I'm not saying anything further. Just do your job and find him. Don't rely on me to do your job. May I go?"

The deputy took his boot out from the door and the door closed. Ben walked over to a front window and watched as four deputy sheriff's cars made their way out of his driveway. At least for now, the coast was clear.

CHAPTER 72

THE WARDEN'S DAUGHTER

As the deputy drove away, he called the warden at the prison. The warden was in his car and answered on his cell phone.

"Warden? Deputy James here."

"Hey, thanks for getting back to me. Tell me."

"Well, we went there again. Looks like Ben's got a new girlfriend."

"Interesting. Tell me about her."

"Very beautiful, brunette, blue-eyed, princess-looking. Really quite a ravishing doll. I get the idea the relationship is rather new."

"Why do you think that?"

"She was kind of flirtatious with us. I think a girl that was really with him would not have acted in that manner."

"You sound like such an expert on flirtatious women."

"Let's just say, been there, done that."

"Okay."

The warden continued driving to his suburban home. He entered the front door and was greeted by a golden retriever, bushy, overweight and named Sandy.

"Hello, Sandy."

Sandy jumped up on him -- the only beast on the planet that this warden would ever allow to jump him. Then the light of his life came out, his 14-year-old daughter Lilith, named after his former wife.

"Daddy, daddy."

She ran and gave him a big hug.

In the background, there was one of her favorite songs by Evanescence, "Bring Me to Life."

The single dad warden, his lovely daughter Lilith and their bushy dog Sandy remained together as the song played.

CHAPTER 73

THE GUITAR CENTER, SAN DIEGO

Ben and Hazel got into his dad's Mercedes. Hazel was wearing a lovely dress and sunglasses. She had a small purse and was extremely excited. She loved the outdoors. She was a prisoner getting a weekend release. But mostly she liked having her brain back, as Ben had agreed no more Valium shots. She had about a three day hangover, which was now released. She turned to Ben and blew him a kiss.

"Thank you for getting me off the Valium. I hate that shit."

She brushed her hair, which moved with the wind. She was thinking clear. Today was the beginning of a new phase in her life.

Ben drove her to downtown. She looked pretty good in a slate gray Mercedes. They drove down to the Guitar Center store, which was in a shopping mall. They walked in. Nobody really noticed them. Ben looked like a bohemian guy with his chick. The only assumption was that Ben was the guitar player and Hazel was his roadie.

Hazel looked to the back wall and saw the candy that she couldn't resist -- a wall of guitars. She walked at a man's speed, right by the front cash register, right by a bunch of amplifiers directly to that wall. Ben had a hard time keeping up with her.

She studied the guitars like a scientist and found the one she wanted. There was no mistaking it. It glowed out from the others. It had silver metal on the front, making it look bullet-proof. It had a handle. It was made by Fender Stratocaster, and had the impressive price tag of $6,200. She pointed up to it. She was on one foot and on the tiptoes of another, pointing up to the high guitar.

A salesman came over.

"Can I help you, ma'am?"

She continued pointing.

"That one."

He looked up and he looked at her.

"You know how to play that?"

"Try me," she smiled.

The salesman could only say yes to that. He got a small ladder, brought it over to the area by the guitar wall, climbed up it and removed the $6,200 Fender silver-plated guitar and handed it to Hazel.

Hazel put it in her hand. It was like a mother whose lost baby had finally been returned. She cradled it, touched it, felt it. She didn't play a note yet. She just held it. A tear came to Hazel's eye.

Ben had no idea what he was in for. He didn't know if Hazel was just a little hobbyist guitar player or some kind of majorly talented person. But he had a little hint. If you can build a guitar, you probably knew how to play it.

The salesman looked at her holding the guitar. It seemed like an hour, but it was only a couple of moments. It was a long time for that kind of silence.

The store, meanwhile, was quite busy. They had amplifiers, guitars all over, all kinds of accessories. In one room they had the amplifiers set up with a drum set right there and a microphone. Hazel easily gravitated into that room. There was a man in there playing beautifully on a set of electronic drums.

Hazel walked in. There was an amplifier with a cord. She walked up to a foot pedal, removed her shoe and put her foot directly on it. The man playing the drums, out of some kind of musician to musician respect, stopped. He put the sticks down. He was captivated by her look -- the hot girl about to do what? Belt out a song? Play the guitar?

Ben had no idea what he was about to hear, nor did anyone else in the store.

Hazel started right after she plugged the guitar in. She played the intro reverberation to a song that not many recall. It was a song that came out in the early 1970s, but it was a song that meant a lot to Hazel. It was a song about the endless quest for forgiveness, the desire for forgiveness, and how attaining forgiveness can take a million years and then some. It was a song that had connected with the youth of the early '70s, as so many of them sought redemption and forgiveness from their own failings. There was a connection that brought literally millions of new fans together, to adore coming out of nowhere a completely unknown band by the name of Robin Trower, who played an earth shattering song by the name of "Bridge of Sighs."

That day, Hazel would play it in a way that caused mouths to open, drums to stop, and the store to come to a halt as she began singing the earthly, soulful blues tune. People from outside the store came in. Within a matter of moments, she had a crowd of about 200 people listening.

The guy on the drums picked up and played drums. Hazel hadn't been much a singer before as Henry. There was something about his voice that wasn't so good. He was a tremendous guitarist, but his voice just wasn't right -- but with his new hormones, he could now sing half man, half woman, and was able to belt out these words in a mesmerizing, captivating voice that literally stopped the shopping center.

Bridge of Sighs
By Robin Trower
[Used with permission]

The sun don't shine
The moon don't move the tides,
to wash me clean
Sun don't shine
The moon don't move the tides,
to wash me clean
Why so unforgiving and why so cold
Been a long time crossing Bridge of Sighs
Cold wind blows
The Gods look down in anger,
on this poor child
Cold wind blows
And Gods look down in anger,
on this poor child
Why so unforgiving and why so cold
Been a long time crossing Bridge of Sighs

Hazel grinned as the drummer grinned back. She appreciated his backup. He smiled.

"Do it again."

This time, on this second shot, she would sing it even better. She would play it even better. One of the shoppers who had wandered in, a teenage girl opened up her iPhone's video camera to film Hazel's concert. Hazel would become known to literally tens of thousands of youth.

The video clip was uploaded onto YouTube and played by kids all over, wondering who this mystery woman was, where she got her voice, and what had she done in her quest for forgiveness. They knew that nobody could sing that song that way unless they were seeking forgiveness.

One of those girls listening away and thoroughly enjoying the YouTube video was the warden's daughter, Lilith. She smiled and rocked and swayed with Hazel. She played an air guitar as Hazel played, and played it over and over again.

This song would have been completely unknown to the warden himself, had it not been for the fact that Henry had sung it for him before. It was a different voice, but within that different voice, there was a DNA imprint that came to the warden forensically. The warden stopped. He rarely would listen to his daughter's music. He had come to terms with some of it, enjoyed some it, disliked most of it, but this song hit him like a raw nerve. Not because he enjoyed it, but because he knew in his own quest to find Henry that this song was along the path.

He came into his daughter's room.

"Hun?"

The daughter was lost in song. He was surprised to see on the computer screen a woman singing. It sounded like a man. He saw how his daughter's agility blended perfectly with the movements of Hazel. She was lost in the emotion of the song.

But it couldn't be Henry. That was a woman. But make no mistake about it, there was no one else on this planet who could sing this song that way. He remembered it. Henry sang it to him. Though Henry had an acoustic guitar at that time and sang in a different voice, there was a level of oneness between that voice and that song that no other musician could achieve. It was Henry.

The warden stood in front of the computer screen, blocking his daughter. He found the volume control and turned it down. Lilith became angry.

"Sorry, hun. I gotta ask ya -- this is important. Where did you get this?"

"YouTube."

"Okay, YouTube -- but I mean, where is it from?"

"Guitar Center at the Galleria Shopping Center downtown."

"Someone filmed this down there?"

"Yeah, it was uploaded from their iPhone."

"How do you know all that?"

"You can see it in the comments right there."

"Can you find that poster?"

"No, but you can send her an email."

"Wait a minute. This person was playing this song in a shopping center right downtown in San Diego?"

"Dad, why do you care?"

"I think she is someone I've been looking for."

Now Lilith was interested.

"You know her? Dad, I would love to meet her."

The warden was searching for words.

"Talk to me, dad," Lilith interrupted. "Let's go see her. If you know her, take me to her. I want to talk to her."

"So do I."

"Okay, let's go."

They got into his car, and proceeded to the Guitar Center at the Galleria Mall.

CHAPTER 74

FISH OUT OF WATER

The warden and his daughter drove straight from Calapatria to San Diego, a matter of a several hour car drive.

Lilith kept questioning her dad relentlessly.

"What is it, daddy? Where are we going?"

"I told you, we're going to go to the mall. We're going to check it out."

"But why? Why do you care? I don't understand."

He decided to come clean.

"Honey, I think that woman is actually a man. I think she was a former prisoner of mine, and I think someone is keeping her or him against his will."

Lilith was not expecting that answer.

"Wow, daddy -- are you on drugs?"

The warden realized how ridiculous it all sounded, but he also knew what he knew. He knew that Henry had gone missing, and he knew that whoever was singing that song was either Henry or somehow mysteriously connected to Henry.

"Bear with me, Lilith."

They drove to the shopping mall and entered the Guitar Center. Here was a fish out of water: the warden in a guitar shop. He was as straightlaced as they come, former military, and was now surrounded by a bunch of super cool dudes strumming on guitars. He reeked of law enforcement.

The other shoppers immediately noticed. Though his daughter was a little on the hip side, he was in another world. The sales guy approached him.

"Officer, can I help you?"

The warden smiled. "That obvious, huh?"

The salesman was polite. "Oh yeah."

The warden explained, "Well, you're almost right. I'm a peace officer, but I'm not a police officer."

The salesman was curious. "Oh, let me guess. Sheriff?"

"Nope."

"FBI?"

"No. Okay, you want to stop guessing?"

The salesman gave up. "Yeah, maybe I better."

"Warden."

"Warden?"

"Yeah."

"As in --"

"As in prison."

Now he was feeling curious. "Oh. And what, you're a rocker?"

The warden answered, "No."

"Oh, you're buying a guitar for your daughter."

"No. Are you done guessing?"

"Yes, I think I'll stop guessing."

"I want to know about something."

"Okay."

The warden asked his daughter, "Honey, can you show him?"

"You guys got a computer?"

"Yeah."

She went to the computer, brought up YouTube, searched, found the video and played it. The salesperson smiled.

"Oh, yeah. That was pretty cool, huh?"

"Yeah, tell me about it."

"That gal was here yesterday -- unbelievable. We've never had so much business in the store since. Look at the place."

Indeed, there were many people in the store shopping for guitars and drugs. It was a good time for Guitar Center.

"What can I do for you about that?"

"I want to know where she is."

"Oh, okay."

Lilith turned.

"I would love to meet her. She just seemed so hot and so cool and I want to know her. Can you help us?"

Normally they would never allow such an intrusion into a customer's private affairs, but there was something inviting about the cool daughter and the uptight warden. This salesperson couldn't resist the notion of bringing them all together. He walked to the invoice tickets from the day before, and thumbed through them. He knew the guitar she had purchased. It was the same guitar that was being played. It was a rather unique guitar, not the kind that sold every day.

"Okay, here it is. Yes, they bought this yesterday. It was purchased by Ben Nightingale. He paid cash. Here's his address, right in La Jolla."

The warden took a look.

"Hun, can you write that down?"

His daughter took out her cell phone and wrote it onto a text message. She sent the text to her father's phone. His phone vibrated. He brought it up and there it was, the address.

"You want directions, dad?" She quickly went into her GPS and entered in the address. "What's the address of this store?"

The sales guy gave it to her.

They would arrive at Ben's house in half an hour.

CHAPTER 75

CATATONIC AND TELEPATHIC

There is a theory that people with disabilities often receive a corresponding enhancement in some other ability: The blind person that can hear five times as well. In the case of Erica, she was a vegetable with a quiet brain, seemingly doing nothing. People still don't know what goes on in the mind of a person in these so-called vegetative states. Are they really "brain dead" or are they just overtaken by some type of physical paralysis and still highly active mentally?

Yet she received a new ability: telepathy and its near cousin, remote viewing. This condition will permit a person to see things out of their line of sight, to hear things well out of earshot, and to receive communications from others through silence.

There are quite a few reported cases where a mother suddenly wakes up in the middle of the night at the exact time when one of her children has become endangered, such as being in a terrible automobile accident. They just know something terrible has happened. They don't know what. They don't know where. They don't know how, but they have this feeling.

Then there are those who can actually see it. There are those that are elsewhere in between of two extremes. Erica was one of those in betweens. She couldn't see it, she couldn't hear it perfectly, but it was way more than just a feeling. It wasn't just a concept; it was specific, concrete and hit her like a ton of sand.

The doctors would have no idea what would finally awaken her. The truth was, it was her own sense of loss, the loss of Ben. She knew he was being taken by another woman. She knew he was being taken by another woman who had moved into the very house in the photo on the table in her room.

For the first time since the night of her rape, Erica did something that appeared to be consciously driven. She picked up the photo. She touched it with her hands. There was glass on top of it. She put her index finger around it. She made her index finger go into circles and then into lines and then into diagonals. She touched every molecule of that glass. She wanted to get closer. She removed the back of the frame, removed the photo -- being careful not to scratch it, tear it or bend it. She held it like you would hold a mouse's tail, dangling that mouse in front of you.

The photo looked so real to her. She started to hallucinate what was going on in that photo. She saw an image, an image of Ben with Hazel. Hazel looked positively gorgeous walking through the house, wearing a black dress and heels. They looked like they were going somewhere.

She followed Hazel as she walked down to the living room and stopped by something that she was not expecting to see -- Hazel's guitar and an amplifier.

Ben was behind her with car keys. It looked like they were going somewhere. Hazel was picking up the guitar. She held it in her hands. She looked so strong. She held it like a man.

She did not see the path of transformation of Hazel from a man into this woman. She did not have the slightest clue that this new woman taking her man, taking her house, taking her life was also the man who had raped her. It was a second time destruction of her life, only she didn't even know it. She thought this woman was a first time taker of her life and she wasn't going to allow it.

She placed the photo down onto the table.. She got up on her own, and walked around. There was a small window in her door. Erica looked out that window -- those cobalt blue eyes, so mystical, so unearthly, peered out into the hallway of this antiseptic asylum. She was searching for help, searching for someone who would realize that at long last, she was ready to leave.

There was no one in the hallway. She looked up and down and around. For the next hour, she went out there again and again to the window, looking for someone -- searching and hoping, but no one would come. She banged on the door. The door was made of a special kind of pad on the inside to prevent the very occurrence that she was trying to make happen: the sound of someone beating on the door.

The asylum did not want to hear endless banging on the door. They placed padding in these rooms. A patient could pound on that door all they wanted, but wouldn't make a sound.

She saw the chair in her room. The chair leg might be able to break through that glass. They had left the chair in her room thinking there was no way she would ever pick it up and use it. Most of the other people in this place didn't have a chair for that very reason. The one point of vulnerability she found in this whole ultra security system was that little square of glass on the padded door, and the steel leg of the chair by her table.

She picked up the chair. She had a look of want, of desire, of self-protection, of the kind of motivation that nature puts in us. She was a force of nature. She was a hurricane. She was a tornado. She was an earthquake. She was a forest fire. She was regenerating. She was creating life. There was nothing any human could do to stop her room length charge at that little window.

If she had lived during the times of the Renaissance when there was jousting, where people would ride on a horse and try to slam the other off the horse with a pole, she would have done well.

She showed the exact same skill set of riding on a horse and sticking someone in the chest with a pole, by charging that small square of a window with the chair leg in front of her. She held the chair above her head level. She charged the window with a possessed look -- saliva-filled mouth, tense arms, white knuckles, fingertips wrapped around the chair arms. This would not take two takes, three takes or four takes. The first time would be it.

The chair leg SMASHED through that little window, sending the glass forward into that previously antiseptic hallway, into pieces.

The sound of the glass hitting the floor was not that impressive. It alone would not have alerted anyone. What alerted everyone was the fact that these doors and that glass are connected to an extensive security system. Once that glass shattered, the security system was ignited into action. The alarm bells rang, the noise was huge. It wasn't just a fire, it was a far worse danger -- the danger of a psychotic person on the loose.

Only this time, at long last, a person was actually coming out of their psychosis. This was a sane person coming loose -- perhaps even more dangerous. A sane person bent on saving what was left of her life, bent on an idea that no new woman would take her Ben away, would take her home away, would take her life away. That period of loss was coming to an end. It was now time for Erica to stand up, to come out of this asylum and reclaim her life. That is, if these men in the white suits would let her.

CHAPTER 76

CAN I SEE YOUR YOU-KNOW-WHAT?

The warden and his lovely daughter Lilith arrived at Ben's house just about the time the men in white suits were strapping poor Erica down to her bed. It would be impossible for Erica to explain to them that she was healed, she was okay, she could be released, everything was fine -- *just let me go; I'm going to be okay.* Forget about it. They would shoot her up with a cocktail of drugs, far more powerful than whatever it was that Henry had given her. It knocked her out like a light, and kept her down for about 12 hours.

The doctor saw the undeniable physical evidence -- there was a photo removed from a frame, conspicuously laying on a table. There was a chair top sided by the door and there was woman who, before this day, wouldn't lift a finger, wouldn't even get up to pee -- but yet here she was, studying a photo, charging the chair and breaking the window. The doctor looked at the window, fixed the chair, looked at the photo, looked at the empty frame, looked at the back of the frame and looked at the ultimate clue of wellness -- the still body of Erica.

The warden and his daughter were at Ben's front door. The warden looked positively like law enforcement. What was his undercover excuse for being at Ben's home? He had a great excuse -- his daughter.

Ben answered the door.

"May I help you?"

"Hi. I hope I'm not disturbing you."

Ben saw another [unreadable] and became defensive.

"Well, that depends. What are you here for?"

"This is my daughter, Lilith."

"Hello."

"She saw, I believe, somebody who lives here on a YouTube video."

Lilith spoke, "It was awesome. The guitar was out of this world. I loved her. I would give anything to meet her, to say hi to her. Is that possible?"

Ben smiled. Oh boy, what had he created? A mentor to young girls? This was an involuntary transsexual turned mentor to young girls. What's the downside of that? Who knows? Ben realized that being rude right now would not be the proper course.

"HAAAAAZEL!" he yelled out.

Hazel walked up quickly. She was wearing a black dress and heels. Wow. She looked awesome. Even the warden was hit a little by her presence. Hazel was movie star quality, the sort that you could never find on Gilligan's Island.

"Hi, you must be --"

"I'm Hazel. Nice to meet you."

She shook Lilith's hand, then the warden's.

The first thing the warden noticed was that the grip on that hand was a little stronger than he had expected. He looked up at those eyes and had this huge question in his mind that he could not utter. *Can I see your you-know-what?* He wouldn't ask it. He would think it. He would plan it. So how could he possibly make that question a reality?

The warden took his glasses off and studied Hazel's eyes. They were Henry's eyes, but the warden couldn't recall them. The reality was, back at the prison, they would study the paperwork endlessly. They would know the person's docket, his jacket, his C-file (as it's called) and all the crimes that person has committed, all his probation violations, all his parole violations, all his in prison violations. They would know it all, but they wouldn't know the man. They wouldn't stare into his eyes, look into his soul or learn who he really was. They knew him by his paperwork only. Had Hazel been wearing her prison C-file on her little black dress, the warden would have been in a position to know that was Henry.

The one piece of Henry that still existed, unchanged by Ben, was Henry's eyes -- blue, scintillating -- they were exactly the same. But the warden didn't know that. Wouldn't know it, but could have known it. Perhaps there was a lesson there. Whomever you are dealing with, look at them in the eyes and know them.

Hazel knew very well who this man was. Here was the interesting facet of her existence. If she screamed out right then and there, help me, help me -- I'm a prisoner of this evil man who's changed me from a man into a woman -- please take me away from him -- save me from him -- give me my freedom -- what would the warden do?

The warden had already been suspicious that maybe that's exactly what was going on. The warden would have believed her 1000%, and probably would have taken Hazel and gone somewhere where he could ask the question, please show me your you-know-what.

But Hazel didn't do it. She didn't cry out for the warden's help. Why not?

CHAPTER 77

SERENDIPITY

Serendipity is the accidental discovery of something. It can be a thing, such as the Grand Canyon. You might be looking for something else and stumble upon it. It also can be a scientific breakthrough, such as the invention of the telephone when Alexander Graham Bell voiced the first telephonic transmission, 'Come here, Watson, I need you,' during which the phone was discovered.

Or it can be, as often is the case, a scientific breakthrough. Something that could never be solved is solved. The way the discovery is made is not out of an intent to solve the problem. Instead during the process of examining some other completely unrelated issue, a discovery can drop.

A great example of this is the pill, so famous now, called Viagra. Nobody hired a bunch of scientists to figure out how to change or solve the problem of erectile dysfunction. Instead, scientists were hired to solve a blood flow problem for heart attack victims and other heart diseases. That project resulted in a rather odd discovery -- that blood flow through the lower abdomen could solve the problem of erectile dysfunction. Viagra was born, not because they tried to solve ED, but because they accidentally stumbled upon it.

Which brings us to Hazel and the statement of a judge made in open court on the issue of sexual offender therapy: "It never works."

It's a sad reality. We should probably never say never, but when it comes to sexual offender therapy, sadly, the word may be correct. It may be a DNA issue. It may be a gene issue. It may not be a behavioral issue. Whatever it is, it is a fact that the rate of recidivism among sexual offenders is in the 90th percentile. Perhaps if all violations were reported, it would be an even 100%.

Here was a serendipitous discovery made by Ben and Hazel. If you transform the male rapist into a she, she will no longer want to rape. Hazel knew it, but Ben didn't know that Hazel knew this.

Before, not a day would go by when Henry didn't have some idea, some plan to do something terrible. He would plan, he would plot, he would seek out a victim. He would hunt them. There were more than 1,000 attempts by Henry where he got a hold of himself at the end and walked away without committing the violence.

There are two known occasions when he connected -- with the veterinarian and with Erica.

But one thing Henry knew, and he knew all too well, was he was possessed by his desire, his drive and need to take a woman against her will. The therapy regimen, though good and well thought out, would not assure a complete cessation of these thoughts, of these desires, of these drives and these occurrences. That was the sad truth and Henry knew it. He knew when he left prison. He was the first to say he wasn't ready. He didn't know enough. He hadn't practiced enough. He could re-offend.

Inside Henry was a good guy. He truly did not want to re-offend, and also a smart guy that knew he couldn't control it. There was an impulse. There was some kind of genetic DNA disposition within him that he couldn't control.

Now that he'd become Hazel, amazingly, he never had the desire to take a woman, to pull up her dress and insert himself into her, pump back and forth. Those images never appeared. They were gone.

Hazel thought about it, and figured out that just as Erica was on a path to reclaim her life, Henry reclaimed his life in the form of a woman -- and as this woman, named Hazel, he lost the need, the want to ever rape another woman again.

Release the Demon
By Hazel Emerson

Someone help me.
There's a demon in me,
that won't set free.

Release this demon in me.

Points on his head,
razors on his teeth.
eyes of red;
Arrow on his tail.

He makes me fail;
He makes me fail.

I listen to what he says.
He always gets his way.
Every night, every day.

I can be a good man,
without this demon.

Can't do it alone,
he's in my bones.

Someone help me.
There's a demon in me,
that won't set free.

Release this demon in me.

CHAPTER 78

TWELVE HOURS LATER

Erica was coming to. She was strapped down in a chair with those leather belts at her wrists, at her upper arms, her ankles and one around her waist. She could not move an inch.

The doctor had given orders before, "The minute she awakens, call me."

The men in the little white coats, if nothing else, were obedient to the doctor.

"Doctor McNally."

"Yes, is she up?"

"She's up."

"Okay, I'll be right there."

He came storming down the hallway. Not just walking, running. This was, to him, a revelation of medical science. Something, God knows what, had caused Erica to come alive again.

At the same time, and given to Erica telepathically, Hazel had agreed to play a song for the warden's daughter. It was a beautiful song that had captured many. It was one by a group called Evanescence, called "Bring Me to Life."

"Bring Me To Life" by Evanescence
[Used with permission]

How can you see into my eyes like open doors
Leading you down into my core
Where I've become so numb without a soul my spirit sleeping Somewhere cold
Until you find it there and lead it back home

(Wake me up)
Wake me up inside
(I can't wake up)
Wake me up inside
(Save me)
Call my name and save me from the dark
(Wake me up)
Bid my blood to run
(I can't wake up)
Before I come undone
(Save me)
Save me from the nothing I've become

Now that I know what I'm without
You can't just leave me
Breathe into me and make me real
Bring me to life

(Wake me up)
Wake me up inside
(I can't wake up)
Wake me up inside
(Save me)
Call my name and save me from the dark
(Wake me up)
Bid my blood to run
(I can't wake up)
Before I come undone

(Save me)

Save me from the nothing I've become

Bring me to life

(I've been living a lie, there's nothing inside)

Bring me to life

Frozen inside without your touch without your love darling only you are the life among the dead

All this time I can't believe I couldn't see

Kept in the dark but you were there in front of me

I've been sleeping a thousand years it seems

Got to open my eyes to everything

Without a thought without a voice without a soul

Don't let me die here

There must be something more

Bring me to life

(Wake me up)

Wake me up inside

(I can't wake up)

Wake me up inside

(Save me)

Call my name and save me from the dark

(Wake me up)

Bid my blood to run

(I can't wake up)

Before I come undone

(Save me)

Save me from the nothing I've become

(Bring me to life)

I've been living a lie, there's nothing inside

(Bring me to life)

Before Hazel had turned into Hazel, when she was Henry, she could play excellent guitar, but her singing wasn't so hot. The hormones now had changed her voice. It was a combination she-male male voice that came out like a bird. It would stop you in the middle of a crosswalk, even with two semis coming from either direction.

Erica awoke with her cobalt eyes wide open to this song. She became doubly worried as she saw Ben in this remote viewing session, the warden and the warden's daughter, Lilith. Any person who could make this kind of music would have a competitive edge over Erica. Erica was, at this point, superhuman.

Erica had her own ability of being, literally, a dead person who had awoken. This awakening would create in her a new kind of writing style, a new kind of ability. Before, she had written about angst, the anger developing between a mother and daughter who were filled with expectations of one another, expectations that were never realized. She wrote books that had found their audience in that core belief system of mothers and daughters who had wanted so much and had received so little. The good news for her publisher was that there were many out there in that category.

But now, as Erica would rise up, she had a newfound super ability and Ben, being a writer himself, would see it in a nanosecond. As much as Hazel could mesmerize in her singing and her guitar, Erica could do the same in a new stratosphere of writing ability -- but before she could do that, she would have to get these leather straps off her wrists, off her ankles, off her waist. That's where the good Doctor had to help.

"Hello, Erica. Welcome back."

"Hello, doctor."

The doctor saw it right away -- the tone, the language, everything. This was no deranged human.

"How are you feeling?"

"I'm feeling tied up."

The doctor couldn't help but laugh.

"Erica, I saw that you were looking at the picture over there. You want to tell me about that?"

"That's Ben's home."

"Oh, okay. Your former fiance?"

The engagement ring was not removed by Erica. It was removed by one of the men in white suits. As standard protocol, you do not allow asylum patients to wear any kind of jewelry.

"Erica, I need you to tell me if it's safe to let you have the ring."

"Well, doctor, look at that frame over there."

The frame was unbroken.

"Yes, but look at what you did to the window."

"Sorry about that, doctor, but no one was paying attention to me. I was trying to get your attention. Did it work?"

"Oh, yes, it worked."

"So your first reaction, as I finally woke up, was to fill me full of drugs, to put me back down under?"

Doctor McNally took his glasses off.

"It was the wrong decision, no question about it."

Shoot and then ask questions 12 hours later? No. He should have just restrained her, asked her questions, figured out where her head was at and then gone through a deep therapeutic series to determine if she was doing okay. Instead, they just shot her full of drugs. She was humming the song by Evanescence.

Dr. McNally asked her, "Ben has a new girl?"

Erica knew, "He does."

"How do you know?"

"Because I can see her. I can hear her."

Erica's voice was nothing even close to Hazel's. There was this connection between the two voices. What Hazel sang, Erica heard. Dr. McNally misinterpreted it as evidence of a continuing psychosis; some kind of hallucination, a delusion. That's what he would write in his report. The last thing he would consider writing would be something like, `patient has newfound ability to engage in telepathy and remote viewing.' That's not in his science book, but that was exactly what Erica was doing.

She would remain, belts wrapped around her wrists and ankles, surrounded by men in white coats and a doctor that had unfortunately misdiagnosed her as having psychotic delusions.

Hazel was mesmerizing Ben with incredible music, music that tortured Erica. She knew Hazel was stealing the love of her life. If Erica could get out of that room, she could win Ben back. She had the power of words, that once delivered to Ben, would win him back, if only they would let her go.

The warden's daughter found a new mentor in Hazel. Lilith would become a guitar student. The warden's daughter, her dream was to be the greatest musician ever. A typical goal of a young person, but with the guidance of Hazel, who knew? Maybe it would happen. The warden's goal? To determine if Hazel was really Hazel and not Henry. He was happy that his daughter would take up this undercover operation. This would give him plenty of access to Hazel.

Hazel, in the throes of a betrayal bond, stuck to a man who had violated her, who had kidnapped her, who had drugged her and who had turned her into someone she wasn't -- a new person, a female -- all against her will. She was the involuntary transsexual. We read about betrayal bonds all the time. Abused wives continue to go back to their husbands. Cheated on husbands continue to go back to their wives. Ben had betrayed Hazel in every way imaginable, except for two -- he wouldn't beat her and he would be completely loyal to her. She loved him. In transforming her into this new person, he had destroyed the old Henry and in that, eliminated the monster that resided in Henry. Ben had released Henry's demon. Hazel was no longer a rapist and for that, she was forever grateful to Ben. She fell in love with him, and loved him in a way that only a she-male could love a man -- firmly, rock-solidly and with a sexual aggressiveness that left Ben often speechless, mouth full, vibrating, pulsating and endlessly delirious. There was no woman on this planet that could ever take Ben away from Hazel. Except, of course, Erica.

CHAPTER 79

WHAT IT'S LIKE TO BE DEAD

Erica convinced the doctor to give her a ream of paper.

She took the top one and wrote the title to a book that would catapult her to the A-list of writers: What It's Like to Be Dead.

WHAT IT'S LIKE TO BE DEAD

BY ERICA LAZARUS

She did not pause, and began chapter one.

CHAPTER ONE

INTRODUCTION

It has been a little more than a year since my death. During this time, I have had the unique opportunity to see death and life, and to compare the two side by side. I now give you this comparison.

CHAPTER TWO

HOW I LIVED

I lived my life filled with expectations and constant disappointment over unrealized dreams. I wanted, I desired, I never got. It was tumultuous. I was anxiety-prone. I was a walking zombie. I couldn't help it. I couldn't stop it, until one today somebody murdered me.

CHAPTER THREE

HOW I DIED

(She started the first sentence without trepidation.)

I will never forget the day that a man murdered me. I will now explain every detail of what he did to me.

Erica wrote like a forest fire. The next chapter filled up 50 pages in her small, super neat handwriting. She would number each page before she started the next one. She wrote of when Henry got her at the Tasterilla. How it happened and her reaction to it would be something that would send the coldest, commercialist literary agents and editors of publishing houses into a flow of tears. When Ben read it, he literally fell down onto his knees sobbing and crying over the love of his life, who had been murdered one night at a place called the Tasterilla.

CHAPTER 80

THE LITERARY AGENT MAKES IT HAPPEN

If Erica had been a first time author, this process would have taken over a year. She would have had to magically find somebody to type up her handwritten manuscript. That alone could take a year. Then she would have had to submit it to about a thousand literary agents, of which 999 would turn her down, most of them without even reading it.

But Erica was not a first time author. She had already placed two books on the bestseller list. She was already connected as a proven writer. She wrote a somewhat cryptic letter to her agent, "Come see me."

Within a day, the agent was there in the asylum. She picked up the first 400 handwritten pages of her third novel, an earth shattering explanation of the thoughts, emotions and deliberations of a person in a near death state known as catatonic schizophrenia.

The truth that she told in these pages was that this was a very lively emotional state, one in which she excitedly considered a thousand times more information than she could have ever done in a normal, earthly conscious state. This was a semi-dream state, a semi-death state -- somewhere in limbo in between consciousness and a vegetative state. This phrase, given by medical professionals of a vegetative state, is quite a misnomer. The proper word should be enhanced consciousness.

Erica would explain all this, play by play, step by step in this never ending book. It was a book she wrote feverishly, page after page. There was no stopping, no wondering what was going to happen next, no searching for insights, no throwing away paper after paper after each page was not quite perfect. Every page that was whipped off was in a perfect form. There could be no imperfection here, as she was simply telling a truth that she knew all too well. She had lived it, she had experienced it, she knew it. She knew the simple reality that during this period in her state, she had thought about many things, including not the least of which was her own primal emotional quest for something called revenge.

She wrote about it, she thought about it, she planned it. There was one thing this broken person with a super heightened sense of consciousness would absolutely need and desire and would absolutely be unstoppable in getting -- her own revenge against the rapist that had put her there. There would be no mercy. There would be no second thoughts. There would be no compassion. There would be no philosophical thinkings of, 'isn't revenge really bad?' Doesn't revenge just turn you into the monster that you are trying to eradicate and punish? Doesn't revenge leave you with an empty hollow feeling?

Make no mistake about it, she would get her revenge against the man who had put her in this asylum. That is, if she could find him.

CHAPTER 81

BEN GETS THE BOOK

At Erica's request, the literary agent delivered the typewritten version of Erica's manuscript to Ben. It was hand delivered by the agent herself.

Ben answered the door, expecting to see anything from a warden to a sheriff's deputy, but not a literary agent. She was dressed in a white outfit and had in her hand a box with some scotch tape holding the top to the bottom.

"Ben?"

"Yes."

"Erica asked me to deliver this to you."

"Erica?"

"Yes."

"Really?"

"Yes."

Hazel stepped behind Ben. The agent looked in, smiled.

"Good morning."

Hazel responded, "Hello."

It was a semi-low, semi-high voice; took the agent a little bit off guard.

Erica was trying to tune in to this discussion from her remote place of viewing in the asylum. Somehow it was blocked, but she smiled, knowing that the delivery was being made. This was part of her plan to win Ben back. She knew full well that when he read this book, he would be floored. It didn't matter what the rest of the world might think of the book. What mattered is what happened with Ben.

He opened the top of the box to see the somewhat alluring and frightening title, "What It's Like to Be Dead" by Erica Lazarus.

"Oh my," Ben said out loud.

Hazel peered over.

"Wow, what's that?"

"It's a book by Erica."

Hazel became somber. She was still filled with the teachings of her sexual offender therapy program, one of which was that the impact of a rape was huge and has many ripples. She looked at the tome, a rather substantial document. There were well over 500 pages.

Ben noted its thickness, and looked at the end. He noted one thing.

"Missing from the last page --"

"Yes?"

"Are two words."

"What two words?"

"The end."

"They're not there?"

"They're not there."

"Which means?"

"Which means it isn't quite over yet."

They wondered how much more there was to write.

Meanwhile, Erica was back at the asylum, cranking out more and more handwritten pages. She had to constantly request further pencils -- so many that Doctor McNally just didn't believe she was really using them up.

He had to come in and see himself.

"Erica, how are you today?"

"Fine. Did you bring the pencils?"

He showed her a group of five. They were already sharpened. He looked at her wrist, looked at her hands. There were no signs of any puncture wounds or any other misconduct with the pencils.

"So far, so good, Erica. Tell me, what are you writing about?"

"Well, if you really want to know, call up my agent and she'll give you a copy of the manuscript."

"I just may do that. But why don't you go ahead and explain it to me?"

"Well, doctor, you may be interested in knowing this as a medical professional. Did it ever occur to you what people are thinking about when they're lying here, staring blankly out into space?"

"I would like to know that. I have no idea what you're thinking."

"That is the subject of my book. The title -- 'What It's Like to Be Dead.'"

"That's rather negative, isn't it?"

"That presumes death is negative, doesn't it? I submit to you that perhaps it is not negative."

"Now you're worrying me, Erica. You sound like you're expressing thoughts of suicide."

"No, doctor. You don't understand. I've already been dead. I'm now back from it. I've done the opposite of a suicide. I've done a lificide. I'm here again. My eyes are open. My brain is open. I'm back on Earth. How about that?"

The doctor was silent and mulled over his thoughts.

"Hmm," he said. "A schizophrenic catatonic comes back to reality, so to speak, and then writes about it. Well, that ought to catch on."

He looked at Erica's new pile.

"Looks like you've got, what, 140 or so pages there? Wait a minute. Why are these numbered starting with 511?"

"The other 510 pages were picked up by my agent and have been typed up."

"Oh, I see. This is the next part of it?"

"Yes."

"I don't even want to ask this question, but I feel compelled to. How long is this book going to be?"

"I don't know, doctor. I've got a lot to say about this stuff."

"Okay. Well, why don't we proceed like this: You continue writing. Here are your pencils. I've brought you another ream of paper. Good luck on all that. I'm going to continue to monitor you."

"Doctor, at some point, you've got to let me out of here."

"I know, I know. You're doing great, but I'm a little bit frightened of your state."

"Just because you're scared of what I may have in my brain, I don't think that's a proper reason to keep me here. Ask yourself this, doctor -- am I a danger to myself? Am I a danger to others? What do you think?"

"The answer is, I don't know."

"But doctor, isn't an, 'I don't know' rather insufficient as far as a basis to keep me here? Don't you have to have an answer of, 'I do know and with some kind of medical certainty, I reasonably believe that this person is a danger to herself and/or to others'? I mean, 'I don't know' doesn't quite cut it, does it?"

The doctor was silent. He knew, of course, she was right.

"Listen, doc. Let's do this the easy way," Erica pointed out to the doctor. "You let me go. If you don't want to do it the easy way, as you know, there's a legal way. I've got some resources at my disposal, so you don't want to mess around with me. I could make it rough for you."

"Erica, don't threaten me. That's no way to get any favor from me."

"Oh, doctor, please understand -- I am not asking for a favor. I'm asking for my legal right to be let free of this place. I am well. I am fine. I have been fine for several months now and you're keeping me here against my will. Let me go."

The doctor thought about it. He didn't want to let her go -- and not for any particular reason, but it just seemed she was somehow dangerous.

"I'll tell you what I'll do. Have your agent deliver the book to me. I'll read it. That will give me some insight into your condition. How about that?"

"Call her. Here's her name and number."

Erica scribbled out her agent's name and phone number and handed it to the doctor.

The doctor called her. Within several hours, another copy of the 510 pages that had been delivered to Ben not long ago was delivered to Doctor McNally. He would read them -- at first, somewhat slowly, but as he got into it, it was truly a book he could not put down. He devoured it, he ate it up, he loved it, he hated it, it made him laugh, it made him cry, it made him happy, it made him angry, it made him hate, it made him love, it made him want to scream, it made him want to go to sleep. It got him way up, it got him way down -- exactly as a good book should.

The same was occurring to Ben. At some points, the book was quite entertaining, cheerful, relaxing and even funny, but then there were times when the story got into Erica's inner sanctum of what she was going through in her catatonic state and some of the very dark thoughts she was having -- of how she felt so compacted with emotion. It was like being, as she said, "30,000 leagues under the sea with no submarine. The pressure of the water above was insurmountable. I couldn't swim up and I couldn't swim down. I was frozen, like a fossil."

Ben was able to picture Erica as a fossil, stuck in the sediment of hundreds of feet of dirt, oil and granite, crushed together over several millennia and turned into stone. It was here in this petrified state that Erica would have some of the deepest emotions that she had ever had. In those emotions, one that just kept coming forward was the emotion of revenge and fate. You might think that in this enlightened state, there would be some concept of forgiveness and a spiritual awareness that says, live and let live. But this enlightened state was primal in nature. It brought Erica closer to the human animal that we are first. It brought her to a notion of self-preservation and of vindication, of making what was very wrong right.

CHAPTER 82

HI HONEY, I'M HOME

Ben found himself in great grief over this book. He decided he of course would have to go and see Erica. While Erica had been going through the throes of this inner darkness, Ben had been having a perfectly lovely time with his new female. There was a complete love affair at this point between the two of them. Hazel and Ben had become quite an item. They would go out all the time. They would have a lot of fun. He would watch in amazement as she played the guitar. The warden and his daughter were coming over as well. The warden's daughter was learning excellent guitar from Hazel. There were constant flows of awesome and beautiful music in the household. Beautiful women, good people, good conversation -- everything was positive and in a good way.

While he was experiencing all of these positive emotions, now he was exposed to the hugely negative emotions experienced by Erica. Was his happiness at her expense? Was he guilty for exacerbating and compounding her pain? Maybe yes, maybe no -- but for him, it was absolutely yes. He felt a pang of guilt. He became enraged at himself. He was angry. He was supposed to be a good guy.

This was Ben, the bohemian journalist, the finder of truth, the man who would bring down the evil giants, toss out the monsters and let good win over evil. Now look at him. He'd become a perpetrator of injustice. He'd become a kidnapper. He'd become a man who forced drugs into a person and then he turned that person into a person of the opposite sex.

There is not presently a criminal law statute that covers this sort of thing, but if word ever got out that somebody did this, some kind of forced transgender penal code would have to be developed. Forcing a person who is a man into being a woman may not be a crime under the penal code, but it does qualify as a crime against nature. A crime that Ben was 1000% guilty of.

He had set her up on a rape and in doing that, had become a rapist. He was a perpetrator or as the criminal law says in abbreviated form, a perp. Kidnapper, rapist, drugger, forced transgenderer -- these were all the crimes that Ben had committed.

But the biggest one, the one that he could never forgive himself for, was the man who had found pleasure in the aftermath of all these crimes, who had lived on top of his bounty eating grape after grape, carefully peeled by slaves, big smile on his face and enjoying his life in the sun. His father's beautiful home, rolling in money and now with this sexy lover playing beautiful music to his ears. And all this was being enjoyed during Erica's darkest hour. Where was Ben when Erica was in this pain? Ben was enjoying himself.

He looked at himself in the mirror and for the first time in his life thought, *I just gotta kill myself.*

He then looked over at Hazel. As people do, they blame others for their own misconduct. It's a tendency in people that goes back thousands of years -- rationalize, justify, do whatever you want, blame others for what you've done. Ben argued with Hazel. The thing about arguing with Hazel is that she was a valedictorian of a sexual offender program and had learned that there was no such thing as argument. There was only admission.

"You're right, Ben. I'm a piece of shit. I don't have any question about that. I know what I did, but Ben, step back a second and ask yourself, do you know what you've done? Let's look at it. Just look at it square. Let's see what we can do about it."

The last thing Ben wanted to do was to look at himself square. He needed someone to reflect his own misconduct off of and that would be Hazel. Hazel saw Ben look at the guitar. Was he going to pick it up and swing it at her? Would Hazel duck or just let it happen?

"Ben, go ahead. You want to hit me, hit me. You want to pound me into the floor, pound me into the floor. You want to blame me for everything you've done, go ahead and blame me. I will tell you right now, you're right. It's my fault. I did it. I made you do these things. I made you do all of these things. Go ahead, say it. I'll agree. I'll help you here, Ben. I'll agree with you 1000%. I'm at fault, not you. You want that, Ben? You want to beat me? Do you want to destroy what you have made? A thing of beauty must be destroyed. Do you know who said that, Ben? My dad did. That's what he believed. Something's too beautiful, you just can't handle it -- you have got to destroy it."

Hazel brought her beautiful figure before Ben. She pulled off her dress and exposed her beautiful body.

"Go ahead, Ben. Destroy me. Kick my ass. Beat me. Bruise me. Cut me. Go for it because remember, Ben, I've already lived and died. I've lived again. I've died again. I've gone to the low of the low. I've gone to the high of the high. And if you want to bring me back down to the low, hey, been there, done that. I'm ready to go again."

Ben was about to explode. He realized, of course, Hazel was completely correct. He realized beating her was not the right answer, even though he truly wanted to do that. He put the guitar down. He would not smash her head with it.

He pictured her in the aftermath of that blame, a bloody mess. He realized he would be guilty of yet another crime -- this one, felony domestic violence, assault and battery with a deadly weapon. He would have turned beauty into ugliness -- and as far as Ben could see, he had already done quite enough of that.

He turned, got his car keys and did something you're not supposed to do when you're filled with anger and hate and thoughts of suicide. He got into his father's car and drove off to the mental asylum. He was going to see Erica, still the love of his life.

"Hi honey, I'm home."

CHAPTER 83

HONESTY IS NOT THE BEST POLICY

Ben immediately broke into tears upon seeing Erica.

She was strong and smiled. She would not cry. She held him, hugged him. He curled up into her like a little infant. She could sense his guilt and understood all about it.

"It's okay, Ben. It's okay. I understand."

He looked up at her, eyes bloodshot red, streaming with tears.

"What do you mean, you understand? What do you understand?"

"I understand everything, Ben. You read my book?"

"Oh, honey, did I. Oh, my God. I, I can't --"

She put her hand on his mouth and shushed him.

"Shh. Look darling, it's okay. Just relax. Everything is going to be okay. Let's just be here for each other. Let's just hold each other and please listen very carefully to these words: I love you."

Ben looked up at his amazing fiancée Erica. He was overwhelmed with her genius, her courage, her stamina and for still being there after all she had gone through, and all the additional garbage that he was now putting her through. He had become an enemy of the woman that he loved and that was the last thing he wanted to do.

"Honey, please forgive me. Please forgive me. I love you. I love you. You have no idea how much I love you."

"Oh Ben, I do know. I can feel it. It's flowing into me right now. It's going into my veins. It's going into my bones, into my bone marrow. You and I, we are marrow to marrow."

Ben got the idea that Erica had some kind of sixth sense ability and it scared the hell out of him. He did not want to confess to her the truth that his new girlfriend was her rapist so how could he not think about it? The minute that he thought, *I cannot think about it*, of course, the first thing he did was to think about it.

But these thoughts weren't all getting to Erica. What had gotten to her was the fact that Ben had a new woman in his life.

304

"Ben, look. You moved on, and I understand that," she explained to him. "I forgive you for that. I understand it and indeed, Ben, I apologize."

"Apologize? What are you apologizing for? You haven't done anything."

"I wish I had been psychologically stronger so that what happened to me did not put me here. I mean, come on, people get raped, they go to therapy, they move on. They don't become catatonic. They don't stay in an asylum for what, 15 months?"

"16."

"That was my weakness. A weakness of mine that put me here, kept me from you and delivered you into the arms of another woman."

Ben closed his eyes. He didn't want to think about her. He couldn't think about her. *Please don't think about her. Please don't have an image of what she looks like. Please don't have an image of what she looks like naked -- no, no, no, don't go there. Oh my God, there it is.* It was lack of control Ben had over his own thoughts. Whenever he didn't want to think about something, of course he thought about it. There in his mind was Hazel's awesome naked body. He hoped to God that Erica could not see this.

It appeared that she couldn't. If she had seen those erotic images in his mind, she probably would've slapped him. The fact that she didn't slap him showed either incredible control on her part or that in the process of all this emotional roller coaster writing that she'd been doing, that somehow the part of the brain that produces the emotion called jealousy had been eliminated.

Ben already knew this was not the truth. She had written on jealousy in her book. There was jealousy, envy, revenge all over the place -- jealousy about losing what she had, envy about wanting to gain what others had, and revenge for wanting to destroy the person who took it all from her. All that was very neatly and expressly laid out in her book.

The fact that she didn't slap him right then and there meant that somehow, with whatever sixth sense capability she had, she could receive some but not all of what he was thinking.

She looked at him and saw his relief.

"What?"

"Oh, nothing."

He put his hands out. He held her. He smiled.

"Erica, are we back?"

She smiled.

"Yes Ben, we're back."

"Thank God. There's nothing more that I want than to be back with you."

Doctor McNally walked in at this point. He had finished reading the book.

"Hello, Ben. How are you?"

"Fine, thank you, doctor."

"Erica?"

Erica nodded. "Hello, doctor. Did you finish it?"

"I did."

Ben looked at the doctor.

"Can you believe that book?"

The doctor shook his head in disbelief.

"I can't believe it, but then, I know who wrote it, so yes, I can believe it. Erica, let me tell you, it's a masterpiece. Not only is it a masterpiece of literature, but it's a masterpiece of medical science. You are a test case to show an answer to a question which we doctors have been examining for decades. Now we have an answer from you. Thank you for that."

Ben looked at the doctor. "Does this mean --"

"Just a second. Erica, would you like to go home now?"

"Now?" Erica cried.

The tone in the doctor's voice said that his answer was yes. She would be released of this prison. She turned to the doctor, tears welling down her eyes -- those cobalt blue eyes turning red, white and blue.

"Yes, doctor. I would love to go home. May I?"

"Yes, you may," the doctor responded.

Erica held Ben's hands. The doctor witnessed a reuniting of souls that should have never been separated in the first place. The two of them cried tears of love as the little men in white suits came in to prepare her for her exit from the asylum.

CHAPTER 84

HONEY, I'M HOME

Ben had already forewarned Hazel about the arrival of Erica. Hazel, unlike most women, was completely accepting of Erica's rightful place in this home. It hardly needed explanation.

"I know, Ben. Don't even worry about it. In fact, let me know what you want me to do. You want me to go, I'll go. Remember, I've got a house not far from here just sitting there."

Ben looked at Hazel's incredible beauty. Though he did have a real love for Erica, it was quite clear that he also had a real love for Hazel.

"No, you stay," he explained to her. "We'll talk."

Erica was looking out the car window. She put her hand on his thigh, realizing that there were certain parts of Ben's life that would need to be changed and that this change could be expected to take some time. She wouldn't even question it. She smiled out the window and felt the salty breeze of the ocean wind for the first time in many months.

They pulled into Ben's lengthy driveway, drove up to the front, and Erica got out of the car. She could hear the sound that she had previously heard remotely, and would now witness first hand -- the sound of Hazel playing guitar along with the warden's daughter. They were playing the song "Suite Madame Blue."

Erica walked in the house right in the middle of the song. Hazel looked at her and nodded. During the rape by Henry, he was not looking at Erica eye to eye. He had been from her backside. She had some opportunity to see Henry, but didn't recall his eyes, those piercing blue eyes. Just like the warden didn't know them, she didn't know them. There was really no hint of Henry in Hazel. Henry had a shaved head, Hazel had gorgeous hair, gorgeous blue eyes, lovely pouty lips, an awesome figure. There was no way anybody would ever imagine that this woman was a man. Impossible. The warden didn't know it. The warden's daughter didn't know it. The only people in the room who knew it were Hazel and Ben.

She listened to the rest of the song. It was beautiful. She didn't know it was about her, but it didn't matter. When it was done, Hazel put down the guitar and walked over to Erica.

"Welcome."

Erica smiled ethereally. This was a rather strange meeting. The old fiancée and the new love, both in competition for Ben's heart. One being more than willing to let him go out of a sense of debt to the other, a debt that the other, Erica, had no idea was due and owing. She looked at Erica. They hugged each other. Erica was tense, loosened a little bit.

"I am Lilith," the warden's daughter introduced herself. "Hazel's teaching me guitar."

"You're quite good, Lilith."

"And this is Lilith's father."

The warden shook her hand -- a delicate touch. He had forgotten how a woman could be delicate.

"So shall we get some tea?"

They all sat down, with the warden presiding over this odd meeting between two lovers after the same heart. After the small talk was exhausted, Erica decided to chime in on the rather obvious question of what they were going to do.

"So Hazel, how do you feel about all this?"

"I feel good."

"Good about what?"

"That Ben is in love."

"You can tell?"

"Oh, yes. I know him. He's in love with you."

"You know, I was about to say the same thing. I also know him and I can just tell ya, he's madly in love with you. Ben is so obvious."

Ben was very shy about this. He was, first of all, dead guilty of being in love with two women at the same time. He didn't know what to do. It, of course, could only be in his wildest dreams that he could somehow have the two of them. This was not reality. He would have to choose.

He looked over to the warden. The warden, a practical man, an honorable man, shook his head.

"You know, Ben, you're going to have to choose."

Ben looked up.

"I know."

"So what's your choice, Ben?"

"Well, listen. Do I actually need to choose right now?"

Erica smiled.

"No, you don't."

Hazel smiled.

"Right, you don't need to right now. Take your time."

"The reality is, to be honest with the two of you, I love you both. Let me just be honest. I do."

"I know, Ben."

Hazel knew. Erica knew. The warden knew.

Lilith knew, most of all. She learned a lot about love that day. One of the things Lilith learned is that a man could love two women at the same time. Probably a woman can do the same.

"Well, tell you what. There's plenty of room here. Erica, you stay. Hazel, you stay and we'll just carry forth and at some point we're going to figure out the best way to handle this situation. How about that?"

Erica looked up and smiled.

"Okay."

Hazel was pleased to see this agreement. She was, of course, willing to do just about anything.

"So be it. May I play you another song?"

"Please do."

Hazel and Lilith walked over to the music room, picked up their guitars and sang the song that had come to Erica as she was being released from her catatonic state, a song that she recalled then and adored and was very happy to hear once again -- the song by Evanescence, "Bring me To Life."

Lilith started on the piano.

The cool part of Hazel's voice was shown in this type of song, where there are lyrics sang in part by a man and in part by a woman. Hazel surprised everyone by singing both parts perfectly.

The warden smiled as he watched his daughter play beautiful music. It was a pleasure seeing such talent.

Ben smiled with Erica as they watched two budding superstars show a combined spirit that could probably overtake the world.

They were all smiling in happiness in a situation that everyone knew could not possibly go on. Something would have to give.

CHAPTER 85

LET'S BAKE A PIE

One day while Ben was at work, Erica and Hazel got the idea to bake a pie. They were sitting around the living room awkwardly staring at each other, both realizing that idle hands are the devil's workshop.

"For some reason, I feel like a blueberry pie."

Erica came up with this rather off the cuff idea. Hazel was happy to do anything for Erica.

"A blueberry pie? In my entire life, I do not think I've ever had one."

"Do you think you would like blueberries?" Erica asked.

"I'm sure I would like it."

Hazel sounded very certain.

"Well," said Erica. "How about you and I go to the store and get one?"

Hazel stood up. She was wearing shorts, which showed her long legs, still fairly muscular from her man side. Erica pretended not to notice.

"How about you make the pie?" Hazel suggested.

"Well, that's what I was thinking."

"Oh, okay. I thought you were just going to go buy one."

"No. Let's make one."

"I like that idea."

Hazel then came up with another suggestion.

"I'll tell you what. You make the pie of your choice -- sounds like that's going to be a blueberry pie."

"Yes. I would like to make a blueberry pie. And you?"

"I have a different kind of pie in mind."

"Okay. What's that?"

"I want to make a cheesecake."

"Ooh. That sounds yummy. What kind of cheesecake?"

"I want to make a strawberry cheesecake."

310

Erica got excited. "Oh, I love strawberry cheesecake."

"Okay then."

Erica was wearing a light sundress, beige in color, nearly matching her skin tone. It made her look practically naked.

"Then let's go." She was happy to have a project.

Hazel grabbed the car keys, her purse and a pair of knock-off Chanel sunglasses. Erica grabbed a real Hermes scarf and wrapped it around the top of her head. She was tying it when Hazel walked over behind her.

"Here, let me."

Hazel tied it into a cute little bow. "Now you look like somebody's gift."

The girls looked at each other in the mirror. They were both positively gorgeous and ready to awe people at the grocery store. They took the Mercedes. Ben, still in his Bohemian state, continued to drive his Corvair. This left the slate gray Mercedes for Hazel and Erica to drive off in. The girls looked pretty cool driving to the store in their fake Chanel glasses, real Hermes scarf tied in a bow, both with mouth-watering missions in mind. There was a spirit of competition in both of them. They thought in parallel, almost like sisters.

Hazel said it first. "I wonder --"

And then Erica quickly interrupted, "Which one will Ben prefer?"

Hazel expanded, "Your blueberry?"

Erica finished it, "Or your strawberry cheesecake?"

CHAPTER 86

SHOPPING FOR PIE MATERIAL

Neither Erica nor Hazel was much of a cook. They parked the car and proceeded into the grocery store. It was a beautiful sunny day in San Diego -- busy, shoppers all about, each trying to outdo the other in good looks. Few would top Erica and Hazel. In front of the grocery store door was a rubber mat. When you step on the mat, the door automatically opens. Several people walked in front of them and opened the door in this way.

Erica, in a show of her mindset at the moment, took a surprise running leap in about four steps and jumped over the entire automatic door pad, broad jump style, landing inside the store. Hazel laughed, but did not follow her example. Instead, she grabbed a grocery cart and calmly walked inside.

She turned directly to the produce department. "First stop, blueberries."

Hazel proceeded to the produce section and found a display of blueberries in those cute little plastic boxes. She examined them like an agri-scientist, opening the plastic containers, smelling them, bringing them close to her eye -- doing everything but tasting them. It then occurred to her that Erica had strayed.

Hmm. Where did she go?

Within a couple moments, Erica came back into the produce section, proudly displaying a box of prepackaged strawberry cheesecake mix and a can of blueberry pie filler.

"Look, these are ready to go. All we need are some pie crusts."

Hazel shook her head. "Hun, why don't you just buy a pie? I mean, if we're going to bake a pie, let's bake a pie. That's not baking a pie. That's just dumping a can into another can and turning the oven on."

"Well, what did you have in mind?"

Erica was perplexed. She wasn't much of a cook. To her, following the directions on a box of prepackaged pie mix absolutely qualified as cooking.

Hazel showed Erica her hands. "You see these hands?"

Hazel's hands had some pretty large veins running through them.

"Out of these hands, I hand built a guitar from scratch. These same hands will make a pie from scratch -- and I will show you how to do it as well."

"Step one," she grabbed the strawberry cheesecake box from Erica, "is to put this down. Step two -- let me introduce you to something. You see this over here? That's a real strawberry. Look at it. Pick it up. Smell it. Feel it. That's what you're going to make your cheesecake out of." ((I thought Erica was making the blueberry pie...?))

Erica held the beautiful plastic canister of strawberries and compared them to the nickel blueberries. "Mine are bigger than yours."

Hazel laughed. "Whatever."

Erica was a bit troubled by this cook from scratch concept. The best she had done before was a peanut butter sandwich and a grilled cheese sandwich. This was new territory for her.

"Don't worry," Hazel reassured her. "Look what I have here."

She turned her cell phone to face Erica. She had Googled how to make a strawberry cheesecake. Amazingly enough, there were no fewer than 15 websites out there giving her a play by play of what was needed ingredients-wise and a step by step on how to cook it.

Erica was impressed. "Wow. You got that on your phone?"

"I got that off Google."

"Okay, so what's the first thing I need?"

"Apparently you'll need strawberries for a strawberry cheesecake. Go figure."

"Okay. Strawberries, check. What else?"

"Well, according to this -- and this may be a shocker -- you need cream cheese."

"So cheesecake really is made out of cheese?"

"It's made out of cream cheese. And you need some lemon."

"Okie dokie."

"You need some sugar."

"Don't we have sugar?"

"Let's assume we have nothing. Let's basically buy every single ingredient that we need. If there's something left over, don't worry about it; we can use it. Let's see -- it needs a dash of lemon. I guess that makes it a little bit tart. It needs some butter. It needs some salt, a dash of cinnamon, some brown sugar and -- let's see now. The crust mix -- you want to go graham cracker or regular pie?"

"Oh, let's do graham cracker. That sounds great."

"Okay then. You go get a box of graham crackers. Get some starch, some butter and some flour."

They walked over and looked at the flour bags.

"Wow, there's so many different kinds. What do we get?"

Hazel cut to it right away and found a bag of what you'd call regular white flour, one pound bag.

"This will be enough for both pie crusts, I'm sure. I think we got all the stuff you need. Let's check out what you need for a blueberry pie."

"Oh, you don't know?"

"Believe me, I don't know how to do anything other than how to do a Google search -- but nowadays, that's all a girl needs to know."

She typed in the words, "how to make a blueberry pie" and sure enough, there were quite a few websites showing how to do it, what ingredients were needed and even providing a YouTube video display of it.

"Can you believe that?"

They played the video for just a second and then went back to the previous site to get the basic ingredients. Hazel looked at the instructions and planned:

"Let's see now -- three or four cups of blueberries. That's kind of tricky. These come in ounces, so how many cups in an ounce? Eight, right? So that means I need -- wow maybe eight of these packages. That's a lot of blueberries."

Erica peered over Hazel's shoulders, and became so close that their hair intertwined.

"It says we need cornstarch," she continued. "We've already got that. And some grape juice--grape juice for a blueberry pie? How odd."

They proceeded to the juice section and saw the impressive array of all the juice products.

"Now I guess we will get -- what? White grape? I don't know. Let's get white grape."

They picked up a quart size bottle of white grape juice.

"Let's see. We need some lemon juice."

They found a small bottle of lemon juice.

"Spices -- let's go over to the spice section."

They walk over there.

"We need a little bit of cinnamon and we need a little bit of allspice."

Erica was wondering. Hazel answered the unasked question, "I know what you're thinking. What is allspice? The answer is, I don't know, but here it is so let's just get it."

Hazel had to reach over Erica to pluck the bottle of allspice. They both studied this mysterious bottle and nodded.

Hazel was proud to conclude, "Okay, that should cover it."

They proceeded to the cashier. As they waited in line, Hazel suddenly remembered something.

"Oh my goodness."

"What?"

"Stay right here. I'll be right back."

Hazel loped away like a deer and came back in a matter of half a minute with an essential ingredient for this project.

"Look, pie pans."

"Oh yes, I'm sure Ben does not have those."

"I'm sure he doesn't."

She had two shiny, foil pie pans. They were deep dish and expendable-- the type that you would use for one project only and then toss. They placed their items on the grocery store conveyer belt.

The elderly cashier was pleasant. "Pie night, huh?"

Erica laughed. "We'll see if this really works."

Hazel reassured, "Oh, it'll work alright."

CHAPTER 87

THE INTRUDER

They tossed the bags into the backseat of the Mercedes and proceeded home. The iron gate in front of Ben's home was supposed to open up via the remote control device in the car. For some reason, it wasn't working. Hazel pushed it once and then pushed it a second time.

"What the hell?"

She got out of the car and walked over to the gate. Right away, she could see the problem. It wasn't completely closed and locked. The remote required the gate to be closed in order to open. Hazel grabbed two bars of the gate and manually closed it. She returned to the car, pushed the remote and the gate then opened.

Erica was impressed. "You fixed it."

"Yeah, the thing didn't close all the way."

"Oh. That's a problem. I don't know how that happened."

The girls thought nothing of it and proceeded to the front door. Hazel tested the security of the front door. It was locked tight as a drum. She opened it and allowed Erica to enter first. They brought the groceries in, three bags altogether. Hazel took two. Erica took one. They closed the front door and proceeded into the kitchen.

"Okay, now the fun part. Let's start with the crust."

"Oh boy, here we go."

"We're going to need a little equipment here," Hazel again had her phone open to the how to make a graham cracker crust page. Hazel took out a large size Ziploc bag. "Here, you'll need this."

Erica held up the bag. "What's this going to do?"

"Okay, open up that box of graham crackers."

Erica followed.

"Take about ten of them out of there."

She counted them. "One, two, three --"

"Here, just use the whole package like this. I think there's twelve there. Don't worry about it. Okay, break them in half."

"Okay."

"Put them in the bag."

"Great."

"Ziploc the bag."

"Okay. Now what?"

Hazel handed Erica the flour roller. "Take this and beat the crap out of it."

"Ooh, that sounds fun."

Erica took the rolling pin like a hammer and was about to slam down on it when Hazel stopped her. "No, no, no, no. Don't do it like that. Just gently roll over it."

Erica took the rolling pin in both hands and steamrolled over the graham crackers in a gentle, delicate way.

Hazel put her hands behind Erica. "No, like this." She put more weight on it. "Put a little elbow in it. Put a little shoulder in it. Put a little hip in it. Put a little oomph in it."

Erica was not the least bit bothered by Hazel's closeness to her. She pushed and rolled and turned and massaged the graham crackers from flat baked crackers into a near-powder. She held the bag up proudly and showed it to Hazel.

"Shake and bake."

"Okay, looking good. Now next step." Hazel handed Erica a large mixing bowl. "Dump the crushed up graham crackers into this bowl."

Erica followed and dumped them all in there. "Wow, look at them." She was so impressed with her transformation of the graham crackers into dust.

"Here you go. I want you to take this margarine and use this butter knife and cut off enough for one-third of a cup."

Hazel watched as Erica followed her instructions.

"Very good. Put that in the microwave for one minute. Turn on the microwave and watch that cube of butter melt into liquid."

They both watched as the butter melted down. It didn't take long. Hazel continued.

"I want you to take this sugar bag and -- let's see here. Put in a quarter cup of sugar."

Erica dumped the sugar from the bag directly into the melted butter. Hazel was going to get mad, but then caught herself.

"I don't know why you did it like that. We don't know how much sugar you put in there."

"Oh, whatever. It's got some sugar. It's got to be sweet so it'll be fine."

Hazel laughed. "Okay, it's your pie. Now pour that into the bowl with the graham crackers."

Erica started pouring it drop by drop, watching as though it were blood dripping from a wound.

Hazel gently held Erica's wrist and tilted the cup to splash it all out. "Moving right along. Okay, now -- oh, before I forget -- Erica, please turn the oven on to 375."

Ben had one of those top and bottom ovens. There was one oven on top and one on the bottom. Erica studied the oven as though she were looking at the inner workings of a submarine.

Hazel smiled and shook her head. "Okay, I'll handle this one. You want top or bottom?"

Erica paused as though it were some kind of trick question, and then smiled, "Bottom."

"Very well."

Hazel turned the bottom oven on to 375 and clicked on bake.

"Next step -- we get this stirred up."

She took a wood spoon and started stirring it ever so slowly.

Hazel took Erica's hand. "Let's go a little faster, like this."

They stirred together. Erica decided to be cute for some reason and took a spoonful of this moosh and tossed it at Hazel's face. It landed right on her cheek.

"Oh, you little bitch!"

Erica laughed. "It was an accident."

"Oh sure it was. Don't worry. I'm not going to get back at you."

"Oh yeah? No tit for tat?"

"No tat for tit. Continue please."

Erica stopped. "What about your pie?"

"I'll tell you what. The first step is getting this crust together. Why don't we get your crust done, then we'll do my crust, then we'll work on your pie and then we'll work on my pie."

Erica disagreed.

"I don't think so. I think I know what to do from here." She grabbed the phone from Hazel.

"It's simple. It says here I just pour it in a pie dish." She grabbed one of the brand spanking new shiny pie dishes, nine inches diameter, two inches tall.

"Pour in and distribute onto the bottom and push it all onto the sides. I think I can handle that." Erica poured it in and then massaged the graham cracker crumbs up onto the entire perimeter of the pie dish.

"Just a minute." Hazel inspected. "Hmm. You missed a spot. Look."

Erica looked. "Indeed I did."

She pushed some graham cracker crumbs over to cover the entire perimeter. It was near perfect, as long as this was a home job and not to be considered restaurant-grade. She put it into the oven at 375.

"Let's see. How long's this got to cook? Half hour? One hour?"

Hazel laughed. "How about eight minutes?"

"Oh, okay."

They set the timer for eight minutes.

"Now let us proceed to the crust for my pie. I'm not doing a graham cracker crust. This is going to be a regular flour dough crust. Do you want to help?"

"Sure. You helped me on mine so I'm going to help you on yours. What do you need?"

"Step one, get me the flour, and do not throw it on me."

"Do I look like the kind of girl that would so such a thing?"

Hazel continued unfazed. "We're going to need four cups of flour. Take that measuring cup and wash it out. It's got that butter and sugar in it."

Erica washed it out in a half-assed way and handed it back to Hazel. Hazel went back to the faucet and washed it better, took out a towel and dried it.

"I need it to be free from what you did. Otherwise, I'm going to have a blueberry pie tasting like graham crackers."

Erica shrugged her shoulders. "Whatever."

"Okay, first step -- can you pour four cups of flour into that measuring cup and then put it into this bowl?"

Erica picked up the one pound bag of flour and OOPS! She poured out the entire one pound bag right on top of the table into a small mound. It made a big poof followed by a bellowing of white smoke. Instantly the girls had flour all over the place.

Hazel looked at Erica, who had this "sorry I screwed up" look on her face. The two laughed it off.

"Whoa," Hazel said. "We were not expecting that to happen. Okay. Now don't worry, Erica. Let's go like this. Just pick up that first cup right of your mountain here. Pour it in the bowl here. There's one. Now pick up another one and just do it like that."

Erica took it four times -- one, two, three, four -- and had four cups of flour in the bowl.

"Now at some point, we will put the rest of the flour back into the bag. Let's not worry about that right now. We'll just leave it right there." Erica nodded.

Hazel continued. "Okay, I need a tablespoon of sugar. Now if you don't mind, I'll handle this operation. This is the delicate stuff. Allow me."

She measured a tablespoon of sugar and a teaspoon of salt. She took out a bottle of Crisco, measured one and three-quarters cups and poured it into the bowl.

"A little bit of ice water." She dumped in some cold water right from the refrigerator.

"One large egg."

She took the egg and spun it on the table, showing that it moved slowly -- definitely not a hardboiled egg. She took it and with one hand, cracked it on the side of the bowl, in went the yolk, both halves of shell were in her hand, which she gently tossed into the sink to go into the disposal.

"Oh, one other item -- apple cider vinegar. Shoot. I don't think we have that."

She looked through Ben's kitchen cabinets.

"No, definitely no apple cider vinegar. Well, I hope that's going to be okay. I just don't have it. You know what I think I'll use instead? Lemon juice. Let me just try a little bit of this."

She poured a teaspoon and dumped it in the bowl.

"Okay, now the fun part. We've got to mix it all up."

Erica handed the mixing spoon that she had used. Hazel looked at it.

"No. I'll get my own spoon."

She got a new spoon. Erica watched as Hazel used some impressive hand and forearm strength and a wood spoon to mix up that flour bowl. She turned it to the left, spun it to the right, up and down, all around until it was all mixed up.

"Now it says here I'm supposed to make it into four small balls."

She took out a big hunk of it in her hand, shook it into a ball and splat onto the kitchen table it went. She made four such balls.

"Okay, it says here I'm supposed to refrigerate this for about an hour. Let's put the balls in the fridge. The refrigerator door was opened, the little balls of dough went in, and the door was closed. Hazel turned back to the kitchen table. "Next step is to make the cheesecake. Are you ready?"

Erica smiled. "Ready when you are."

"Let's see now. First, get a new mixing bowl, and bring me those strawberries. Put them right here."

Just then, they heard a ding. It was the oven alarm clock going off.

Erica was excited. "The crust is done."

She walked over, opened up the oven and was about to grab the pie with her hands. Hazel was quick to grab her wrists.

"Whoa, that's hot." She handed her a mitt. "Please use this."

Erica looked at Hazel's strong hand on her wrist, looked up at Hazel and smiled. "Thank you."

She took the mitt and then brought the pie pan carefully out onto the kitchen table.

"Okay, now what?"

"It says here --"

Erica took the phone from Hazel. "I'll handle this."

"Very well."

320

Erica read it out loud. "Let's see. Slice up the strawberries. Use two cups."

Erica took a knife out and was about to slice the strawberries when Hazel stopped her.

"Whoa, you're missing a step."

"What's that?"

"Please wash the strawberries. You see those little green tops? While you're washing them, take those off."

"Well, it doesn't say that here."

"Just trust me. You need to do that."

"Okay."

Erica followed the directions given by Hazel, washed off the strawberries, took the little green tops off, put them in a little bowl and brought them back to the table. She took her knife out and began ably cutting them into small slices. She scooped those slices up with the knife blade, put them back into a measuring cup and saw that they equaled about two and a half cups.

"Think that's okay?"

"Perfect."

She placed that into the pie container.

"Let's see. Add a tablespoon of sugar."

She took out a tablespoon and measured a heaping double tablespoon and put it in.

"And the important ingredient."

She pulled out the cream cheese.

"It says to use eight ounces." She noted that the cream cheese itself came in an eight ounce container.

"Well, I guess I'll use it all." She dumped it all into a mixing bowl.

"Let's see. Add two cups of cold milk." She put that into the mixing bowl as well.

"And some instant vanilla pudding mix. Hmm. That's what that's for."

She stirred it all in there for a couple of minutes. She then poured in the strawberries and continued stirring. Hazel was about to reach to help her stir harder when Erica hissed like a cat.

"I'll handle this."

Hazel backed off. "Very well."

She watched carefully as Erica did a wonderful job of beating the crap out of this mix. Once it was all mixed together, Erica gently poured it drop by drop into the pie pan. She was just bothering Hazel. Hazel reached over to pour it all in when she backed off.

"I'll do it."

She then poured it all in one whoosh. It filled right to the top, almost perfectly level.

"Wow, look at that."

They both studied it. It was quite impressive -- strawberries floated about in the thick cream cheese. It was deep, it was gooey, it was bright red and gooey white. It was hot from the baked crust, and was about to be cold.

"Last step -- put a plate over it and stick it in the fridge for about two hours."

They did just that.

"Beautiful. Your pie is now done -- except we have to just let it wait. So let's work on the blueberry pie next."

"Very well."

"First of all, let's take these doughballs out."

They took the four balls of dough.

"Here, you do two, I'll do two."

She put the two balls in front of Erica.

"First, here's the Ziploc bag. Put the two balls in here. Put a little flour in there and shake them up again."

Erica shook up the bag with two balls in it and white flour. Hazel watched with some amusement as Erica did this. Hazel then did her two balls in the same manner.

"Now take the flour covered balls and put them right in front of you. Now pick up the rolling pin and roll that out flat."

Erica took the roller pin and began flattening out the ball of flour. She made it into an almost perfect circle. Before long, they had four circular smashes of what used to be a sphere of dough. Hazel picked the two pancake items from Erica's side of the table and put them into her pie crust and then the other and then the other and then the other. She gently used her fingers to piece it together seamlessly. She put it up on the perimeter of the pie pan and then used a fork to make a series of perfect Vs that went around the perimeter. Erica was mesmerized as she watched Hazel work in such an incredibly detailed and perfect manner.

"Wow. Now cook?"

"No. We have to make the blueberry mix first and then we pour it all in. Then we cook the whole pie together."

"I see."

"Let's get the blueberries."

Erica quickly announced, "First step, wash the blueberries."

"Exactly. Please do that."

Erica took the blueberry boxes over to the sink and did a wonderful job of washing all of them. She was trying to pull out the little tiny tops on the blueberries when Hazel stopped her. "Don't worry about those. Just pour them into the bowl."

She put them into the bowl.

"Okay, add in three tablespoons of grape juice."

Hazel measured the white grape juice and poured it in.

"Two tablespoons of lemon juice."

Hazel measured that and poured it in.

"A little sugar."

"Let's see -- two-thirds of a cup."

Erica got excited about that. "Oh, let me do the sugar."

"Very well."

She took out the cup, cleaned it extremely well, dried it off just like Hazel did before, and lifted up the bag of sugar. Hazel then intervened and pointed to the still awesome pile of flour. Erica got the message and gently poured into the cup a measured two-thirds of a cup of sugar. Erica poured then poured the cup into the bowl.

"And add half a teaspoon of cinnamon and half a teaspoon of allspice and stir." Hazel handled the spices. They both watched as the allspice came out.

Hazel began stirring. Erica reached in with her hands and just started fluffing it all up manually. Hazel stopped and watched this. It was kind of fun seeing Erica get her hands all wet and gooey. Erica looked up for a smile and Hazel gave her one. She continued mixing in this manual way for several minutes.

"I think that'll about cover it."

"Okay now, let's pour this into the pie container."

Hazel picked it up. Erica wanted to do it, but allowed Hazel to proceed. She poured the contents into the pie bowl. There was a little bit more than what was needed. She piled it up.

"Don't worry. It'll cook down."

They then took the remaining piece of pie dough and put it over the top of this pie as a cover. Erica saw the result and was very pleased. They cut a little X on the tip of the cover.

"Okay now, turn the oven to 400."

They took the oven that was still on 375 and just turned it on to 400.

Erica asked, "Is it okay to cook it in the same oven?"

Hazel figured "sure, why not. Put it in."

Hazel held one side of the pie and Erica held the other. They both gently put it in the oven. Hazel closed the door.

"Now mark the time -- 60 minutes."

They put the alarm on for 60. Hazel looked at Erica's hands. They were blueberry-stained all over. Erica had this idea of putting both of her hands onto Hazel's face, but Hazel could see that coming from a mile away.

"Oh no, you don't."

Erica laughed and screamed and started chasing her around the kitchen.

"Oh no, oh no."

Hazel ran around the table. Erica followed. As Hazel got a little bit further away from Erica, she backhanded the pile of flour and it poofed up into Erica's face and hair.

"Now you're going to get it."

Erica ran after Hazel with her blueberry hands, white puffy face and put two blue paw prints right on the back of Hazel's shirt.

"Gotcha!"

Hazel turned around, heart beating, confronting the playful Erica. They both stopped. They looked at each other. They laughed. The kitchen was a mess. There was flour everywhere. Blueberries were on the floor mixed with the strawberries. There was melted butter on the table. The sugar bag had fallen over, mixing in with the flour. It was all a complete, fun mess.

Suddenly, the mood went from playful to serious. They heard the sounds of footsteps upstairs.

"What the fuck?"

Hazel turned around, too late. There were two men in the house. They were wearing black. They each had a bag filled with stuff from Ben's room. There was a camera. There was a laptop. There was a small color TV. There was a wallet and a watch. There were two small frames of artwork. Oddly, they even took a plain photo of Ben's father. They were trying to make their way out on their tiptoes when they were caught by Hazel and Erica.

CHAPTER 88

HAZEL'S REVERSION BACK TO HENRY

There was a path of nature where a (awkward) domesticated animal like a dog or cat will revert back to its wild state. The cutest dog in the world, when confronted by a wild rabbit, will turn into a wolf. It will chase that rabbit down, catch it, rip off its head and eat it. If any other animal tried to come and share it with them, they will bark, hiss and fight them away as though their life depended on capturing and eating that rabbit.

Humans can also go through this reversion process. The adrenaline rush created by the two men suddenly being found in Ben's home started a process of reverting Hazel back to Henry.

"Who the fuck are you?"

Henry walked over. One of the men took the bag and swung it at Henry. Henry dodged out of the way. The bag hit the wall and burst at its seams. All the contents of Ben's room went flying out everywhere. The watch, the laptop, the small color TV, the artwork and glass covered photos crashed against the wall and then to the ground.

Erica had Hazel's cell phone with the pie recipe on it. She acted quickly, picked up the cell phone and called 911. One of the thieves saw that and grabbed the phone from her.

"You bitch, you calling the cops?"

The thief cocked back his arm, ready to punch Erica right in the face. Hazel went off at the sight. The other thief ran like a scared animal out the front door, leaving his bag behind. This left Hazel, Erica and the one thief. Hazel jumped on the thief's back and grabbed his arm before it could strike Erica. They all came tumbling down, one, two, three -- with Erica underneath. Hazel rolled the man over onto the floor. The man elbowed Hazel right in the gut.

Erica scooped up a bunch of flour dough and threw it right in the guy's eyes. This temporarily blinded him. He shook it off and looked at Erica again.

"You bitch; I'm going to get you now."

He walked over to her as though he was going to kick her ass. Hazel shook off the abdomen wound and walked over.

"Motherfucker, I'm going to get you now."

She grabbed the guy by the head and twisted his neck as hard as she could. She was trying to kill him, but it didn't work. The man turned around quickly, shrugged off Hazel's hands and faced off Hazel. He threw a punch, it missed. He threw another punch, it missed. Hazel was dodging, one and two. Erica was amazed at how quick Hazel could dodge these punches. Then Hazel blocked one, blocked another. The other guy unfortunately was quite a good fighter. He started kicking. Hazel then turned with a surprise move, dodging a kick with a twist and in one swoop, grabbed the rolling pin off the table and with a roundhouse back slap, smashed the guy right in the cheek with it.

The guy was dazed, but still standing. He shook his head and then pointed at Hazel. "You're dead, bitch."

Hazel still had the rolling pin and put it in her hand as the man looked at her. Hazel did something the guy completely was not expecting. She took that rolling pin, put it straight out like a baseball bat, brought it backwards and then forward again as hard as she could and released it. It swung end by end. The dazed thief was not quick enough to get out of the way. It hit him right on the forehead. This knocked him down and drew blood.

Hazel then went off on the guy. She rolled him over, and got on his back. "You motherfucker, I'm going to fuck you up your ass." She pulled his pants downs to his knees, pulled off the guy's boxer shorts and propped up his ass. She grabbed the guy's butt cheeks, spread them apart. She was looking around for something. She saw some melted butter and a bottle of Crisco oil, either of which would do.

Erica couldn't believe what she was seeing. "What the hell are you doing?"

The guy tried to get up. He groaned. Hazel grabbed him on the back of his head, shoved it backwards and then forward—whack--onto the kitchen floor. The man was now out out. While he was like this, Hazel poured some Crisco on his butt, and was about to start a rape of his ass.

Erica, thank God, was able to stop it. "Hazel, no, no. What are you doing? Stop."

At that moment, the police arrived. Erica's call did get through. The cops walked in to a very unusual sight. The front door was open from the fleeing felon. There were blueberries, strawberries, and flour mixed everywhere. There was a man on the floor with his pants down, shiny butt up in the air, and two messy hot girls. The cops didn't know who to shoot, but figured someone should be shot. They looked over to the girls for reassurance.

"Officer, this man is a burglar," Erica explained. "He came in to steal stuff. We live here. We were cooking. We caught him. He swung the bag at us. That's why all that stuff is there and we took him down."

The cops looked at the situation. They came to the guy. He was groaning in pain.

"Hey you. You alright?"

"Motherfucker tried to fuck me."

The guy turned around. He was trying to pull his pants up. The cop grabbed him.

"Hold on there. Bentley, cuff him."

Officer Bentley put the cuffs on the man.

"Alright, pull his pants up, Bentley."

Bentley hated being the younger officer. He had to do all the dirty work. He pulled the pants up and buttoned them up.

"Let's see his ID."

Bentley pulled out his wallet from his back pocket.

"Call it in."

"Alfonso Ramirez, CELC59157."

The radio call came back soon. "Be advised, there is a parole hold no bail warrant for this fugitive, recently paroled from San Quentin Prison on six counts of residential burglary in the San Francisco area."

The officer looked over at this man. "I guess you moved South?"

Alfonso pointed his head toward Hazel. "I want that bitch arrested for attempted rape."

Bentley walked over and looked at Hazel, every millimeter of her. Here was this gorgeous woman and somehow she was going to rape this guy.

"I just don't know how that would have been accomplished, sir, so we're going to have to decline your suggested criminal action. But don't worry -- something good will come out of this today. You're going to go to prison for probably a long, long time."

Just then Erica screamed at the top of her lungs. Bentley reacted.

"What now?"

Bentley and his partner looked over.

"What, what? What is it?"

She pointed at Hazel's side. In Hazel's abdomen, there was a slice of glass from one of the picture frames. It had been smashed against the wall and somehow in the melee, managed to find its way right into Hazel's gut. Hazel didn't even know about it. She looked down and saw it.

"Oh crap."

She pulled it out. As she was pulling it out, Officer Bentley put his palm out.

"No. Leave it there. Leave it there."

It was too late. She pulled it out. The glass actually held the blood in. Now the blood started spurting out and making a huge mess.

"Oh shit."

Officer Bentley got on his radio.

"Send an ambulance by ASAP. We've got a woman bleeding here."

Hazel put her hand on her abdomen. Erica came over and placed her hand over Hazel's hand. They both held the blood back. It was not long, though, before Hazel collapsed. Officer Bentley was right there to catch her.

"Man, this girl's heavy."

He gently placed her onto the ground. The other officer went into the living room, found a pillow from the couch and put it under her head.

"Here, just rest right here until the ambulance gets here. Don't worry. Everything's going to be okay."

CHAPTER 89

THE HOSPITAL

Paramedics arrived soon enough. Two men, early 30s, both wearing powder blue surgical gloves and navy blue uniforms crouched down before Hazel. There was quite a bit of blood on her blouse. They knew what to do.

First step, rip that blouse off. They were not delicate. Hazel's abdomen was a little bit strange to see. First of all, it was a bloody mess. Second, Hazel was sporting a six-pack. Erica tried not to worry about it, and instead focused on the medical emergency at hand.

The paramedic instructed his partner, "Let's get a drip and get her patched up ASAP."

They first used a bottle of hydrogen peroxide to irrigate the wound. They poured the entire bottle onto the wound. It was about two and a half inches long, and had gone through the abdominal wall. They put a square cloth bandage over it, and taped it down. The white bandage quickly turned blood red. The paramedic took Erica's hand and put it back on to the bandage.

"Hold here."

Right then, there was a DING!

Hazel looked up. "The pie!"

Officer Bentley wondered, "What pie?"

Erica continued.

"In the oven, there's a pie! Oh, officer, please take it out. I don't want to burn it. We did a lot of work on that."

Bentley turned around and looked at the huge mess.

"I can see."

The senior officer grabbed a mitten and handed it to Bentley.

"There you go, officer."

He opened the lower oven, carefully removed the perfectly cooked blueberry pie, put it on the middle of the kitchen table, turned the oven off and closed the door. It was a perfect looking blueberry pie.

The other paramedic brought in a gurney. They put Hazel onto the gurney, blouse off. She was wearing a black bra and had her shorts on.

"One, two, three."

They picked her up. The paramedics were a little bit surprised at how heavy she was.

Officer Bentley came over and gave a hand. The three of them, with Erica holding the bandage still, brought her onto the gurney, lifted her up, put an IV into her arm and wheeled her out into the ambulance. Erica got in the back and was whisked away to the hospital.

En route, Erica used Hazel's cell phone to call Ben at work. Ben, of course, was oblivious to all of these events. He was in a meeting with his editor, talking about another case of political corruption, this one involving some immigrations officials looking the other way at boatloads of illegal immigrants.

"I just don't understand why ICE is allowing these boatloads of immigrants into the harbor."

The editor looked up. "There must be some payola. Let's find it."

Ben wondered, "Maybe we could do a sting?"

Just then, his phone rang. He saw it was Hazel and was surprised to hear Erica on the line. "Oh Erica, it's you."

"Ben, Ben!" she was screaming hysterically.

The editor could hear it over the speakerphone on the cell phone. "Is everything okay?"

"What's up? Erica, what happened?"

"Oh my God, Ben, it was awful. We had some robbers in the house and one of them hurt Hazel."

"What happened to Hazel?"

"She got stabbed."

"Stabbed? With a knife?"

"No, with glass from a picture frame. It's in her, but they got it out."

"Are there doctors there?"

"No, we're in the ambulance right now going to the hospital."

"What hospital are you going to?"

"I don't know. Let me see. Where are we going, guys?

The paramedic advised, "Mercy."

Erica told Ben, "We're going to Mercy."

Ben didn't even say bye to the editor. He was out the door, into his Corvair, and flying down the road to Mercy Hospital. He was there before they got there. He waited out in front of the ER. Each ambulance that drove up was quickly met by Ben. The first one was a pregnancy, the second one was a gunshot wound, and the third one was Hazel.

"Oh my God, Hazel, are you okay?"

She had an oxygen mask on. She had an IV in her arm. She had her shirt off. Erica's bloody hand was on the wound. The paramedics greeted Ben, acknowledged him and wheeled her right into the ER.

They quickly went into the hospital doors that opened together, back into the area where doctors do immediate fixes to people who are all broken apart. The doctors would not allow Ben and Erica back into the surgery room area. They waited in the waiting room along with other anxious people.

In the quiet time during the wait, Erica turned to Ben. "How well do you know Hazel?"

"Uh, I know her. I mean, I don't know."

"Well, I mean, do you know anything about where she comes from, who she is? What her past is?"

"No. Why? What is it?"

"Ben, something really weird happened back at the house."

"Like what?"

"Hazel went off on this burglar guy."

"Well, good. The guy's robbing my house."

"Yeah, but I mean, she went off in, like, a really weird way."

"What kind of way?"

"It was a sexual thing."

"A sexual thing?"

"She pulled down the guy's pants. She was about to do him. If the cops hadn't arrived, I don't know what would've happened."

"Well, I don't think much would've happened."

"I'm telling you, I saw the look in her eyes. She was possessed. She was on a mission. Somehow -- and I don't know how -- she was going to fuck that guy. She was going to rape him."

Just then, the doctor came out. "Ben, Erica?"

They both looked up. They came over to see the doctor.

The doctor looked at Ben. "Can I talk to you -- alone?"

"Sure."

Ben walked over with the doctor.

"This girl?"

"Yeah."

"Her name is Hazel?"

"Yeah. Is she okay?"

"Yeah. Medically, no problems. We had to do a surgical repair. The wound went into her abdominal wall -- it pierced it, but didn't go through any organs. We did some internal sutures. We did some skin sutures. We got her all bandaged up. She's going to need to stay here for about a day and then you can bring her home. So she is fine."

Ben was so happy. Thank God. He turned to Erica, standing out of earshot, and gave her a thumbs up. Erica was expecting a good report, and remained somber.

The doctor continued to Ben. "I've got a question for you."

Ben knew the question and answered it. "I know, doctor."

"You know?"

"I know."

"Does she know?" The doctor pointed his head in the direction of Erica.

"No, And I'd like to keep it that way."

"Very well."

Ben ushered Erica over.

"Good news, Erica. Hazel's going to be fine."

"Oh doctor, thank you."

Erica gave the doctor a big hug. The doctor backed away. He didn't like this touchy-feely stuff.

"Everything's going to be fine. Don't worry," the doctor told her. "Hey, I know who you are. You're the author."

Erica smiled. "Yes, I am."

The doctor put his hand out.

"Loved your book."

He shook her hand. The doctor then turned and went through the double doors to save the lives of several other men and women, and at least one that was a little bit in between.

CHAPTER 90

A DAY LATER

Ben and Erica stayed in the recovery room with Hazel. They both slept in the chairs while Hazel remained in the bed.

The following day, the doctor came out and announced, "Hazel, you're doing fine. You can go home now. Here are some antibiotics I want you to take four times a day. I want you to just take it easy. Obviously you can't do any heavy lifting -- and don't do anything that would require you to breathe hard."

The doctor looked over to Ben as he said that. Ben tried not to smile, but couldn't help it. They placed Hazel into a wheelchair per hospital protocol. She did not want to be in a wheelchair.

"I'm sorry, ma'am. Hospital rules -- all patients leave in a wheelchair no matter how healthy, strong and able."

Hazel complied. "Fine, treat me like an old lady."

Ben got behind the wheelchair, but Erica stopped him.

"I'll handle this." Erica patted Hazel on the shoulder.

Hazel put her hand on Erica's hand, looked up and said, "Thank you for stopping the bleeding."

Erica looked at Hazel and said, "Thank you for saving me from those criminals."

They both smiled at each other. Ben realized right away that something was going on between these two. They proceeded out the hospital corridor to Ben's awaiting Corvair. Erica got in back. They gently placed Hazel in the passenger seat and the three of them drove home. The gate was securely locked. Ben used his remote control to open it and drove into the driveway. The three of them got out of the car and went into the house.

Ben saw for the first time the incredible mess that was left in his home. There was a broken bag of his things from his bedroom. There was a crashed and broken photograph of his father. There was a bunch of blood on the entry doorway. He walked into the kitchen and saw an even bigger mess. There was stuff everywhere -- flour, sugar, butter, eggs -- and suspiciously in perfect shape, right in the middle of the kitchen table, was a perfectly placed blueberry pie.

"What's the story on the pie?"

Erica and Hazel couldn't help but start hysterically laughing. It was hurting Hazel.

"Stop. I can't laugh anymore. It's hurting."

"Okay, what's so funny?" Ben had no clue.

Hazel then thought of something. "Oh, wait a minute. Open the fridge."

Ben opened the refrigerator. Inside he saw a perfectly cooled strawberry cheesecake.

"Please bring it out and place it right next to the blueberry pie."

The girls smiled.   They wouldn't say a word, but Ben heard the question: "Which pie do you prefer?"

Ben looked at the two pies. He took his two hands out as though he was holding two pistols. Each index finger went into each pie, the left into the strawberry cheesecake, and the right into the blue berry. He put both fingers into his mouth, and tasted the pies. He walked over to his favorite women in the world, and gave each a big kiss right on the lips.

"I love you and I love you -- and that's my answer."

He then walked out of the kitchen and began the job of mopping up Hazel's blood from the floor.

The girls looked at each other and smiled. They watched Ben scrubbing away. They brought over some towels, some sponges and some Lysol, and helped him as he cleaned up the mess.

CHAPTER 91

IT WAS A DARK AND STORMY NIGHT...

Several months later, the rain came down like a judgment. Hazel, Ben and Erica watched the news reports of evacuations up in Carlsbad. Unfortunately, many of these homes up there were built on cliffs overlooking the beach and the gorgeous Pacific Ocean. When the rains came, the dirt would be washed away, and sometimes the homes would come a tumblin' down.

The dangers were many. Gas pipes were ruptured. Methane gas would be released, highly flammable. Electrical wires would be pulled and broken. In the process, they could swing around and become ignited into the methane gas. There's a big problem: electrical fire, methane gas fire all being extinguished by the strong rains. Who would win? The water from the heavens or the fire from the earth?

The county knew very well that people would have to be evacuated. The news accounts showed the evacuation scenes up and down the very road where Hazel's home was. Helicopters flew around. People were coming out and being taken away in droves. They had next to nothing. Some people grabbed the only thing that they could never replace -- the photos.

It was then that Hazel remembered the shrine she had built for her parents, Henry's parents in the home that Henry had lived. There was a picture of his mother, a picture of his father, some candles and a piece of cloth. They were absolutely irreplaceable. She didn't care about the house; the ocean could open up and beat up that place all it wanted. But those photos, she had to have.

As they watched the news about the rain, they could hear it almost in stereo as it pounded on the roof, coming down, in front of the windows and hitting the lawn, machine gun-style.

Erica could sense a huge level of anxiety with Hazel.

"What's wrong?"

Hazel didn't know what to say, but she had to say something.

"My, my house."

Ben was very nervous.

"We can't go there. It's way too dangerous."

"You have a house up there?"

Erica had no clue.

"Yeah, I have a house up there."

"In Carlsbad?"

"Yes."

"Is it gonna be okay?"

"I don't know. You tell me."

The news accounts suggested it would not be okay. There was one image of a home on fire, crashing into the ocean, people running away, going into a van and being driven to safety.

Hazel looked in horror to Ben for help. Ben had his palms out in a 'there's nothing I can do about it' gesture, but Ben didn't understand what it was that Hazel wanted to protect.

"Listen, I've got photos, pictures of my mom and dad," she told Ben. "I have a piece of cloth from my mom. I can't lose that. It's all I have of her."

Erica was starting to get clued in to Hazel's anxiety.

"Your parents are --"

"Yes, they're dead."

"I'm sorry -- and this, these photos, that's it?"

"That's it."

Erica looked over to Ben.

"Oh Ben, we've gotta do something."

"But look, it's all cordoned off. You can't get in there. Look at the cop cars all over the place."

Indeed, it was teeming with sheriff's deputies, emergency vehicles, the Federal Emergency Management Agency (FEMA), even helicopters flying all over.

"You can't get there. There's no way."

Hazel looked over to Ben.

"Hey Ben, there's a back way. Isn't that right?"

Ben knew, of course, what Hazel was talking about. Erica didn't.

"A back way?"

"Well, kind of."

"What is it?"

"We can take my dad's boat and go by ocean."

Erica knew that to be the perfect answer.

"Yes, let's do it. That's the way. Let's go right now."

Ben rolled his eyes.

"Look at the rain -- you want to go out in this kind of weather --"

"Look Ben, we gotta do something here," Erica interrupted. "We have to save those photos."

Hazel looked over to Erica.

"Thank you. They mean the world to me."

Ben shook his head in disbelief. *I can't believe it. I can't believe it.* But he realized he had to go.

He grabbed his car keys and they went out into his dad's Mercedes. They drove down to the marina. Of course, no one in their right mind would be out at this time. The ocean swells were huge. The tide was in. The rain kept coming down relentlessly, pounding on them. Forget about an umbrella. The good news is that the driver's seat was inside a rather impressive cabin, so at least they wouldn't be driving with rain pounding on their heads.

Erica and Hazel walked into the cabin first. Ben saw them soaking wet and handed them both towels and bathrobes.

"We're going to have to dry these clothes."

"Why bother?"

"We're going to have to get into something to go run in and grab those photos. I mean, I've got two wet suits aboard, but they're not for girls."

Hazel looked down and Ben realized right away that, in fact, his father's wet suit would probably kind of sort of fit Hazel.

"Okay, put it on."

He threw the wet suit down on the ground in front of Hazel.

She would not strip naked right there and put it on. Instead, she shyly walked into the bathroom, took off her soaking wet clothes and put the wet suit on. There was a little bit of a trick to hide the outline of Hazel's penis. She had to bring it straight up. Luckily, the suit was a bit on the loose side. Sam was a slightly heavier guy, but still somewhat skinny.

Erica had removed her clothes right in the cabin, and was wearing a terry cloth bathrobe that Ben had given her. She looked comfortable and warm.

Ben explained, "We've got to get you something else, unless you want to wait on the boat."

"No, find me something else."

He went into the bedroom and went through the clothes. There were several outfits that his mother had left. One of them would work just fine. It was a nylon sports pants with stripes up and down and a half-torso neoprene top. Over that went a blue cotton shirt. This would have to work, at least for now.

He brought it out to Erica, who was not shy to strip right in front of Hazel. Hazel pretended not to notice, but the remnant of Henry still inside her was fully aware that this was the body he had raped.

The seas were big at night with swells going way up and way down. Rain coming down, lightning in the distance, the scene of fires on the shoreline all made for a kind of a scenery that gave all three of them goose bumps. Of course, they shouldn't even be out there, but of course they were. It was simply ridiculous. All this for a couple of photos?

Ben looked over at Hazel and Erica, resting safely in the dining room of the ship, sitting on brown leather seats, comfortable, soothing each other, helping each other. For Ben, this was an amazing sight. These two should be the biggest enemies on the planet and yet, here they were BFFs.

CHAPTER 92

DISCOVERY, REVENGE AND REDEMPTION

It took about 45 minutes to get from the shoreline to the place where Henry's home was. There was quite a bit of activity just down the road from Henry's place. One of the homes had caught on fire. Another home nearby had crashed into the ocean. The helicopters and Coast Guard both were focused on that home and not Henry's.

Ben was left with a clear shot right from the back into the beachfront that laid before the ice plants and the cliff that went up to Henry's home. The small Zodiac was the only way in to shore. This time, Ben would get his ship as close to shore as possible. There was nobody there to detect them so he was able to get right up to a sandbar within 30 feet.

They came empty-handed, except for one item held around Hazel's neck: The house keys. There were two keys; one for the little house and one for the big house.

He put the Zodiac into the water. It immediately was tossed by a wave and did a complete somersault. They were still safe onboard the mother ship, but they couldn't help but wonder, my goodness, do we really want to get in this little boat and ride it even this short distance to the land?

They looked down the way. They saw the fiery homes, the crashing homes. They could see the reflection of the red, blue and green police lights, the lights coming down from the helicopters and the megaphone loudspeaker ordering people, "You must leave your home at once."

Hazel took out the life preservers, handed one to Ben. He strapped it on. She handed one to Erica and helped Erica put it on. Then she put one on herself.

They brought the small boat back. It was upside down. As it got to the back of the boat, they were able to stand on the platform.

"One, two, three, go!"

They picked that little boat up and turned it over, right side up. The water poured out, and it was ready to make this short trip into the beach. The anchor had been placed down. The ship was secured, wobbling to and fro in the huge waves, going up and down with each of them.

They stepped from the platform onto the Zodiac. The weight of the three of them would keep the Zodiac from flipping over again. Ben started the little engine on the boat, and turned it full throttle. On the way in, they caught a wave that jetted them like a slingshot would throw a pellet. They scooted up well onto the beachfront, landing halfway between where the water used to stop and the cliff began.

It was quite a ride. Erica had never done anything quite so exhilarating in her life. Most of her existence was spent cranially and not in the physical world. This was a first for her, and it really turned her on like a light. Adrenaline was flowing. She got out of the boat. She looked at her hands. She looked at Hazel. She looked at Ben.

And she screamed, "I love it!"

It was the happiest moment that Erica had experienced in several years, if not her entire life.

Ben laughed in the rain before the danger.

Hazel had more serious thoughts. She smiled, held the two keys in her hands, still wrapped around her key and reminded all of them that there was important business to attend to.

The three made their way up the ice plant-surrounded walkway. It was quite a physical feat to reach the top of the cliff. It was a distance of about 100 feet, but the zigzag of the path made it more like 300 feet. This required physical strength and endurance, which Erica did not have. She had spent so much time in a hospital bed that by the time she made the top, she could barely walk, she could barely crawl. They would have to wait there for a second and let her catch her breath. She breathed hard, in and out. It upset her to be the weak link of this rescue team.

"Look, go, go. Leave me here. I'll be fine."

Hazel did not like that idea at all. She noted the direct path of the small house right on to where Erica was standing. She saw the house where Henry used to live. It was creaking. It was trembling. It was shaking. It was wobbling. It was quite literally teetering on disaster.

"No, we're waiting right here for you. Don't worry about it. Catch your breath."

The rain pelted on them, relentlessly, mercilessly. They all caught their breath.

At last, Erica turned.

"I'm ready. Let's go."

They fought the beast of the wind and rain going forward to the small house. Erica noticed how Ben seemed to know his way around this area. He had walked right to the door of the small house. She didn't ask him about how he knew. She could just tell he did.

There wasn't much time. The house was shaking, cracking. One window had already broken. A lamp had fallen down and several pieces of the roof were already flying off. A few more flew off. A few more cracks were heard. Another window broke.

Hazel was not one to fail in the moment. She unlocked the door, but it had become stuck. The shaking of the home had shifted the frame to the point where it would not open. Hazel still had Henry's finish carpenter brain in her. She quickly analyzed the perimeter of the doorway and could see a rather easy solution.

She looked to the front pathway of the home, where there were several large rocks. She picked one up. It was an impressive sight to see Hazel smash that rock into the doorknob. It was a direct hit. The doorknob shot right through, but still the door did not open. It remained stuck.

A rafter flew off the side of the home. One crashed down in front of them. There was more creaking, more teetering. The cliff that they had just ran up started to collapse, with large chunks of mud and dirt flying down 100 feet to the sand on the beach.

The helicopters that were down several homes away did not see the calamity occurring at this house. They were left alone.

Hazel swung the rock back and smashed it again into the door. The door didn't budge.

"Jesus, this thing is stuck."

She realized, of course, that she had built it that way. She looked at the moulding again on the perimeter and saw how tight it was. She looked around for some other kind of tool. What she needed was a hammer and a screwdriver, but there was none lying around. There was something though. There was a tree that had a vertical stake holding it up. She walked over to that tree, grabbed the stake and sympathetically advised the tree, "I don't think you'll be needing this anymore."

She ripped that stake up. She walked back to the door, around the perimeter and smashed the stake into the moulding that made the doorway waterproof. It took some doing, but that moulding started to fly off. She chopped one part of it off, another part of it off. It began finally to unravel. This allowed her one more fourth play. She picked up that rock again and smashed the door, again and again. At last the door opened about half an inch, then an inch, then several inches and then about a foot. It still wouldn't open all the way. It was wide enough for three skinny people to get through and they did. Erica went last, Ben was second and of course, Hazel was first.

Once inside the house, it became all the more obvious to the three of them how wobbly it was. "Whoa."

The floor was surfing, waving like a magic carpet. There were gaps in the roof where it had flown off. Rain was coming in. The house was about to leave the land.

Ben shouted out the obvious, "Move it!"

"Where are the photos?" Erica yelled.

They followed Ben as he ran into the workshop area. Still there was a beautiful cabinet he had been working on before, untouched, unsanded. It was a strong piece of wood, perfectly flat, propped up against the wall. Another one lay on two sawhorses. They were both works in progress, waiting to be finished.

In a room adjoining this room, there was a shrine made by Hazel in memory of Henry's mother and father. All three of them walked in. It was peaceful, religious, and simple, and it had to be kept.

Erica reached for a photo when Ben intervened and stopped her arm. He ushered her back. "Let Hazel do it."

Hazel quickly grabbed the photo of her mother and the photo of her father. There was a nearby blanket. She wrapped the photos in the blanket. There were three unlit candles and a piece of cloth. It was white. It was something from Henry's mother that he just had to keep. It was placed in front of the photos and was surrounded by the candles. These items were all very carefully wrapped into the blanket. Hazel held them close to her.

They ran back out of this shrine room, through the workshop that Henry had spent so many hours in. She stopped only for a second to take her last look at it. She saw the carpentry work she had done so effortlessly before. She saw her cabinets. This was unfinished work that would remain unfinished, but they were still gorgeous.

Ben knew what Hazel was thinking. This was Henry's life. This was Henry's workshop. This was a part of Hazel's life that tonight, at last, would be literally washed off the face of the earth.

They ran back out to the front part of the house to get through that small opening in the door. Unfortunately, it was enough for their bodies, but not enough for the blanket filled with pictures, candles and a piece of cloth.

Hazel tried to rearrange the contents of that bag slightly to get it so it could slide through the small crack in the door. She quickly completed this process.

Once outside, Hazel sprinted to the main house, clutching that blanket close to her all of the way. Ben and Erica followed behind. They ran up the pathway, to the area where the pool was, around the side of the pool. They could see the raindrops connecting with the pool water. It looked as though the pool was shooting rain up instead of rain coming down. They passed the pool and went to the sliding glass door leading into the kitchen.

Once they got to the sliding glass door, there was an overhang of a roof. At last a dry moment. Hazel took the other key and opened the sliding glass door. This slid open without any problem. They walked into the home and went to the living room area where Henry's grandfather had built his own little shrine to his wife.

Ben didn't see that shrine on his first and last trip to Henry's home. Had he seen it, he would have never allowed Erica to follow Hazel into the room, because right next to the beautiful photo of Henry's grandmother, there was a photo of Henry.

Erica suddenly found herself in front of a photo of the man who had raped her -- shaved head Henry, clean in every way, not a speck of hair anywhere, with a set of scintillating blue eyes that could immediately be matched up with Hazel's. It was right then and there that Erica discovered the ultimate act of betrayal that Ben had committed.

"What the fuck?"

She pointed at the picture.

She walked right up to it and put her hand right to the eyes.

"Those eyes, this picture. Those are his eyes. Those are her eyes. This is the man that raped me. How come my rapist -- how come his photo is here and how come he's got the exact same eyes as Hazel?"

Erica's brain was going 40,000 miles an hour. The adrenaline was flowing through her.

Hazel had placed a blanket onto the ground. It opened up and the photos of her mom and dad rested safely against a wall, to the side of where there was a photo of him. This was a photo she did not like. Hazel was not interested to allow the old Henry to exist. She walked up to that photo, took it off the wall. She would not say a word to Erica.

She walked outside into the pouring rain. Erica followed. Ben didn't know what to do, but he followed.

This was the moment that Henry's house would begin the final process of being wiped from the face of the earth. It was no longer creaking. It was tearing. It was splintering. The wood was flying. Pipes were bursting. The house was falling off the cliff, going down to the ocean.

Hazel took the photo of Henry and threw it like a frisbee to the inside of the tumbling house, where it would meet with its proper destiny along a pathway to infinity.

CHAPTER 93

THE REVENGE PART

Erica looked at Ben.

"How could you?"

"You don't understand."

"I don't understand? What did you do? I don't understand. What did you do?"

She walked over to Hazel and with one quick maneuver, ripped down Hazel's wet suit, exposing Hazel's pelvic area and in there was a small, super soft penis.

She walked over and pointed at it.

"*WHAT DID YOU DO?*"

The rain would not let up.

Ben showed his guilt by just looking down at his feet. What could he say?

"You don't understand."

"I don't understand? Then explain it to me. Is this the man?"

And then she turned to Hazel and realized that her true anger would be directed at Hazel, not Ben.

With a prosecutor's sense of blood, she needled Hazel.

"Are you the man from that picture?"

Hazel was quiet, but she was not in denial. She was not about to be deceptive. If there was anything the sexual offender therapy had taught her, it was honesty -- especially about your true self and saying who you are, what you are, what you had been and what you had done.

"Yes, that is me."

Hazel couldn't even say a word of explanation about how that was the old Henry and how that Henry no longer existed and had been replaced with a new Hazel or about the whole serendipity of discovery that the one way to truly solve the problem of a rapist that they had discovered was to turn the man into a woman. She would not be given this chance.

Hazel's eyes met with a new kind of look on Erica. The full force of her anger, her feeling of betrayal, her quest for revenge came forward with a gust. At the same moment, the wind flared up, the rain came down more, more pieces of the house dropped down.

Erica, without warning, ran to Hazel, hit her as a full body shot right in the chest, and knocked Hazel off a walkway in front of where Henry's home used to be. There was now an empty space there and below that space, a bunch of broken wood that was making its way down a cliff. Hazel flew off into this crevice.

Ben could not believe what he had just seen.

Erica's adrenaline was pumping. She was shaking. Whenever you kill, you shake. She looked down and smiled. At last, she had obtained her revenge. She didn't feel guilty. She didn't feel bad. She didn't feel empty. This feeling was quickly interrupted when suddenly the very ground that she stood upon gave way.

She teetered and lost her balance. Ben quickly reacted and ran to her. He grabbed her hand. His hand was wet. Her hand was wet. It was too slippery. She fell off. He couldn't hang on, and she followed the very path that she had just sent Hazel upon, a path of certain death.

Ben stood from the top area and looked down into a black hole where the two loves of his life had just fallen into.

He screamed out, "NOOOOOOOOO!!!!!!!"

He looked down to the disaster of his life that lay below and realized it was truly 100% all his fault. He fell to his knees, put his head into his hands and cried like a baby. Then he stopped. He got up with great anger. He wasn't convinced of anything at this moment. He had to get back down that cliff, back down to beach and look through the rubble to see if he could find Erica and Hazel.

Getting back down the cliff through the zigzags -- forget it. He went in a vertical line. Just like the dollar signs have two lines that go through it vertically, he made the same vertical line through that zigzag and made it down, sliding across the ice plants, hydroplaning to the bottom. He flipped in the sand, tumbled over several times, got back up and turned around.

Much of the house had slid down like lava through the mud into the water. There was a kind of roadway here, a roadway of mud, ice plants, sand, water, broken house, pipes, walls and somewhere within all of it, two beautiful and hopefully still alive women.

Ben searched frantically through the rubble. It was dark out. He saw the helicopter and lights, still several homes away.

He screamed out, "Help! Help!"

But it was no use. There were too far away. His voice was not nearly loud enough. He was alone and would have to search for them on his own.

The pieces of wood from Henry's old home were snapped, splintered, cracked. Several of the two by fours came into a point. Ben held it up like a sword, threw it down. He picked up another one like a spear and threw it down. Another one was like a dagger and he threw it down. He was frantically searching, pulling up muck, pulling up pieces of the house, but not seeing the slightest evidence of two women.

He came upon the sawhorses that had held the unfinished cabinet, but there was no piece of unfinished cabinet around. It was lost.

CHAPTER 94

REDEMPTION

Ben could not handle this loss. The guilt over having caused it, the impact over having lost it and the permanent scarring that this huge guilt and loss would have on him for the rest of his life. There was no way.

He picked up another piece of splintered wood. It was formerly a two by four, now a jagged edge sharper than a spear. It was stuck in the mud at an angle. Ben looked at it. It invited him. He could so easily put himself out of misery. All he had to do was fall on it. It would take him. He put his palm on the top of the tip, put a little pressure on it and quickly snapped it back. Ouch! It was sharp.

He walked up and put it right to his ribcage, right where his heart was. That was the bullseye. He knew it could go right through. He took three steps back, trembling with fear.

Ben was not a brave man. He was not a courageous man. Taking his life would take a level of courage and bravery that he did not possess.

He backed up. He would take a running start. There was no way this was not going to work. He would have to run and jump on it, make sure it did what needed to be done.

When the adrenaline flows through your body in these moments, everything turns into slow motion. He ran, but it seemed like walking. His chest was out, yelling out, "Take me! Take me!"

Just then he heard the scream of Erica. It was a bloodcurdling scream. "NOOOOOO!!!!!!"

Ben stopped, but the mud beneath his feet wouldn't let him stop. He slid closer to the spear in the mud.

Erica was in Hazel's arms, resting safely on half of an unfinished cabinet door. She had managed to hop on it as she slid through the mud and the debris. When Hazel saw Erica coming down behind her, she managed to grab her. She had placed herself on top of her, sandwiching her between Hazel and the board and the two of them rode it out into the sea.

Once in the ocean, they were able to turn it around and ride it back in to the dry ground. She put her on the board of a stretcher. They both coughed up water. Hazel walked her out of the ocean, carrying her on this flat cabinet board. Erica screamed at the top of her lungs for Ben to stop what he was about to do.

Ben heard it just in time to consciously make the decision to stop. But physically, the momentum took him closer to his own death. He saw he would not be able to stop in time to avoid the spear. He placed his left palm out in front of him, just the same way as he had done moments ago to test the sharpness of that spear. Like a gymnast, when the spear pierced into his palm, he was able to use that as a fulcrum point. It caught his palm. He sprung upward with his two knees, and catapulted up and over that spear.

The spear let go of his bloody palm. He did a complete flip and landed on his butt, facing before a wide-eyed Hazel and Erica. Two sets of different blue eyes watched him as they would all begin the first day of the rest of their lives.

The moon would move the tides to wash them clean.

CHAPTER 95

EPILOGUE

Can these three live someway somehow after all?

Ben threw a coming out party for Hazel. It was time to let the world know who Hazel was, and to come clean on the facts. The warden is there with his daughter Lillith, and Hazel's former prison sexual offender doctor/therapist, Dr. Abigail Miller. Ben's co workers and bosses from the newspaper are there, along with several of the folks from the Guitar Center. There are deputy sheriffs there as well.

They are watching and listening to Hazel on guitar, Lillith on bass, and that black guy from the Guitar Center on drums.

The Warden loves his daughter so much, which impresses Dr. Miller. He doesn't even notice how she admires him. Her swaying into him during the force of the music makes it unmistakable. He smiles, and sways back.

The band plays *Too Rolling Stoned* from Robin Trower's *Bridge of Sighs.* The song is an electric ride, and allows Hazel and Lillith to shine as performers.

During a play break, Dr. Miller asks Hazel to do some work with the many sex offenders at the prison. She wants other offenders to consider female hormone therapy as a way to release their demons.

Dr. Miller explains, "This may be the one and only way to actually release the demon."

Hazel of course agrees. The following week, Ben drives her there in his Corvair, with Erica in the passenger seat.

The Warden and Dr. Miller greeted Erica, Hazel and Ben at the prison lobby. Erica placed her book, *What Its Like to Be Dead*, through the X-ray machine. They went through the metal detector, and out to the prison yard. They entered into another building, proceeded down a hallway, and into a room with eight carefully guarded rapists.

After the rapists got over the initial euphoria and amazement of seeing Henry as a woman, they got down to the hard business of listening to Erica read from her book. The Warden offered Erica a chair, but she declined. She stood and delivered the story of what its like to be a rape victim and have your entire life taken away from you.

There wasn't a dry eye in the room.